Drop Dead Gorgeous

a novel by
Wayne Simmons

edited & designed by
Travis Adkins

cover art by
Michael Brack

Permuted Press
The formula has been changed...
Shifted... Altered... *Twisted.*™
www.permutedpress.com

A Permuted Press book
published by arrangement with the author

Drop Dead Gorgeous

©2008 Wayne Simmons. All Rights Reserved.

ISBN-10: 1-934861-05-7
ISBN-13: 978-1-934861-05-9
Library of Congress Control Number: 2008927567

For everyone who doesn't feel
DROP DEAD GORGEOUS...

Belfast City
Sunday, 5th June 2005

"THAT ONE WAS A FUCKIN' BLOKE."

He'd been at it all day. They'd been in town since half nine in the bloody morning and all Jimmy had done was gawk at every single tit and arse they happened to walk by.

Siobhan was getting a bit sick of it. She didn't consider herself the jealous type, by any stretch of the imagination, but this was taking the piss.

Every fucking girl...

And he wasn't even subtle about it. His beady wee eyes were blatantly undressing every female in Belfast between the ages of fifteen and forty.

The last one he had looked at was a bloke. Siobhan was sure of it. It had been one of those wee emos that seemed to congregate around the city hall every Saturday and Sunday. The place was crawling with them these days, their baggy-jeaned arses spilling out in drips and drabs, shuffling downtown to pick up whatever release-of-the-minute MTV was whoring...

Pasty-faced. Lank-haired. Eyelinered to fuck.

It had been one of them her boyfriend was perving on. Siobhan reckoned Jimmy had seen the make-up on the lad, automatically giving his tits—or lack of them—the once over, and deciding he was a looker.

"I said that one was a fuckin' *bloke*," she repeated, slowly and loudly, spelling it out to him as if he was a child.

"What are you on about?" Jimmy muttered back, without even looking at her.

It had got to the stage where he didn't even realise what he was doing. Sometimes he forgot himself and nudged Siobhan, as if to let her in on the secret, as some half decent blonde wandered by.

It made Siobhan's heart sink. She didn't feel sexual anymore. It was like their relationship had deteriorated to that of a mother and child. All Jimmy seemed to need these days was someone to wash his clothes, cook his dinner, and provide the occasional hole to fuck in.

"Never mind," she said, deflated.

Sighing, she slipped her credit card back in her purse, suddenly remembering about the bills coming out this month. Swiping plastic about town wasn't going to pay the electric.

"Is it not time to go home?" Jimmy said, sniffing. Siobhan could see him look at her shopping bags, wondering, no doubt, just how much she'd clocked up this time on the card. "There's footie on tonight and I told Frankie to call round at about seven. You need to get dinner ready and all."

Yeah, I need to get dinner ready. That'll be right.

He'd hardly lifted a hand around the house in all the time they'd been together. Siobhan often wondered why she even bothered with him at all. But life with Jimmy was just kind of the norm. She couldn't imagine him not being around every day, not scratching his bollocks audibly in bed every night, not burping loudly after a good feed of dinner.

And, of course, Siobhan saw another side to Jimmy.

She still remembered their first night out all those years ago when Jimmy had been a skinny bundle of nerves, palms sweating, voice stuttering, trying so hard to be some version of romantic. He'd taken her out to Burger King. It was the first time she'd been there, what with it having only come to Belfast in the nineties. She remembered him choking on his Coke, he was so nervous. That had made her giggle.

Were she to think real hard, Siobhan might still be able to recall that big teddy bear he'd sent into her work on their first St. Valentine's Day together, and how all the girls in the office told her how much he must have loved her.

And then more recently, of course, Siobhan still remembered (how could she forget?) that dark day around Halloween last year when Jimmy had found her in hysterics standing in the rain outside the house, hands gripped tightly around her mobile phone, bawling her eyes out. He hadn't even had to ask Siobhan what was wrong. He had just taken her in his arms and held her for days, rocking her to and fro. He had fixed it so that her mother's funeral seemed to somehow just happen all around her.

That was her Jimmy and he wasn't all bad, Siobhan decided, as they marched towards the car, bags of shopping tripping them.

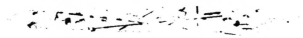

Caz's mind was meandering freely as she sat cross-legged on the 11.20 train to Belfast Central. She was daydreaming indulgently, a collage of all-things-bright-and-beautiful dancing a merry jig to the humdrum rhythm of the train. She was sixteen years old, and as something of a romantic, Caz savoured these moments when her quasi-adult mind would dip back into its inner child.

Her token trashy magazine was lying face down on her lap, as if dead. Her eyes glazed over as she traveled to Cloud Nine. The mish-mash view of her own reflection, some grassy banks and rail track, did little to bring Caz back to reality—that was the way she liked it. Her mind swirled like a spiral, inside-and-outside, as the train continued its northern journey to Belfast. The world blew by like smoke in the wind, fields and roads intermingling like a Cesar salad as the train moved gracefully along its track, gently humming.

Caz remembered that famous quote about some writer staring out the window of his room. "What are you doing?" someone had asked him. "Writing," came the reply.

—*Or maybe it was painting?*

It didn't matter. The story had always struck her as extremely bland. Not just because it didn't make sense to her, but because it shouldn't make sense to anyone. For Caz, there was nothing more natural in the world than unleashing the imagination, than uncorking the creative juices and letting them flood over you, just for the hell of it—just because you could.

But then again, she was sixteen.

Somewhere close by, a random noise... something falling... or a door opening... made her look up. One glance at the train's sliding, automatic door and Caz's hormones were bouncing, shaking her out of a self-induced trance. Her heart skipped with instant and sudden euphoria as the tall, gangly frame of Tim Adamson, the cutest lad in her GCSE History class—and possibly the whole damn school—slouched into the car she was in. His MP3 player was playing loud enough to be heard over the train's jiggy-jigging.

Caz crossed her legs, picking up her magazine like it was a weapon of some sort. She watched, under her fringe, and pretended not to care as Tim sat down in the seat opposite her.

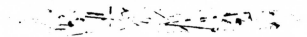

Even though it was barely noon, the car park was a lot more packed than it had been when they'd first arrived. The afternoon was always the busiest time.

That's why Siobhan had dragged Jimmy's hungover arse out of bed to drive her into town in the morning. She hated crowds. So did he, truth be told.

When they'd first opened the town on Sundays, it had been fairly quiet all day. The place had been like a ghost town. Siobhan had once told him that she felt like one of those celebrities who could get shops to stay open just for them. Meant fuck all to Jimmy. He just did what he was told. He was good at that.

Like clockwork, Jimmy unloaded the bags off his bird's arms and packed them into the car. It was a well-practiced routine, carried out methodically without any need for communication between the couple. All the usual suspects were present and accounted for: Topshop, TK Maxx, and Siobhan's personal favourite for that cheap and cheerful bargain, Primark.

Jimmy had absolutely no interest in the contents of those bags. He just needed to get them into the car in order to get home quickly.

Fashion, to a man like Jimmy, was a dark art. Usually he just wore whatever his sister or ma bought him. Day-to-day wear consisted of trackie bottoms and trainers. A night out usually called for one of the stripy shirts his ma had got him for Christmas and a pair of jeans. A trip downtown also merited the latter, Siobhan insisting on it, of course.

You needn't think you're going out like that.

Yeah, whatever. He just did what he was told. Made life a lot easier.

Siobhan and Jimmy lived about fifteen minutes drive out of town, a place called Finaghy. It was just south of the city centre, an area wavering between the middle class suburbia of the Upper Malone Road (or "Mauuulone Rowd" as Jimmy called it, effecting his usual broad Belfast sneer) and the all too familiar tribalism of Taughmonagh's red, white and blue stained pavements. Where Jimmy and Siobhan lived sported a different colour scheme, with similar looking wall murals featuring a more autumnal green, white and orange.

The colour of paint set the boundaries in Belfast. Like piss against lamp posts, murals, stripy pavements, flags and buntings were painted and erected by respective community leaders. Only the colour schemes were different.

Jimmy had once entertained the thought that the same bloke could be painting wall murals and pavements for both sides of the community (tenner an hour, mate. Cash in hand. Not bad work if you can get it) but it wouldn't have mattered to him, even if it was true. Jimmy thought it best just to ignore all that shite and fucking get on with life. Politics was as dark an art to Jimmy as shopping was, truth be told.

Sometimes he pretended to give a fuck, just to go with the flow, indulging his friends who, like most people in Belfast, had a certain sectarianism inherent within their blood, but underneath it all he couldn't give a rat's arse.

Beer. Birds. Football.

Siobhan changed the radio station as Jimmy was driving. A sudden tut showed it wasn't a move he liked.

"Fuckin' gay music's what that is," he muttered, eyes still firmly fixed on the road.

"No gayer than that hip hop shite you listen to," Siobhan replied, putting on her usual indignant face as she turned the volume up on whatever cock rock Real FM was churning out.

"Aye, whatever you say."

"Just you keep driving and never mind what fuckin' music's playing."

And there it was. Their third conversation of the day wrapped up in seconds.

Had it went on, Jimmy would have said he was too tired to bicker. He might have pointed out the fact that he'd been tripping around town for the better part of two hours and it hadn't helped either his hangover or his mood.

Siobhan then would have brought up the fact that he had spent most of this time perving on other girls, and might even have mentioned how one of them was a bloke—and a bloke that wore make-up, for that matter. But they hardly even argued anymore, such was their predicament. Their relationship was stale, like out-of-date milk. It looked okay, but smelled funny.

Jimmy's belly growled a little, reminding him that he'd missed breakfast, his beer-soaked gut not having felt up to it earlier. His mind began to think of food as he turned onto the Lisburn Road, finally getting a bit of speed up.

"We stopping for a fry-up on the way home?" he asked Siobhan, hoping to win her back out of her huff with an offer to pay for it.

Then he dropped dead at the steering wheel.

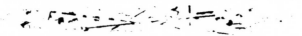

Tim Adamson, lead vocalist with The Muckwits, was sitting right across from Caz. His band had played at the Christmas party in school, although word had it that Tim had quit them. He was without a doubt the most talented one amongst them. Everyone said it. Even Kelly Cullen, who had once also told Caz that she thought Tim was a dick. Of course, Caz knew she really wanted to jump Tim's bones.

Kelly Cullen was one stupid cow.

As all of this rushed though her head, Caz sat with a defiant expression of nonchalance painted on her face. Tim had barely noticed her. His eyes wore the same glazed expression that Caz's had only five minutes ago. Lost in all that stupid music, his MP3 player boring through his brain like some kind of drill.

Fixing her glasses, Caz ventured a look at him. He lay back in the seat opposite, arms crossed over his belly. The sound of gum bouncing around his mouth was even more annoying than his MP3.

I mean, geez... Really...

He was probably going down to the City Hall, no doubt to hang out with Bonzo and all those arseholes. She hated that crowd, hated how effected they all were, with their heavy make-up, kitsch backpacks and stripy tights. God, they were getting younger and younger, too. Even her little brother was starting to hang around there with all his teeny-goth mates, and he was barely fourteen.

It pissed Caz off to no end that she found a guy like Tim Adamson so attractive. He was, like, a nemesis to her, so image-conscious with his baggy jeans, sneakers and the constant drone of MP3 being the only thing resembling vocabulary to come out of his head. He was so below her.

The train jerked suddenly, causing Caz to clumsily fall forward into the unsuspecting personal space of Tim. She had barely time to recover herself, hardly even the time to go red with the absolute humiliation of it all, before another much more violent jerk sent her sprawling down the aisle of the train car. As if having some sort of seizure, the train jerked a few more times before coming to an abrupt halt somewhere close to Balmoral Station.

Caz was just about to pick herself up, confused and absolutely mortified with embarrassment, when the limp body of an old lady, the only other occupant of the train car apart from herself and Tim, fell on top of her like a discarded rag doll.

Siobhan was just about to give in and answer Jimmy's question about the fry-up when she noticed his head bobbing up and down. His hands were no longer on the steering wheel. It looked as if he'd literally fallen asleep.

"Fuck! Jimmy!" she screeched, leaning across and grabbing the wheel, steadying it to keep the car from mounting the pavement. "Are you taking the piss?!"

It seemed not. His heavy-set, hungover eyes peeked out of his bouncing, lopsided head, staring at her the way dead people did in movies. It was almost funny, were it not so fucking grim. Her boyfriend of nine years and two months had simply expired before her very eyes, without even as much as a whisper.

He was gone. Kaput. Fucked.

And it was too weird to take in, so Siobhan just didn't. She put it out of her mind, deciding to deal with one problem at a time.

She had never bothered to take driving lessons, what with Jimmy usually being on hand to do all the driving. And that was definitely a problem demanding her attention.

Ironically, even now, Jimmy was pissing her off, his lifeless (useless, big, stupid) foot still keeping the car at a good 40+ MPH. She battled with him, trying to shake him off the wheel the same way she would have shook his drunken, lecherous hands off her tits. Only with less success.

A car in front swerved right, dramatically crashing through a shop window. One of the new minis (Siobhan had always loved how cute they looked) could be seen in her rear mirror, jittering then slowing down, the limp body of a cyclist somehow strewn across its bonnet. Another car, this one bigger, jerked violently, as it crashed into a lamp post, uprooting an attached waste paper bin.

As the contents of the bin spilled into the light wind, crisp bags, sweets wrappers and cigarette butts flailing about merrily, a small car in front of Siobhan crumpled clumsily into a car in front of it. Siobhan stretched further across her boyfriend's body, jerking the wheel again in time to narrowly avoid collision. But Jimmy (good ol' Jimmy) kept the pride of his life (afforded more affection than Siobhan, lately) revving like a bastard, tearing up the Lisburn Road. A road going to hell right before Siobhan's panicked eyes.

Birdhouse In Your Soul by They Might Be Giants played merrily on the radio, its quirky innocence taking on a whole new sinister undertone as its famous drum beat bounced in time with Jimmy's bobbing head.

Siobhan didn't even hear the song. It was lost in the riot of her brain, the spinning of her own engine as it tried to work out how to deal with this new and sudden insanity.

Another car swerved dramatically in front of her, mounting the pavement. A dog stood barking, its owner seemingly having collapsed. Siobhan turned her head as the swerving car made a beeline for the dog.

It stopped barking.

Siobhan wouldn't have made much of a driver, of that she was sure. Truth be told, she knew damn all about cars—how they moved, why they needed water as well as petrol...

(*Does it get... thirsty?*)

Frankly, she couldn't tell a brake pedal from a carrot.

As if mocking her, Jimmy's body remained rigid, his ever-increasing beer belly providing much of the weight that was currently pressing one foot on the accelerator pedal. The speed of the small car held, maybe even increased, as Siobhan struggled with the steering wheel.

"Come on Jimmy..." Siobhan whimpered, tears messing up her mascara. "Wake up, for fuck's sake!" But it was no good. Jimmy's sleep was the eternal type. His eyes remained fixed at some indeterminable spot, his head bouncing comically on the steering wheel, twisting eerily as Siobhan turned the wheel this way and that.

The long road stretched out ahead, deadly straight. Carnage was building as the light traffic ground to a halt, cars smashing against each other like some fucked-up demolition derby. The sound of metal against metal and breaking glass seemed to echo, in stereo, somewhere beyond the noise of the radio.

The body of a motorcyclist lay on the stretch of road dead ahead. It was ironed out like something out of a sick cartoon. His corpse was contorted, having already suffered some injuries from the fucked up road rage. The leather of his jacket succeeded only to keep his arm in its sleeve as Jimmy's much loved Suzuki Swift drove over him like a rolling pin.

The poor bastard didn't feel his lifeless body shake, nor hear it squelch against the hard tarmac road as two wheels cut a perfect line through his neck, the second wheel separating his head from his body like the popping of a cork.

Siobhan's eyes shut only momentarily, only whilst she felt their blue Suzuki Swift—recently polished by a doting Jimmy—bumping over the hard bone and soft flesh of the motorcyclist. Only long enough to avoid a glimpse of the scarlet spray against her rear window.

But it was enough time for her to lose what control she had left of the car.

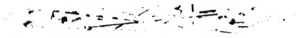

Caz screamed as the old lady tumbled over her, the pensioner's body and arms flapping around the sixteen year-old's petite frame like a broken puppet. She struggled, frantically, brushing the body away as if it were a spider crawling up her leg.

"Holy s-shit..." Caz stammered. "Fuck!" she added, not normally one to swear. Or swear so loudly.

Staring at the woman's ridiculously vacant face, Caz began to fear the worst. It was something about the eyes. They were peacefully content, as if the old lady didn't know she was dead yet, as if some part of her still sat on the 11.20 train, reading The Times.

She was so quiet... so doll-like...

Is this what death was like?

In the sudden silence, Caz could hear her heart beating fiercely in her chest. Her breathing was heavy. Her eyes wide. Steam had filled up her glasses, somehow remaining undamaged by the drama.

Caz paused briefly to clean them, her hands shaking profusely as she wiped the lenses down with a tissue.

Then she thought of Tim Adamson.

The train hadn't crashed, as such, but for some reason, Caz worried that Tim might also be dead, thrown aside by life without any realisation of it. She looked again at the body of the old lady, drawn to it in one way, repulsed in another. Then, gingerly, she approached the seats where Tim had been.

Nothing stirred. The train remained still, as if waiting for someone important to get on.

As she got closer, Caz could make out the profile of Tim draped across the hard plastic, his MP3 headphones still blasting out an audible track. It was the only noise spoiling the otherwise deathly silence.

Closer. Heart still beating. Until she could see him more clearly. There he lay. Completely still. No movement. No sound.

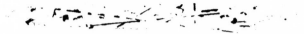

Siobhan watched helplessly as her and Jimmy's blue Suzuki Swift soared onto the pavement, seeming to actually gather speed as it revved angrily towards the railings of the Balmoral railway bridge.

Unlike Jimmy, Siobhan was very much aware of her impending death. She had almost time to rehearse it. Time seemed to slow down for her, offering a clichéd attempt to grab every last second and pull each and every breath close to her chest in a final embrace. She had all but given up the fight for her life in that last second or two, her previously flailing hands no longer struggling with the wheel, instead reaching to tossle Jimmy's curls one last time. She was satisfied that she had done all she could.

(*A good effort*, as Jimmy might have said.)

As urine trickled freely down the legs of her Primark jeans, Siobhan watched the last moments of her life pass by like some old movie.

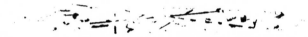

Caroline Donaldson (Caz to her mates) stared at Tim Adamson with a creeping fear of loss. She suddenly missed him more than she'd ever missed anything or anyone in her life. All her embarrassment was gone, all her teenage immaturity suspended as she stared at what looked to her like the second body she had witnessed within two minutes.

A sudden sound, breaking through the silence dramatically, turned her attention to a window somewhere behind. As Caz gazed wide-eyed towards its source, she caught the incredible sight of a small blue car soaring through the air from the bridge above the train. She watched, helplessly, as the car hurtled towards the train carriage immediately in front of her.

The blue Suzuki Swift containing Siobhan Laney and Jimmy Ferris crumpled brutally against the driver car of the 11.20 to Belfast. The whole train shook wildly again, throwing Caz on top of Tim Adamson for the second time that morning, then slapping her hard against a nearby plastic window.

There was no explosion, even though Caz thought that there should be.

That's how it happens in the movies, doesn't it?

But she could definitely smell smoke. She could feel a sudden heat looming up from the train car in front, and a dull throbbing pain at the back of her skull.

A sharp movement to her immediate left startled her. Her heart was playing constant leapfrog with her throat, and Caz wondered just how much more she could take before she completely lost it.

She felt for the small silver crucifix around her neck. Her mother had given it to her a few years ago, telling her to grip it tight it when she needed extra strength.

(God knows it hadn't helped her through her French exams last summer.)

As Caz's hands felt the naked torso of her little silver Jesus, everything changed.

Tim Adamson casually lifted his head and stared vacantly at the flames lapping against the door straight ahead.

"*Fuck me,*" he muttered, somehow capturing it all perfectly.

PART
1

"Here's to the crazy ones.
The misfits. The rebels.
The troublemakers..."

(Jack Kerouac)

one

ERE MOMENTS AFTER NINETY-NINE PERCENT OF Belfast's population stopped dead like wound-down clocks, The Silence descended. Nothing moved. Small, isolated pockets of carnage gave a sombre accompaniment to an otherwise dead city. Flames flickered here; a soft (almost mourning) wind whistled there...

But nothing moved.

Behind Queens University, in the usually vibrant Botanic Gardens, a flock of dead birds lay sprinkled across the lawn. Littered through the flock was the occasional man, woman or child. It was like art gone wrong. Beautiful, abstract—yet wrong.

Somewhere, a dog barked. Somewhere else, another dog replied. A warm breeze whispered through the trees, their leaves flourishing with late Spring, whilst branches danced quietly in the morning sun's smile. Then there was nothing again.

Nothing was the new something.

A constant flow of silence was now the dominant species in the eternal tug of war between that which could be heard and that which drowns such out to become more heard.

Nothing breathed.

Outer city generators remained active, faintly buzzing on their own whilst employees slept-on-the-job. Lights of shops shone seductively, their sveltely pale mannequins perhaps more life-like now than the fallen shoppers slumped quietly around them. Factory production lines kept moving, comically transporting fallen workers, amongst incomplete products, up the line to nowhere. Well, nowhere useful, anyway.

Nothing.

Was.

The.

New.

Something.

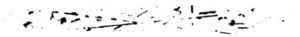

A sudden fuzz from various radios throughout Belfast snapped back at The Silence, briefly off the air for some unknown reason. The fuzz evolved quickly, soon forming a unified sound, distinctive and defined. Like a vicious rumour, the noise spread with haste and defiance. Before long it took definite shape, blaring obnoxiously from radios in cars, houses, offices, and shops across the city, finally dissolving into the all too familiar form of the Thin Lizzy classic, *Whiskey In My Jar*.

Utterly clueless to events outside, Sean Magee reclined back into his chair. The disc spun in the player, his mic turned away from him as he whistled along with the record. Swiveling his chair around, (this one was comfy, not like the last one the station had left him sitting in for the best part of a decade) Sean stretched across his vinyl-cluttered desk for the small mug of coffee he'd left cooling for the last ten minutes. He hated things being too hot, always had. Swigging on his drink, secretly livened up with a sizable nip of vodka from his hip flask, Sean picked up the sleeve of the single currently rolling.

Man, oh man... how he loved this tune! Over the course of his twenty years as a DJ, Sean had played this particular wee gem an incredible two thousand, one hundred and twenty-one times. Not that he (or anyone else for that matter) was counting, of course.

Sean was an old school DJ. A veteran, with the receding ponytail to prove it. His style was minimalist. No fancy quizzes, no phone-in competitions, less talking bullshit and more good tunes. He liked to think he enjoyed his job. Hell, he lived for it.

Real FM weren't that difficult to work for. Sure, there had been a few changes over the years, most of them for the worst, and the music output on the whole was questionable, to say the least, but Sean had always felt that his years of experience earned him the respect of his fellow DJs, grudging though that may be. More importantly, Sean knew he had the respect of the listeners...

(But not the respect of his ex-wife).

No matter how often his time slot had been changed, Sean's listening figures remained fairly consistent, proving his show was one of the station's most popular. The suits, of course, weren't fans. They wanted a more contemporary sound, a lively programme including promotional interviews with local celebrities plugging their wares, and political satire. Listeners weren't enough. They wanted *active* listeners, an audience not shy of phoning in with their questions, their praise, their fifty-pence-per-call opinions on whatever bullshit news-of-the-day negativity the local politicians were dragging out. The suits wanted revenue, and lots of it, because that's what their bosses wanted. Sean couldn't give a high-flying-fuck, of course. He'd watched one suit change to another suit over the years, one grand plan getting shot out of the water by another. He'd slept through enough staff meetings, where the direction and vision of the station had been hammered out ad nauseum, only to return to his swivel chair, fix himself a coffee (not too hot, with a nip of vodka) and wire on some solid tunes.

He largely ignored the play list that was encouraged by management, sticking to what he knew best himself, what he had learned to be the music that Belfast wanted to hear, over his twenty years as a DJ.

He had defiantly ignored the station's no-alcohol policy since its inception. Sean had always drank, always would drink—so fuck anyone royal who told him that he couldn't enjoy a tipple whilst spinning his favourite vinyl.

Whiskey In My Jar? How could you not drink along to a tune like that?!

As Thin Lizzy faded out, Sean expertly faded *Free Falling*, by Tom Petty, in. *Perfect*, he thought to himself, taking a heavy swig of his drink and looking up at the window facing him. It surprised him to find no one looking back in through the glass. Round about this time, of a Sunday morning, the most recent time slot for his unashamedly folk-rock show, the room opposite would always be occupied by his producer and whatever news reader was working. Noon would be coming up soon, yet there wasn't a news, sports or weather reader anywhere to be seen.

So, where the hell were they?

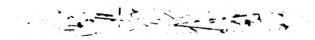

Star wore something akin to a bemused scowl as she sat uselessly poised for action, leaning forward on her small, wooden stool. Her hand, famously steady, with the ability to draw inhumanly straight lines for up to one hour (before needing a ciggie break) shook suddenly and briefly, before becoming still again. The sound of her machine whined hungrily, hungry for the naked flesh (good skin, excellent tone) now flat out on the floor in front of her. A tall, thin punky girl lay face down, half of the outline of a pentagram etched into her spine, her skin still red and enflamed from the needle's incision.

What the...?!

Star suddenly sniggered. It was a snigger pitched somewhere between nervous and amused. She wasn't green, by any means. She'd seen it all over the years; Big bouncer-type lads screeching like banshees as the letters 'F.U.C.K.' were inked onto their knuckles; Teenagers, with their pungent reek of hormones, giggling and sweating their way through having respective names burned onto each other's arms; Sombre-looking, menopausal women almost orgasming with delight as a pair of hearts, or the words 'Bite Me', were branded onto their pelvic area. She'd watched people scream, cry, laugh hysterically, puke, faint, urinate, even leap from their seats with horror as that first sting of the needle bit into them, as that little taste of adrenaline surged through their arms/legs/backs/pelvis/neck/whatever.

But she had never—not in the ten years she had been working as a professional tattooist—had someone fuckin' die on her.

This was new.

It wasn't like this client, this particular client, to be nervous. Punky Girl was something of a regular. Star had always thought she had the look and attitude of an art student, probably from York Street Art College around the corner. Somehow sensing a quiet day, the Punky Girl (was her name Melanie, maybe—or Melissa?) would often casually weigh in, gum bouncing around her mouth, A2-sized folder by her side, quietly asking for more black (always black) occultic symbols to be tattooed. This was her first Sunday appointment, a slot normally reserved for regulars. Like a lot of regulars, the real serious tattoo addicts, Punky Girl never spoke much, staring into space as the work was done. Occasionally Star would have noticed her arm getting a slight bout of shakes when she was feeling the bite of the needle. But she had never made a noise, never complained, never even as much as winced until today.

Fuckin' weird.

And she was dead, all right.

Perhaps it was the shape of her body on the floor, almost hog-tied, arms and legs somehow having crossed behind her back and curvaceous arse (yes, Star had noticed; yes, she had leered) as she had fallen. Perhaps it was the stillness, not just a lack of movement, but an almost statuesque stiffness, no gentle rising and falling of the lower back, no rhythmic whisper of breathing—all things a tattooist, like Star, would be working closely with, and against, every day.

Either way, Star was quite sure this bitch was dead.

Gone. Kaput. Fucked.

She turned the radio off. There was the distant sound of something colliding with something else, a hint of momentary madness, then nothing. Belfast became strangely silent.

A veritable drop-in centre for the torn-skinned and disenfranchised of Belfast, Starcrossed Tattoos would normally be filled with thirty-something drop-outs and twenty-something stoners. In a gaff normally bouncing, This Absence, This Lack, This Silence seemed wrong. In a shop normally so full of life, a dead body was like heresy.

In this place—*her* place. It sure as fuck wasn't going to be good for business.

Star sat her machine down, carefully, on the workstation beside her and rose gingerly from her stool. She bent down slowly, studying the fallen girl's pentagram. What had been done so far was fine, a little frayed at the corner where Star was inking when the girl had suddenly fallen, but otherwise in good shape. She had got most of the outline sorted. She was just about to change to another machine for filling in colour. As it stood now, however, the pentagram was unfinished, incomplete, unprofessional.

On dead skin.

She pulled her latex gloves off and discarded them in a nearby bin. Rubbing her shorn head quickly, a habit Star had developed when thinking on some shit that needed sorted, she strolled over to the door of her gaff and slowly opened it. Lighting up her third ciggie of the morning, Star casually stepped outside, sweeping her eyes left, then right, as she took her first drag. She sniffed ambivalently, spitting on the pavement after catching sight of the crooked outlines of two fallen people nearby. A dog lay sleeping, (*or dead?*) its leash twisting and turning to meet the hand of its collapsed owner. Along the long street, Star could make out more crumpled bodies. Just a few, what with it being early enough on a Sunday. But it was enough to reinforce what she already feared: This wasn't just some new, drastic reaction to the needle.

Continuing her brief stroll, Star discovered a Sunday more quiet than any she had ever known. She had never been a fan of Sundays, (for that very reason) but this was taking the Mickey. A handful of cars had stalled, untidily, across the city centre. More people were sprawled like homeless refugees on street corners and sidewalks alike. Several birds lay like fallen confetti outside a nearby church building.

Gingerly, she opened the gothic-looking doors. Inside, an entire congregation slept the sleep of the dead.

Star shivered, a cold and tingling sweat breaking out across her body. *This bollocks would have to happen now*, she thought, breathing the last drag of her ciggie in deeply then flicking it down the aisle of the cursed church. Why not last year? Why not when she was living in a squat in London, snorting Charlie like sherbet, moving from one fucked-up relationship to another. Not knowing whether she was straight, gay, heathen or holy, artist or junkie.

Why did this shite have to happen when she had finally got her arse in gear, finally made something of her life, found her niche, found her passion? She'd even taken out a bloody mortgage on her shop!

A mortgage for Christ's sake?! So, why now?!

Star lit another cigarette and smoked indulgently, sucking the nicotine and tar out of the damn thing until she was burning filter. Returning to the shop, she walked decisively over to her stool. She sat down before reassessing her posture and choosing instead to sit cross-legged on the floor. She pulled on another pair of gloves. Settled and once again poised, Star retrieved her second custom-made iron from the nearby workstation. She inserted a new needle, then revved the whole lot up again. She ran a critical eye over the half-completed pentagram on the dead girl's back, checking the line work. Her hands were shaking, nervous energy rattling through them. She breathed in, steadied them, then began.

She'd never left a job looking unfinished and she sure as hell wasn't going to start now. Apocalypse or no fucking apocalypse.

Several miles south of Starcrossed Tattoos, Tim Adamson helped Caroline Donaldson clamber out of the window of their stalled train. Flames still licked against the side of the carriage next to theirs.

The ridiculous sight of a car, burrowed into one of the train's carriages, both excited and terrified Tim. He heard the girl beside him giggle, then cry mere seconds later. She looked at him, hoping for some sort of comfort, but he offered nothing. (What could he offer?) Instead he ran a long-fingered hand through his hair, shaking his head and breathing out in one complete motion.

"Fucking mental," he muttered, staring at the car. "Did you see that?!" he added quickly, looking at the girl. "It was... *mad*... I'm telling you, that's... like... *mad*..."

Tim was trying to make some sort of sense from a nonsense. He knew the old lady on the floor of their carriage was dead. He knew it even before the girl had told him, explaining all that happened when he'd briefly passed out. He knew that a car had buried itself in the side of the train, now smothered in flames, and he knew that his MP3 player was broken. He didn't know the name of the mousy girl standing, shivering in front of him, although he had the sneaking suspicion that she was in his Biology class. Or was it Chemistry?

Whoever she was, she was crying. And Tim hated it when girls cried. He didn't know what to do, what to give her. He searched his pockets, finding a half-eaten Snickers. He didn't reckon that was the answer. Finally, he pulled his hoody off and handed it to her.

"Here," he muttered, reaching the hoody over, still shivering a little himself.

"Thanks," the girl replied, sniffing. She took the hoody, pulling it close at first as if it were a cuddly toy, before throwing it over her head.

She was cute. Tim noticed that right away. He even thought he could remember her name. *Caz.* Yeah, that was it. Funny name for a girl.

Tim looked at Caz, who was staring back at him, then around the Balmoral train halt, noticing several more bodies, each as peaceful looking as the old lady had been. Apart from the defined crackle of flames nearby, neither of the two kids could hear anything. There maybe was the faint sound of a radio playing, perhaps from the headphones lying beside one of the fallen bodies. But there were no cars, no people. Nothing alive stirred, neither from the streets below nor the bridge above. Nothing.

Tim slowly approached one of the bodies. A young lad, not much older than himself. Bending down gingerly, as if worried the dead lad might jump up suddenly, (BOO!) he prodded, with one finger only. Nothing happened. The poor bastard didn't stir. Braver now, Tim cautiously placed his hand on the lad's shoulder, finally working with both hands to roll the body over onto its back. The lad's face was nonchalant, almost as if he was still tuned into the headphones. Touching him was strangely a non-event to the teenager. Tim had thought that there would be some kind of definite chill to be gained from handling the dead. But the body was still warm. The dead lad might as well have been asleep.

"Is he..." Caz began, seeming to be searching for the right words, "like... *dead*, or what?"

"Aye... Think so..." Tim touched the body again, as if making sure. Still no reaction. Nonchalantly, he picked up the headphones, placing them on his ears. It was one of those portable radios, it seemed. Digital, maybe. Some granpa rock was playing, somewhere between country and Bryan Adams. Nasty stuff. But it would do.

"You're not taking that off him?! What are you like?!" Caz barked, seemingly appalled.

Before Tim could reply, both kids suddenly jumped, simultaneously startled.

"THE NEXT TRAIN FROM PLATFORM ONE WILL BE THE TEN FORTY-THREE FROM LISBURN TO BELFAST, STOPPING AT BALMORAL, CITY HOSPITAL, BOTANIC AND GREAT VICTORIA STREET."

It was the train station tannoy, an automated voice all too familiar. Its cold, pre-recorded tones rang out through the still train halt, slaughtering The Silence with an almost visceral shredding.

The two teens heard only the echo of the tinny voice and their own hearts beating, alone, among the fallen majority. Once the tannoy had quietened, its mechanical fuzz snapping like an electronic twig, there were only their beating hearts to be heard, seeming to almost harmonise each other.

Caz giggled again. This time, Tim joined in.

Professor Herbert Matthews sat up in his bed, the lines in his face reflecting more of his bemusement than the years on his clock. He realised how bloody late in the day it was on feeling the chronic rumbling in his belly (meaning he hadn't been served his Sunday morning fry-up in bed) and a precarious stillness in his head (meaning a heck of a lot of time had passed since setting his eighth glass of bourbon down the previous night and the opening of his eyes now).

His wife, Muriel, was nowhere to be seen and the sun was not only shining brightly, but splitting through the partially closed curtains of his bedroom. In short, Herb had no hangover. Herb was hungry. Muriel was nowhere to be seen and so, he surmised, something was most definitely amiss.

By all accounts, it seemed that Muriel hadn't joined him in bed on Saturday evening at all. There, on her dressing table, the Victorian one that she had fought tooth-and-nail to secure at the auction that day (against Herb's better judgement and the good health of his bank balance), was the same night dress that his good wife had ironed just yesterday afternoon. It definitely hadn't moved since then. Not only that, but her book wasn't on her bedside cabinet and the lamp (and this one was the clincher for the good Professor) which Herb had forgotten to turn off by his bedside table (because that was Muriel's job) was still shining uselessly in the sun-split bedroom.

Something was definitely amiss. Yes siree.

Feeling for his spectacles, Herb climbed painfully (damn arthritis!) out of the four poster bed he had shared with his wife for forty years, peering around for his dressing gown and slippers combo. He frowned upon seeing that the aforementioned slippers still lay where he had kicked them the previous night, and the aforementioned dressing gown (not washed, not ironed) lay across the chair of his desk. His papers littered said desk, a half-drank bottle of bourbon still sitting, bottle-top still removed, beside a half-empty glass.

The entire room stank of him, and not Muriel. There was no trace of her inane (yet easily missed, it seemed) need for tidying. There wasn't even a hint of her floral perfume in the room, or that pungent hairspray she insisted on spraying on her hair every morning regardless of whether or not she intended to go into town for shopping. There was nothing of her here, no evidence at all that she had passed through their bedroom in the last twelve hours and every evidence that she hadn't. And, frankly, that more than anything else that Professor Herbert Matthews would see, hear, or think from that time onwards, was utterly terrifying.

Ever since retiring from his position as Head of Faculty (Engineering) at Queens University Belfast, Professor Herbert Matthews no longer saw any reason to hide from the rest of the world behind the door of his office and weekly bottle of bourbon. He had figured the countryside would make a much better retreat for him, and Muriel (being something of a fan of solitude herself) had seen no reason to object. So lock, stock (four-poster bed and mauve suite of chairs) and barrel they had upped-and-away'd from middle-class Malone Road, Belfast, to the wilds of Ballyclare.

For Herb, it was an idyllic life. Semi-retired on health grounds (he had three years left to go until the official time to go), Herb had been trying to put the latter part of his career behind him. He had preferred to linger on the glory days, the days before academia when he had worked in industry, refining the very nature of engines and propellers and any other bloody thing which had cogs and wheels and gears. Herb had made those things run almost magically, lending him the reputation of something of a mystic within the linear world of engineering. He had been trying to rediscover that creative part of him, the part of him which had earned him such a name for himself that even his signature at the bottom of a research paper would lead to its immediate publishing in any journal across the globe.

At first the students loved him. His reputation had preceded him, meaning that you could have heard the grass grow at one of his lectures, such was the utter zeal of the young undergraduates that lapped up every syllable that came from Herbert Matthews' mouth. But times changed and students became more interested in partying than an old-school scholar like him. No longer did they remember the major feats of engineering he had pioneered. No longer did they care for his tales (dressed in pomp and ceremony for effect) of how much the mechanical world owed to Herbert Matthews. As time went by, Herb became less of a pioneer and more of a drunk, his lectures losing much of their old vitality, becoming out-of-date and irrelevant to an audience becoming increasingly less impressionable. With more time passing, he became accustomed to remaining in his office, drinking, as opposed to turning up for lectures.

Soon questions were asked about Herb's mental health and doctors called in to assess his suitability for work. The result was a diagnosis of alcoholism and agoraphobia, leading the professor to review his whole lifestyle. Retirement to the country had been seen by his doctor as a helpful first step to defeating his demons, but for Herb it was to be the only step. Within the last ten years he hadn't gone as far as the garden gate of his house, relying heavily on Muriel to look after his needs both inside and out.

Until today, that was.

Gingerly, Herb crept down the stairs, his pace and posture dictated more by poor health and lack of exercise than any perceived need for stealth. The countryside, usually quiet (as was Herb's preference), was unbelievably still this Sunday morning. Even the birds were on strike, the wind whistling, unchallenged, through the trees surrounding the

Matthews' small two-storey cottage. The sun shone magnificently bright through the front door's stained-glass window, casting a red and green glow against the pale walls of the hall and landing. Nothing could be heard. All was still.

Herb turned the handle of the living room door.

"Muriel?" he called. There was no reply. "Muri-eeel?" he tried, singing her name in that way he did when she was trying to ignore him. There was still nothing.

He opened the door wider, allowing some of the flickering light, from what appeared to be the television, to catch his eye. The curtains in the living room remained closed even though it was now early afternoon. Light from the television bounced around the walls, courting the shadows.

"Muriel? Are you in there?"

As the door opened further, Herb could just about make out the familiar frame of his wife sitting on her chair—the one opposite that bloody idiot box that seemed to entertain her so much. On closer inspection, Herb realised that the television was simply broadcasting a snowy picture, as if the channel had been tuned in wrongly. Muriel remained in the shadows, the sunlight unable to get past the living room's heavy-drawn curtains.

"Muriel, do you know what time it is?" Herb asked, the shaking in his voice coming more from a state of nervousness than any kind of impertinence. But Muriel wasn't listening. Her eyes remained fixed on the idiot box as if it were broadcasting something entirely revolutionary in the way of entertainment. Biscuit crumbs littered her lap, leading Herb to believe that her latest macrobiotic diet (or whatever it was this week) had fallen by the wayside yet again. A cup of tea rested in her hand, some of its contents having spilled onto the mauve armchair, drying, unchecked, to create a dark stain. Yet Muriel herself didn't move. Nor *had* she moved.

"M-Muriel?" Herb said again, this time his voice shaking.

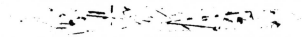

Star packed only a few things to take with her. She didn't need a lot.

What the fuck were you meant to pack for the end of the world, anyway?

Her small cloth satchel, tattered through years of airport abuse, now held her portable radio, a couple of hats—*never leave home without at least a couple*—and her ciggies. Just the essentials, really. She'd seen enough END-OF-THE-WORLD-AS-WE-KNOW-IT movies to realise that you could grab whatever you needed as you went along. It was one of the benefits to an apocalypse, of course—everything's free.

Pulling one of her hats on, this one a small, khaki peak cap, Star stepped out of Starcrossed Tattoos, deciding to head to the city centre. She would stop at whatever shop she could find along the way which had a television. She wasn't sure why the radio was still playing music, but she knew that noon had passed by with no news broadcast. In order to work out just how wide-scale this whole PEOPLE-DROPPING-DEAD thing was, she'd be needing the use of a television.

A fuckin' telly of all things.

She hated them, usually. She didn't even own one. Music was her thing. Star would usually have her I-Pod with her, but this morning she had mistakenly grabbed her radio instead. It didn't bother her, of course, because she quite liked that bloke who DJ-ed on Real every Sunday morning.

Music—*any* music, really—helped her work. It put her in the zone. It helped her focus on cutting those incredibly straight lines she was respected for. And it had allowed the whole fucking world to end without her even knowing.

The louder, the better. Block out the world around ye.

She was currently going through a weird phase of listening to movie soundtracks, *Betty Blue* being the current favourite. The lads who usually hung around Starcrossed were very amused, of course. She absolutely loved that film, but some of those philistines hadn't even heard of it—a veritable classic, a piece of cinematic history and those jokers could only sing *Groove is in The House* when she put the soundtrack on in the shop.

Fuckin' arseholes.

Walking along the deserted streets of Belfast, occasionally peppered by a crashed car here and a dead body there, Star suddenly felt grief for those a-holes at her shop. It was early on a Sunday, so most of them probably hadn't even got out of bed yet. Fuckin' alcos, the lot of them. She could imagine it, all right—those clowns had slept right through the end of the fuckin' world. A part of her smiled at that, of course.

Typical, really, she thought, whilst lighting up another cigarette.

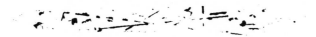

Tim and Caz made their way into Belfast, the added thrill of walking on a rail track racing their pulses further. Their youthful hearts were dancing with emotion, mostly excitement. They hadn't got to THE-WORLD-HAS-ENDED-AND-MY-MUM-IS-DEAD stage, although they were fast approaching OH-MY-GOD-THE-WORLD-HAS-ENDED.

There was a difference, of course. The former related directly to their own situation, and the true horror of it. The latter, however, still had a certain Hollywood romantic notion to it. With the former, they were victims, yet with the latter they were survivors. Different. Special, even.

The two teens ventured off the track onto the nearby streets, crossing the Adelaide halt bridge to reach the Lisburn Road. There was death in the air, the normally bustling slice of student accommodation and middle class coffee shops providing not even a whisper of life. The Silence reigned, the tall early-Elizabethan houses seeming to take on a new sinister quality when stripped of activity. Beer cans littered the streets, their rattling echoing through cul-de-sac after cul-de-sac, no longer smothered by laughter or spontaneous shouting, music or traffic. Everything and everyone that had once brought life to these formal, stern-looking houses, with their high ceilings and angular roofs, had died, leaving the houses themselves as the only survivors. Weather-beaten, sombre and persistent, only brick and mortar remained, when all of life was spent.

Nothing had passed. An occasional car was clumsily mounted on the pavement, spewing paper out of bins and glass out of windows. A light breeze carried the remnants of several post-boozing take-aways scuttling up the road. It was the only activity on an otherwise still road.

The teens had been walking for about ten minutes, Caz at times calling out her throat-scorching *helloooos* as she marched, tutting each time she didn't get a reply, Tim busy with his mobile as he dandered behind her, texting one minute, dialing the next, each time having no joy. Seemed no one was in anymore.

They had seen a few more bodies, Tim checking each of them for signs of life. He was getting braver with every one he checked, now lifting and rolling them over if necessary rather than just prodding them.

One of the bodies had made him a little curious. It belonged to a girl in her twenties. An attractive girl. She was dead. He was almost sure of that. Yet she still seemed very alive to him, almost radiant. She wasn't pale like the others. In fact, Tim had even wondered if she was just unconscious, if maybe this one had somehow, like Caz and him, been immune to—

What was it, anyway? Some kind of plague? Bird Flu?

He bent down to touch her. Her body was hot. Not just warm, like some of the others, cooling as time passed, but actually hot. And there was something about her face. It wasn't peaceful like the other bodies. No part of it seemed content with death, like all the other corpses they had seen thus far were. Instead, this body—this small, petite female, with ginger hair and a faint peppering of freckles—seemed almost angry.

Tim reached his fingers towards a lock of her hair. It glistened in the sun, gently dancing in the light, warm breeze. He ran each strand of ginger through his hand, almost expecting her to look up at him—a prince to awaken her from her still, angry sleep.

"Excuse me!"

Tim looked up to find his classmate, Caz, glaring at him. He had almost forgotten she was with him, such was his fascination with the corpse.

"Look... what are we going to do?" she blurted out.

Tim ignored her. He started texting again, sending message after message. He'd worked his way through all of the other Muckwits, anyone else he knocked around with. Everyone, really. Everyone except his dad. A part of him hoped his dad was dead. Another part of him grimaced at that thought. Truth be told, he was still confused by what had gone on over the years, unsaid, unchallenged, unexplained—how that bastard—that *hypocrite*—had come into his bed each night, when he was shivering and pissing himself to sleep. How his mum had known about it, yet said nothing.

"Tim!" Caz persisted.

"What?!" he shouted back. He hadn't even asked the girl her name, and Caz hadn't offered it. Neither had he clocked the fact that she seemed to know his, even though he hadn't offered it. Names seemed somewhat trivial during a time like this.

"I just think we should have a plan, or something... an idea of where we're going. I mean... are we going into town? Or some police station? Yes, that's it... we should go see the police, shouldn't we?"

Tim laughed in reply to this idea, picking up a police hat he'd found lying on the ground right next to its owner. He placed the hat on his head and performed a mock salute.

"Oh fuck off, Tim!" she swore, tears building again in her eyes. She obviously didn't appreciate him acting the dick.

Tim was only trying to help, of course. Maybe lighten the situation up a bit. But he decided this wasn't the time for pissing about. They needed to find someone who would know what to do. Someone they could trust. They needed to find an adult, someone who could explain to them what the hell was going on here—like why all of those people were dead and what happened to the train and that car that had somehow flown over the bridge.

He needed to stop being a kid and act more responsible. This girl— the cute one from his school—was depending on him.

Throwing the hat to the ground, Tim bent down beside the policeman's body and studied the gun by his waist. For a few short moments, he simply stared. Then, somewhat in awe, the lad carefully removed the gun from its holster. It was a handgun, that much Tim knew. It had a bit in the middle with six chambers, like the ones you saw cops carrying around in American cop dramas, and the like. It felt a lot heavier than he expected, and holding it gave Tim both a sense of power and nervousness. Rather than tucking the thing in his belt, like he'd seen cops do in movies, he put the gun in his shoulder bag.

He looked up to find Caz watching on without saying a word.

As one disc played out, Sean lined up another, fading music in and out without as much as a cough for his adoring public. Even for a DJ as economic with chat as he was, five songs without a single word was kinda pushing it a little.

Sean tipped a little more vodka from his hip flask into his coffee. All this stress was getting to him. He needed another drink. The twelve o'clock news hadn't happened. He didn't know why it hadn't happened, and with the sudden lack of producer or newsreader to ask, it didn't seem that anyone was awfully bothered about this monumental gaff.

And that just didn't make sense.

A part of Sean knew that something was wrong, that something had happened since the end of *Teenage Kicks* and the start of *Whiskey In My Jar*. He knew deep inside that something had gone badly askew, affecting more than just his playing list. He knew all of this because the twelve o'clock news hadn't gone out and not one listener, not a single sinner from the twenty-odd thousand good citizens of Belfast he seemed to play to most Sundays had rang in to complain.

Sean stared at the mic hanging several centimetres away from him. It was one of the old school mics, probably from the eighties when mics had got fairly minimalist-looking. Although it was the least modern studio of the two in the Real FM building, Sean still favoured this one. Its walls were wooden, littered with old pictures of celebrities over the years who had been interviewed there. A large plastic clock kept silent watch over time, never out of synch with the hourly pips, faithful to the very second. A small window high up in the back wall was blacked out, designed to keep passers-by from peeking in and upsetting the flow of broadcasting. A yellow lamp shed a little light on the dark studio, providing just enough illumination for Sean to pour coffee and undress vinyl, with the effect that it always seemed like night time. That's what Sean liked about this studio. It had a smoky Memphis jazz-club feel to it.

Sean looked again at the mic. He didn't know what to say, but he knew this shit demanded he say something. Maybe he should ask for someone to ring in and let him know what was going on out there... or maybe that would make him sound like a daft git. Maybe he should let everyone know that he was still here, still playing good music like he always did, just to see if anyone would then ring in.

Someone like your ex-wife... eh, Sean?

Sean decided he needed to think about things for a bit, and then decide what to do. He poured himself the last of the coffee, adding another generous drop of vodka to help him concentrate. He put some thinking music on.

The Silence was all that could be heard from inside the Matthews' cottage home in rural Ballyclare. The distinct (and for some reason now violently nauseating) sound of silence, its deafening vacuum giving Professor Herbert Matthews the headache from hell. Herb reached, almost automatically, for his bottle of bourbon, a cure for many ills. And God knows there was many-an-ill that Herb had woken up to this particular Sunday.

He was still in his pyjamas and dressing gown, what with Muriel not having taken the time to set out his clothes for the day like she usually did. Instead, his wife remained perfectly still and lifeless on the easy armchair opposite the sofa.

The crumbs were annoying him.

Muriel would not have liked to have been found like this. She was far too meticulous a person to be found in this way. It said little about how she was in life. It wasn't the Muriel that Herb had known and loved and shared his life with all these years. That Muriel was the Muriel that Herb really wanted to be with now and so, based on this simple logic, he did something which didn't come naturally to him.

He tidied.

He started with Muriel herself. Carefully, Herb brushed every last crumb off her lap then prised the tea cup from her stiffening fingers. She never flinched, of course, her listless eyes remaining fixed on the television which was still flickering soundlessly in the corner of the living room. She didn't even so much as breathe as Herb continued with his mission, folding out the collar of her blouse, replacing her slippers with her favourite shoes and sliding on her wedding ring. (She sometimes removed it for comfort). Herb wasn't sure why he expected her to move or breathe or talk. He knew deep down that she would never do any of those things again, but a part of him still expected it—*longed for it*—all the same.

Stepping back like some sort of artist, Herb examined his work. He looked at the corpse of his wife with the same critical eye that had won him a reputation for spotting the flaws in the blueprint plans of prototype engines all those years ago. And, as was the case all too often with the blueprint, he found the image wanting.

The crumbs were still there. They were all over the floor and Muriel wouldn't like that.

And so it continued, Herb working out how to use a vacuum cleaner for the first time ever, in order to suck up the offending crumbs before moving onto every other thing that remained out of place in their home; every unseemly thing that remained unattended to by the meticulous eye of his wife. He cleaned the small two-story cottage from top to bottom, learning the uses of many machines and potions (that he would have noticed Muriel using through the years) for the first time in his life. He did it for her, but also for himself, noticing (again for the first time) how therapeutic cleaning and tidying could be.

Once done, Herb sat himself down on the sofa opposite his wife. There was nothing else left to do.

So he cried.

Barry Rogan woke with a start, smelling his hangover before he felt its nasty effects on his body. The room stunk of beer and dope, nastily mixing with the definitive taste of last night's Chinese in his mouth. Suddenly he knew he was going to be sick, jumping out of bed and running to the communal bathroom outside his bedroom just in the nick of time. He stumbled back into his room, wiping the puke from his stubbly face.

Running one hand through his mop of unkempt hair, Barry adjusted his eyes to the semi-dark bedroom. The curtains remained wisely closed, offering a little protection for him and his hangover against the cruel sun.

Barry made a move towards his bed, again, thinking another couple of hours sleep might be in order before he could face any of the remaining day. It was then that he noticed the shape of someone else—a girl, he hoped—under the duvet. Closer inspection revealed the well rounded body of a female. Blonde, big tits, from what he could see, and a cracking arse.

Still have it in ye, boyo.

Barry had been feeling a little washed out since he'd graduated from Queens University. He wasn't quite ready for the BIG-BAD-WORLD yet, but felt too much of a hanger-on to keep doing the student circuit. He had known this day would come, dreaded it all the years of his degree.

BA Honours in English Lit. Waste of fuckin' paper.

But this little honey in his bed, this additional notch on his bedpost... well, it kinda showed him he still had his old mojo.

Events were starting to come back to him now. That ninth pint of Harp had really nailed him, it seemed, but he was beginning to recall actually meeting this little honey. She had been sitting across from him, in his usual spot, to the left of the dance floor at local indie haven, The Limelight. The Jam had been playing, and Barry was just about to get up and throw some drunken shapes to it before she caught his eye. She was looking back. Small, blonde, skirt up to her neck, this bitch had looked slutty enough to be his type. She was drunk enough too. Barry had sprung into action, grabbing his beer from the table, then casually strutting over to her table. The rest was history, as they say.

Girls loved a lad with confidence, a lad who would waltz over to their table practically smelling of sexual prowess. Barry was convinced of it. That was his secret. He'd learnt it through trial and error over the years whilst studying (*yeah, right*) his degree in English Lit, most of it spent getting pissed whilst researching the art of pulling birds—women, girls, whatever you wanted to call them. They were the only thing that Barry had really learned anything about during his three years of mounting up Student Loans and beer cans.

The don'ts as well as the do's, ain't that right, Barry-Boy? But you don't want to think of all that, now... Do you?

Slipping back into bed, his duvet cover still in need of a good laundering, Barry smugly threw one arm around the corpse lying beside him.

FOR THE NEXT FEW HOURS, BEFORE THE RAIN CAME DOWN, many of those who had survived whatever-it-was-that-they-had-survived found themselves in a sort of limbo. There were different reactions to what had happened, some people screaming uncontrollably at dead relatives, their primal keens ripping, briefly, through the pungent silence. Others seemed almost shell-shocked, staring at empty TV screens, or lifeless streets from their bedroom windows, lost in a melancholic daze.

Some people started moving.

From the outskirts of Belfast, they cautiously made their way into the city centre, hoping that whatever help was going to be sent (sent from where?) would arrive there. Likewise, others outside of Belfast, from towns like Omagh and Enniskillen in the west, and even Lisburn and Newry in the south, made their way carefully up the motorways, driving around the dead and broken, like skittles, to reach The Big Smoke.

Some people, of course, found themselves unable to move.

Ken Fitzpatrick, recovering from a road traffic accident which had left him in traction, had spent the last couple of weeks completely immobile at Craigavon Area Hospital, twenty-odd miles south of Belfast. He was unable to wash, feed, piss, or control himself when the nurse gave him a bed bath. Ken had been completely dependent upon the staff to meet his each and every need, with only a short cord close to his bed to allow him to call for help. Help hadn't come, of course, even though he had been pulling that bloody cord for the better part of three hours.

Ken was on a heavy prescription of painkillers, and would have been for some time, had this whole end-of-the-world thing not fucked things up for him. Four times daily, one of the nurses would come to give him both pills and a drink to wash them down with. The nurses would come at other times as well, brandishing a bed pan for him to do his business in. That hadn't arrived lately either, meaning that (what with all this nervousness) Ken had soiled his pyjamas.

The lack of painkillers was starting to have an effect on him. He could feel a mild tingle in his arms and legs. Within an hour, this tingle became an irritating itch, an itch he couldn't scratch, what with being strung up like a turkey in a butcher's shop window at Christmas. The itch, of course, soon gave way to a throbbing pain, growing in intensity until he was unable to stand any more, passing in and out of consciousness. Before long a fever broke on his brow and his breathing intensified, this combination leading to violent nausea. Within twenty four hours, Ken was dead, choked on his own vomit, his pain finally— and *eternally*—killed.

Quite a few miles above where Ken lay, passed the BMS26 flight from Edinburgh to Dublin. A Scottish lass by the name of Susan had recently discovered herself to be the sole surviving passenger onboard. Forty-one bodies rested around her. Susan would have thought they were sleeping, save for the fact that they had all nodded off at exactly the same moment.

And then there were the air stewards lying across the aisles.

For Susan, the faint hope that someone alive was flying the plane would evolve slowly over the next thirty minutes or so, the autopilot taking her safely towards a runway at Dublin airport. That hope would eventually fade, of course, as a dead pilot failed to take manual control for landing and the plane simply wandered south of Galway, using up more and more precious fuel. Although traveling at quite a speed and covering quite a lot of land, Susan was ultimately on her way to nowhere.

Sean Magee chose not to move, still spinning discs from his recliner chair in the Real FM studios. After exhausting the various emergency service numbers, Talking Pages, and for some reason his mother—*none of whom answered*—Sean had spent the last hour lifting and replacing the phone, debating as to whether or not he should call his ex-wife. His hip flask was pretty much empty now, giving his brain the jolt it needed to work things out a little better. He definitely knew something was wrong. Very wrong—so very wrong that he wasn't sure he wanted to know what exactly it was.

Terrorist attacks? Chemical warfare?

It was only when Sean had discovered the bodies of his producer and newsreader slumped at their desks in the office next to the studio that he really began to fret.

His hip flask was empty. His play list was nearing exhaustion. There was nothing doing. He knew now that he had to make that call to his wife.

A couple of minutes walk from Sean's studio was Barry Rogan's house. Barry, of course, also chose not to move.

He'd spent the morning in bed, sleeping through both hangover and Armageddon (which was worse?), one arm slung around the corpse beside him. When he finally awoke, dragging himself off to the bogs for another piss, it took him a while to readjust before inspecting the shape in his bed more thoroughly. It was then that a good ol' slap of *what-the-fuck?!* woke him up properly.

Of course, it wasn't the first time Barry had found someone incapacitated lying in his bed. Before he had learned how to charm his way into a girl's pants, Barry had used other, less noble methods. His mate, Dave, had got him into it, scoring him the drug Retinol. He'd only done it three times, only to see what it was like, and, as he'd said to Dave afterwards, the girls he'd used it on were dead keen anyway.

But he'd never forgotten their faces. Each of them had burned a permanent stain on his soul, occasionally leading to sporadic bouts of depression and self-reproach whenever dark, guilty thoughts wormed their way to the forefront of his mind. Barry lived in a constant state of denial learning to reason his ever-creeping conscience back into its box each time it threatened to stab him. It was a mistake he'd made (okay, *mistakes*) but it was all behind him now, wasn't it? Just a part of growing up that he regretted. Everyone had regrets. These were his.

What did it matter now, anyway?

But fact was, the girl in his bed *now*, at this very moment, looked drugged. There was no denying it.

This began to eat away at him. He felt the first wave of guilt wash through him, threatening to break down his well-protected dam. It was a familiar feeling. He looked, fearfully, towards the bed again. She looked just like the others had looked: peaceful, oblivious to what he was doing and where he was doing it, oblivious to his unprotected cock sliding up her leg...

No! That wasn't what happened last night!

More waves of guilt beat against his dam, stronger now and threatening to tear it down, but he knew—he simply *knew*—he hadn't used that shit, not for years now. In fact, Barry hadn't even seen Dave in years, not since he'd decided to put all that shit behind him.

Barry gently shook the girl for the best part of two hours, feeling like a total shit whenever he realised he couldn't remember her name. Guilt rose within him with every caress of her dead cheek, every gentle embrace of her dead body. He needed someone to comfort him. Unable to wake her, he curled up in a ball beside her cold, dead corpse, shivering with disgust at himself.

As the afternoon sun rose over a dead city, Barry's dam broke down. He cried his eyes sore.

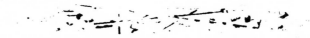

Star had seen enough bodies and crumpled cars around town to know that something was definitely not right with Belfast. Now she wondered about the rest of the planet.

Stepping carefully over two corpses at her feet belonging to an elderly couple, Star pressed her hands and face against an electrical shop's window. Her shorn head reflected in the large pane of glass, piercings and random zips of her urban combats glittering in the sharp sunlight. Her heavily blackened eyes narrowed as every television set in Dixons lost their reception, giving up life as simply and peacefully as every corpse seemed to have done. Snowy screens washed over every set like some kind of fucked-up Mexican wave. Star didn't move from her spot, simply staring at the fuzzy nonsense on each television set through the window. This was the stuff of horror movies. Opening the door of the shop, Star stepped inside, determined against the odds to find any fucking channel she could.

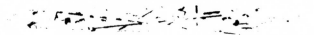

Roy Beggs was one of the survivors who was moving, gradually working his way up the M1 motorway. He was traveling in his Army Land Rover, packed to the brim with chemical toilets, canned foods, bottled water and other essentials. Hidden under all of this stuff was a small armoury, including several SLR rifles, a couple of pistols and two top-of-the-range sniper rifles.

A veritable veteran of the Royal Irish Regiment (although if you asked Roy, he would still have called them the Ulster Defence Regiment,) Roy had been somewhat trained for such eventualities as an epidemic/ bird flu/gas warfare attack or whatever the fuck this was. He had taken action rather than just sitting back. He had sorted things out directly, the way things needed to be sorted out. That was his way. Always had been.

Sitting beside Roy was Mairead Burns, a staunch Republican who had spent more than a few hours in the back of one of these Land Rovers. In days gone by, she would have kicked and screamed as she was roughly thrown in through their back doors during the Hunger Striker protests in the early eighties, manhandled by soldiers like Roy. Mairead also was a veteran—a veteran troublemaker for the likes of Roy, for the so-called security forces who had blighted her land for too many decades. She had spat, stoned and swore at pseudo-soldiers like Roy, calling them traitors and murderers. She had stored weapons and bomb-making equipment in her modest terrace house on the Garvaghy Road, hiding bombers and key figures of the Irish Republican Army (IRA) before and after operations. These weapons and bombs had been used to blow people like Roy to pieces as they investigated false emergency calls in key Republican areas.

An apocalypse was the only thing in the world that would bring the likes of Roy and Mairead together, Roy with the sleeves of his combat jacket rolled up, proudly showing-off his loyalist tattoos (REM 1690) and Mairead with her Sinn Fein necklace (limited edition) hanging outside of her blouse. These two were like oil and water, hated by and hating each other in a merry-go-round-of-misery grinding Northern Ireland into a political quagmire that was a fucker to get out of.

After basic introductions, conversation between the pair had been limited, for obvious reasons. Ironically, though, they shared quite a bit in common. Both believed in their retrospective cause with a passion like no other. Both had broken the rules—even broken the law—to further their cause. Both came from Portadown, described once by a key Republican politician as 'The Alabama of the North' (and neither Roy nor Mairead could argue with that). Yet, since Roy had picked Mairead up, somewhere on the Seagoe Road of said Alabama, hardly a word had passed between them.

Mairead had been in a car with her husband Mickey when the shit-hit-the-fan, managing to steer off the road when he had taken a nose-dive for the dashboard. She had tried everything to wake him up, then cried heavy-hearted tears for her Mickey, rinsing out twenty years of marriage in a desperate and vulnerable keen that one wouldn't expect from a hard-nosed battle-axe like her.

And yet it wasn't the first time this morning Mairead had cried. Dressed head-to-toe in black, she and Mickey had been on their way back from their son's grave. He would have been eighteen years old today, and for that reason Mairead's tears had been particularly stingy this year. They had dried quickly, of course, when Roy had shown up. She wasn't going to let one of his sort see her showing any emotion, any weakness, any humanity, so she clogged those tears up quick-smart, slipping on her Easter Rising face as smoothly as changing gears.

She was scared and confused and so, God forgive her, Mairead had taken help from the first person who had come along. Even if that person was the devil himself.

Mickey would have turned in his grave, (were he to have had one) if he could have seen his wife getting into a Land Rover with a Brit Bastard like Roy. But Mairead knew deep down that she had been left with no other choice.

Slowly and quietly, the pair traveled up the M1 motorway to Belfast. A small convoy of cars gathered behind them as they went, somehow thinking that following a military vehicle might lead to help of some sort.

Star was sitting alone, nestling a cup of coffee she'd got from a machine. Her drink had cooled even though she'd hardly had any of it. On the floor beside her lay her shoulder bag, containing the few possessions she'd taken with her. Beside that, a couple of Marks And Spencer bags, containing a few edibles and bottles of water.

It was there, the Marks And Spencer Food Hall in the city centre, that she'd seen it: A pram, dead mother draped over it like a fallen curtain. Of all of the horror Star had encountered since leaving her shop earlier on, all of the bodies she had stepped over, walked around, even searched for valuables (hell, it was the end of the fuckin' world, what did it matter?!) only that image had burned deep into her head. Only that picture was etched permanently in her mind. All the other bodies, all the other faces were like a sea of blanks, merging into each other.

But that child...

Like a tattoo, it stung and itched whenever she thought about it. It brought home to her the seriousness of what was happening all around her.

Those little hands, static, immobile...

That little face, peaceful, silent...

She tried to blank it out, tried to think of something—anything—else.

She hadn't found any sign of life so far, having wandered around the city centre for the best part of the morning and early afternoon. The hoarse crackle of flame here, a radio blaring there.

And those fuckin' televisions.

Belfast's buzz had suddenly been snuffed out, leaving only a messy and broken landscape. As she had gingerly tiptoed, opening the odd shop door here, checking the odd crashed car there, Star couldn't help but think how similar this desolation was to the aftermath of IRA bombs from days gone by. Only difference was that bombs made a sound.

Almost automatically, perhaps due to her love of travelling, Star had made her way, unintentionally, to The Europa Bus Station at Great Victoria Street. It had been renovated considerably within the last few years. (The good years, the years of peace). The Great Victoria Street Station was the centre of all travel from and to Belfast, hosting both Bus Centre and Train Station within its modern metal and glass structure. A small shopping mall occupied those entering the station's main entrance, but many preferred the side entrance, where the taxi depot serviced, close to the station's main coffee shop and café. Countless times Star had caught the popular Airbus from Great Victoria Street, taking her to Belfast's International Airport. That bus had been the first step to many a journey to near-and-far.

Now, of course, Great Victoria Street's constant hubbub was as dead as everything else, the bodies of queuing holiday-makers and business-men sprinkled around its spacious interiors, coffee shop and shopping centre like spent dominoes. An occasional suitcase had fallen hard on the floor, spilling clothes and toiletries messily onto the well-polished, cream tiles.

Star sat in the main café area, sipping her cooling coffee silently, taking a break from all the thoughts and theories spinning around her head. She ran her tongue over the back of the stud piercing her bottom lip, remembering for some reason that she had forgotten to brush her teeth that morning.

A sudden, shrill noise of breaking glass nearby, by the taxi rank, snapped Star out of her trance, her eyes widening with both fear and excitement.

Sean picked up the phone, this time with surety. He was going to ring his wife—

Ex-wife, Sean, don't forget the EX.

—and find out what just what the hell was going on. It had been hours now, but the phone was still working. Whatever insanity that was rife outside hadn't affected the phone yet. That was a good sign, wasn't it? He dialed the number, a number he hadn't rang in five years, not since that Christmas she had told him there was no need anymore.

No need?!

Yet still he knew it off by heart.

A panicked voice answered quickly. "H-Hello?!"

It was her. He'd never forget her voice. Never forget how he'd heard it the first time, singing with that folk band all those years ago.

"Sharon," he began, the vodka in his coffee having slurred his speech a little, "it's—"

"*Sean!? Oh, Sean... everything's wrong!*"

"What? Slow down, Sharon..."

"*They're all dead!*"

"Who's dead?!" She wasn't making sense. Her voice sounded hysterical.

"*Everyone!*"

Sean could hear Sharon sobbing violently between words. On and on she rambled. The words 'dead', 'everyone', 'hell', and 'fucked' being all Sean could make out. He couldn't get a word in; it was difficult to know whether she even heard him anymore. Finally she calmed somewhat, sniffing snot away loudly. "*Everyone's dead,*" she said more quietly.

"Sharon, just tell me what's happened. Is it a bomb?"

She ignored Sean's question, seeming to be lost in some sort of trance all of a sudden.

"We're all dead..." she said, eerily.

Sean's eyes widened, his hands starting to shake as he realised what was happening. It had been eight years ago, just before they'd broken up. He'd phoned home one night just to check up on her before he started the show. He'd been doing the evening slot then, having been moved during yet another one of the suits' shake-ups. When he'd rang, Sharon was in weird form, talking a lot of bollocks and generally not making sense. Then there was that voice—an ethereal and lifeless whisper. Half in the world, half out of it.

Drugged.

Sean had been able to get an ambulance to her just in time. She had taken enough sleeping pills to kill an elephant, but they were able to pump them all out of her stomach. Ironically, after saving her life, Sean lost his marriage. By the time the shrinks had picked Sharon's bones and brains, session after session of whys and wherefores, there was nothing left for Sean.

Depression, she'd told them. A feeling of disenfranchisement. And Sean had been the reason for all that, of course—the late nights, the morose, subdued lack of conversation, the bad sex.

The bad sex?!

She needed more, she'd told them. And then she told him that she was leaving, that it was part of her recovery to put behind her all the things that were wrong in her life.

Like her marriage... her marriage to you, Sean...

"Sharon, listen to me.. Did you take anything?! Sharon?!"

There was no response.

"Sharon!"

The sound of a phone falling from the other end of the line. Then nothing.

(Nothing was the new something.)

"Sharon! Nooooo! Sharon!"

The last song had ended, perhaps minutes ago. Sean hadn't even noticed. It had been *Don't Fear The Reaper* by Blue Oyster Cult. Later, Sean would see the humour in that. Later, he'd remember every last song he'd played in those final hours, the hours when the world had ended, when everything had changed.

But now...

Now only The Silence ruled the airwaves, The Absence... The Lack... It seemed to overpower everything. It started with the radio going QT, every electric radio and ignored alarm clock throughout Belfast now gently humming. Even static became a thing of the past. Then the power stations gave up, no longer able to hold out to the demands of a dead city's indulgent waste of electricity. Unmanned, unkempt and uncared for, computers simply stopped telling machinery what to do.

And then came the black-out. Like toy soldiers falling, the lights throughout Belfast dimmed one by one until there was nothing but shadow. Heaters and television sets around the country powered down. Electronic billboards gave up their relentless campaign of marketing whilst arrival and departure times at Belfast's two airports finally dulled.

Everything and everyone was officially pronounced deceased within seconds. In the dipping sun of the late afternoon, Sean buried his head in his hands whilst Belfast became a new city.

A city without power.

A city without Sharon.

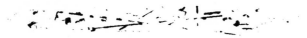

In The Silence, now seeming even quieter since the power went down, the shrill noise of breaking glass seemed amplified.

"Shit!"

Caz stepped away from the glass her foot had come down heavily upon. She was lucky not to have sliced herself. She had to be more careful, what with glass and wreckage dotted everywhere now.

"You all right?" Tim asked her, suddenly sounding quite alpha-male for a sixteen year-old lad.

"Fine," she replied. "Never even noticed that."

"You have to be more careful," he snapped back.

(Me-Tarzan-you-Jane).

Caz smiled, surprised at how much she appreciated his concern, no matter how badly expressed it was. They had been together for the last few hours, wandering through the torn city centre, avoiding the bodies and wreckage as best they could. A strange and foreboding sense of exactly what was happening was fading in and out of their post-adolescent minds like summer rain. But even in silence, even when neither teen knew the other or what exactly the other was thinking, to be going through it with a peer made things that tiny bit easier.

They didn't know why they had chosen to come to the station on Great Victoria Street. Maybe it was because they had met on the train, where everything had gone to hell. Maybe it was because they had heard that automated voice over the tannoy.

("THE NEXT APOCALYPSE WILL BE LEAVING FROM PLATFORM TWO.")

Regardless of the reason, they had found themselves drawn to this place—a place of transition—a place where journeys began and ended, yet rarely felt completed. In that way, it made perfect sense to come here. This was the place of the disenfranchised. This was where you waited for something else to happen, somewhere else to go.

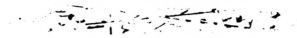

Star watched both kids as they opened the side door, spotting the first body at the entrance. The young lad held one large, glass door open as the girl made her way through. Star lit up another ciggie as she watched the lad bend down to search through the contents of a split-open suitcase. As the tattooist looked on, slightly amused, she watched him rummage through a dead man's belongings, picking a few things out and shoving them into his own shoulder bag. Star waited until they had walked a few metres beyond the entrance. Then she stood up, moving her chair away with her foot.

Bloody kids...

She took another drag, smiling wryly as the two teens literally stopped in their tracks, studying her as if they couldn't believe their eyes. The shorn-headed tattooist was used to people looking at her in that way, of course, her colourful image both shocking and attractive to Belfast's conformed-looking majority.

"Hey," Star called, somewhat lack-lustre. The two kids gawking back at her were the first living people she'd laid eyes upon.

"Hey," the lad replied.

three

T HEN CAME THE RAIN.

It came down like cats and dogs. Torrential. Sombre. Purifying. It put out every fire, every little flicker of flame. It wiped clean every blood stain from where the fallen had hit the ground, sterilising the pavements and roads as if Baby Jesus was trying to clean up his mess before Daddy saw it.

It came down hard and fast, and Roy Beggs found it difficult to see through the windscreen of his armoured Land Rover in order to continue his crawl up the M1 motorway.

The small convoy of survivors behind Roy's Land Rover mostly had their headlamps on. All except Steve Marshall, who hadn't bothered his arse replacing a broken headlamp since his shambles of a car failed its MOT last week. Steve had to make do with one headlamp, straining against the poor light and rain-stained vision in order to follow the military vehicle in front.

In the front seat of Steve's car was his dead wife, Kirsty. Her corpse was surprisingly radiant. Steve could still smell her distinctive brand of perfume, mixing with the sickly, sweet smell of death and shit coming from the small cot in the back seat of the car, where their son Nicky lay. Kirsty was wearing a simple white blouse and short mini-skirt, its subtle gem effect having glimmered in the same sun that had tanned her long, shapely legs. Even with the rain coming down, Kirsty's tan still glowed, her legs resting slightly to the left of the gear stick. Steve felt the hairs on the back of his hand brush gently against them each time he changed gear.

They were setting out for a Sunday drive when the madness had struck, sending the light traffic on the Lurgan Road wayward as Steve skidded to an abrupt stop. He couldn't wake either his wife or son, and was frightened to get out of his car to see what had become of the other vehicles that had skidded and spiralled out of control as his wife and child had seemingly fallen asleep.

It was just sleep, wasn't it?

Steve hadn't given up, of course. He couldn't give up on them. This was his family and it was his responsibility to care for them.

This thing could be curable, he told himself between heavy breaths and loud heartbeats, chasing the military vehicle in front. He hoped the police or the army would know what to do in a situation like this. He hoped they would bring him to a doctor, or a hospital, no doubt set up to deal with whatever the fuck had just happened.

They can do anything these days, those doctors. Anything.

Sean had to get out of there. He couldn't sit anymore in that damn room, surrounded by his ever-growing collection of vinyl and CDs, in a radio station that could no longer broadcast. With the lights now down, it was difficult to even see anything. He was virtually sitting in the dark, surrounded by useless equipment. After more years than he cared to count in the business, Sean's job was over. He had finally been retired, making the transition from crowd favourite to has-been a lot quicker than he previously thought possible. He was no longer useful as a DJ in a world without radio.

In the sombre twilight, the rain's constant and furious drone being the only soundtrack available, the once popular Real FM DJ packed a few CDs, some vinyl, and his last bottle of vodka into a strong plastic bag. Then he left this godforsaken studio. He walked purposefully through the small corridor to reception, stepping over the bodies of his receptionist, opening the door to the outside world for the first time in nine hours.

There... that wasn't so hard, was it?

Sean made every move with a numbness in his head and a heaviness in his heart. The Rain beat down upon him, unacknowledged. Trickles of moisture ran down his expressionless face, unchallenged. He was a shadow of a man now. All around him, spread throughout Northern Ireland, the vast majority of his twenty thousand listeners lay peacefully dead.

With one destination in mind, Sean wandered into the damp twilight of the evening.

"Do you know what's happening?" Caz asked, not entirely convinced that the pierced, shorn and tattooed young woman opposite her would know much more than she herself did.

They were all sitting at the small coffee shop built within the station's mall. The constant patter of rain kept a steady, sombre rhythm to an otherwise silent tune. A single candle burned in defiance against the ebbing blackness of nightfall.

They'd exchanged the basic pleasantries—names, etcetera—but little else. It seemed to Caz that this wasn't a girl who enjoyed talking much.

"End of the word, doll," Star replied, seeming utterly convinced. "The way this place was going, I'm just surprised it didn't happen sooner."

"But how?" Caz persisted, not entirely sure she agreed. "Maybe it's just something that's happened in Belfast?" Sure, something bad had gone down, but had it affected everywhere? Caz hadn't travelled that much in her sixteen years, but she knew the world was a much bigger place than the eye could see. Who was to say what was going on in, say Portadown, or Ballymena, never mind Melbourne, Australia.

"Television's gone," her new 'friend' replied, drawing on that damn cigarette again. "Not a single channel broadcasting. I tried them all, BBC, RTE, Channel bloody Four, Sky... even the fucking shopping channels. None of them are working. No TV... no world." She subbed her cigarette out in the ashtray on their table. "Much as I hate to fucking admit it, television's our window to the rest of the world. The news, the communication. Only thing that beats it is the internet." She searched through her pockets, finally producing another cigarette. "And the internet's fucked too. Not a dickie-bird about any of this on there, either. A lot of sites not connecting at all."

Caz looked over to Tim. He was playing about with Star's lighter, striking flame, then blowing it out. Striking flame again, then blowing out. It was starting to irritate her.

"Tim, *don't*," she scolded, before turning to the other survivor again. "Why are we still alive, then? This disease, virus, gas attack—whatever it is. Why hasn't it affected us?"

Star laughed cynically. "Who's to say it hasn't?"

"Well, we're still here, aren't we?"

"For now, yes." She lit up the other cigarette after grabbing her lighter back from Tim. "But how do you know we're always going to be immune to—well, whatever the fuck it is we're immune to? We could drop dead at any minute."

"You might, if you keep smoking like that," Caz snapped, somewhat frustrated by the morose attitude. The shorn-headed girl laughed, blowing a cloud of smoke into the teenager's face. It was enough to push Caz over the edge. She stood up, kicking her chair away in anger. "Star!? That's your name, isn't it?! I thought a star was a symbol of *hope*," she hissed, then walked away, sniffing away the tears.

She stood, looking out at the rain-stained streets to an empty void of Belfast.

Hope?

That first night was difficult. Difficult for them all. The seats at the bus station were comfortable enough, and roomy enough, to use as beds. They stretched generously in rows, offering plenty of leg room for even the gangly frame of Tim Adamson. A leather look finish offered a hard, yet firm, mattress. But it wasn't exactly The Ritz. Sure, the Europa Hotel was just next door, a mere stone's throw away from the bus station, but none of the three really fancied dragging dead guests out of bed before lying down in more comfortable surroundings. They weren't quite there yet, so here they remained, in this huge glass building. Clinical-looking. Minimalist décor. Its inoffensive, beige flooring and pale walls perhaps providing the subtle serenity that the three needed. In a way, staying at the station, sleeping there like travellers waiting for the next bus or train, helped them feel alien to this new and strange, dead world. Separate from it. Just passing through. In the courtyard outside, as if in response to the survivors' sub-conscious meanderings, lines of buses, uselessly primed, were parked neatly beside each other.

Neither the teens nor Star had come prepared, so they just used their coats as blankets. Comfy duvets had seemed unimportant, somehow, during their retrospective scavenging throughout the city centre earlier that afternoon. Sleep had been the last thing on their minds.

Whilst the night drew in, the torrential rain seeming to make the skies look even darker, the three survivors made their makeshift beds on adjacent aisles of seats. No one spoke or said goodnight to each other. And although all three were utterly exhausted, none of them slept a wink that night.

Sean Magee walked with purpose, almost oblivious to the dark, the rain and the few bodies he passed along the way. He was seeking closure, and in a world which seemed to have completely closed down, his quest seemed ridiculously ironic. Yet for Sean, it wasn't just closure from the phone call that was needed, but closure for his entire marriage. Closure for everything since that fateful night she had taken those pills.

He'd treated her well. Never hit her, never left her lacking anything. She had had everything materially that she could want. As long as Sean had a few quid every week to spend on CDs (hell, most of them he got for free, anyway) he was happy. The rest of his paypacket (which, let's face it, wasn't too bad after all his years at the station, and his pension was mounting up nicely, too) had been hers to spend as she pleased. Clothes, books, things for the house, whatever. She had it all.

But she didn't have you, Sean, did she?

Eventually he reached Sharon's house. He'd drove past it a few times in the past, sometimes pissed up, intending to call in. But he'd never had the balls. Now, of course, he had no apprehension at all. He opened the door quickly and assertively, quite confident that no one indoors would mind all that much.

From the inside, it didn't look anything like the house Sharon had shared with him all those years ago. He wasn't sure who's taste it was decorated according to, but it sure as hell wasn't Sharon's. Well, not the Sharon he knew, anyway. The walls of every room were white, almost blending into the ceiling like a sea of blandness. Random and abstract artwork cluttered the place, a painting here, some weird sculpture... *thing...* there.

In the living room, he found a photograph. It was Sharon and some arty-looking bloke. Smart pinstripe suit paired with trainers. Fancy Britpop haircut. Bit of a poncy looking fucker for a man of his age. Sean guessed it was this dude that Sharon had shacked up with. For how long this had been the arrangement, he couldn't tell. He realised, suddenly, how little he actually knew about Sharon.

Since that Christmas...

Gingerly turning the handle of the kitchen door, noticing the phone missing from its hands-free base in the hallway, Sean soon got the closure he was looking for. There, sprawled on the checkered-tile floor, still in her pyjamas, the phone resting in one hand, lay the only woman he'd actually ever cared for. On the kitchen table near where she lay, a tub of pills had spilled. Sean didn't need to read the prescription label on their side to know what they were.

The aging DJ pulled a chair out and sat himself down. For long moments he simply stared at his wife's corpse, one hand over his mouth.

"Oh, Sharon," he muttered, his hand muffling the words. "Sharon, Sharon, Sharon..."

Four

THE SMALL CONVOY FOLLOWING Roy Beggs and Mairead Burns turned off the Motorway, into Lisburn. They were about ten miles shy of Belfast, but the torrential rain and choking darkness was making the difficult enough job of driving through sporadic wreckage very hazardous indeed. Roy figured they needed to find shelter for the night.

Then Mairead spoke, maybe for the first time since getting into the Land Rover. "What are ye doing?"

"Pulling into Lisburn, love," he replied, eyes still on the road, windscreen wipers going like the hammers. "It's too dangerous to go on."

"But, what if they send some helicopters or whatever to Belfast, and we're not there?" Mairead was starting to panic. "What then?!"

"Well, just you leave that all to me, love. Nothing to worry about." Roy checked the mirror to make sure his band-of-merry-men were following him. "And besides, don't you want to meet all of this crowd?" He smiled over at the stern look on Mairead's face before adding, rather facetiously, "Never know... May even be a few more provos in there for you to chat with, eh?"

Mairead was seething at his remark, finding it difficult to hold back her anger. Provos, of course, was slang for the Provisional IRA.

Roy knew Mairead Burns. He'd dealt with her before, back in the 80's, when they had been investigating a lead from one of their grasses.

The deal was that the little fucker told Roy and his boys about any local IRA weapon stores in the area. Striking gold would slice a good five years off the bastard's life sentence.

Sure enough, they struck gold.

Mairead and her husband had been hiding a shitload of mortars in the greenhouse in the garden of her council house, just off the Garvaghy Road. She had pleaded innocence, of course, when they had knocked her door in one night. Spat, screamed and scratched at the soldiers who were throwing her in the back of the Land Rover, her young child crying uncontrollably as he stood in his pyjamas, watching the scene unfold.

Of course, she didn't recognize Roy. He had just been another Brit Bastard, no doubt, tearing her house apart. Another camouflaged goon. The Enemy.

It made Roy laugh.

That was twenty odd years ago, when both of them were a lot younger and even more bitter and entrenched. Yet even now, neither spoke as Roy continued driving down the slip road, looking for somewhere to rest up for the night, somewhere for them all to be comfortable. Somewhere where they could maybe even wash or grab a bite to eat. Somewhere, of course, without dead people.

Before long, Roy had found the perfect spot, straining against the poor light to make out a signpost nearby. It signed towards a primary school, just off the slip road, close to the motorway. Roy pulled over next to the school's gates, using his indicator lights to let those behind him know what he was doing.

Home sweet home.

Sean couldn't bring himself to get up. To leave. This was not the closure he was hoping for. He had dreamed of being in this house, went over in his head what he would have said to Sharon when she would have answered the door. But here he was. In her kitchen, staring right at her. A corpse. Just like all the others.

Only whatever had got everyone else, in the end, hadn't been pills.

It would have been better for Sean if she'd have gone like all the others, taken away without rhyme or reason. Unpreventable. Completely random. Yet this—this again?! What kind of a God would do this to him? Was Armageddon not enough for that Mother Fucker in the sky? Did he have to piss all over Sean twice in one day?

A noise. Creaking of a door. Was it locked? Did he close it when he came in? Sean couldn't be sure. Maybe it was just the wind. Or a cat.

Did Sharon own a cat?

No. There it was again. The noise. Footsteps. Coming closer. Coming towards the kitchen.

Carefully, Sean rose from his seat. Slowly, he moved his hand to the rolling pin sitting on the draining board.

In a world with nothing but corpses, Sean thought, *I ain't trusting no one.*

Roy stepped out of the Land Rover and gestured to all the cars pulling up behind him that he wanted them to stay put. It was incredible how much power you held when you wore a uniform in a crisis. Nobody even as much as wound their windows down.

Roy pulled a raincoat out from under the seat of his Land Rover. Sliding it on, fighting against the aggressive rain, he moved towards the school's front gates, keen to check the place out before allowing anyone else in. He unlatched the gate, opened it, and jogged the few metres across the playground to the school's front doors. His considerable beer belly meant he was out of breath by the time he had covered even that short distance.

The gates were locked. Roy gave them a good shake, but they held tight. He would have to find another way in. Squinting against the heavy rain, he pulled out a torch and snapped its beam on. He was going to have to go around back, and the Land Rover's headlamps weren't going to illuminate anything for him there.

The heavy-set soldier stepped carefully, lighting his way with the torch as he took each step around to the back entrance of the school. If the back door wasn't open (and why would any door of a school be open after midnight on a Sunday?) then he might have to break open a window.

It was locked tight, just as he thought. Scaling the walls leading back around to the front of the building, Roy searched for a suitably located window to bust through. Of course, he hadn't banked on one already being broken.

Someone had gotten there before them.

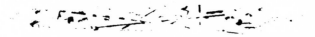

As the intruder made their way down the hall, Sean readied himself with his makeshift weapon, hiding as best as he could behind his dead ex-wife's fridge. Slowly the door opened, revealing a soaking, yet familiar, face.

It didn't take Sean long to realise who it was. Sean remembered him from the photo. The only difference being that the man (Sean didn't even know his name, and that seemed odd to him all of a sudden) was broken, and wore his face morosely to prove it. The once-perfectly-styled hair was glued to a furrowed forehead by cold, sickly-smelling sweat. The man's skin was pale, as if he'd just seen a thousand ghosts, and not one of them knew his name. His eyes hung out of their over-exerted sockets, a crude display of fear and loss peppering each pupil.

As he entered, the newcomer's mental health dissipated to an all-time low, catching sight of his sweetheart sprawled on the floor.

"Sharon," the man gasped, weakly. "Oh... my god... My gorgeous Sharon..."

Sure, it's Sharon okay... but she's not your *Sharon, mate...*

Sean followed the man's eyes, almost seeming to illustrate what he himself was feeling inside. He knew the man's pain, having experienced it himself just minutes ago. Like Sean, this man had come here chasing hope, fearing the worst, no doubt, after everything else that he had seen happen earlier. Unlike Sean, this man had likely been in the middle of the madness just as it was happening. Sean watched his nemesis (of a sort) deal with the same horror that he had dealt with himself. He followed the man's eyes as they poured upon the lovely, dead face of Sharon Magee.

Sean began to miss everything about her. All those phone calls he had cut short. The endless amount of nights he had left her in the house, by herself, while he was out pretending he was still twenty-one at some random club night. Sean longed for every one of those wasted seconds to be available to him again. Like some form of credit, he resented those minutes having been spent. Wasted. Squandered.

A sudden tearful choke gave Sean's position away. As the grieving man turned sharply, hearing the noise, his eyes widened. His sullen face changed on seeing Sean hunched behind the fridge, rolling pin raised weakly above his head.

"Bastard!" Sharon's partner screamed in a posh accent. It was perhaps the poshest version of bastard Sean had ever heard.

He lunged for the DJ, a fiery vengeance in his eyes. This whole end-of-the-world thing obviously wasn't sitting well with Sharon's hunny-kins, the man she would have shared her life with for the best part of five years, shared her bed with...

Good sex...

He looked like a man who had snapped, the sight of seeing his girlfriend dead on their kitchen floor perhaps adding to whatever other horrors he'd already been dealt thus far. Sean didn't know if the guy had recognised him, or knew who he was. He couldn't tell if his attacker knew that he had once been able to make his partner happy.

Make her cum...

But the way his hands locked around Sean's throat, it sure felt like he had.

Roy opened up the Land Rover door, passenger side. "Come on. Get out."

The torrential rain invaded, soaking her like a car driving through a puddle. Mairead Burns stared back at Roy Beggs, part incredulous, part surprised. "Thought you said to stay here!" she shouted over the wet din.

Roy laughed ruefully. "You think I'd really trust you to stay here by yourself? You'd probably build a bomb from one of those toilets or something." He opened the door wider, stepping aside to let her climb down. "Look, provo... I changed my mind. Come on. I want you where I can see you."

Mairead climbed out, snapping her coat out of the back as she did so. Fuming, she watched Roy go around to the back of the Land Rover and pick something out. He seemed to take ages, rummaging through all the gear in the back. The rain continued to hammer down and Mairead was growing impatient. She was also growing scared. Was he going to shoot her? A part of her really didn't give a fuck whether or not he did, yet another part—the fighting part, the soldier within—was already hatching out escape routes.

"Come on," Roy gestured, pointing to the school across the forecourt-come-playground.

Mairead felt his eyes lingering on the back of her head as she walked through the school gates, Roy following closely behind her. They made their way through the rain and splattering puddles until they reached the front doors of the school.

Roy showed Mairead the broken window. "Listen," he said, speaking in a low voice, "I know we're very different, you and me... Very, very different."

Mairead looked back at him, bemused, and still a little scared.

"But we're both the same, too."

"Look, where is this going?" Mairead snapped, losing patience. Nervously, she watched Roy take a handgun out of his pocket.

"We're both soldiers, you and me," Roy replied, his face taking on a deadly serious expression. "That's what I mean."

Mairead laughed nervously. "You're not going to get all love-thy-enemy on me, are you?" Her eyes fell back to the gun. It seemed more like he was going to shoot her than hug her. Give some bullshit speech about honour, then shoot her. His face seemed forlorn. For the first time since they had met, Mairead realised that he was talking straight with her. And it scared her.

"Don't think I don't know what you are and your kind have done to people like me in the past," he spat. His hand gripped the gun tightly, and it looked for a second as if he was going to use it, right there and then. "But there's no law here, not anymore."

Nothing happened. For a few stalactite moments, Mairead and Roy stood poised in the stark, rain-stained school grounds. The rain bounced off them as if illustrating the building tension. Roy's hand was still clenched around the gun, Mairead's eyes stuck to it like glue.

It was an ironic choice of venue, given what was being said. It was where it had all started for adults. The playground. All their politics and bullshit opinions about themselves. All their rules and regulations. All their games. But none of that mattered now in this broken-down world. Stripped of people, society's conformities and structures seemed pointless. No politics. No borders.

There was only this window. This school. A small crowd of frightened people huddled in their cars, waiting for someone to help them. A man standing beside a woman with a gun which he may or may not use against her.

It was Roy who broke the stalemate.

"God only knows who or what's inside there," he said, eyeing Mairead, "but they got here before us and I'd prefer to have back-up before I check it out."

Mairead stared back, matching his gaze, trying to work out if any part of him was talking shit. His rugged, yet not altogether unattractive, face strained against the rain. Water had dampened his thick moustache, making it look heavy.

Mairead went to snatch the weapon. Roy held onto it tight.

"Can I trust you, provo?"

Mairead glared at him, her hand firmly gripped around the gun's barrel. The two of them looked for a second as if they might suddenly struggle for it. In days gone by, they almost certainly would have.

"You can trust me," Mairead replied, finally.

Roy's grip loosened.

Mairead hadn't lied. They needed each other. Both realised it. He hated her as much as she hated him. Fuck, the way he talked to her was as if she was dirt on his shoe. This peace between them wouldn't last forever, but it was needed now.

Roy Beggs relaxed his grip completely, allowing the weapon to be taken from his grasp. As his eyes remained fixed on her, Mairead Burns checked that the weapon was loaded before nodding back at him. It was a series of motions so fluid, so calculated, that she knew he'd be unnerved.

A part of Roy Beggs, she reckoned, regretted giving her the gun right there and then.

Another part of him would regret it later.

Sean fought to prise the madman's hands from around his neck, panicking somewhat when he realised that this middle-class toffee had the power of a goddamn legion. His attacker's mental health was weak, ironically making his grip stronger. There was no doubt about it. He was tanked up on crazy juice, mad as a firework, crazy as a biscuit. But strong as a fucking ox.

Sean couldn't breathe at all now. The man's grip was tightening around his throat, rinsing more and more life out. Sean swung weakly at him, grabbing his damp, slick hair with one hand and punching him with the other. It hardly seemed to affect the crazed attacker. He probably didn't even feel it, such was his fury.

A string of incomprehensible obscenities and abuse spat constantly in Sean's face, creating a collage of terror. The words seemed lost to him, swimming away from him as if part of a dream. He began to feel his own grip on the attacker go limp. His throat had dried up, starved of air. It began to numb against the onslaught of pressure. He couldn't breath, couldn't move, couldn't shake this son of a bitch off.

This is it, Seany-boy. Say your goodbyes to your dead wife.

The room was going dark, spinning. The noise of the man yelling at him was fading in and out.

Ex-wife, Sean. Don't forget the EX.

His mind began the slow-but-sure journey through life. His eyes began to blur, stars shimmering and dancing all around him, his lungs giving up the fight against the pressure of the madman's grip. Sean could feel the tightness in his chest intensifying, years of heavy drinking seeming to kill him that little bit quicker, that little bit sooner.

And then came the jolt. A sudden and almighty halt to proceedings. As if the pause button had been pressed, the words stopped attacking him, spit stopped soaking him. The grip loosened, the madman's eyes becoming still and startled suddenly.

Another jolt. Then another.

Sean grabbed his moment, kicking his attacker away with a desperate burst of energy. The crazy man's body fell lifeless to the floor beside Sharon, Sean landing immediately on top, spitting and coughing, recovering his breath.

As his eyes regained focus, the dizziness gradually clearing, giving way to nausea, Sean was able to make out the wide-eyed profile of a young man staring down at him, bloodied kitchen knife in one hand.

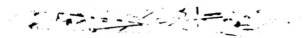

Mairead squeezed her small, stocky frame through the broken window, helped by Roy, dropping down onto the tiled floor below. The room she landed in was dark, and it took her eyes a while to accustom to her surroundings. In the poor light, she couldn't make out much short of the room's shape, a doorway and little else. However, she worked out fairly quickly that she must be in a locker room of some sort. The smell give it away.

Sweaty socks.

That smell brought her back to several years ago, just before her son, Pat, had got too big. Just before he had started washing more than his face, combing his hair more often, asking for whatever trainers were fashionable at the time. Just before he had left school, got himself in with a bad crowd, found himself in more trouble with the pigs than even Mairead would have liked.

—Just before he blew himself up.

Mairead put the thought out of her head, sliding it into the same box her dead husband was currently residing in, unchecked, unmarked. A box that would have read 'Briefly Mourned', had someone the time to mark it such, but for Mairead all of this stuff had happened so quickly that such a box hadn't even been built yet. Thoughts circled freely around her broken mind, body and soul. Nothing had settled. She felt almost dizzy with the chaos of it all, yet valiantly fought to steady herself. This was the first time she had been alone, the first moment of solitude, and it didn't bode well for the future.

Mairead had to focus, concentrate. She checked her handgun. It was a standard Glock. One she was familiar with, possibly even having fired during IRA training.

Accustomed a little better to the dark, Mairead slowly and quietly moved towards the door of the locker room. Leaning back against the wall, she held her gun up with one hand as the other slowly opened the door. It creaked obnoxiously, causing her to freeze. She held her breath, listening for signs of life or alarm.

None. Nothing.

(The new something.)

Mairead crouched, stealthily sneaking her way through the double doors, out into the school's main corridor. It wasn't far to the back entry, where she had agreed as her rendezvous point with Roy.

Fucking brit.

Finally she reached the back entryway. A door stood, solidly. A key was precariously resting in its heavy-set lock, carelessly left by a caretaker who was probably dead now. With little sound or trouble, Mairead undid the latch, turned the key, opening the door to the somewhat rain-soaked and bemused face of Roy Beggs. Without even as much as a nod to her, she watched as Roy crept in, pulling the door quietly shut behind him.

Together they moved discretely along the school's main corridor, checking each door they came to for signs of life or death. It was Sunday, so the classrooms normally stocked full of screaming children were empty today. Each chair was stacked neatly on top of its respective desk, nice and tidy for the cleaner on Monday morning. Yet the floors remained as they had been left the previous Friday. Specks of glitter from the Friday afternoon artwork glistened in the poor light. Desks remained unpolished. A thin veil of dust hovered in the musky air. The cleaner, a Miss Evelyn Johnston, currently lying dead in her bed, had a similar attitude to death that she'd had in life. Do as little as possible—as little as you can get away with.

She hadn't even bothered to wake up in order to die.

A sudden noise. Something falling, or tapping against a table stopped the two unlikely allies in their tracks.

Roy drew his handgun and prepped himself for action. He looked to Mairead. She shrugged her shoulders, signaling to him that it was the first time she had heard the sound. Taking the lead, Roy inched his way back down the corridor.

Mairead slowly followed, suddenly thinking how easy it would be to shoot Roy in the back were she to take the notion.

There, again. Same sound.

Roy glanced back, his eyes straining against the darkness, no doubt finding the frame of Mairead, gun ready, several feet behind him. She fought back a smile. He was clearly freaking out. Hers was a profile that would ordinarily have struck terror into him. A profile that could have meant his death were it to have been several years ago in the heart of West Belfast. Tonight, however, it provided support, albeit uneasily.

The noise, again. This time louder.

The door to a classroom further down the corridor gently swayed open, as if invitingly. Roy stared at the door's movement, pausing briefly, before looking back to Mairead. She shook her head in response. She felt just as apprehensive as he looked.

Roy gestured to her that he was going to make a move. Mairead nodded back, indicating that she understood. She was prepared to back him up. This time.

As the door to the classroom flapped gently in the draft, the heavy rain seeming to drown out any sound it was making, both soldiers caught an earful of that noise again. It was like tapping, a nervous rhythm being drilled out on wood. It drummed out eerily within the still, lifeless corridor of the school, darkness cloaking every painting, every photograph and every trophy no doubt lining the walls. This was their guy, Roy seemed sure of it, and Mairead readied her gun in agreement. This was whoever had broken in and was, therefore, a threat to them.

This was someone they needed to take out.

Following close behind, Mairead watched Roy darting through the door, handgun raised threateningly. His voice rang out, aggressive and full of venom.

"On the fuckin' floor! *Now!*"

Sprinting in from behind, Mairead could see that he'd almost pulled his trigger, stalling at the last second and lifting his gun high into the air, almost as if surrendering.

What the fuck is...

And then, with the pale moonlight spilling through the classroom's opened curtains, Mairead could see the reason for Roy's bizarre about-turn. The small profile of a child, terrified, looked back at her. Alone at a desk. Her hand holding a pencil, as if it bore the meaning of life itself.

For a moment, there was silence. The child had stopped scribbling with her pencil.

So that's what that noise was.

Instead, she screeched on seeing Roy's large frame, on catching sight of the gun that had been aimed at her only seconds ago.

The sudden, shrill noise of the child screaming clearly startled Roy even more than being met with the fully-grown threat he had expected. Mairead watched, agape, as the heavy-set soldier almost tripped over himself like some kind of big green clown, dropping his weapon in the process.

Using the torch Roy had given to her earlier, Mairead made a bee-line for the distraught child. With the desperate, maternal instinct of a mother robbed of a child in its prime—

("There's been an explosion, Mrs Burns...")

—Mairead wrapped its small frame in her arms, immediately making soothing noises. She looked to Roy with even more disgust in her eyes than he was, no doubt, used to.

"For fuck's sake, Roy, she's just a child."

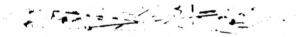

Sean finally set himself down at the kitchen table. There were two bodies on the floor now, lying in almost romantic proximity to each other, as if part of some kind of Sid-And-Nancy hoo-haa.

Yeah, Romeo and fucking Juliet.

He went to speak, realised he couldn't, instead pouring himself a drink from a jug of water on the table. He gestured to his rescuer, checking to see if the young man wanted the same.

"Oh, fuck," came the reply, the young stranger staring with horror at the corpse he had just created, not even seeming to notice Sean. "Oh, fuck me..."

The lad began to whimper, huge terror-stricken tears filling his eyes quickly. "I... I didn't mean... I tried to shake him off you..." He turned to look at Sean, desperation in his face. "*I had to!*"

Finally getting his voice back, Sean stood up, pulling another chair to the table. "Don't look at it. Here. Sit down a minute."

The young dark-haired man went to sit down, then seeming to realise he was still holding the blood-stained kitchen knife, jumped back up again. He all but threw the knife to the ground as if suddenly discovering it to be a hot coal.

"Fuck!" he yelled, wide-eyed and breathless.

"Listen, the guy was a nut," Sean offered, trying to calm the lad down. "You had to do it, just like you said."

The young man looked at Sean, squarely. Bizarrely, and untimely, it seemed to click with him just who he was talking to, just whose life he had violently saved.

"You're that DJ, aren't you?" he said, somewhat inappropriately considering what had just happened. He ran one shaking hand through his lank, wet hair. "Fuck me... I used to listen to your show..."

Sean was about to answer when the lad suddenly jumped back to his original train of thought, launching himself into another full-on keening session. As Sean watched on, clearly powerless, his unlikely saviour cried hard and heavy, like a child. An overgrown, heavy-sobbing child. With stupid-looking hair.

"What... the fuck... is going on here?" the lad finally managed, through sobs.

Sean insisted they both sit at the table. The lad finally obliged, seeming only semi-aware of his movements. Still traumatized, obviously.

Sean fixed them both a drink from the fridge. Two cold beers. For several long and much-needed seconds, the two men sipped at their drinks, shaking and shivering almost in time with each other.

Sean told the lad everything that had happened to him. Every event in the finest of detail, from the minute he had put on *Whiskey In My Jar* to the second he thought his life was over. He told him all about there being no news bulletin, about the sudden and unmistakeable silence that descended. About the vodka and coffee he had consumed. About the dead news reader and his ex-wife's phone call. About the music he had played.

(A lot about the music he had played.)

He told him about the bodies he had seen on the streets and the quiet carnage. About the rain, and the madman who had attacked him.

He told the lad everything, because he reckoned the lad deserved to hear it all, what with having saved his hide. He also thought it might calm him down. Hell, calm them both down.

The young man listened, eyes constantly wide, occasionally wandering back to steal a glance of the man he had just killed.

"Fuck me," he said again, having heard Sean's tale. His vocabulary was understandably limited. "There's some very serious shit going on here..."

For a few more moments they both sat, glaring at the two bodies on the kitchen floor. It was as if they were watching something on television, drinking beer and shooting the breeze. Father and son. Watching the footie on the box.

"What's your name, by the way?" Sean asked, setting his beer down and offering the lad his hand. "Figured I should really shake with the guy who saved my life."

"Barry," replied the young dark-haired man, shaking Sean's hand limply. "Barry Rogan."

THE PREACHER MAN SHIELDED HIMSELF AGAINST THE WIND, a lone figure amongst the dead and rain-stained streets. He was soaked through, hardly having noticed the incessant downpour whilst it had drenched him. Now that the rain had ceased he could actually hear himself breathe again. Heavy, solemn breaths. Despondent. Guilty. Full of the spirit.

The Preacher Man's brow was furrowed, although that was nothing new. Daily his brow furrowed, as he stood where he stood now, the Band Stand at Cornmarket, preaching the good word. His voice would have carried across four streets of sinners, some cursing him audibly as his campaign of blood and thunder was waged. Daily he had toiled, mostly in vain, what with people these days having a new religion—that of commercialism.

The streets in this part of town were full of things to compete against. Clothes, jewelry, shoes, games, DVDs. All manner of shiny, sparkly things. The devil's grip on Belfast was strong, that was for sure.

In days gone by, The Preacher Man had preached often and long about what was now happening.

The Second Coming. Judgement Day. Wages Day. Armageddon.

His well-worn Bible—King James version, of course—providing evidence sufficient of how hard he had worked to save sinners, some of whom were now lying dead around him.

For the wages of sin is death.

But he failed to see why he had been left behind to suffer along with them, why he wasn't snatched greedily away in the Great Rapture by his Lord and Saviour, why Jesus fucking Christ hadn't taken him by the hand.

Like you promised, Lord?!

His dead wife and mother provided further evidence that Great Jehovah had pissed all over him from a great height. Shat upon him, his family and all that he had worked hard to create. He had preached about God's wrath, yes. But he'd also told the good news of God's mercy— God's love for those who were faithful to him.

His rod and staff to comfort them as they walk though the valley of the shadow of death.

Yet here he stood. Alone. Broken. Rejected.

Why me, Lord? Why?

That was the only question to be asked now. That was the only prayer worth praying. He had stood in this very spot. Daily. Microphone in hand, his brothers and sisters in Christ around him. They had sang many songs of praise, many of the old gospel hymns, their voices joining together in sombre worship of their Saviour. Yet the only song he could find it in his heart to sing now was one of sheer desperation.

Lord, have mercy upon me, a sinner!

Numerous doubts wormed their way into his mind as The Preacher Man stepped under the old Band Stand's ornate roof for shelter. Hadn't he been faithful enough? Hadn't he preached enough, won enough souls for his Lord Jesus? Hadn't he himself been blameless? Or had he let the Devil get under his skin, and bowed to temptation?

The sex, the drink, all the evils of the world…

As The Preacher Man stood at his faithful spot, searching desperately through his well-oiled Bible for clues as to why he had been abandoned, left to rot amongst the damned—*a sheep amongst goats*—the incessant rain continued to fall.

THE SURVIVORS FROM THE CARS GATHERED IN THE SCHOOL'S small assembly hall, strangely silent regardless of their impressive number. Roy was busy herding them, showing them where to get some water, helping to open up the larders and free some tinned foods, tasking some of the more 'together' survivors with simple jobs, such as wrapping torches together with masking tape, creating makeshift lamps to illuminate the dark corridors, canteen, and hall. For the most part, they seemed happier to be led, content to be occupying themselves with small responsibilities, striving to keep their minds from dwelling on individual tales of woe.

Except for Mairead. She was still fussing over the child she and Roy had discovered a short time ago sitting in the dark at the very desk she had spent most of her third year at Primary School. Her school uniform had been sloppily hanging around her tiny frame, back-to-front, so Mairead was fixing it for her, helping her look smart.

She was called Clare McAfee. She was from the area, mere minutes away from the school. Clare had told Mairead that she didn't know what to do when her mommy had fallen asleep. She had forgotten that it was a Sunday, worrying that she would get into trouble for not going to school. So that's where she went. She had washed herself, made herself some cereal and dressed herself, before hurrying out into the dead world.

The school gates were locked, probably to keep her out because she was late, Clare told Mairead, so she had climbed over them. The doors were locked too, so Clare had broken the window, climbed onto the bin and clambered through. She didn't remember that part, probably due to the shock, but it was obvious to Mairead, in retrospect, because the child's arms were scratched where the glass had sliced her, leaving her white blouse slightly stained by blood. Luckily, apart from that and a few bruises from dropping down into the changing rooms, Clare was relatively unharmed.

It seemed that the child had sat all day at her desk, in the classroom where she had spent the best part of the last year, scribbling nonsensical words into her homework jotter. When the jotter had filled up, she had started on the desk. That's what the noise had been—that insidious scratching noise that had freaked Roy Beggs out, almost leading to...

(*"There's been an explosion, Mrs Burns..."*)

The poor child. Zoned out, catatonic with fear and loneliness. Half-dressed and hungry, her clothes soiled and her tiny heart broken. Sitting at her desk, scribbling like a maniac as the night drew in and the rain opened up.

"I think it's still okay..."

Mairead looked up from where she and the child were sitting to find Roy awkwardly offering Clare a glass of milk. Roy had that friendly look painted over his red, puffy face. Mairead had seen it before. It suited him. I made him look more approachable and less like a fucking brit thug.

"You can smell it, if you like," he added, stooping awkwardly as he reached his peace offering down to the little girl's level.

As Mairead watched, Clare obediently took the glass and sniffed it, smiling up at Roy to let him know the milk was okay.

He smiled back, producing a chocolate bar from his back pocket like some kind of bargain-basement magician. He whispered, conspiratorially, as he offered her the chocolate, "Don't tell anyone I gave you this, all right?"

The soldier's voice was gruff, but heavy with affection. His large-boned, poorly exercised profile seemed almost bear-like compared to the tiny frame of the child. Mairead smiled weakly at his almost creepy efforts to comfort the girl. Despite herself, she knew Roy was genuinely feeling bad for scaring her earlier with his unnecessary assault on the classroom.

"Say 'thank you'," Mairead encouraged, more for the child's benefit than for Roy's.

"Thank you," Clare repeated, parrot-style.

The hungry-looking child made very short work of the milk and chocolate. Her innocent little face swallowed the bar in a few bites, her cheeks filling up like a gerbil. She gurgled the milk down, loudly, both Mairead and Roy watching her every little move as if it might be her last.

Mairead reached one hand into the pocket of her jacket, feeling the handgun Roy had given to her earlier. She gripped it tightly. Its cool, smooth metal now represented a duty to protect as opposed to a means to fight. With a child's life in the balance, Mairead's mindset was changing. She had seen Roy as her enemy—in many ways, her captor. The handgun had made her an equal to him, perhaps even a threat, and she wouldn't have hesitated to use it against him. Yet now, as she watched the burly soldier fuss and gush over the child he had literally tripped over himself to save, Mairead realized that, at least for now, they both wanted the same thing: To protect the innocent.

The very definition of innocence.

It remained to be seen who or what the new threat was, but as her hands curled around the familiar shape of the Glock, Mairead knew she would be ready, waiting to take out any bastard who threatened her child's safety.

("There's been an explosion, Mrs Burns...")

("...an explosion.")

("...an EXPLOSION.")

And as she watched the soldier cooing like a granny, she was pretty much sure Roy Beggs would too.

The enemy of my enemy, she mused, smiling.

She had eaten nothing since breakfast so Clare was very hungry. She had forgotten just how hungry she was, how much she had missed her coco-pops in the morning and jam-drenched soldiers.

She was starting to relax a little now, contented somewhat by the attention given to her by these nice adults. They were strangers, she knew that. And strangers were normally bad. But there were a lot of them, and they couldn't all be bad.

It seemed like something was definitely wrong with the world. None of the people Clare knew and trusted seemed to be around anymore. Her mummy must still be asleep. There was no Granny and Granpa visiting at twelve, bringing her a new toy, like every other Sunday. Even the TV wasn't working. Everything was different.

She remembered how quiet the streets had been when she set off for the school. No other children playing, like there normally was. No cars driving by, roaring down the busy road that her Mummy and Granny and the teacher and Mr. Gillespie, the lollipop man, had all told her to be very careful on. Clare had stopped, looked and listened for ages, but no cars came

Nothing was normal.

It seemed best to go to school. She remembered that time that Mummy had been late, and all the other children had gone home, leaving her the last child in school. She had stayed with the teacher, doing some painting. Mummy had been very sorry for being late, but she had told Clare that she did the right thing. *If I'm not there*, she had said, *just stay in school until I get there. Always stay in school.*

So that's what this was like, really. She would stay in school until Mummy woke up and came to get her. She would stay with these people...

That's what Mummy would want.

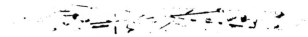

"How's she doing?" Roy asked Mairead, lowering his voice enough to avoid the child overhearing him.

"She's okay," Mairead whispered back. "Probably still in denial."

Roy shook his head. He felt for the child. She had retreated into her routine to escape dealing with all that had happened to her, retreated into the only place she could feel secure when things went belly-up at home. Roy figured that deep inside this little girl knew what had happened, knew the scale to which this was going to affect her young life, but was refusing to confront it. A glass of milk and bar of chocolate wasn't going to help much when she decided to deal. *If* she decided to deal.

"I'll get her a camp bed made up so she can get some sleep. It's after midnight, so we should all rest up here anyway. At least for tonight."

Mairead agreed, smiling over to Clare as the young child drained her glass of milk.

Looking around, the two ragtag leaders could see small groups of survivors working together to make the assembly hall as comfortable as possible. It was to be the birth of a new community. One, perhaps, without colours, or flags or murals on walls. One simply about survival, and the struggle for such, both emotionally and physically. They wondered, briefly, if it was possible, even in their situation, to build a community like that.

"Finished!" Clare suddenly exclaimed, proudly offering her empty glass to Roy. His eyes welled up as he took the glass back, walking away without so much as a word. Roy Beggs, a man roughened around the edges by the hard-dealt hand of the so-called Troubles and his own self-fulfilling bitterness. A man not normally accustomed to displays of emotion. Yet even he was melted by the total innocence of this little child, and the sheer hell she'd been through.

"Good girl," he heard Mairead say, throwing an arm around the child.

Roy wandered out onto the damp tarmac playground, finally grabbing a minute to be alone and take a few breaths. He often felt claustrophobic whenever conditions were cramped. And boy were they cramped, now, in the school's small assembly hall. Sometimes he just needed to get away and literally take a breather.

The rain was still hammering down, and Roy took shelter under a nearby bike shed. He looked over at the small convoy of cars and other vehicles parked randomly just inside the school grounds, near the trees. These people were his people now. They looked to him, obeyed him whenever he asked them to do something. And now there was this child, Clare. Fuck, she was just a baby. Not normally a man given to self-doubt, Roy Beggs suddenly began to feel every ounce of the responsibility resting on his shoulders. In his heart of hearts, as his mother would have said (God rest her soul), he knew—he simply *knew* that there were no helicopters waiting for them in Belfast. No ships at the docks, full of British troops—*Real soldiers, Roy, not glorified TA like you*—ushering hordes of survivors onto boats to be shipped over to The Mainland (RULE BRITANNIA!) where everything was just hunky-dory. No, Roy knew that this was their lot. Small groups of survivors gathering. Rebuilding. Restoring what was left of an over-saturated world.

Taking in another long, deep breath of air, Roy thought about these things. Breathing out, he caught a glimpse of movement by one of the cars. Squinting against the poor light and pouring rain, Roy was able to make out the figure of Steve Marshall, one of the survivors.

Steve was the one who had driven behind Roy's Land Rover in his beat-out Fiesta, with the one headlamp. Roy remembered his car, like a one-eyed bandit, battling defiantly against the downpour of rain as it travelled behind him. He had met Steve earlier, the two of them having recovered some canned food from the school's kitchen. Roy had found him uneasy company, but put it down to the catastrophe rather than any other factors.

Hell, they were all uneasy company today.

But now, whilst the others thrived on being together, comforting each other, quietly, in a shared hour of need, this guy was just sitting in his old, beat-out car.

"You okay over there?" Roy called out, suddenly back on duty again.

"I'm dead on, mate," Steve replied, smiling back. He stuck his head out of the open door of his car. "Rain's still holding up, I see."

Roy realised that it was the first time someone had mentioned something as trivial as the weather to him.

"Yeah," he muttered, half-heartedly. "Guess it is."

Small talk like this didn't seem appropriate in this brave new world. It didn't fit. Didn't mean anything. The shock of normality reminded Roy too much of what they all had lost, and it was too soon for that. But, sure enough, the rain of earlier was still holding strong. Despite this, the clouds had cleared a little, peeling off their grey skin to reveal a treasure of stars. For Roy, seeing the stars offered some kind of hope. Some kind of reassurance that whatever God was up there looking down on them still had his hand in the game. Still cared enough to make the moon and stars come out at night, despite the rain.

Roy glanced over to Steve before turning to walk back inside again.

Steve Marshall sat in the driver seat of his car. He had the radio on, but only a dull-pitched static could be heard playing over the tip-tap of the rain's constant beat. Steve watched, carefully, as Roy Beggs turned back, the heavy-set soldier awkwardly jogging the short distance from the old bike shed to the poorly lit school building. He closed the door of his car, blotting out the rain.

Steve leaned back in his driver's seat, looking over at the body of his beautiful wife, Kirsty. Her blonde locks glimmered in the fading twilight. Goosepimples rose above the smooth silk of her snow-white legs, an oblivious reaction to the crystal chill of the star-filled night.

"I think we're going to make it," he said to Kirsty, hardly caring that she was beyond replying. "I know we've had it tough, what with Nicky being born and all, but I just know, somehow, that it's going to be all right."

He smiled, stroking Kirsty's usually rosy cheek with one hand.

She said nothing, still staring into the ether as if daydreaming.

It was one of the things that Steve had loved about her—yet feared. Those Wonderland eyes, an ethereal quality that separated her from just about every other woman that had ever been in Steve Marshall's life. It made her all the more mysterious to him, all the more beautiful. It was as if she was an angel, or some other otherworldly creature, that had been sent to enchant him, to love him—and, ultimately—to leave him. A creature like this couldn't be held by one man for too long. He knew that. Still, even now, he held onto her. He loved her and held her, even in death.

Steve turned to the back seat of his beat-out Fiesta, picking up the little bundle carefully wrapped in blankets. Gently and lovingly, he began to nurse his dead son, smiling over at his beautiful wife's corpse in the seat beside him.

"Wake up, Nicky," he whispered. "Come on, son."

STAR OPENED HER EYES TO THE GLARE OF EARLY-MORNING SUN blazing through the bus station's huge glass windows. She yawned, loudly, wondering whether she had slept at all, or whether the whole sorry mess she now thought was reality was just a very bad fucking dream. One look at the nearest body, a middle-aged woman with a very poor idea of colour coordination, and the idea of this being a dream was well and truly gone.

Kaput. Fucked.

The building she had slept in had been fairly recently built, with exteriors that seemed to comprise of nothing but metal and glass. Minimalist and modern, Great Victoria Street station, encompassing rail and bus travel (the old Europa Bus Station) stood beside the most bombed hotel in Europe. Yet its design and architecture was an expression of Belfast's new era of peace, the post 9/11 era, when the gun and the balaclava no longer had a place in Western Society.

Caz and Tim were already up, sitting in the station's café with an orange juice each. They seemed subdued, Caz in particular wearing all the body language of someone whose world had fallen down around her. Literally. As something of a reminder of the brutal reality of her situation, a scattering of corpses littered the tiled floor throughout the station. Seems the station had been busy, even on a Sunday.

"We need to do something about these bodies," Star said, without even as much as a good morning. "I don't know about you two, but I'm starting to notice a nasty smell around here." Smiling sarcastically at Tim, she added, "And I'm sure it's more than your crusty old cacks that's causing it."

Tim muttered something in response, seeming more bemused than amused. As Star drew closer to the pair, she noticed that Caz was crying, her young face blotchy and red with fresh tears.

"What's wrong with you?" she asked, coldly, pulling up a chair and searching in her pockets for her cigarettes.

"What's *right*?!" Caz replied, sniffling. "With *anything*?!"

"Sun's up," Star remarked, lighting up her ciggie.

Caz suddenly flared up. "Our families are dead! Our friends are dead! Even the bloody teachers are dead!" She looked at Star, incredulously, seeming appalled by the tattooist's apathy. "How the hell can you just sit there smoking as if it's just another day?!"

Tim rubbed his nose, but added nothing.

"Well..." Star began, leaning back in one of the café's comfy chairs, "I haven't got any family. Not anymore, anyway. No significant others and all my mates are probably as happy in death as they were in life." Star looked at Caz's tear-stained cheeks without even a hint of emotion in her own eyes. "I wasn't much of a people-person, shall we say."

Caz buried her head in her hands, emotion once again taking its toll on her. Star studied her face, pretty as it was, all blotchy and bubbling with tears. She had the sudden urge to paint it.

The poor wee bitch just couldn't put a brave face on, couldn't look for the positive anymore. She had probably reached that stage of grief where denial was out the window, no longer the crutch it needed to be when the shit had well and truly smashed into the fan. Not only was everyone dead, but here she was sitting with some punk who didn't seem to care as to whether they were alive or dead. To top it all off, she was making a prize tit of herself in front of the boy.

Star smiled into herself. Why she saw humour in this poor girl's predicament, she didn't know. Why she, herself, wasn't blubbing along with her, she didn't know either. But she could make a pretty good guess.

And then there was the boy. Yeah, he seemed nervous, but something within him, something Star couldn't just put her finger on yet, seemed to make him a little more hardened to this whole world-ending hoo-haa. Sheepishly, he looked to Star, and then to Caz, seeming unsure what to do or what to say. He still seemed lost in something of a daze, perhaps well used to burying shit like this—*Like this?! What could be like this?!*—deep beneath within his brain. Whilst Star reckoned it wasn't the healthiest way of dealing with things, normally, it was definitely an attribute in this situation.

She watched as the lad cautiously put one hand on the shoulder of the girl. "It's okay," he lied, consoling her awkwardly. He probably knew it was a lie even as he said it. Yet Star liked him, almost immediately, for at least trying to make things better for his friend. He was a good kid. That much she knew, from the start.

The rest she would know later.

Dragging on her ciggie, Star watched the little drama unfold before her tired, blackened eyes. She wondered, briefly, why she couldn't jump right in there. Create some sort of group-hug, like you might see in some episode of *Friends* or something. She entertained the idea that these two kids, and her, might be the only people left in Belfast. Perhaps the whole fucking world. And that was a bad situation, bad enough to warrant a little display of emotion.

The truth was, of course, that things were going to get a hell of a lot worse for all of them.

"So what was she like, then?" Barry asked, his hand shaking less now as he downed his seventh beer. "When you were together, I mean."

The two men had sat up all night, drinking every last drop of booze in Sharon's fridge and drinks cabinet. They hadn't moved from the kitchen, where two bodies lay side-by-side on the floor nearby. In a sense, it helped to get used to the bodies, two at a time, before going outside.

Sean gave the question the consideration it was due.

What was *Sharon like?*

He remembered mainly the bad times, of late. Perhaps as some sort of defense mechanism dictated by his brain (and heart) to help him put their sorry marriage behind him. To allow him to move on the way *she* had so very obviously been able to do. Running a hand through his receding and unkempt mane of hair, the aging DJ shot a glance around what used to be *his* kitchen, *his* home with Sharon. Yet now, sitting at the table, his dead wife at his feet, he barely recognised the god-awful poncy, middle-class décor.

"She was..." he began, hardly knowing how he could end his sentence, "*funny*, I suppose."

"Like, funny ha-ha?" Barry offered, bleary-eyed and very obviously pissed.

"Well, yeah," Sean continued. "We did make each other laugh. In the early days, anyway."

"But then it all went sour, yeah?"

Sean could see that Barry's mind was only half on what he was asking. But half was good enough, given their particular circumstances. 'Half' was also bloody apt to describe his relationship with Sharon. A woman whom he had loved. A woman whom he had only given 'half' of himself over to.

"Yeah," he replied, finally. "*Sour* wasn't the word for it."

A couple of moments passed drunkenly between the two. Sean realized that he hadn't even put any music on the boom-boom box. They had sat for hours without a single track playing in the background.

How fucking weird is that?!

Barry spoke next. "I had this girl once, right?" he said. "She wasn't half bad-looking. Blonde, yeah? Great tits and all the rest." He smiled, probably thinking back on his misspent youth and a girl that was more than likely dead now. "Thing was, she was a real arrogant bitch. Or so I thought, anyway. She was one for flirting with other blokes, and stuff. She'd be grand when she was sober, talking and kissing me, and stuff. But then she would get pissed and start acting the arsehole."

Barry stopped short. Sean noticed he was staring at Sharon's body while he talked. He seemed fascinated by her stillness, perhaps slightly perturbed by how attractive he found her long brown hair, still gleaming in the virgin light of the new day.

Sean wiped a quiet tear from his eye, trying to hide behind his can of beer as he did so.

Barry continued, "Thing was, Sean, this girl had Eczema. You know, that disease that makes all your skin peel off, like..."

Sean nodded. He was beginning to wonder where Barry was going with this story, if anywhere.

"Well, I think she should have been happy with any fucking fella looking at her twice, never mind the whole fucking bar! But she was, like, always looking for attention. Always looking for someone else's eyes to give her the once over."

Barry swigged at his beer again. His speech was slurring, his eyes completely bloodshot. But he had lost that panicked, frantic quality from the night before. Sean reckoned that was a plus.

"It was because she was insecure, of course," the lank-haired youth continued. "I realised that later. I guess I just couldn't understand why my eyes weren't enough for her."

Sean nodded, the feeling of tiredness and drunkenness seeming to wash over him simultaneously.

"And what did I do, fucking arsehole that I was? Well, I started a whole bullshit ignore-her right-back thing." He looked Sean in the eye, drunken sincerity plastered all over his skinny face. "Even though I really fancied her... *really* was into her, big-time, man... I ignored her. And she was doing the same to me."

Sean's eyes narrowed, fighting the drink, his attention flipping between the two images of Barry in front of his own red eyes. This was an odd character. Couldn't be over twenty-five, with a face somewhere between angelic and demonic. The kind of guy who would live life to the full, riddling his body with every last narcotic and vice known to man in order to chase the dragon. He was probably the very nemesis of Sean's own nerdy youth, pissed away in independent music shops and mild-mannered prog-rock gigs.

Barry drained his can of beer dry, burped, then finished his spiel. "I could have sworn, mate, that the longer we spent together, the more circles we spun in that bullshit merry-go-around, the more fucking skin she shed with that Eczema shit... It was like being with me was literally wasting her away."

Sean said nothing, but he knew exactly what Barry was talking about. He too had ignored Sharon, his greatest love, cheating on her with another passion—that of his music. The music was safe. It made no demands. But his wife was dangerous. She demanded to know him, inside as well as out.

Sharon didn't have Eczema. And she certainly hadn't wasted away, visually. Even now she looked radiant, her skin still rich and soft-looking. Her hair still shining, and glittering, like some kind of movie star. But as the years of their marriage rolled by, the very essence of what she had truly felt for Sean had wilted away to nothing.

All of the survivors at the school had gathered in the canteen for breakfast. It was a clinical and somber-looking place, gray and depressing, from crudely polished floors to damp-stained ceiling. Roy began to think back of his earlier days in the barracks, where downbeat mess halls would be norm. Somewhere to grab a cup of tea and put your feet up between patrols. Somewhere to talk about the fucking mess going on outside that you were expected to deal with, somewhere to get your head down, shelter from the bombs and bullets and fucking petrol bombs that IRA terrorists like—

Roy was reminded of earlier. He searched the large room for their newest addition—the child, Clare, the wee girl he had very nearly put a bullet through. She was sitting with Mairead, the two of them getting on like a house on fire. Mairead was platting her hair, stroking and petting her as if she was a puppy. And that didn't look right. To see someone like Mairead, who had been so cold, so hardened—so fucking *dangerous*—getting on like some kind of Sesame Street reject was odd. Roy wasn't sure if he liked it. He might have preferred the old Mairead. At least you knew what to expect, then.

One of the older survivors, a large, ever-smiling bear of a woman by the name of Sylvia Patterson, had helped to organise a simple meal of juice, cornflakes and tinned fruit. The juice was lukewarm, the fruit sugary, but those gathered were very grateful. Almost everyone ate hungrily.

Roy sat at one table, Steve Marshall beside him, whilst Mairead and Clare sat at another, somewhere near the back. Others littered the small canteen in groups of three and four. The survivors seemed to need each other's company. Safety in numbers.

Conversation had been sparse at first, but eventually excited voices had started up at all the tables, everyone telling their stories. In a way, it was cathartic.

Steve had finished his meal, leaving only a spoonful of cornflakes in his bowl. His eyes had something of a thousand-yard stare. To Roy, the younger man seemed lost in his own world, whistling and tapping his fingers on the table to an unknown tune.

Fucking do your head in.

A little conversation was needed to chill the poor bastard out.

"So where're you from, Steve?" Roy asked, more to break the silence than out of genuine interest.

"Portadown," Steve replied. "Killicomaine direction," he added, perhaps knowing that a man with a name like Roy Beggs wasn't going to be from the *other* side of town.

"Oh, right," Roy replied. "I have a cousin lives around there. Just near the High School."

The younger survivor looked at him.

Roy realized his mistake, and corrected himself. "*Had* a cousin, I meant. Funnily enough, I don't think I've chatted to her in a while. She mightn't even live there anymore, to tell you the truth." Again he corrected himself. "Fuck's sake. She definitely doesn't live there now, let's face it."

Steve smiled awkwardly, obviously becoming uncomfortable with Roy's forced and clumsy attempts at conversation. Within seconds his eyes had glazed over again, that inane whistling and tapping returning.

Another silent moment passed, painfully. Roy noticed the cook, Sylvia, looking at the two of them uneasily. Theirs was the only table where no one was talking or crying—or, weirdly, laughing. It must have looked odd.

Roy tried again, this time more out of suspicion. "So had you any family, Steve?"

The soldier's question was as insensitive as you could get, given what had happened to them all. Yet it hit an even rawer nerve that most with Steve Marshall. The young survivor thought first of his little son Nicky. He recalled the wonderful cocktail of emotions he had gone through when Nicky was born only a couple of months ago. Joy, fear, love... the panicked sense of responsibility. It had been a difficult pregnancy with his wife, Kirsty, eventually giving birth prematurely. He remembered holding her hand as she screamed, and cried, her relatively small belly seeming so strained that it might explode.

Steve loved her more that night than ever, her face all blotchy and tear-stained, her nose and mouth glistening with snot. It felt primal to be with her during the birth. As if a part of them was to be joined together, forever, through that experience. Now, of course, the corpses of Nicky and Kirsty were in his car. His little bundle of joy had festered in the cruelly ambivalent sun. His beautiful wife still sleeping, oblivious to it all.

Steve looked up at Roy's face staring back at him. He realised that he hadn't answered his question.

He knew that he had to be careful with these people. Sure, they might be his only hope to find some help for his family—some *real* help— but he still had to be careful. They might not understand him, might not see the bigger picture.

(Might try to take his family—his beautiful wife and baby—away from him.)

So he needed to play his cards close to his chest.

His mind drifted back to the first time he had met Kirsty. They had been at some student dive, and she was part of a larger group of friends (and friends-of-friends) that had all been sinking the pints together. It was pound-a-pint, so everyone (regardless of how little of their student loans were left) was able to get pretty tanked. His favourite song at the time had come on (*Cannonball* by The Breeders), the DJ finally wiring it on after being plagued all night for it, and Stevie-Boy was all primed to throw some drunken moves.

He turned to hit the floor, and there she was. Standing on her own, like some kind of mannequin. Tall, elevated above all of those around her. Moving, slowly and dreamily, as if the music was flowing through her heart and soul, slowly and beautifully washing her long, lithe body.

On that first day—just like her last day—she was without blemish, her eyes lighting the fuse of her paleness.

Her eyes.

"Steve?" the soldier beside him persisted.

Careful, Stevie-Boy, careful.

"Em... Sorry, mate," he muttered, suddenly getting up from the table. "Gotta take a piss. I'll see you later, right?"

Roy watched as Steve shuffled out of the canteen towards the bathrooms where the chemical toilets had been laid out. From another corner, Sylvia watched too. Neither of them could work him out. At times Steve seemed a little too bright and chirpy, and then he'd freak out a bit like he'd just done now. Were Roy to be truthful, he wasn't sure whether he liked a man like Steve Marshall being around. Inconsistent. Jumpy. Someone he couldn't read. But grief took its toll on them all in different ways, of course. The more generous part of the soldier settled on that, calling check on his gut instinct.

For Roy, grief seemed to be something worth avoiding, and that made someone as emotionally raw and unkempt as Steve Marshall unsavoury to him. Truth be told, Roy was seeing in Steve Marshall the kind of pent-up fear and insecurity that he felt within himself. Roy wasn't ready to face his demons just yet. Steve was obviously already wrestling with them. But for the soldier, there was too much needed doing, and doing was proving to be a great way of avoiding the real dangers of thinking.

He watched the survivors at the other tables continue to console each other, some crying, others comforting, then switching roles, everyone getting a chance to tell their stories to each other. People of all ages, all religions (men as well as women) were shedding tears for themselves, their loved ones and one another. They were bonding. Building a new community. A community with a shared grief. Shared history. Shared loss.

Still sipping on his morning tea, Roy looked over to where Mairead and Clare were sitting. Mairead's eyes were looking right back at him. Stern, cold, and unforgiving. It was as if she blamed him for everything that had happened, refusing to move on from her petty resentment of him. Refusing to recognize how everything had changed.

Even things between them.

Fuck her. She isn't worth the hassle.

Roy looked away, not bothered by whatever the hell her problem was. He'd more important things to think about, like what their next move would be.

By 10am, talk amongst the tables had moved on to what had caused the disaster and how widespread it was. Different people had different ideas. For those still crying it was too much to think about, so they drifted off back to the assembly hall or out into the school's grounds. For others, the very act of talking about what had happened helped them deal with it, even avoid the reality of it.

Talks and talks about talks.

"It's got to be them Arabs," commented an older man named Trevor Steele, his face pale and unkempt. "Probably one of them gas attacks, or something."

John McElroy, slightly younger but equally as bigoted as Steele, joined in. He shook his head, then added, "Too many foreigners running around these days."

One of the group's few ethnic minorities, a young Egyptian woman named Aida Hussein, shook her head in response to Steele's comment. In days gone by, she'd suffered several racist attacks on her home in South Belfast. It grieved her to think that even at a time like this, racist attitudes were still rife.

"For fuck's sake," snapped a young, studious-looking girl beside him, noticing how uncomfortable Aida looked, "have a bit of tact, would you?"

"Well what do you think happened, then?" Steele protested.

The young girl sighed heavily. "Well, I'll tell you this, Trevor," she began, "if it was a gas attack you'd fuckin' smell something, wouldn't you?" She laughed, sarcastically, before whispering under her breath, "Or maybe you wouldn't, you sweaty ol' bastard."

Roy had to laugh at that one. A few others, who had heard the quip, joined in. It was the first genuine laughter amongst the group and it seemed to echo, almost inappropriately, around the room. It felt like laughing in church. Someone looked at Roy and smiled. Suddenly, others were joining in, even Aida. For the first time since the disaster had hit, it seemed to Roy that people were beginning to loosen up a little.

As they spoke, Roy realised, the survivors all seemed to look at him, almost as if for reassurance, or permission to continue. But he said little, simply listening as the talk bounced back and forth through various theories. Chemical attacks, nuclear meltdowns, bird flu, food poison, something in the fucking water. All the clichés were present and accounted for. One man, an austere-looking bloke with eyes that would bore through you, suggested that this was the wrath of God. That humanity had got too big for its boots. Although not a religious man, Roy thought this was probably one of the more believable theories.

Yet, regardless of what caused it, everyone seemed to take for granted that this disaster was nationwide, perhaps even global. One survivor, a young fellow who had actually joined the convoy of cars fairly late in the day, commented about how the internet seemed to go a little askew shortly before the power shut down. He had been online, trying to contact people through messenger, message boards, and MySpace. To his surprise, however, one of his message boards, a huge online community of sci-fi and horror fans, displayed a worrying lack of active members. Those who were signed in didn't seem to be posting. The young lad regaled everyone of how he watched as, one-by-one, all those signed-in were logged out, their names dropping off the screen like dominoes. Soon his own power had shut down, logging him too off permanently.

Another man, Eastern European with a relatively poor command of English, explained how he had tried to phone his family and friends back in Riga, Latvia. He'd only been in Northern Ireland for a month, working in a meat factory in Portadown. His first purchase on getting his pay cheque had been some new clothes. His second had been a flashy new mobile phone. He'd spent the whole journey to Belfast, sharing a lift with a co-worker from the factory (they had been on the same overtime shift when it all went south) ringing all of his friends and family back in Latvia. None of them—not a single one of the twenty odd numbers he rang—actually answered.

The man, a large, burly giant named Peter Stokenbergs, started crying as he told his story. As Roy silently watched on, Sylvia, (the group's emerging cook and maternal type), immediately comforted Stefan as he wept.

Regardless of the occasional bickering and outbursts of raw emotion, the survivors seemed to be making themselves at home at the school. No one seemed to be too keen on moving, perhaps craving the security and comfort this little haven provided. It made sense, of course. The school had been deserted when things had gone belly-up, meaning there were no bodies lying around. Even the school's fairly spacious grounds, consisting of some gardens, a football field and gravel sports track, were relatively untouched by signs of death, a couple of dead birds and a hedgehog being the only dead things in sight.

The assembly hall's polished wooden floor was large enough to provide the survivors with adequate space to set up makeshift camp beds, piling their few belongings next to such, and from what Roy could tell from overhearing something Sylvia had said, talking to a small group of similarly-aged women and the Eastern European man, talk was already starting to move towards what could be rustled up for lunch.

"So what's the plan, then?"

The voice came from behind him, but he was quite sure who it belonged to. Turning, Roy was met by Mairead, the young Clare hanging off her arm shyly. She still had the handgun Roy had given to her, tucked neatly but noticeably inside a pocket of her jacket. Roy clocked it, nervously, before answering.

"Seems everyone's happy here for a bit," he muttered, ruffling in his pockets for a bit of chewing gum for the child.

"Here?! But didn't we agree that help would come to Belfast? That we should gather in the city?" Mairead lowered her voice, not wanting to upset Clare. "Roy, if anyone comes, they're not going to find us here. We're over ten miles from Belfast."

"Who's going to come?!" Roy snapped back, suddenly irritated by Mairead challenging him. He recovered his composure, quickly, smiling down at the child, unable to find any gum.

"I don't know… Emergency Services? Rescue? Helicopters?" A scowl drew across her face as she added, "God knows we had a shit load of helicopters here in the eighties when they damn well *weren't* needed. Surely they'll send them now they *are* needed?!" Mairead, of course, was referring to days gone by, when the British Troops had pulled out all the stops to deal with the terrorist threat in Northern Ireland. To Roy Beggs, a comment like that was like a red rag to a bull.

"*Typical*," he sighed, turning and walking away from Mairead. He shook his head as he walked. "Fucking *typical*."

She followed him, defiantly, Clare still hanging onto her arm.

"Whenever something goes wrong, there you are, rabbitin' on about what the brits did or didn't do. Never anyone else's fault, just the brits." Roy laughed sarcastically before adding, "I bet you think this whole thing is some British or loyalist attack, don't you?"

"Don't be fuckin'—"

"*No*! You listen to me!" Roy yelled at her, suddenly very riled, "No one's going to fucking come! Not the British! Not even the fucking *Americans*! No-fucking-body! All right!?" His face was purple with rage. He noticed Mairead stepping back, Clare cowering close to her. "This is it," he stressed, firmly. "This is our lot. And we stay here until I say otherwise. That clear?!"

He felt Mairead's eyes burning into him. The sleeves of his camouflage uniform were rolled up and he noticed her looking at his tattoos, proudly boasting affiliation with loyalist paramilitary groups. What he'd said earlier had been right. They weren't too different from each other. They had been fighting the same war, just from different sides. But she couldn't let it lie—couldn't show him some respect—and that riled a man like Roy Beggs. A bitter man, a man to whom women didn't give backchat. A man who was no stranger to showing a woman who was boss, especially a woman like Mairead Burns.

"Fuck you, Roy," she whispered before turning and walking away from him.

"You provos are all the same!" Roy called after her, still seething.

Without even turning around, Mairead graced his last comment with a one-fingered salute.

He couldn't have hated her more.

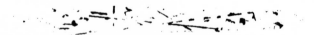

It took Caz, Star and Tim the better part of an hour to clear the sixteen bodies out of the small mall at Great Victoria Street, Star somehow seeming to haul some on her own, whilst the teens worked together. They didn't drag them far, just out to the courtyard where all the buses were parked. A few fire blankets were used to cover some of the dead, whilst a large waterproof canvas sheet (discovered in the storeroom of the little newsagents in the station) could cover the rest. In a huge, plastic mass grave, the bodies began their final rest.

Some of them had started off on their summer holidays only to finish prematurely. Their sunglasses, ipods, and handheld game consoles littered the beige tiled floor, where Tim and Star had ransacked every suitcase. As Caz watched on, disgusted, arms folded and face like thunder, the two built a pile of technological treasure. She was slightly placated when Star threw her a pair of curling tongs.

After the clear-out, the three survivors found some cleaning materials and gave the place a freshen up. The clinically-pale tiles shone after being mopped, reflecting the gleam of the sun through the huge glass windows quite beautifully. A railway-come-bus station was a strange place to call home, and each of the three saw each other as strange bedfellows to share it with, but they could relax a little better now the bodies had gone. The clear-out had been a release, of sorts, so at around noon they treated themselves to yet another junk food lunch of potato crisps, chocolate and Coke to celebrate a job well done. They dined at the same empty coffee shop in the station where they had initially met.

Each of the three were starting to talk a little more now, mostly about banal stuff at first. Talk had come around to what everyone had done before the disaster had hit, with Caz and Tim laughing about teachers and classmates they both knew. Star listened, quietly, smoking her way through yet another box of ciggies liberated from the newsagents. It was one of the benefits of being at the station. Plenty of smokes on stand-by.

Despite herself, the tattooist was glad to see the two kids livening up a little. A part of her had felt a little guilty about not doing much to console them. It was a lot to go through at any age, this whole end-of-the-world thing, but to go through it as a teenager, with all those hormones popping off at the same time?! It had to be fucking *gruesome*...

"So what did you do, Star?" Caz asked, smiling for the first time since they'd met. She had a very pretty face. Innocent, a little bookish, maybe, but with a certain quirky appeal that Star couldn't help but find attractive.

"I scar people, make them bleed," Star replied, smiling mischievously.

Caz looked back, confused and a little scared.

Tim's eyes widened as it clicked with him what she meant. "Shit... I knew I recognised you! You're that tattooist chick, aren't you?" He leaned forward, beaming. "My mate Andy went to see you a couple of months ago. You know Andy? Goth kid, with eyeliner..."

For a brief moment all three were quiet, sharing the same realisation that Andy was probably dead now.

"I always wanted a tat myself, but my ma wouldn't let me," Tim added ruefully, breaking the silence.

Star took another drag, winking at the lad with a mischievous look in her eye. "Still want one now?"

"Fuck yeah!"

It was the first time Star had seen the lad really animated. Tim Adamson reminded her a lot of some of the goth kids who'd come in to her place in the past to get tats. People like Andy, no doubt. Quiet, awkward, gangly. They had usually sat sweating whilst she got her stuff ready, stinking the place out. After three of those wee gits in a row, Star had to open the windows wide for a bit to get rid of the stench. But Tim was nothing but excited by the notion. Even Caz, the stuffy little bitch that she was, seemed to be encouraging him.

"Yeah! Go on Tim!" she egged, showing more of her playful, teenage side. Star saw a new dynamic come into play. It was obvious to her, even if not to Tim, that Caz was besought by the lad.

"What would you get?" Caz whispered, as if it was a sin they were talking about—a secret, adult sin.

Tim's smile seem to fade, perhaps knocked on the head by having to actually think about something to get tattooed. Like a lot of kids that would have come to her, Star reckoned he had never taken the idea any further than 'how-cool-would-it-be-if'.

His face furrowed as he, no doubt, thought about all the things in the world he could get tattooed. It struck Star as pretty funny. Although, ironically, he literally had all the time in the world to make up his mind, it seemed very important for him to make a decision right now.

"What can you do?" he asked Star, after a short while contemplating.

Star laughed. This kid was cute. She liked him.

"Not a lot here, that's for sure..." Star replied. "We'd need to go back to the shop. I'd need all my gear."

Suddenly, the idea of getting tattooed became about as realistic as grabbing the morning paper. Or watching television. Or making fucking breakfast—or anything that people used to do to pass the time in the world before... *this*. The faces of the kids seemed to echo this dawning realisation of Star's. No one was getting a tattoo today. Not here, not anywhere else. It was probably the first day in a hell of a long time that no tattoos had ever been done.

The finality of what they were all facing continued its journey towards hitting home, pushing along the queue with the little pram from the supermarket and the punky girl nose-diving the floor and the televisions going on the blink and the train. Normal, everyday stuff had changed. Everything was fucked-up.

Star looked up at the blank, petrified faces looking towards her. These people—these kids—seemed to be looking to her, hoping she would be able to offer something to blot out the inevitable smack of reality threatening to spit in their tired eyes. Each of their faces was steeped in denial and all-consuming fear. Yet she had nothing to offer them.

Without another word, Star simply got up and wandered out into the courtyard. A waft of death, singing of the festering bodies across Belfast, whistled through her nostrils. It seemed almost familiar.

Sin. Everywhere.

It was all The Preacher Man could see. Billboards with their whoring sluts flaunting themselves. Dancing with the devil, selling their ill gotten gains with their sex.

(SALE! Buy Now Pay Later! All Items Must Go! New Season's Selection in Store Now!)

And what did it all mean now? Where was the rush *today*?

A handful of corpses stained polished shop floors, their flesh having festered somewhat in the early sun. A few cars crisscrossed over five sparsely-filled streets. Although the streets had been pedestrian, some cars had ventured into their cobble-paved no-no for parking. With the disaster hitting, a couple of other cars had lost control, flailing wildly onto the paved area. Fallen pedestrians sprinkled randomly around the cars, meeting at Cornmarket's Band Stand.

The ornate, Victorian structure had been a focal point for Belfast's amateur street theatre. Music, mime artists, buskers, charity collections and protesters had all gathered there. It had been a stage for all the wares of Belfast's wannabe thespians, quasi-musicians and wheeler-dealer types.

It had also been The Preacher Man's pulpit. His Rock Of Ages, his Anchor From The Storm. Now, however, the bandstand was nothing. No meeting place. No stage. No storm and sure-as-fuck no anchor. Post-apocalyptic Cornmarket was but a focal point for death.

Death and the shadows of death. Closing in on him. Coming to take him.

Like Job in the Old Testament, the poor bastard who had been infamously stripped of his entire world in a wager between The Good Lord and Satan, everything had been taken from The Preacher Man. Gone were his friends, his family and (most importantly) his audience.

The Preacher Man had been left nothing. Even sin was dead, its dark memories splashed over the odd billboard here, and glistening like fool's gold from the odd shop window there. No more voices to battle against, no more insults to suffer. It was difficult to find a purpose.

Why the fuck, God? Why?!

The Preacher Man knew he had to have been left behind for some reason. Surely God hadn't just abandoned him to rot in the scum-infested world with all the sinful.

Shadows... getting closer... drawing nearer...

All the sinners?! God wouldn't, simply, dump *him*, a faithful servant... left like a *dirty* ragdoll to be raped and tormented by Satan.

Shadows... almost upon him, like a cloak...

No. No! There was something else to it... The Preacher Man's work wasn't done here yet.

Not yet... Not just yet...

As the shadows around him drew closer, their bodies and faces now tangible, The Preacher Man set up his stall for business again.

Here was his purpose.

Thank you, Lord! Oh, thank you, Jesus!

Here were souls needing saving.

Tim was in the station's bathrooms, the large steel urinals providing more than enough space for him to aim. He'd taken a piss, too self-consumed to give a thought to how the plumbing continued to work, washing away his urine and spat-out gum with its usual ferocious-waterfall flush. He had then been staring in the huge mirrors behind the sinks.

They had come hard and fast, like the rain. They poured down his face, almost burning him with their salty sharpness, rinsing out a bucket-load of teenage hormones and pent-up grief.

Family, friends... the whole world... all dead.

It had finally hit home.

He mourned his mother, his sister, his friends, the other members of the Muckwits, the guys he went to school with, even the camp guy who used to sit beside him in GCSE maths. The loss burned a sharp, flaming blade of grief down his chest, choking him, stabbing him over and over again, as if to make sure he was well and truly dead—well and truly finished off.

He mourned everyone he had ever known in that mother of all outbursts. Everyone he would have met in his daily routine. The stony-faced bus driver, Bertie the caretaker at his school, his teachers, even that callous bitch, Mrs. McCabe. The girl with the cute arse, who worked at the newsagents near his house—all of them were finally pronounced as deceased and given their send-off with undefiled bereft.

Yet when it came to his father, Tim Adamson spat out a more complex cocktail of emotions amongst the tears and piss—love and hate and fear. Those nights spent in his daddy's arms as a small child. Love one minute, abuse the next. Such memories had receded deep into Tim's young mind, peeking out briefly and dangerously on occasion, only to be hammered back in with angry music or violent video games. It literally took the end of the world for them to finally flood his young mind.

And eyes.

Tim didn't know he had been screaming and wasn't aware he was on the hard bathroom's floor. Everything was a blur, suddenly, lost in the mist of his tears and dirge of his mind. Voices were straining to be heard above the sheer shriek of his polluted heart, voices he would never hear again.

(His mother his sister friends and bandmates the girls he had fondled clumsily behind walls at school those who had rejected him those he had rejected teachers uncles the bus driver the girl at the newsagents)

He put his fist through the large mirror above the metal sink. Again and again he bashed, splitting both glass and skin, crunching against bone—and heart and soul and mind—shredding fingernails like dried glue. Glass burrowed into his fists, and blood was both flowing and spraying all over the broken mirror, sink and perfectly-polished tile floor.

He couldn't feel any pain. Blood was seeping freely, unchecked, from his scathed hands and yet Tim couldn't feel any pain. He couldn't feel any shame, either, his aching heart having burst through the thin veneer dividing what he *really* felt from what he wanted others to *think* he felt.

But Tim *could* feel himself being held, the small arms of Caroline Donaldson gripping around his broken body, tightly, with desperation and love.

She had sprinted quickly to the bathrooms on hearing the screams, sparing no thought for what could be causing them, grabbing Tim almost violently on seeing his broken and heavy heart.

She held Tim with passion, her own tears erupting as if inspired, mixing in with the boy's own concoction. And there the two teens remained, in that bittersweet embrace, for the best part of an hour.

In the brutal honesty of that time, no words were spoken or needed to be spoken.

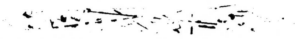

She smiled. Star actually *smiled*, lighting the last candle of the thirty-two she had laid out around the bus station, neatly arranged to provide a mellow glow to fight off the deathly black of the incoming night. She lit a joint to celebrate, having realised that she still held a scrap of weed in her pocket. Good stuff, too. Scored from her old mate Stumpy, an odious-looking little toe rag who used to loiter around her shop, preventing her from ever getting any work done.

Like a lot of the motley crew that had littered her gaff, Stumpy had eventually grown on Star, becoming part of the furniture in both body and voice. Now the poor fucker was dead.

(Doped to his eyeballs, of course, but dead nonetheless.)

Finding the weed had given Star's form a much-needed lift. She had felt inspired to liberate some scented candles from the craft shop in the station's small mall. It had seemed a shame to use the boring ones so Star had laid out all different types, colours and scents of candle, creating a pungent (but not altogether unpleasant) aroma, and distinct mystical glow against the evening sky.

The tall glass walls of the station came alive with the light, almost radiating. From quite a distance, the station's illumination stood out amongst the clouding backdrop of Belfast, a single expression of life and hope amongst the darkening backdrop.

Star sat on the floor, cross-legged, at one of the station's side doors, looking out onto the courtyard. It was still populated by several buses and the makeshift graveyard for all the corpses they had cleared out.

Somewhere in the station she could hear crying—or was it laughing? The smoke was really beginning to take effect, numbing her brain blissfully, yet opening up her imagination like a veritable Pandora's Box.

From somewhere else, another voice carried in the light breeze, almost audible. It didn't matter, of course, where these voices or cries or laughs were coming from.

In the faintly cheerful moment of draw, nothing really mattered much.

"Hope, eh?" Star whispered to herself, taking another drag of her joint. Smiling, she leaned back, feeling the night air blowing in against her face with the first pitter-patter of The Rain.

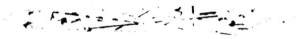

"Wash me!" screamed The Preacher Man. "Wash me in your blood!"

The Rain came down again, precisely the same time as it had descended the night before. With it came enlightenment, The Preacher Man's theology encompassing a new strand of transubstantiation.

The Rain had been sent to cleanse the filth from the world. The sex, the greed. This was one last clean-up operation, a decontamination of sin-stained streets before God released his angels. It was Judgement Day, and The Preacher Man had one last mission before the choir of heaven would sing out in celebration of Christ's new reign.

There was still time.

He had to prepare a path for the Lord. He had to cleanse and baptise any sinners who remained (hidden and ashamed) in the shadows, before God's beautiful Angels came down to reclaim him. To lift him to Glory, where he would reign with all those who prophesised before him.

This was his mission, his gift, his privilege.

Whilst the rain carried out its cleansing work, the blood of Jesus spilling once again onto the earth, The Preacher Man stepped out into the drawing evening, Bible in hand, and began to preach. His new mission beginning, a new flock soon to be gathering from the shadows, The Preacher Man's voice once more echoed through the death-stained and rain-polished streets of Belfast.

"There's power in the blood!"

Roy Beggs took a minute to listen to the pitter-patter on the school's high windows. It was always something he had loved to do, listening to The Rain beating off the roof of his car or windows of his flat. Once upon a time, when the world had been alive, he had enjoyed that simple pleasure with his ex-wife, it being their thing. Now he simply saw the bucketing rain as another element to take into consideration when securing the small Lisburn school where he and his followers had gathered.

The group would have been lost without him, of course—him and his stuff. Although the toilets in the school still seemed to flush, Roy had feared they would start to really smell if the survivors continued to use them, the sewer system no longer being maintained. He had insisted that everyone use chemical toilets, which could then be disposed. It was a small thing, of course, but all too important when trying to maintain hygiene and prevent disease.

Piss and shit were the least of his worries, though. Roy was coming to realise that with a breakdown of society came a breakdown of law. There would inevitably be looters, rapists, and opportunists only too willing to prey upon a community such as theirs. Preparation was needed, and—as with all preparation—security was imperative.

Roy's trainee militia had blackened out most of the windows of the school, erected some simple tripwires on the football pitch and gravel track, and moved most of the cars outside the school grounds. They couldn't remove all evidence of their presence, what with that festering silence highlighting every little whisper from each of the nineteen mouths assembled in the school, but they could minimize signs of life and prepare themselves, as best as possible, for anything untoward.

The soldier had spent the remainder of his day around the school, planning his defence strategy, showing some of the more trustworthy and balanced-looking survivors how to use simple firearms such as the Glock 19 handgun and SLR rifle. Roy had gathered a basic armory from his base when the world had gone to hell, storing the weapons in the back of his Land Rover, along with all the other supplies they had found all-too-useful.

Avoiding his nemesis hadn't been that difficult. Mairead had taken herself off to nearby shopping centre, Bow Street Mall, to get some supplies. That was what she had told the others, anyway. He suspected differently. For Roy, the main reason for her excursion was to bond with Clare, her newly adopted daughter. Roy shivered to think how the former IRA operative would corrupt the youngster.

Start them young.

Tired and light-headed from all of the grafting and thinking, Roy sat quietly with the survivors who had been helping him, enjoying a cup of tea. One of them, an older man named Tom, had been an electrician before he had retired. Working with a retired engineer named

Fred, and a shitload of fuel from the garage down the road, Tom had kick-started an old generator they found around the back of the school. The result was a little electricity, enough to comfortably power a cooker, a water heater, and one or two lights.

The first thing that had been heated, of course, was a huge flask of tea. Sylvia (large as life and bubbling with chat) had brewed it for the men, washing out a whole sink of mugs to make sure they all had something clean to drink from. Even though they didn't have any fresh milk, and the extra sugar had made the brew taste saccharine, Roy was still enjoying his caffeine hit.

A flash of spontaneous lightning suddenly illuminated the door to the canteen. It had been unexpected, and Roy jumped a little. Whilst The Rain had been heavy and loud, creeping in before dusk, it had never been accompanied by thunder or lightning. The effect was kind of horror-film-esque, and it made Roy edgy.

Roy sat his tea down.

A man. By the door.

Roy squinted against the darkness at the door. Lightning, again, affirmed what he was seeing. Roy's eyes narrowed, trying to make out who the profile belonged to.

Shushing the suddenly panicked survivors around him, the soldier reached for his rifle, some of the other men following his lead. Soon Roy's makeshift army were all armed, trying to remember their training, feeling clumsily and nervously around the metal and wood of their firearms.

The doors burst open as another sudden blast of lightning preceded a gruff and stuttered roll of thunder. It was like a scene from some fucked-up gothic fairytale as the sorry silhouette finally revealed itself to those gathered.

There, in the dimmed down light stood Steve Marshall, dripping wet from head to toe. In his arms was the small, clearly dead body of a child.

"I tried..." Steve said, half to himself and half to those gathered. "I tried everything. I sang to him, bounced him on my knee, kissed his beautiful little face. But no matter how much I talked to him, how much I rocked him..." Steve looked up, a thousand yard stare being the only expression present. "I just couldn't wake him up..."

PART
2

"...from so simple a beginning endless forms most beautiful and most wonderful have been, and are being, evolved."

(from *The Origin of Species* by Charles Darwin)

one

AT FIRST THE SILENCE WAS STIFLING. WASHING ACROSS BELFAST like a tiptoeing tsunami, it shushed everything and everyone in its path, sweeping all evidence of life under the carpet. Battery-powered radios and automated streetlamps, ignored, eventually powered down. Most of the dead decayed slowly and quietly, their death more like a curious sleep, their bodies hoping to blend into the earth just as apathetically as they had given up on life, simply and without protest. Occasionally, though, more explicit sights of trashed cars and broken people could be seen mangled together. Even then, what was left of crash-test human faces was generally expressionless.

On the whole, it seemed, the human race had died without caring.

After a post-Millenium sway away from devil-may-care diets and lifestyle towards a more holistic way of life, after an almost feverish obsession with all things environmental, all things organic, the human race had finally thrown in the towel. Mother Nature, like the Great Divine Whore She is, had simply fucked humanity without rhyme or reason. In her trail, even the initial signs of devastation had given up.

At first, flames and smoke had bellowed out of engines. Before long, even that had died away. A foul stench of barbecued flesh and petrol seeped into the quiet night air. All that could be heard was the pitter-patter of daily evening rain and the whistle of a gentle summer breeze.

More survivors crawled out of the woodwork as time went by. Some had cowered in their homes throughout the city, staring deliriously at dead relatives and failing TVs. Others had remained for days and weeks in deep, dark depression, caring little for anything or anyone, including themselves.

Eventually, they moved. Short trips around their estates or apartment blocks soon gave way to longer trips into the city centre, to see what, if anything, was happening. They were mostly unsociable, eyeing each other up suspiciously. Some gathered in small groups feverishly gathering supplies as if a nuclear winter was on the horizon. Most, however, remained in the shadows. Alone. Scared. Barely alive. Barely seen or heard.

The Silence, thick and foreboding, discouraged conversation. It was as if the world was one giant library—or church—where talking was seen as uncouth and disrespectful. Random mad people, largely ignored, shouted, laughed or cried in shadowy street corners. They were despised for their candidacy. Their public nuisance would last only so long before a random shot in the night, or curious scream, spelled their sweet demise.

No one questioned it. No one cared.

Occasional fights would break out, sporadically, seemingly over nothing. It was probably more to do with frustration than anything else. Even these were largely ignored, reaching their conclusion within a very short space of time, one brawler lying bleeding and ignored in the street. Sometimes they picked themselves up again. At other times, they didn't.

Fresh bodies were ignored as much as the older, staler ones. What was another body in a world now fortified with death? It was meaningless, like another leaf in a forest, another blade of grass, another cloud in the rain-clogged sky.

The Preacher Man was doing good business, of course, his religious doomsday writ now more believable in a world reeking of apocalypse. One by one, tearful and repentant sinners had seeped out of the shadows to join him. Some, like 29 year-old rocker Gavin Cummings, were simply unable to think clearly for themselves, needing a strong leader to help make sense of things. Others were terrified that God would shit upon them the same way He had, obviously, shat upon their friends and family.

Great Victoria Street was largely avoided, Star's laissez faire attitude and solo boozing sessions unnerving most of the somber majority...

(Suited just fine.)

Days, then weeks, passed by.

The same routine had kicked in for Star, almost as if the apocalypse hadn't happened. By day, she inked. By night, she drank.

It was not her intention to invite others to join her, and her two compatriots... but that's exactly the impression that her nightly routine of lighting candles gave to Barry Rogan and Sean Magee.

Or maybe they just smelled the dope.

The eclectic twosome had arrived one night, sick of moving from one pub to the next, weighed down with gifts of expensive booze and cigars. With hardly any need for introduction, the two likely lads and Star bonded, wasting no time in setting a precedent for how they were going to deal with the End-Of-The-World. They partied endlessly, blasting out angry music from a pilfered, portable CD player, defiantly pissing all over The Silence's morose parade. Before long, even Tim and Caz could stand no more, moving next door to the Europa Hotel and finding a room without any of those pesky festering bodies to worry about. Alas, the three amigos followed their lead, stumbling drunkenly through the hotel doors, seeking out rooms with mini-bars and king-size beds for their insatiable campaign of hedonism.

And so it continued, life finding its own sub-niche amongst the ever-rotting death thickly coating the streets. Unlike Lisburn, where the school's community continued to evolve and develop, few in Belfast tried to take control. Few tried to build anything amongst the nothing. Instead, pockets of survivors carried on living their own lives, ignoring those—alive or dead—around them, simply making do.

In a way, things weren't that different from before.

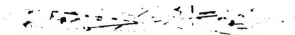

Trevor Steele peered through one of the school's front windows, his eye focused on a small patch of flames and glass just by the main entrance. Slung across his shoulder was an SLR rifle, a weapon he had been recently trained how to use by Royal Irish Ranger, Roy Beggs.

Steele sighed heavily, allowing the single Venetian blind he held open to fall closed. He had counted at least four strangers out there but there were probably more of them. They had no visible weapons apart from the petrol bombs that were lying on the ground, but that had been enough to keep the likes of Roy Beggs busy of a Saturday evening back in the day.

Steele really didn't like the look of this.

"How many?" It was the voice of Roy Beggs. Steele slowly turned around to face him. The soldier was as formidable looking as ever, his rolled-up sleeves flashing aging tattoos that all but sang of his past association with loyalist paramilitaries. That suited Steele just fine, of course.

"Four that I can see. But there's likely to be more of them."

"Weapons?" Roy asked, studying Steele's face in a way that was slightly intimidating. As he spoke, the soldier continued to play around with a small, two-way radio. Steele hadn't seen it before.

"Nothing visible, apart from the petrol bombs. But I couldn't be sure."

"I want everyone in the assembly hall. There are only a few windows there, so it'll be fairly safe. If things go badly wrong, there's always the fire exit nearby."

Steele nodded before heading off to get everyone together.

"Oh, and Trevor?"

"Yes, Roy?"

"Tell Mairead that I want her."

Roy walked through the panicked school with all the importance of a headmaster, yet none of the finesse. He carried his portable two-way radio in one hand and a small handgun in the other. The fear was heavy in the air. These people had suffered way too much to have to go through a situation like this. Roy knew there could be pandemonium were he not to sort this situation out quick smart.

The soldier helped to herd survivors into the assembly hall, aided by other members of his freshly trained militia. He tried shushing those who gasped at the bursts of gunfire coming from outside, but it was no good. His patience was wearing thin and he was about to move on towards the main entrance of the school, at least happy that everyone was safe in the hall, when he noticed the child, Clare, hiding under one of the tables outside the assembly hall. Roy stopped for a moment, sighing.

"You know, it's very naughty for little girls to hide," he said, leaning down to look under the table.

"I'm not a little girl anymore," came the reply.

"Well, then," Roy began, thinking how true her words were—how very poignant and true, "maybe you should join all the adults in the assembly hall. How about it, eh?"

The soldier offered his hand to the cowering child. After a moment or two, he felt her small fingers grip it, tightly, allowing him to gently pull her to her feet. Another burst of gunfire rang out and Clare hugged Roy suddenly, the fear causing her small body to shake.

"Now go into the assembly hall like a good girl," Roy said, sternly. He felt in his pocket for the Mars bar he had been saving for himself, and gave it to the nervous child. "Go on, now."

She took the chocolate bar and smiled, no doubt happy to get a little attention from the burly soldier who she was beginning to see as something of a daddy figure. Tears were welling up in her eyes yet she seemed reluctant for them to escape, perhaps trying to maintain her composure in front of the soldier. Roy felt for her. She was so very innocent.

Sighing heavily, he watched her walk into the assembly hall where the group's cook, Sylvia, was waiting to look after her.

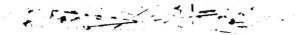

Roy walked briskly towards the main entrance of the school. The door was open from when Trevor Steele and John McElroy, two of Roy's recently trained militia, had exited like the inexperienced idiots they were, firing wildly into the air as they sought cover behind nearby undergrowth. One petrol bomb had landed by the open door, the carpet in the hall already having caught fire, but Roy was able to quickly stamp the flames out and close the heavy door over again.

Retreating to the window, Roy gingerly peered out at the carnage outside. Steele and McElroy were pinned down by one of the trees now, taking pot-shots wherever they saw a flash of gunfire emerge. Several spent petrol bombs littered the grass nearby, the large tree shielding the two men from the worst of their threat.

From where Roy was, he guessed that there were probably ten of the fuckers out there, working together with a shitload of petrol and at least one gun. It was probably a semi-automatic from the sounds he was hearing, likely stolen from the body of a member of the security forces. That made Roy seethe even more. He didn't care why these bastards were attacking them—although he guessed it was to steal their powered-up base—but the thought that they had the gall to steal weapons off men like him, men who dedicated their lives to protecting people, really riled the soldier.

Roy sat his two-way radio down and lifted the rifle leaning against the wall. Carefully, he fitted it with a scope and then, lifting one of the blinds, opened the window slowly, allowing both nuzzle and scope to slide out under cover of the Venetian blinds.

Through the scope, he picked his first target, a twenty-something male with a football scarf covering his mouth. Roy took aim, removed the safety, and fired. Through the scope, he watched the bullet tear through the man's chest, a short burst of blood spitting into the air as he fell.

One down.

Now he had to act fast.

Reloading quickly, Roy repeated the action of adjusting his scope, seeking out a target and firing. This time he found the skull of a thirty-something fat bastard, spilling his brain over the bonnet of a car the fucker was taking cover behind.

A second look told Roy that another man was hiding there, too. And this one had a shooter. Roy ducked quickly as he spotted the other guy standing to fire. The bullets were well-aimed, suggesting some training, and Roy had to cover his head as pieces of glass from his window vantage point splintered around the room he was in.

The cheeky bastard.

Further shots and then a petrol bomb followed, taking advantage of the destroyed window, landing just behind the table of the office Roy was in. Roy crawled out of the room, cursing as he went. He had only time to grab his two-way radio before the heat from the licking flames had built to a dangerous level. He closed the door, retreating down the corridor to relative safety.

As he retreated, Roy passed another survivor who was moving in to tackle the flames, armed with a fire extinguisher. "Keep your head down, for fuck's sake!" Roy barked at her, ducking in behind the main corridor wall.

He caught his breath before raising the radio to his mouth.

"Mairead, you there?"

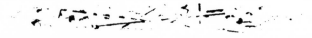

The entirety of Mairead Burns was sprawled out on the school's rooftops, drinking up the splendour of the action on the ground. She had been waiting for Roy's word before opening up with her own sniper rifle, resenting the fact that—yet again—he was calling the shots, but respecting his ability as a soldier enough to play along. She needed to protect Clare and working with Roy Beggs, in this case, was going to be the best way to achieve that. It didn't mean she had to like him.

Testing her scope, Mairead picked out her future targets, almost laughing at the pathetic mess that McElroy and Steele had got themselves into. Not a bad thing, of course. It had provided Roy and her with an excellent decoy to distract these rank amateurs before they mounted the main offensive.

Two shots rang out, almost in succession, Mairead noticing how two men that she had hoped to take a pop at, hit the deck, dead.

"Beggs, you're a damn good shot," she muttered to herself. "Even if you are a complete shit."

Then came the surprise.

Another man had jumped up from behind a car and sprayed the school grounds with semi-automatic fire, providing cover for a third fucker to let go with another petrol bomb. This one struck gold, Mairead watching as it glided through the air toward the school's entrance.

Come on, Roy, just give me the word.

A moment passed before she got what she was looking for.

Pzzt. "Mairead, you there?" *Pzzt.*

Picking up her two-way radio, the former IRA operative answered.

"I'm here," she said. "Looks like you're knocked out of the game, though." It was a cheap shot and she knew it. But it gave her pleasure to put Roy down at every opportunity.

Pzzt. "Just take the remainder of them out. There's a wee bastard behind that car with a shooter. Take him out first then we can see how many of them have real weapons." *Pzzt.*

Mairead didn't bother to reply. She set her radio down and retrieved her rifle. From her bird's eye vantage point, she picked her targets with ease. The silly cunt who was cocky enough to come out from behind his cover, firing wildly towards the hapless Steele and McElroy, was first to go. One shot from Mairead took him out of the game, sending him sprawling across the pavement. Another idiot had made a beeline for the first man's weapon but Mairead had already reloaded before he was even able to pick it up. A shot to the back of the head put him down, too.

That was all was needed. Mairead watched as the remainder of the posse upped and legged it, pouring out of the various hiding holes they'd taken for themselves outside the school grounds. She smiled as she watched them run, picking up her radio again.

"It's clean-up time, Roy. Let's get busy."

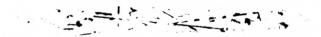

Roy listened from inside the school as the two shots from Mairead rang out, signifying the end of the road for another two of their opponents. Her next message, delivered swiftly after the shots, was all that the soldier needed to hear. Pulling a handgun from his belt, Roy bolted for the door as quick as his heavy build would allow him.

The front lawn of the school grounds was charred from the petrol bombs and Roy had to be careful not to step on any patches that were still smouldering, fully aware of how easy it was to catch fire from these bloody things. Smoke was still heavy in the air, providing Roy with some cover yet also making it difficult for him to see.

"Steele! McElroy!" he yelled as he ran, "Move out! Let's finish this!"

The poorly-prepared militia grabbed their SLR rifles, huffing and puffing towards the school gates, following Roy's lead. As they moved out into the open, the smoke cleared and all three men were able to make out a small group running towards Lisburn's town centre.

A shot rang out, suddenly, dropping one of their number to the ground. Roy knew it was Mairead, picking the exposed fleeing men off like the chicken shit they were. As Roy gave chase, he, too, fired at will, cutting down another guy. His screams sounded brutal, Roy's smaller calibre bullets tearing through various parts of the man's anatomy before silencing him for good.

Steele and McElroy had taken cover, again, behind a car. Noting this, Roy ducked behind a lamppost, worried more about the wild shooting of his militia than that of their fleeing opponents. Both men opened fire, their own semi-automatic gunfire cutting through the air to take down another runner. Another burst from Mairead took down yet another man who was trying to force a shop door open, leaving only one young woman in flight.

Roy waved to the others, signaling that he wanted her for himself.

He made good his chase, catching his opponent due more to her tiredness and fear of being gunned down than his own athletic ability. By the time he reached her she had put her weapon down and was on her knees, facing Roy with both hands on her head. She was crying and a stain spreading across the front of her combat trousers suggested that she was in the process of pissing herself.

Roy paused to catch his breath before addressing her. "How many of you are there?"

The woman sniffed away her tears, trying to compose herself before answering. "There's only me, now. Everyone else is gone."

"You're lying," Roy said.

"I'm not!" she screamed, terrified. "Please don't hurt me."

"What, like you wouldn't do the same to any of my lot?" Roy said, incredulously. "I've got people who depend on me. People I need to protect. If I was to let you go, I wouldn't be doing my job, now, would I?"

"Please, I—"

"Just shut up and listen to me," Roy said, his patience all but dried up. "I'm going to need you to do something for me."

"Anything!" she begged. "Just say it and I'll do it."

The woman remained on her knees, looking up at the formidable frame of the soldier. She was in her thirties, Roy reckoned. Nothing especially remarkable about her struck him. Just another drop-out trying to make her way in the broken-down world. Dirty hair, wide-eyed hunger about her face. Slovenly clothes and skinny, malnourished arms. Possibly a drug user or hooker, working for some Big Man in order to get some kind of reward.

He knew she was playing along with anything he said. Fear was making her tremble all over, but the soldier (Protector? Leader?) couldn't feel anything but anger for her.

"Here's the message," he said, clearly. But where there should have been words to follow, Roy wasn't forthcoming. Instead, two bullets pierced her forehead, a jet of blood and brain spewing from the back of her skull as she fell, dead, to the ground.

Roy couldn't be sure that she was lying about there being others, and that didn't bother him. She couldn't be trusted not to seek some kind of revenge, even if on her own. And if there were any others nearby cowering in the shadows, the fear of God pissing out their dicks, they too would have witnessed how Roy Beggs deals with anyone who crosses him. It would set an example, a precedent that would show how those who prey upon his community end up.

And that was the kind of rep he needed to be a leader.

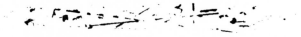

Roy started back towards the school, his heavy boots echoing out throughout the dead, grey backdrop of Lisburn. A few flames flickered around him, the remnants of the various petrol bombs that had been thrown. A distant sound of a barking dog shattered the stillness, briefly.

Roy spotted the face of a beautiful woman on a billboard, advertising perfume. Despite its colourful-looking bottle cradled in the palm of her hand, the soldier could smell only death.

Death and more death and more death and more.

He didn't see the point of covering over the bodies of the attackers. There were dead scattered throughout the whole world now, it seemed. Some of them reeked of too many days in the sunshine, festering as could be predicted. Others, Roy had noticed, were better preserved, perhaps even as fresh as the day they had fallen. That was fucking weird for a man like Roy to take in. It was fucking weird for *anyone* to take in. Yet the more thought he gave these things, Roy wondered whether anything could be weirder than the entire population suddenly falling dead.

For Roy, it was simple. As long as people stayed with him, protected inside the school grounds, none of this would matter. The smell of death—*or not*, as the case might be—would be hidden from them. They didn't need to know about it. It would only freak the survivors out even more. Others, perhaps, would crack under the pressure like Steve Marshall.

And God knows they didn't need another fuckin' case like Steve Marshall.

Roy would be there for them. No matter what creepy horror-movie bullshit came to get them, Roy would take care of it. That was his job, after all. A trained soldier. Their protector. Their leader.

Toying these things over in his head, Roy walked slowly back towards his base—their haven. A glint in the distance gave away the position of Mairead Burns on the school's rooftop and, for a moment, Roy wondered whether or not she would fire upon him, taking him down with the same precision that had spelled doom for their attackers.

But she didn't.

TWO

DAYS HAD GONE BY, MAYBE WEEKS, AND YET HERB HADN'T changed from the pyjamas and dressing gown he had woken up in on that fateful Sunday. Muriel hadn't left any clothes out for him. He had kept the kitchen clean, along with the rest of the house, simply filling the outside bin with the remains of every tin of Spam he left half-eaten. He even kept Muriel clean, giving his wife's corpse a bed-bath from time to time to keep her looking her best, but he never even as much as splashed water over his own unshorn face. It just didn't seem a worthwhile thing to do.

Perhaps it was the shock, or the fact that with his condition (that's how the doctor had described it) Herb had refrained from checking to see what was happening in the outside world. He just couldn't physically do it. Sure, he had rang for an ambulance at one stage (although thinking back on it, he couldn't be sure if he had done that on the first day... or even the second), he had turned on the television, getting nothing but fuzz from every channel, but even then he hadn't considered for an instant that there might be something wrong with the rest of world—only *his* world—the world which had began and ended each day with Muriel.

A part of him didn't want to be found, didn't want to have to give her up to the doctors and the funeral directors who would, no doubt, need to take her away. He didn't want to have to welcome all those strangers into his house (their home) and entertain them with cups of tea and grateful smiles, the way those things needed to be done. Herb didn't want or need any of that (and he was quite sure that Muriel didn't either). Yet, another part of him was growing fearful of The Silence.

The Silence was everywhere. It was in the house. It was in the garden, (which he had gingerly breached in order to kickstart the generator when the lights had gone down. Was that the first day or the third?) It was in his shed, (where he kept all the things which he had been playing with over the years—motorcycle engines, the Amateur radio which he used to tinker about with many moons ago. The Ariel was still erected by the cottage, that old double-barrelled shotgun which Muriel had always been begging him to get rid of).

The Silence—that goddamn *Silence*—was everywhere and, after God knows how many days or weeks, it was starting to grate on Professor Herbert Matthews. In fact, it was beginning to tear away at his very fabric—his very *essence*.

He needed to get out. He needed noise. He didn't realise how much he missed it until it wasn't there.

Herb walked to the front door, sighing. He opened it with relative ease, stepping onto the garden path leading to the world outside for the first time in almost ten years.

There. That wasn't so hard, was it? Those bloody doctors know nothing! Nothing, I tell you!

The old white van that Muriel would have driven remained parked in the driveway. The garden gate (a little rusty from the last time Herb had seen it) was firmly closed. Fields nearby were littered with what appeared to be sleeping livestock. Or were they dead?

It was all enough to give Herb the shivers. He wasn't dressed for the outdoors, having neglected to change from his dressing gown and slippers for his little escapade. It hardly mattered, of course. He didn't make it much further.

First came the heavy breathing, then there were the palpitations. Finally the professor had a full-blown panic attack, complete with dizziness and swirling stars in his eyes.

He passed out, and woke to find himself half in and half out of the front door.

Herb crawled desperately back inside. He closed the front door for what he thought to be the last time, locking it defiantly.

Shan't try that again, that's for sure.

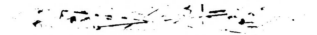

John McElroy stepped out of the school's mobile classroom, looking left and right. Sweat was building on his forehead, darkness in his eyes.

He had done some bad things of late.

It hadn't been his fault, of course. Were he to blame anyone, it would be God. That Royal Fucker had left him alone in this world, without his wife Shauna and that bint, Glory, from work, who he had fucked on a regular basis. What the hell else was he to do?! How was he supposed to control those urges now?

Roy shouldn't have given him the job of cleaning up. McElroy had been sitting at the table with Roy when Steve Marshall—a fucking weirdo, in any case—had burst into the canteen with that foul little bundle in his arms. It was shocking. Nothing short of it.

Roy had seen how maggot-ridden the corpse had been, lumps of dark, yellow skin peeling of it like it had been a plastic doll buried, then unearthed. And they all had caught a whiff of the putrid smell, attacking the senses like a wave of sick. So for Roy to give McElroy that job—the job of cleaning up the car where Marshall had kept the decrepit child for all that time—spoke volumes of how far down the pecking order the soldier saw the ex-civil servant.

But the other corpse in the car—that of Marshall's wife—hadn't been so foul…

John McElroy made it to the makeshift grave where Roy had asked him to bury the bodies. The grave contained the child (and fucking hell, he couldn't bury that thing deep enough…) but he had neglected to bury the woman, Kirsty. She had been Steve's wife, a young thing about half McElroy's age. And damn, even in death she was still pretty hot.

McElroy had kept her hidden, buried under old junk that the survivors had cleared out of the school and thrown into the mobile classroom. No one was ever going to find a black bin liner containing the body. Oddly enough, she didn't smell. In fact, she hadn't deteriorated at all, it seemed. And much as that thrilled John—night after night for several weeks running—it was starting to freak him out now. He was beginning to worry that she wasn't dead at *all*.

It was like those other bodies that Trevor Steele and him had seen during the attack, before Roy had called the curfew. Marshall's wife wasn't decaying (not as far as he could see, anyway) even though she seemed dead. McElroy had heard of comas that were so intense that even the most highly-trained physician couldn't tell if the person was dead or not. He had heard the urban myths of bodies being buried alive, their coffins unearthed by grave robbers to find claw marks on the inside of the lid. He'd heard all of that, and whilst it had once freaked the Bajazus out of him, it hardly mattered now. Not in the Brave New World—a world within which McElroy had witnessed Roy Beggs—their champion—murder an unarmed woman in broad daylight as she begged and pleaded on her knees before him. A world where everyone had fallen dead within minutes.

Everyone.

In a world where the shit had well and truly *murdered* the fucking fan, it hardly mattered what John McElroy, ex-civil servant, was up to.

Did it?

The black bin liner was heavy, and it took all the strength in his squat frame to drag its bulk across the lawn. Yet Johnny-boy worked hard, pausing only to take a breath, mop his brow and keep an eye out for anyone who saw him. It looked all clear. What with John being the sentry for the night, it was likely to be clear anyway. Most people slept well now, what with Roy having made things more secure, scaring the hell out of any would-be attackers, and Sylvia sourcing some comfortable sleeping bags and blankets from the school's main store room.

Fucking Roy and Sylvia... what kind of names...

The two of them were like mummy and daddy to the small group of survivors, meeting their every need in a way which quietly secured blind obedience and allegiance. No one questioned any of their authority, whether it be the quiet, maternal power of Sylvia—the hand that fucking feeds them—or the more in-your-face military presence of Roy Beggs— the hand that smites.

Once at the grave, John McElroy dug hard and fast, still keeping a sneaky (and *guilty*) eye out for anyone watching. Before long he struck the sponge-like body of Marshall's son, Nicky, catching the sickening gust of death off the child's unearthed corpse.

He rolled Kirsty Marshall's corpse in, quickly, and threw the earth back over the grave with as much haste as he could muster.

Out of sight, out of mind.

There. That was it done. No more temptation.

Looking left and right again, John McElroy wandered back to his sentry duties, another job sorted out.

three

ALAN GIBSON REPLACED HIS GLASSES WITH A SLIGHT SIGH.
It was no use. Yet another hour spent without getting a single word from the bowed head sat across from him. Steve Marshall, (the bowed head sat across from him), hadn't spoken a word since Roy Beggs had roughly prised his hands off the rancid, flea-bitten body of his young son, Nicky. At least the tears, then, had been some sort of reaction. A release, perhaps, of pent-up emotion and delusion as the man had tried to ignore the fact that his hopelessly deceased wife and son (slumped, secretly, in the back his car) were gone forever.

But now, and every day since then, there had been nothing. Marshall had simply stared out of the small classroom window, his eyes growing heavier and heavier, his shoulders sinking lower and lower. Countless meals and drinks had been largely ignored, occasionally picked at with an almost autistic fascination, before Marshall returned to the business of staring out the small, cell-like window of his classroom abode.

This was a man who loss had hit, and hit hard. The grief was so vast within Steve Marshall that his mind had shut down, refusing to allow even a single moment of lucid reflection on what had actually happened to his family. Post Traumatic Stress Disorder. As far up the scale as it could go. With no medication to help him, God knows what chaotic thoughts were distracting Steve Marshall from reality, or what he made of the calm tide of words from Alan Gibson's mouth. But one thing was certain: Alan Gibson was getting nowhere with his patient.

Sighing again, rubbing his own tired eyes, Gibson got up, moved toward the classroom door, and slipped out, taking care not to slam the door behind him.

Roy Beggs stood waiting for him in the corridor.

"How is he today?" the soldier asked.

Gibson removed his glasses, cleaned them, then replaced them in a move that had developed more out of habit than necessity.

"Same," he replied. "Still doesn't want to accept his family's gone. It's as if his whole world has caved in. He just can't cope with it or deal with it, so his mind just shuts down. It's what we therapists call—"

"Everyone's world has caved in," Roy interrupted, looking sternly through the classroom door's window at Marshall's glazed expression. "We just have to pick ourselves up and get on with it, don't we?"

Gibson was one of the quieter survivors at the school who had blended easily into the corridor's cream walls and wooden assembly hall floor. Typical counsellor, of course. Quietly spoken. Kind, reassuring smile. Faintly nervous disposition, neither offending nor affecting anyone, until now.

Yet, although Roy couldn't see it, he was the best chance Steve Marshall had of finally letting go of the dead family he'd kept stashed in his car. Buried though they may now be in the school football field, the bleak and embarrassing funeral having lasted only ten minutes before Roy called time on it, their faces still remained extremely vivid in the psyche of the man.

Bottom line, Gibson pondered, was that Steve Marshall was not a well man. And to Roy, a mentally ill man was an unpredictable man. Not good for any community. Not good for morale. And in a place where everyone was hovering on the brink, still smarting from their own fucked-up lives, morale was all too important.

Gibson had Roy worked out, every bit as well as he had himself worked out. And the other one...

He noticed her large frame lingering in the dimly lit corridor. Sylvia Patterson was obviously listening in on his conversation with Roy, even though she was trying to pretend that she was mopping the floor.

Sylvia would agree with Roy concerning the Marshall case. She hadn't said as much, of course. She had a much gentler way of winning over the survivors' respect than Roy did, and therefore a much more subtle way of manipulating the vulnerable community. But manipulative she was.

Gibson had her sussed. His mind built her profile. A mother of seven, and grandmother to ten. Harrassed husband that scuttled to her every whim before the disaster had hit. Sylvia simply couldn't deal with not being in control. She needed to be needed, and so fell very easily into the role of provider within the school's ecosystem. Daily she toiled, washing and cleaning, dusting and wiping, cooking and gathering for all those resident. A solid oak of strength, mother and provider to everyone—except Steve Marshall.

No, Sylvia didn't like him. Marshall had freaked her out from the very first time she had noticed him, gathered in the canteen with all the other survivors on that first evening. A man like Steve Marshall, a man who wore his broken heart on his sleeve (and his dead son in his arms until recently) scared her, frankly. She wanted him out of sight—out of mind—and that worried Alan Gibson. The bespectacled forty-something frowned. He had Roy and Sylvia assessed and diagnosed just like everyone else in the school. It didn't take a man with his intuition to do that, of course. It was written all over their faces what they were thinking—what they were *planning*.

Neither of them liked Steve Marshall and neither of them liked *him*.

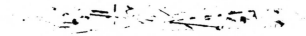

Gently, in that sickeningly nice way of his, Gibson started to tell Roy that locking Marshall up was not going to help him work through his issues. He would need freedom and normality for that, support and encouragement—and all that other fluffy bullshit.

Roy wasn't having any of it. In his opinion, that was precisely what was wrong with the whole fucking world. People had gone too soft, putting up with sickos like rapists and child molesters wandering the streets. A tighter leash needed to be kept on those with something wrong in their heads. Especially now. Especially when the only law remaining was Roy himself.

It wasn't the first time, of course, that Roy had been over-zealous with his law-enforcing. Back in the hey-day of the eighties, a young Roy Beggs had been with his regiment, supporting a police checkpoint in Andi's Town, a well-known hotspot in West Belfast. The cops were looking for someone in particular, following a lead they had got from an informer on a white car which could be transporting some plastic explosives.

Roy's pal, Jordy, had fallen foul of the same type of explosive just a week prior, ending up with him losing his legs after opening the lid of an industrial bin. Roy had watched as the doctor broke the news to the poor bastard that he'd never walk or fuck again.

The night had been cold and icy, and Roy's patience had been wearing thin with every obscene comment and spittle hurled at him from each passing motorist. So whenever a small sporty-looking car failed to slow down when signaled by the cops, instead gathering more speed and bursting through the checkpoint, Roy's trigger finger wasted no time in shredding glass with lead, killing a small town pot-dealer, Gerard, and his cousin Kath almost instantly.

The car wasn't even white, and Roy knew it. But a pro-loyalist judge, anti-narcotics jury, and testimony from a cop who couldn't quite remember how much of a warning Roy had given before opening fire, was enough to exit Roy from court smelling more of rose petal than toilet paper. Not that it mattered what the judge said. To Roy, justice had been served regardless of the outcome of the court case. It was eye-for-an-eye and to hell with anyone who thought differently.

But the boy's mother knew differently. Called Sadie by her friends, although christened Sarah at birth, she was a hardened and weathered woman who spent the whole time during the court case welling up tears behind her bone-dry eyes, as the coroner explained just how badly mutilated Roy's ammo had made her son. The boy's sister, Chris, herself only a child, sat beside her mother, holding her arm with a grip so tight it permanently marked the woman's skin. It was their icy stares that had burned into Roy's head, even to today. The young girl's eyes had been particularly memorable. Deep, deep blue. Slightly crossed, but still beautiful. Full of a deadly combination of anguish, grief and rage that Roy knew only too well to spell out one thing: *revenge.*

Those pretty little eyes had lost Roy many a night's sleep since he walked out of court a free man.

"We keep him locked up," Roy said, finally, to the bespectacled counsellor. "I don't care what your hippy feel-good books say about what he needs, I don't want Marshall wandering free when he's capable of god-knows-what."

Gibson frowned, but nodded.

Roy turned to walk away, then stopped. He slowly turned around, eyeing up Gibson in a similar way that he had eyed up Mairead before handing her a handgun. Shaking his head, as if disappointed with himself, Roy reached into his pocket and took out the bunch of keys that he'd found in the school's principal's office. He sighed heavily before pulling off the key to the classroom that Marshall inhabited, handing it to Gibson.

"I want him kept away from the others, Gibson. You can feed him, give him water, clean out his shit and talk all the psychobabble you want to him. But mark my words: If I ever see him outside of that classroom, I'm holding you personally responsible. Got it?"

Alan Gibson took the key, smiling at Roy in that amicable way that he did.

"You're the boss, Roy."

Roy searched Gibson's eyes for any sense of sarcasm, finding none. Either Gibson was good at hiding such things, or his words had got through. He turned and walked back into the canteen where the other survivors were gathering for another meal.

Gibson knew that Roy wasn't a man to fuck with, but he had his responsibility to his client. Christ, that's all he had now.

Several years ago, Gibson himself needed help. His wife had left him for another man, one that could actually give her what she needed— a home, security, a family, someone who she could speak about proudly to her friends and work colleagues. Someone that wasn't Alan Gibson, borderline alcoholic and disgraced teacher.

Gibson ("Craggy" Gibson to the kids) had been involved in a scandal with one of his pupils. The papers had outed him as something of a pervert, preying upon fourteen year-olds whilst teaching them The Facts Of Life. The story went of how Gibson would lure the prettier girls back to his classroom for some extra study time, feeling them up whilst coaching them in order to help them pass their GCSEs. Mostly these stories came from one particular girl, Chloe Spence, a well-known troublemaker that Gibson had taken something of a shine to. He saw some potential in her eloquent put-downs and smart-arse charm. The little bitch ran rings around even the most experienced of teachers, but she seemed to warm to Gibson's less formal approach to teaching, not to mention his kind eyes and listening ear.

With his relationship with the wife going down the toilet further and further each day, Gibson wasn't in much of a hurry home anymore, so coaching Chloe after hours provided some form of redemption for him, made him feel like the man his wife failed to make him feel. For him, their relationship was paternal. For Chloe, Gibson was yet another idiot in the system that she was only too willing to fuck with. It wasn't her fault, Gibson realised, encouraged by his own therapist to throw away his feelings of hate towards her after she provided the catalyst for his life to spiral uncontrollably, but nevertheless a vicious word or two from her cute little lips spelt doom for his teaching career. One rumour led to another, and soon everyone and their daughter cried abuse at Craggy Gibson, dreaming up all kinds of ways in which his touch on a shoulder or pat on the back was sexual predatory behaviour.

They hadn't enough substantial evidence to do anything about the rumours, but parents were starting to put pressure on the school board of governors, and the principal, who like most of the other teachers had no doubt Gibson was innocent. Finally, the school was left with no other option than to get rid of Alan Gibson. They offered him a good reference and unblemished record if he walked and relocated.

Gibson left the school, his wife left him, then he left England. Having a sister living in Northern Ireland, he figured it was an ideal time to make the break from Rule Britannia altogether. No one knew Gibson well enough to judge him in Northern Ireland, so it was an ideal place to resettle.

At first he had hit the bottle hard, carving out a meagre existence on state benefits as he volunteered sporadically at a local charity shop. Eventually he sought out counselling, finally putting to rest many of the demons that had haunted him since the incident (or lack of) with Chloe Spence. Gibson benefited so much from therapy that he finally went into the profession himself, avoiding working with kids in favour of helping adults with addiction problems and guilt management issues. In a country like Northern Ireland, where many people had got caught up in some way in the so-called Troubles, Gibson soon found himself working with ex-terrorists and members of the security forces alike on the sins of their past. With his quiet, non-judgmental demeanor, he excelled at the job, finally able to do some good without being shafted by his would-be benefactors.

Gibson knew he could turn things around even with the likes of Steve Marshall, even in a world where little made sense, despite what Roy Beggs thought. Tucking his book on cognitive behaviour under his arm, the meek looking counsellor, the teacher formerly known as Craggy, followed the other survivors, quietly, into the canteen. He was feeling peckish.

Mairead Burns and Clare McAfee sat on the swings in the school playground. It was early afternoon and the sun was sitting high and mighty in a deep blue sky. Clare was sucking on a lollipop that Mairead had found in the school's canteen, cooling it in the freezer that some of the survivors had got working again.

It was the first lollipop the child had enjoyed since that fateful Sunday when her mum hadn't woken up. Mairead couldn't believe that that was almost three weeks ago now. It seemed like only yesterday that she had met this little princess, this child that appeared so innocent in the heart of these new, sinister uncertainties. Yet it also felt like years ago that her life had been normal, when she had a husband, two sisters, an annoying mother, a living son, and they didn't live in a school.

"They don't ring the bell any more," Clare said suddenly, swing moving to-and-fro in the delicate summer breeze, lollipop almost devoured.

"They don't need to, sweetie." Mairead ruffled the child's thick, curly hair, wondering if she should perhaps have a go at cutting its split ends, or even asking around to see if any of the survivors had some experience in hairdressing.

Hygiene and vanity were a thing of the past for many. Yet Mairead had kept herself and Clare reasonably clean, even if only for the sake of the child, but she hadn't been brushing either her own or Clare's hair much.

"Aren't we going to do anymore sums? Miss Delaney had been doing money with us, and we all had to bring in some shopping so we could make our own supermarkets. I brought in two packets of cornflakes and a tin of peas, but Miss Delaney said we had to bring in empty boxes and tins, not full ones." Clare looked up at Mairead, her lips toxic-orange with the lollipop. "Do you think Miss Delaney will come back to school?"

Mairead smiled, taking out a tissue to wipe the child's mouth clean. "Why don't I teach you all about money? We could go to the canteen and have a look at the money machines at the counter. Would you like that, love?"

"Yeah! Like going to the supermarket! I used to go with mummy. I'd pack the bags for her. I put all the tins in first then use another bag for the cold things, then another for the smelly things, like soap and stuff." Clare wiped her nose with her sleeve before adding, "That's how mummy likes to pack things. She never puts things that don't go with each other together."

Mairead was worried about Clare. She seemed to talk about her mummy as if she believed she would see her again, yet never actually asked when that might be...

deadDEADdeadDEADdeadDEAD

She was perfectly content with Mairead—that much was obvious. The child rarely left her side, even for a second. Whilst other survivors talked to her or gave her sweets, it was Mairead that the child came to whenever she needed something. Even just a cuddle. And that suited Mairead just fine. She adored Clare, counted her very much her own now. It was a second chance for her to raise a child the way it should be raised.

(*"There's been an explosion, Mrs Burns..."*)

A surrogate daughter.

"Mairead?"

"Yes, sweetie?"

"Could I call you mummy? Just for now, I mean?"

Mairead's eyes watered. She lifted the child up into her arms and hugged her tight.

"Of course you can, sweetie," she whispered into her ear. "All the time, if you like."

Four

THE OLD DX-401 HAM RADIO HADN'T BEEN TOUCHED IN YEARS and a lesser-minded man than Professor Herbert Matthews may not have had the patience that was required to breathe new life into its old circuits. But a machine like this was always going to be a joy for Herb, giving him the opportunity to play God again. He knew precisely how to get this old boy working, just what was needed to resurrect a piece of junk from his shed to become his sole link to the outside world. And, of course, he loved every minute of a challenge such as this.

Once Herb had worked his magic with the internals, teasing his soldering iron around the heart and guts of the machine in an almost flirtatious manner, he turned his attention to the old, rusty Ariel leaning against his house. It hardly seemed fit to be the courier of Herb's desperate SOS signals, but it was all he had, short of a washing line, that could do the job. Of course, Herb knew that with the transmitting and receiving power within the surprisingly small box now resting on his coffee table, the Ariel wouldn't need to do much. Herb's magical add-ons had made his modest HAM radio ten times the machine it would have been on rolling off the production line.

Still have it in you, sir.

Within a few short hours, Herb was ready to power up his rig. He worried about the fact that his entire power depended upon a small generator at the back of his house as opposed to the power station up the road. With his homemade generator's limitations (even Herb couldn't create power out of thin air) it was going to be necessary to ensure that all the power in the house was limited to the radio alone. Especially since receiving its 'special' add-ons.

This baby could burn.

Herb returned to the house and sat himself down by the kitchen table where the radio was rigged up. From the corner of his eye he could see Muriel watching him from the armchair in which she had spent the last days, weeks or months, her eyes as lifeless and expressive as ever, her beauty still unspent. Time, like beauty, was a mystery to Herb now. His clocks seemed to spin around day-in-day-out, going nowhere in particular. Telling him nothing. Meaning nothing. All that meant anything to him now was Muriel and this radio. The only things of any value in the whole house—one dead and the other...

Pzzzzt.

Alive! Herb knew it would work, the electronics of the thing providing him with little challenge at all. Yet he had still felt a little skip in his heartbeat as he had turned the dial.

The airwaves were his now. He could tune in to and listen—*and please, God, talk*—to anyone who was broadcasting, whether they be on a private channel or not. Such was the genius of this machine. Such was the genius of Herbert Matthews, a man whose engineering prowess had led him onto many a confidential conversation in the early 80's when these babies had first come out. A few twists and turns of the dial, listening to the vibrations of sound like a doctor listening for a hearbeat, and Herb was there. He used the same language as these things. Always had and always would—which was perhaps why he was so bad at communicating with people.

Herb flicked through the main channels first, listening carefully for any sign of life from each one he passed through. It took some time, what with the sheer number of channels, but he knew how important it was to try the main frequencies before going all Herb-magical on it.

Pzzt. Pzzt.

The sound was musical to Herb, and he was almost tempted just to listen to an empty channel for a while, perhaps attracted to its sweet serenity. But he knew that enough time had passed where he had given into his almost carnal longing for solitude. He needed to talk, now, no matter how painful it would be for him. He needed to find out just why it was so quiet, why the phones and television and FM radio and Muriel had all died on him. He needed to find out before he decided what needed to be done about it.

Pzzt. Pzzzzzzt.

Each channel breathed the same as the last. Each a desert of activity, a barren soundscape where nothing more than Ballyclare's fresh country air whistled through. Nothing more than the wind and the slight rustle of leaves. Nothing more than the sun-parched clouds evaporating into the skyline, the heavier clouds spitting out their obnoxious belch of rain to create yet another heavy shower at night.

And then it came.

Pzzt. Pzzt. Pzzzzzt. "Ter..." Pzzt. "airfield... calling all..." Pzzt.

Herb was dumbfounded. His jaw dropped, the horn-rimmed spectacles falling, unchecked, off the end of his nose. He reached for his glass of bourbon then realised the last of it had been drained dry hours ago.

"Sweet Lord," he croaked, all moisture seeming to have left his voice. It was contact. He knew it. And what Herb couldn't believe was the channel he had found it on. Channel 40. The most common channel on any Citizen's Band radio.

Scrambling to pick up the mic, Herb cleared his throat before saying his first words in the Brave-New-World.

"H-hello?" he said, simply. "H-hello?! This is Professor H-Herbert Matthews. T-to whom am I speaking?"

ANOTHER PISS-UP.

Ever since Barry and Sean had arrived there had been nothing but drinking, smoking dope, and partying at the station on Great Victoria Street, Sean spinning a few discs in some rig he and Barry had somehow powered up. Star disappeared from time to time, going god-knows-where, to retrieve some weed and a shitload of booze. Repeat ad nauseum. Literally.

Together the three of them had lived the liva-loda, drinking by night at the station, bopping around drunkenly to Sean's bizarre mix of dad-rock and metal, then sleeping it off at the Europa Hotel, next door, during the day. Many of the rooms had been free of bodies, so the three revellers would often rest there to get away from the bright sunlight that would shine in through the high glass walls of the station. Light, as every self-respecting Irish drinker knew, was the arch-enemy of hang-overs.

Tim and Caz had taken one of the rooms in the first floor of the hotel, still looking grand despite having been the most bombed in Europe. Its red carpets and ornate stairways screamed elegance despite the recent downgrading of the entire world.

She and Tim lay on top of the gloriously comfortable bed in one of the hotel's executive suites, listening as Barry, Star and Sean came rolling through the doors, proceedings well underway for yet another night of insatiable hedonism.

"They're early tonight," Tim muttered, eyes closed, lying slightly to the left of where Caz lay.

"Think they started earlier today," Caz reasoned. "I saw Star skulking about the place at about eleven this morning. It's been weeks now. How they keep drinking like that amazes me. Especially Sean. He must be, like, fifty, that bloke."

"That dude's a legend," Tim laughed.

"Yeah, he's old enough anyway." Caz looked over to Tim, sneaking a glimpse at his long, skinny frame sprawled out on the bed. They were both fully clothed, and no one had dared dip below the sheets. She fancied Tim like mad and her young hormones were racing now that they were finally sharing the same bed, but she couldn't bring herself to make a move. That was his job, anyway. Blokes did that, not girls. It was, like, the dating law, or something.

Yet Tim looked about as far away from making a move as Belfast was to Tokyo. He was wearing that same nonchalant expression that he wore most days, whether he was pouring himself a coffee or strolling to the toilet. Reading Tim's emotions was like trying to read Braille whenever you weren't blind. Difficult and bloody frustrating.

"Tim?"

"Yep?" he answered, still keeping his eyes closed and body completely still.

"You know when you were... you know, upset and stuff, the other week?"

Tim looked over to her without saying anything. His body seemed to tense all of a sudden, his feet moving up toward a fetal position. Caz hadn't mentioned that day since it happened. It was an unspoken rule, it seemed, to leave that day where it was. Spent. Clocked. Dealt with. Never to be discussed again.

"Well, I just wanted you to know that I'm always here to listen to you."

For a long and agonising moment, Tim didn't reply. Tears had begun to build up in his eyes again. Finally, he spoke.

"I know," he whispered, almost inaudibly. "You too, you know."

Another awkward moment or two passed. Caz felt very aware of her breathing, and how loud it sounded all of a sudden. The Silence from outside seemed to leak through the windows and creep into bed with them. Even The Rain seemed to shush, a little, its constant pitter-patter gingerly hovering by the window, waiting for something to happen. Something important.

And then it began. At first, she felt Tim's ankle wrap slowly around her own. The mere touch of his socked foot sent ripples of euphoria through her, and Caz's heart started to race like that day, weeks ago, whenever she had watched him walk through the door of her train car. What with all that had happened, she had almost forgotten her crush on Tim Adamson, and how he had made her tingle every time he walked past her in school.

Caz allowed a smile to cross her face as she lay on the bed, now facing the other way from Tim. His ankle seemed to draw closer, snuggly cuddling her own. She began to wonder what colour his socks were, stifling an unexpected giggle of excitement and youth.

"Seahorses," she heard herself whisper.

"What?" Tim replied.

"Seahorses," Caz said again, keeping her face hidden from Tim, her smile beaming quietly and excitedly, her face reddening. "They're one of the few creatures that mate for life. They swim about wrapping their tales around each other, as if holding hands." Caz reached her hand behind her as she spoke, soon finding Tim's own waiting for her. "I always thought it was cute."

"Yeah," Tim said, reaching another hand out to run through Caz's hair. "Dead cute."

SIX

SYLVIA PATTERSON SAT AT THE CANTEEN TABLE, SLEEVES ROLLED up, soiled apron still clinging to her waist. Having taken it upon herself to prepare all of the survivors' meals, helped by the delicate hands of Aida Hussein and the burly strength of Peter Stokenbergs, the group's Latvian, it seemed she was spending every waking minute in this bloody kitchen. Once one meal was finished and the dishes cleaned and tidied, it was almost time to get things sorted for another meal. There was barely time for a cup of tea in between, never mind a walk around the school grounds or jaunt downtown to get any supplies.

She watched Gibson enter the canteen, probably fresh from another session with that madman, Steve Marshall. Marshall wasn't popular with her. Never had been and—since his little sicko revelation—he never would be. Sylvia had lost grandchildren in the whatever-the-fuck-had-happened. When word spread about what Steve Marshall had been up to with his child (the actual details of the story taking a few twists and turns along the way) he become some kind of paedophile. Worse, even. She had been right about him all along.

Yet, were Sylvia to be completely honest with herself, the Marshall incident was more of a shocking reminder of what had happened to her, of what had been snatched from her, and how very sorrowful that made her feel. With everyone in the community caught in some kind of trance, busying themselves with the very basics of survival in order to forget or detach themselves from the traumatic loss each of them had suffered, a stunt like Marshall's seemed all the more grotesque.

The rest of the group had endured their time of grief, comforting and consoling each other that first day, and daily for the ensuing week. They had exorcised those demons in a very tidy way, no one spilling more tears than were absolutely necessary. No shredding of raiment or gnashing of teeth. That time had passed, of course. That box had been ticked, and now they owed it to themselves, and the human race in general, to gradually work towards rising from the ashes. They needed to work on building something from which society could grow, and they needed to do it sooner rather than later. It was as simple as that. Pure, clinically clean, and simple.

However, like some form of fungus thriving in their very dampness, Steve Marshall's tears threatened to seep through and destroy the very necessary foundation that the school's community had been built upon. The façade that everything was getting better, that death was behind them all now. That suffering was in the past, alongside mourning, the present being a time only for rebuilding.

Grief had no place in that mindset, especially a grief so brutal as that shared by Steve Marshall. He was a huge gaping hole in any rebuilding the community planned to do. His rampant emotions had to be locked away as if some form of contagious virus. The less the survivors saw of him, the better. That was Sylvia's opinion and, so, had also become the popular opinion.

And then there was the threat of Gibson, Marshall's long-suffering counsellor and sole ally. Sylvia watched him walk into the canteen, whistling nonchalantly to himself. She cursed under her breath as he spotted her.

"Hello, Sylvia," Gibson said, flashing a toothy, white smile.

"Alan," she replied, guardedly.

"So how's things in the kitchen? I'd say things are a lot easier now the cooker and fridge is up and running again."

Sylvia knew that the counsellor cared nothing about what went on in the kitchen. He was just trying to weasel his way into her good books, the way his type did.

"If only you had a microwave, eh?" he joked.

"We're grand with what we have," she replied, curtly. She poured herself a fresh cup of tea without offering Gibson any. It was as explicit a gesture in Ireland for someone to show you they didn't want you around, as a two-fingered salute would be everywhere else.

"I was wondering, Sylvia," Gibson began, still smiling despite the frosty reception she was giving him, "would there be anything left I could eat? I was... er... busy, you see, and didn't get down..."

Sylvia looked sternly at the counsellor, her normally kind eyes hard and cold. "Sorry, Alan," she said, simply and firmly. "There's nothing left, I'm afraid." She tried to force a smile, failing.

She watched Gibson hold his gaze, eyes fixed on hers. If it was true that the eyes were a window to the soul, then hers were frosted glass. There was no mellowing. She had locked him out and thrown away the keys. And good riddance, too.

Your days are numbered here, Mr. Gibson.

Sylvia was the provider for the group. The hunter-gatherer. Everyone trusted her, and she nurtured them in return for their trust. Such an arrangement wasn't likely to work in Alan Gibson or Steve Marshall's favour. No one would be willing to break away from the security of the group in a world just riddled with insecurity. No one would be prepared to bite the hand that fed them.

Sylvia knew all that. In fact, she had planned all that.

She watched Gibson stand up from the table, smiling. "I'm sure I can make do with some chocolate and crisps," he said, nodding amicably before turning to walk away. Her frosty glance followed him.

Sylvia knew that Alan Gibson wouldn't have been brave enough to force the issue. A part of her realised that the whole scene had been his own way of forcing her hand, working out for sure where he, and Marshall by extension, stood with her. He could sense the power and influence she held, and yet still he had manipulated her. She had fallen for his mind game. She was mad at herself for letting him have his little victory.

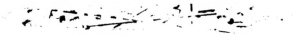

Once the counsellor exited the canteen, Aida Hussein and Peter Stokenbergs gingerly approached. They had both hovered around the scene, listening to the uneasy exchange as they wiped tables down and collected dirty dishes. Neither of them wanted to get involved, yet still they listened in on every word that had been said. It was as close to a soap opera as the survivors would get in the post-television world.

"Are you okay?" Aida asked, speaking first.

"Yes, pet," Sylvia replied, smiling warmly again. "Nothing to worry about."

"Did he mention the crazy man?" Peter asked. He stood awkwardly, his apron seeming to be far too small for him. His hands were full of dishes which he had been reluctant to carry into the kitchen. He hadn't wanted to miss any of the gossip.

"No, sweetheart, he didn't," Sylvia said, looking into space. Even a reference to that Marshall man seemed to upset her. To Sylvia Patterson, Steve Marshall was bad news. People like him should be done away with, or segregated in some way, at the very least. That's what everyone seemed to be thinking. But was it right? Was it not cruel to treat a man like that? *Any* man?

Sylvia looked up to the other two. "In future..." she began, eyeing them up poignantly, "I'll look after any food that's to be prepared for Steve Marshall."

"What do you mean?" Aida asked.

"Oh nothing, love," Sylvia replied, smiling her warm smile. "Just maybe best that I take care of his food, though. You don't mind, do you?"

It was a threat in disguise, and they all knew it. They knew too that were anyone to object to this rather ominous plan, it wouldn't be long until they, too, were ignored and shunned the way Gibson so very obviously was.

Aida wasn't ready for that kind of treatment. Not again. Being a Muslim in Northern Ireland had been challenging. She had put up with racial insults and graffiti being sprayed on her house. Stones being thrown at her children. Strange looks and sniggers whenever she walked down the street in traditional dress. Although young and beautiful, Aida knew what it was like to be isolated, and she sure as hell didn't want to feel that way again. Not now. Not when she had so many other feelings to get used to. Like grief. Fear. Loss. (*Guilt?*) Rejection.

Being made to feel so welcome, now, was a refreshing novelty that Aida wasn't ready to give up, regardless of the price to others. In this new, dangerous age, she had no problem justifying that to herself. But she didn't have to like it.

"Okay." She smiled back at Sylvia, sighing. "I'll make sure to give the Gibson man the food you prepare for Mr. Marshall."

"Great!" Sylvia beamed, as if they'd just decided to organise a party rather than conspire to poison a man to death. "That's it settled, then." She looked at her watch. Aida did similar.

There wasn't much time left until they had to get things started for dinner. There were things needing doing.

SEVEN

"**F**UCKING-A MAN!" BARRY LAUGHED, THE PUPILS OF HIS EYES almost invisible they were so bloodshot. "Where the fuck did you score this from, you filthy bitch?"

Star smiled, carefully cutting the mass of white powder into lines on the elaborate grand piano in The Europa Hotel's main bar. Nearby, ex-DJ, Sean Magee, was getting the rounds in, pillaging a well-stocked bar and pumps to complete his order. On his way back to the other two he almost tripped over a chair, drunkenly struggling in the poor light, managing to spill most of his drinks in the process.

"Geez, girl," he mumbled on catching sight of almost a grand's worth of cocaine being spread out on the piano. "You kept that little find a secret, didn't you?"

"Just waiting for the right time," Star murmured, her hand continuing to draw out perfectly straight lines of snort with a credit card maxed-out to its limit in the old-world, but still nifty for cutting lines in the new. She had snatched the card from the same dealer she'd pillaged the charlie from. An odious-looking little shit she had known from her druggie days. Days that she had thought were long behind her. Until the world ended, that was, and fuck-all seemed to matter any more.

These nights in had been constant since the two guys had shown up at the station, having noticed Star's candles twinkling through the station's tall windows. The first thing they had done on meeting was get stoned, hardly even taking time to exchange pleasantries. Then they got pissed, and so the cycle continued.

As the days had grown into weeks, drunken conversation moved through grief at what had been lost, (Sean often crying hard and long into his pint about his ex-wife) finally reaching the coke-spiked nonchalance of what the three wouldn't miss about the old world.

"That *Raining Men* song," Star said, first to address the question at hand. "You know that one that every girl jumps up to when it's played at weddings, dancing some merry fuckin' jig over the bodies of all their ex-boyfriends?" She ran a little coke under her lips, spoiling one of her perfectly cut lines. "I'll not miss that shit."

"I hear you, girl." It was Barry Rogan speaking. Sarcastically, of course. Sliding by her, he filled his nostril with a line of white. Star watched him sway on his feet slightly, taking a moment to enjoy the hit. "And if ever I tried pulling any of those bitches, they would look at me as if I was a piece of puke."

"You *are* a piece of puke, Barry," Star sneered, smiling wryly, pushing him away from her perfectly laid-out narcotics.

"Fuck you, Ellen," Barry retorted.

"I used to play that song," Sean muttered, finding himself a seat before he fell down. "*Raining Men*, I mean. Hen parties and divorce parties. I kid you not. They lapped it up in equal measure."

"What about you, Sean? What will you not miss?" Star asked, smirking at the aging DJ as he stumbled into his chair. Moonlight spilled through the windows near the grand piano, casting Sean a fairly pleasant profile in the shadows, even when completely pissed. He may have been old enough to be her dad, but he still had that twinkle in his eye that aging veterans like him seemed reluctant to give up.

"Elvis."

"What? Elvis is dead," Barry laughed. He had found his way back over to the coke.

"Go easy on the snort, tiger," Star reprimanded. She was starting to regret sharing this with him. He was getting too hungry for it. Dipping down like that, he reminded her of one of those nature programmes you used to see on TV. A lion tearing on the carcass of a fallen zebra.

"He may be dead," Sean pondered, "but fuck me, he roams free in the hearts of many music listeners. Me? I always hated him. Sounds like a fucking warthog on speed." He guzzled almost half a pint of beer then burped loudly. "And those fucking jumpsuits... What were they all about?! Did he think he was some kind of fucking super hero or something?!"

That one really tickled Star. She almost choked with laughter, stumbling back into one of the bar's chairs. Her nose was raw from snorting yet, like clockwork, the familiar tingle of ecstasy ran through her entire body, shimmering from head to toe as she lounged back.

From where she sat by the window, the city of Belfast could be seen sprawling across the horizon, splashes of moonlight teasing with shadowy glimpses of its dirty secret of death. The Rain continued is nightly assault.

Star recalled the dealer's bedroom she had broken into in order to get the stash that her and Barry were now busy with. The stench of the corpse had been almost unbearable, clouding through the hallway of the dealer's apartment block from the bedroom area of his messy bedsit. Star had tried in vain not to breathe as she stepped into the apartment, unable to blot out the first glimpse of the greasy son of a bitch's rotting mess, half in bed, half out of it, red-raw hands no doubt reaching for the burnt-out spliff, lingering precariously on a large mosaic ashtray by his bedside. Flies had flocked around his body, seeking out new patches of raw, rancid flesh to pick at. Shit had slipped out of the man's bowels, seeping through his boxer shorts onto his jaundiced bed sheets, creating a collage of colour and texture so foul that Star had been forced to take a moment in order to puke over his carpet.

She pushed back a thought that hundreds of residents, equally decrepit, remained within the city. Some on the streets, most in their beds, rotting obnoxiously like some kind of fucking hors d'oeuvre for the cold, deathly main course of Autumn.

It was easy to forget. Weirdly.

Some bodies seemed to just, somehow, disappear. She'd moved a few from the station herself, so she guessed some of the other survivors scuttling about Belfast (those who hid in the shadows or sang their lungs out for the pleasure of their sweet Lordy Jesus) must have moved others.

Yet the ever-present odour in the air was a constant reminder that they hadn't been moved too far.

Not quite out of sight, out of mind.

And then there were the bodies that didn't seem to be rotting. The bodies that seemed as fresh as the day they had fallen. Perhaps fresher. Those ones really freaked Star out. She hadn't mentioned them to any of the others, but she knew she wasn't the only one to notice them.

Truth be told, Star reckoned that the things that didn't click, the bizarre subtleties that came with the territory of watching everyone around you suddenly drop dead, were ignored. It was as if some great hypnotism had been performed on the few remaining survivors, wiping out any ounce of shock ability or awe. Nothing could top what they had gone through. No loss could better the loss they had suffered. Everything else, whether the fiery preaching in Cornmarket or the fresh, perfumed dead lying on the streets, was mere detail to their desolation. Perhaps forming a queue in their post-traumatic brains, behind the very real despair of the current situation.

It was the only way to survive now.

"I'll miss women," Barry wallowed, to the groans of Sean. It was always what it got back to with Barry. "All shapes and sizes of them. Their hair, their smell, their arses, their sweet little titties." His face was all squidged up in that scowl that only men seemed to use when talking about women's breasts. "I can't believe the whole fucking world's gone, leaving me with a shiny-headed punk and sweet little sixteen as the only eligible women around."

"And that Caz one's shagging your wee man now, it seems," Sean added helpfully, before burping loudly again.

"Yeah, cheers, mate." Barry smiled over, receiving only a mock ching-ching from the DJ in response.

"Well, fuck you very much," Star slurred, raising a finger at the lank-haired twenty-something. "And let me tell you, sweetheart... you don't have a fucking hope of getting near my sweet fanny, even if you are the last man on Earth."

"Hey! Don't I count, you crusty bitch?" It was Sean speaking.

Star slapped one hand on the bar table, laughing out loud at his sudden and dramatic outburst. It was unlike the quietly sarcastic DJ to show much enthusiasm about anything, even before the end-of-the-world. "Of course you do, darling," she replied, blowing him a kiss. The cocktail of booze and coke was making her peculiarly affable. "You're a ride and you know it, doll."

Sean smiled over at her, winking like some old, wise sailor, before emptying the dregs from his glass and immediately looking around for something else to drain dry. He quickly found a glass of his favourite tipple of choice, vodka. As a man who had lost his first two loves in the world, (his ex-wife and music), it seemed clear to the other two that Sean was finding bittersweet solace in his third love—that of the bottle.

For a moment no one spoke. As usual the lack of sound filled the room with that edgy quiet that the three seemed to be ever striving to avoid. Sometimes it felt as if they were the only people left who talked any more. Apart from, of course, the mad-arsed Christians at the Bandstand. And god knows, they really didn't count that much in the grand scheme of things to these three.

"So are you a lesbo, Star, or what?" Barry asked out of the blue. It was one of those questions he probably wouldn't have dared ask her if he was sober.

"Charming," the tattooist replied, dryly.

"I bet you say that to all the girls, Bazza," Sean added.

"Nah seriously, though," Barry pressed, "don't you like the cock?"

"I like sex. Who it's with is important... But their gender isn't."

Barry had to think about that for a minute, his brow dramatically furrowed with beer-fuelled contemplation. "But you have to lust after someone, don't you? And you can't like tits and a cock, can you?"

"Why not?" Sean added, slapping a hand on the table as if he'd just invented something new and brilliant. "I know exactly what you mean, Star. There was only ever one person in the world for me, and I sure as fuck never saw her as a gender. Just a person—*my* person." He drained the vodka Barry had given him only moments earlier. "*If only I'd realised that sooner.*"

There was a silence where Barry shared a rolling-of-eyes moment with Star. The ex-wife drone again. They both knew it all too well. Outside the wind howled. Barry suddenly thought of how fitting it would have been to see a little tumbleweed blowing across the bar.

"You know, we were talking about the things we won't miss, weren't we?" Sean said, sweeping the drunken, aimless conversation back on track. "Well, the thing I definitely won't miss is trying so hard all the time to make up for all the fuck-ups I've made."

Barry said nothing. Star paused in the middle of lining up more lines of coke. She looked up at the forlorn DJ, as if surprised. They had both, no doubt, been expecting Sean's usual meandering grief. They hadn't expected a soundbite like that, one which touched them both in different ways, yet on an equally profound level.

For Star, the effort of trying to define herself all the time, a constant struggle in days gone by, was pointless in the new world. She'd been freed of it. It was as if this realisation formed one small needle of hope within this new, chaotic haystack of hopelessness.

For Barry, the sins of the past seemed very far away now. Irrelevant. It was as if he had literally been given a clean slate. He was in the company of people he could trust, and not want to take advantage of. People he could talk to, without being judged. And, hell, Good Mother Nature had fucked over more women in the last week than he had even seen in his life, never mind—

Raped?

No. that was all behind him now.

For a few long quiet minutes, no one spoke. In the sparse hotel bar, the three revelers' slurping of booze and exhaling of smoke was the most that could be heard, the odd cough and wheeze suggesting excess decadence than was healthy. Through the perfectly pale silence of the summer night, another sound rang out, that of drug-curdled daydreaming echoing around the forever buzzing ears of the stoned threesome. Then another howl of wind. Then nothing again. In the bliss of shared feeling, they sat comfortably together, each of them reflecting, nostalgically and drunkenly, on days gone by. Days no longer relevant. Within that one pure moment, each of the three, together, remembered the world for all it was. A bittersweet cocktail of making do and making out. A paddling pool of piss and bliss, for all of mankind to dip its finger and cock into. And for that short time, none of them wanted to be back in there, kicking and splashing amongst the good and the bad, carving out an existence that made a lot less sense, somehow, than drinking and snorting coke in an empty hotel bar.

Star quietly flicked open the grand piano's lid. She had played well since she was a child, music being the only thing other than art that she ever excelled at. In the gentle chill of the evening, she ran her nimble fingers up and down the keys of the piano. She played elegantly for a girl so uncouth-looking, smiling in an almost lady-like manner as she poured her narcotic-enhanced emotion into a few gentle jazz numbers.

For another few minutes, Star played, Sean sipping on yet another drink, whistling quietly along with the sweet piano notes, Barry tapping his foot peacefully.

Outside, The Rain sang along.

eight

AS THE RAIN BEAT UPON HIS WINDOW, HERB SAT BACK IN HIS chair, listening to what the English voice from his Amateur Radio was saying to him. A tear formed in his eye, leading the academic to remove his spectacles, wipe his eye with his handkerchief (ironed to perfection by Muriel) then place them back on the end of his nose. The voice was telling him that the world had changed on that fateful Sunday morning, some weeks ago. Most people had fallen dead, the victims of some unknown plague or something. It spoke so clearly and matter-of-factly and Herb thought, for a moment, that it was all some sick joke. Finally, it stopped and the fuzz of the radio returned.

Herb sat motionless, considering everything that had been said to him. He knew it made sense. The streetlights outside his rural, Ballyclare home hadn't been working. No television broadcasts. No postman calling or any noise of activity outside. The world was dead and to any other man, apart from Herb, it would have been very obvious.

He picked up the mic. "I asked you what your name was, sir. I don't believe you gave it to me."

Pzzt. "Terry. My name is Terry and you, Professor Matthews, are the first Irishman I've made contact with through the radio." *Pzzt.*

"And where are you based, Terry?"

Pzzt. "We're at a small airfield just outside of Manchester." *Pzzt.*

"You said 'we', Terry. How many of you are there?"

Pzzt. "Ten in total, Professor. A couple of pilots. A team of doctors and some others. Is there anyone with you, Professor?" *Pzzzt.*

Herb turned slowly to the armchair behind him. Muriel remained there, still wearing her best shoes—the ones that Herb had put on her feet all those weeks ago. Perhaps it was because he was now talking to the living, but Herb was looking at her, now, in a different light.

He didn't know why it hadn't been obvious to a man of his intelligence that she was, in some way, different than your average dead body. But then again, Herb wasn't accustomed to seeing any bodies, in recent years, dead or alive. The shock of finding Muriel like that had been extensive. Herb could only surmise that his mind hadn't been up to the feat of dwelling on much of anything since he had got out of bed that Sunday.

Pzzt. "Professor?" *Pzzt.*

Herb didn't answer. Instead he stood up, steadying himself by leaning on his desk chair, before making his way to the armchair near where Muriel still sat. Her eyes remained fixed, as usual, on the television across the room, oblivious to the fact that it hadn't broadcast anything in weeks.

Herb sat on the edge of the armchair, removing his spectacles as if about to kiss her. He ran a finger across her face, noticing how soft the skin remained. His other hand ruffled her hair a little, his ailing eyes straining to work out what colour it was. It seemed darker than he remembered and so Herb wondered, for a moment, if she had started dyeing it in recent years without him noticing.

Herb got up, standing back to study Muriel's face against the light beaming in through the front room window. He noticed a framed picture on the mantelpiece, taken many years ago. It was a picture of Muriel at Blackpool pier, taken on their honeymoon. Herb retrieved the picture, looking at it, and then Muriel, in comparison. She had always seemed beautiful to Herb, but in those days she had been a knock-out. Her long, dark hair framed a heart-shaped face. Her eyes had been so pale Herb had almost felt himself swimming in their gaze. Her lips had been full of colour and life, and Herb remembered, again, the first time he had kissed them.

Herb looked at his wife lying on the armchair, slowly realising how much the Muriel there seemed to resemble the Muriel in the picture taken thirty years ago.

Pzzt. "Professor? You still there? I was asking if there was anyone else with you." *Pzzt.*

Herb returned slowly to his desk, picking up the radio mic with one shaking hand, his other still holding the picture.

"My wife, Muriel is with me," he began, bafflement and shock creeping slowly into his voice. "She... she was one of the ones who had fallen yet I wasn't... er... in a position to bury her."

Herb paused for a moment as he choked back the tears. He could hear the rain scraping against the windows and it sounded grotesque to him all of a sudden.

"Terry, I think something's not quite right about her..."

Tim sat in the corner, gazing out through the hotel bedroom window. It was raining. The curtain was mostly closed, save for a slim gap between the corner of the window and wall. Tim shivered as a breeze blew in some random raindrops, his naked skin perhaps creeping against both the chill of the night air and the shame of his flat, useless cock cradled, like a baby, in his clammy hands.

"It's okay, Tim," Caz said from the bed in the middle of the room. It was a clichéd thing to say, and she knew it. Truth was, this was meant to be her first time too and she was every bit as nervous as Tim seemed to be. She knew that what she saw in the movies and on TV was not what it would be like in real life. She knew it from magazines, graduating from the teeny-bop 'position of the fortnight' features to Cosmo's frank, and open discussion of the many, many things that could fuck up when a man and woman get down to it.

But none of that made it easier to hide her disappointment.

Tim said nothing. From where Caz was sitting, the poor evening light gave him an almost ethereal look. His long, slender back curled around the neck as his head bowed in the corner of the room. He looked like someone had told him off and put him in the corner for being naughty. He looked almost dead, the only sign of life being his gentle yet constant shivering. Raindrops continued to blow in on him, sprinkling his pure, white skin like a handful of diamonds. In a melancholic, artistic way, Tim looked more beautiful to Caz than ever. She wanted to tell him that, but couldn't think of any words that sounded right.

"Tim," she called, pathetically.

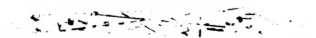

He didn't even hear her. Inside his head were shadows, similar shadows to the ones cast over him whenever his dad would have come in to visit him at night, towering over his bed like a dark cliff. Tim smelt that same stench of whiskey from all those years ago, drifting gently in from the rain-swept night. The curtain caressed his back, swaying with the wind, its touch reminding him of that first experience of sex, the first of too many nights, when he tried to feign sleep to escape those bittersweet touches. He could hear his father's whisper, whimpering apologies for something he couldn't understand. He heard it whistling in the dark-stained wind of night. Tim pulled his legs closer to his chest, suddenly aware of how naked and exposed he was.

Caz watched as the candle they had lit earlier, a feeble attempt at creating the serenity they both needed to make the evening of Caz's seventeenth birthday (she had lied—she was still just sixteen) special, fought bravely against the cold, damp night air before snuffing out. The darkness, The Silence, was suddenly unbearable. Quietly, she got up from the bed, the room having been chosen especially due to its particularly ornate-looking bedposts, and tip-toed over to where Tim was. She covered him with the bed sheets, drawing in close beside him as she wrapped him up.

It was a good touch.

"I want to know what you're thinking, Tim."

"I know... but it's... like... difficult."

"Everything's difficult now, Tim... Difficult for all of us."

She knew it was the wrong thing to say even as she said it. In response, she could feel him withdraw, physically. Yet she persisted, pulling him closer, hoping to bring Tim back from wherever he disappeared to whenever she seemed to reach for him. It was as if squeezing him tighter would stop him from spilling away from her, keep their connection watertight.

"Things happened... a long time ago... I don't want to talk about it."

She noticed him pause. It was as if he was worried that the tears pent up in his stinging eyes might suddenly gush out.

"But, I might need more time to get ... you know... used to us being together, before... before we can do anymore of what we were doing tonight."

She stroked his hair gently as he talked, ready to withdraw if she felt him tense. He didn't, instead slowly leaning his head into her hand.

This, too, was a good touch.

"I need... more of this, I think."

"I know. Me too," she whispered.

It had been peer pressure alone that had made her rush things. She felt, at sixteen, that she should make that transition from girl to woman, go down that clichéd road that every coming-of-age chick-flick told her she needed to take. She had even lied to make it happen. She was suddenly very ashamed of herself. Bowing to peer pressure in a world without peers. Caz couldn't believe how ridiculous that was.

"We've all the time in the world," she comforted. "What else can we do now, apart from spend time together?"

Tim looked around, showing his face for the first time to her in over an hour. In the shadows, he looked even more angelic to her than ever. Light freckles were silhouetted against his pure skin. A faint peppering of stubble made him look a little more mature than his sixteen years. His shiny blue eyes shone like pearls. Tim's innocence and vulnerability was raw to her. Yet absolutely beautiful.

"I... like... love you, and stuff, Caroline," he said, tripping over the words.

Caz felt a sudden warm feeling flow through her body. It was what she expected an orgasm might feel like. A sudden, euphoric glow. A reassurance that everything, even for a moment, was completely, and utterly, perfect.

She felt for the small chain around her neck. It held a silver crucifix, one she had received as a gift whenever she was very young. Carefully, and slowly, she took it off. Carefully and slowly she reached towards Tim, attaching the chain around his neck.

"My mum gave it to me," she said. "She wasn't religious or anything... it just reminded her to keep going, even when things weren't very good."

Tim looked at the figurine of Jesus clinging to the cross. He ran a single finger over the small silver torso, his mind seeming busy with the emotions conjured up by the imagery.

He looked at Caz, smiling weakly. "Faith, hope..." he whispered, as much to himself as to Caz, "...and love."

There was a brief silence between them. Tim's eyes glimmered in the pale moonlight, damp with raindrops and bittersweet emotion. The breeze blew playfully through his unkempt, mousy hair, several strands catching on the newly-acquired chain around his neck. Silver Jesus remained suitably poised. The collage of freshly-inked tattoos on Tim's arms, still healing, made him look very masculine. Caz was thinking just that when he moved towards her. She thought, for a moment, that they might kiss.

But then they heard the explosion.

AS TIME WENT BY, EACH SURVIVOR AT THE SCHOOL IN LISBURN found themselves able to move away from the quiet comfort of the shared assembly hall dormitory and set up their own quarters in small classrooms. Some of the group still chose to share, shacking up with new partners, rushing passionately into fresh and desperate relationships that were more to do with insecurity than love or romance. For others, sharing was not sexual. It was simply because they were afraid to sleep without the presence of someone else. And then there was Alan Gibson. Although he would have preferred to sleep alone, the counsellor had chosen to bunk up with Steve Marshall, regardless of the man's mental health, lack of personal hygiene, and the ever-present stench that such encouraged within his 'cell.'

Gibson had chosen to bunk there for a variety of reasons. First of all, he figured that he could spend more time studying Marshall's habits. As a keen practitioner of cognitive behavioural therapy, Gibson hoped that being able to study the actions and words that Marshall seemed to repeat could help him get to the root of his problems, hopefully speeding up the man's mental recovery. Secondly, with Marshall's physical condition having improved a little (he was starting to eat again and seemed to sleep well at nights) Gibson thought that maybe this public gesture of sharing with the man might encourage others in the group to take an interest in him. In time, people might realise that he posed no threat to them, no danger to their stability. Maybe some of the leaders, even, like Roy and Sylvia, might become less insistent that he stayed locked up.

Out of sight, out of mind.

Thirdly, and a little more pessimistically than the other reasons, Gibson was beginning to fear for both his and Steve Marshall's safety. He had been sidelined almost as much as Marshall, of late, noticing how the whispers stopped as he walked by a group of people talking, or wandered into the canteen for lunch. It was as if he too had been possessed by the same demon they had thought Steve Marshall to be possessed of. As if he too had nurtured a rotting corpse of a child in his arms, a cruel and visceral reminder to all whose loved ones remained somewhere else, unburied and unattended to. It was as if everything that had happened was Alan Gibson's fault as well as Steve Marshall's. Gibson valued the fact that he had the key to Marshall's classroom and took the time to lock themselves in each night. He could deal with their victimisation when he was awake, and able to keep both eyes open. But he sure as hell wasn't going to sleep unsecured.

This was confirmed to him as more than simple paranoia whenever Aida Hussein, who Gibson really hadn't been introduced to yet, approached him one evening before bedtime. There were fewer survivors around, most of them having retired to their classroom quarters for the night. A faint light still spilled out of the canteen, several doors down the corridor from Marshall's room, and it was to this light that Aida kept looking, as if fearful someone might open that door. She caught Gibson just as he was about to lock his classroom up for the evening.

"Mr. Gibson," she whispered, glancing towards the sleeping Marshall behind the half-ajar door.

"Yes.?" Gibson replied, cautiously.

"You have to leave now. Take that man with you. It's not safe." Hearing a sound up the corridor, Aida turned quickly, her eyes searching, her ears listening.

"What do you—"

"Leave!" Aida barked. She turned again to see whether anyone was coming. "Leave now. And don't let that man eat any more food."

She had said 'that man' with a mixture of revulsion and pity in her voice. It was as if she wanted to help Steve Marshall but either felt too scared of him, or too worried about the consequences of doing so. Or both.

"What's wrong with the food?!" Gibson called after her, somewhere between a raised whisper and a shout. But Aida continued down the corridor, back to the canteen without looking back. "*Geez*," Gibson murmured, casting an eye over towards the oblivious Steve Marshall. Had his worst fears been realised? He knew Aida was a friend of Sylvia Patterson, who he had worked out, very recently, was definitely not in his corner. But what was there to be worried about?

Gibson checked the plate Steve had been eating off. He had meant to carry it up to the canteen after supper but had forgotten. Carefully, using a fork, he scraped in between the remnants of food left. It had been some kind of cheese dish. Most of the cheese left had hardened onto the plate, drying up like chalk. As he continued his investigation, Steve Marshall paying him absolutely no attention from the other side of the room, Gibson noticed what looked like a peculiar red powder faintly blended in with the food. It could have been chili pepper, maybe. Putting Steve's plate down, Gibson picked up his own and compared the two. There was no powder on his own. And, now that he thought about it, the cheese macaroni (or whatever the hell it had been) had been distinctly bland tasting. In fact, Gibson remembered splashing more than the usual amount of pepper to liven it up a little.

Gibson sat down on one of the small chairs in the classroom, taking his glasses off and setting them on the desk. He ran one hand through his thinning hair, allowing his head to lean against it. "Oh Steve," he sighed, casting a glance over to his dazed patient.

From a corridor nearby, standing by the door to her own classroom which she shared with the groups' youngest, Clare McAfee, Mairead Burns listened intently. She had watched Aida open the door to the canteen and slip quietly inside. Now she rubbed her eyes, allowing her hands to drop down her face to an almost prayer-like shape over her lips. She had heard everything that had been said. And it worried her.

IT WASN'T AS IF EXPLOSIONS WERE SOMETHING UNHEARD OF IN Belfast. Quite the opposite. Almost all of the survivors could remember at least once, before the shit had hit the fan, whenever a bomb blast near them had rocked the foundations of their home, spilling neighbours onto the streets. Some had even lost relatives, friends, or colleagues to the so-called Troubles, members of the security forces targeted by the IRA's terrorist campaign, innocent bystanders or even mistaken identities. The Omagh bomb in the late nineties, a horrific and ruthless massacre of unbelievable proportion, had been the most recent bomb blast any of them could remember. It was also the most senseless.

For those currently resident in the Europa, this latest blast, seeming to come from somewhere north of the city centre, was even more poignant. Barry, Star, Sean and the two teenagers had taken residence in, of course, the most bombed hotel in Europe. Its four walls had enjoyed many a reworking over the years, shaken by more than its fair share of IRA attacks.

For The Preacher Man and his sombre band of followers in the church, this most recent blast was but a war-cry of the promised return of the Heavenly Host that they prayed for so fervently. Their almost hallucinogenic state, massaged daily by prayer/song/preaching, could see little other than signs and talismans, miracles and curses within the empty, soulless streets of Belfast. Even an explosion, brutal and devastating, with all the trademark telltale signs of the gritty struggle of terrorism from days gone by, now took on a more priestly countenance.

Yet, for those cowering in the shadows, the monosyllabic majority, the explosion was but another reason to remain quiet, hidden and alone.

It was just shy of 4am when the red/yellow blast burst through the navy, pre-dawn skyline, and Barry Rogan was the first of the Europa survivors to wake. He had fallen asleep where he sat, still at the bar table, the smell of cigarettes and booze being the second thing to strike his senses after the explosion. Sean stirred next, his messy shambles of a head simply jolting upright. He had fallen asleep as he did most nights, in the same chair at the same table by the same window, glass or bottle toppled nearby, fierce hangover pending. As his eyes popped open as wide as they could (which was around about halfway, given the lack of sleep and load of booze) the jaded DJ let out a short gasp.

"*Shhhhh,*" Barry motioned to him, one finger over his lips. "I'm trying to work out where it came from."

A noise within the largely silent new world was something of a big deal, but still Sean took a while to gather his senses. His heart was going like the hammers. His whole body ached, particularly his arse. These seats weren't for sleeping in.

"What the hell was it?" he asked before answering his own question. "Sounded like a fucking bomb to me. Well, in my dream it did, anyway."

Barry shushed him again before replying in a whisper, "It was an explosion—that's for sure. Not sure about a bomb. Maybe a fuel tanker going up?"

"Where do you reckon it came from?" Star asked, pulling herself up from behind the grand piano where she had collapsed. Her eyeliner was an even bigger mess than it usually was, having smeared down her gaunt cheeks like tears of ink. Yet she still looked, to Sean, quite beautiful. In an arty kind of way, maybe.

"North, I reckon," Barry replied, still whispering. He had the look of a Native American Indian tracker on his face as he answered her. His head was bent slightly to one side, his ears listening intently to the slight reverberations from the blast in an otherwise soundless air. "I think I'll take a look in the morning, see what happened. It'll give me an excuse to steal a nice car."

Sean was waiting for the inevitable quip, yet Star said nothing. This didn't seem to be a joking matter.

The two teenagers bolted into the bar, joining the others, all of them suddenly brought together by this new and exciting development—this new and startling noise in an otherwise monosyllabic world.

"Looks like a bomb went off out there," Caz whispered, stating the obvious. She spoke in a low voice, as if worried that someone might find out where they were, too, and bomb them. Her glasses were clouded up. She took them off to clean the lenses, revealing her beautiful, china-doll eyes. She had always struck Sean as pretty, in a young and innocent way. Getting on like a kid at a firework display. Excited by noise. Dazzled by light. Hell, just looking at her made him feel old.

In sharp contrast, her boyfriend looked shaken, constantly running the finger and thumb of one hand over the silver crucifix that Caz usually wore around her neck. Sean had clocked it on meeting her. It fitted in with the whole innocent look she seemed to have. He would have thought her to be a Born Again Christian had he not heard her swear so much. Yet now Tim wore the cross, seemingly obsessed by its presence around his neck. His eyes were almost glazed over as if he was drugged. He had moved over towards the front window, looking out onto Great Victoria Street. There he stood, fiddling with the cross, seemingly mesmerized by whatever had caught his eye.

"Did you see where it came from?" Barry asked Caz.

"Somewhere north, I reckon," she replied, pointing. "You can still see the smoke. It's so black."

Star went to the window. "You okay, doll?" she asked Tim, looking out towards where he was looking. Sean followed her gaze. On the street, he could make out a lone figure, tall and formidable-looking. One of the shadow people, maybe. Or those religious nuts from Cornmarket. Sean looked back at Tim. The lad hadn't answered Star. He had hardly even heard her, it seemed.

"Hey Timbo!" she persisted.

He seemed to come out of his daze, flashing the tattooist a weak smile.

"Hang in there, lad," she said, ruffling his messy hair.

The two survivors seemed to have bonded, of late, over a mutual interest in tattooing. Star the teacher, Tim her student. Now Sean was suspecting that there was more than a shared love of body art building in the hearts of the two unlikely friends—Star seemed to have the look of a mother in her tired, fucked-up eyes as she ruffled the lad's hair. And it was nice to see within one so cold normally.

Sean noticed Caz glaring at this exchange. She didn't seem so comfortable about whatever rapport the tattooist and her boy had built up. The tattoo sessions. The things she had no interest in and couldn't even feign an interest in. It was like their own little exclusive club, and Sean could see how that might cause problems for her.

(Like his ex-wife and that fucking—)

Sean thought, again, of his Sharon. How he had felt on seeing new family pictures dotted around the house he used to share with her. Pictures without him. How he had seethed, quietly, on seeing the decor they had chosen, together, changed so dramatically. There had been a different dynamic between Sharon and her new partner, just like the different dynamic between Star and Tim.

To see that had to hurt.

It didn't matter that Star's motives were far from romantic. That she was worried about the look she had seen in Tim's eye. Sean could see this, yet he knew it would be alien to Caz. Even if she had noticed the lad's unnerving look, a look so pungent that it almost felt as if he might pop off, like a cork from a bottle, it would still hurt to see him sharing another look with Star. A look that said something bigger. A look that said there was something between them, a something that wasn't between Caz and him.

Sean sighed at the little drama building, perhaps only in his own head. He looked over to Barry Rogan, standing by the hotel bar's window now, straining to look as far left as the glass would allow facing East.

Outside, a thick plume of black smoke poured across the cityscape. Sure enough, it seemed to be coming from north of the city.

"Fuck me," Barry muttered, echoing everyone else's thoughts with his usual candor. "That's gotta be something big that's just went up."

The Preacher Man stepped out onto Great Victoria Street, his nostrils full of the same stale air that had ran rampant pre-apocalypse. It was the smell of sin. Drifting down from the north of the city, thick with tar. A scent of death. Whatever had just happened to cause such an almighty explosion was pungent and The Preacher Man stood, tall and stoic, drinking it all in.

From his pocket, he took out a small brown bottle, bringing its contents to his lips, slowly and awkwardly. Like a first kiss, he sniffed it first, reassuring himself that whiskey still smelled just how he remembered, just like it did all those years before he had found The Lord. Then he drained it half dry in one swift and fluent motion. A warm rush of relief washed through his tense, sober body, giving sweet release from the pressures of leading his flock, the pressures of preparing for the coming of his Saviour. He looked up to the sky, the smoke (from hell?) having blacked out much of the light, but not enough to prevent him from catching sight of the candles burning from the nearby hotel bar. Inside, no doubt, he would find more souls. More people to lead to The Lord. More converts to his congregation.

(And more temptations of the flesh.)

"Forgive me, Lord," he muttered, almost violently ashamed of himself. He smashed the whiskey bottle in his hand against the side of a wall, bringing the jagged edges of the broken bottleneck against his face as if to slice the evil out of himself. He stood poised, staring at the lethal, sliced glass, eyes fiercely wide, hand shaking with frozen momentum. Then he simply dropped the bottle, a look of resignation spreading across his face.

"Be merciful to me, Lord," he muttered, making back for the church. "Be merciful to me, a sinner."

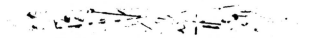

The world seemed even quieter after the explosion. The loud noise had just been a reminder of how loud and obnoxious the world used to be before The Great Silence.

For Star, the sound had been a sudden jolt to the very soul—a call out from the wild saying '*remember what it was like to be alive?*' It injected her with inspiration and she felt the sudden need to tattoo.

The others had drifted off to sleep, finding themselves their own rooms within the hollow-bellied husk that used to be Belfast's busiest hotel. Caz and Tim had shrunk from sight first, followed by the hungover carcass of Sean Magee. Finally Barry Rogan, pausing long enough to steady himself with a swift whisky, disappeared off to bed, his furrowed brow still, no doubt, pondering the mysteries of where the fuck that bomb/plane/nuclear meltdown had gone down.

Star waited a while, drinking up the inspiration that The Silence and The Rain had to offer her before pulling herself out of the empty bar and making her way down to her makeshift studio in the bus station next door.

She flicked on the generator. The old thing whirred into action, its flickering light struggling to illuminate the otherwise black mass of tiled floor and sterile-looking seating. A gentle hum assured Star the generator might just hang in there in order for her to grab another stodgy coffee from the machine, but she sure as hell wasn't going to rely on it to power up her needle.

Pulling up the old stool she had recently nabbed from her shop downtown, along with all of her other stuff, Star began the arduous process of unpacking her gear and connecting the powerpack to the car battery with a couple of leads. Once happy that the power was humming through, Star linked the whole lot up to her foot pedal and clip cord, clicking on/off to make sure everything was working okay. Only then did she click her beautiful girl into place—the old custom made machine that had been passed down to her by the ageing punk that taught her everything she knew.

Her mind drifted back to those days, a time when she had had direction. Just before the drugs and the booze took over, and her art was relegated to third place. She'd done some less-than-great tattoos when she was learning the ropes, yet nothing she would say she was ashamed of. As an artist, she'd grown over the years, honing a particular fondness for tribal tattoos, then black and grey before tackling the boldness of graffiti-style tattooing. Fashions came and went, and as a businesswoman Star had to move with the times, with what people were asking her for. That suited her just fine. She always loved a challenge.

Star was just finishing up her preparations when she heard movement by the door nearest to her. A quick look around revealed Tim Adamson, his head hung low as if he was late for school.

"Hey," Star muttered, half-heartedly.

"Hey," came a similarly lack-lustre reply. "What's going on?"

Star looked up at the lad, a smirk spreading across her face. "I'm having a bath," she mocked. "What does it look like?"

The lad managed a smile, but Star could see almost immediately that he was less than on form for her quips. She had noticed him, earlier, whenever the explosion had happened. Staring out the window, eyes fixed on a particular shadow. A tall, formidable-looking shadow.

"Can I help?" he asked, looking more bashful than she'd ever seen him.

He was a moody lad, that much Star had noticed. Until tonight, she would have put that down to his teenage years. And, hell, what human being was going to be all sweetness and light after the whole fucking world had fallen apart? But, as he spoke, she saw something more sinister going on in his head. The vibes coming off him could have roasted heaven. He was here for a reason, Star realised. Here to cull the demons within his heart and mind.

Star could relate to that.

"Tell you what, go and grab me some of that fake skin we were working on earlier. I'm guessing your arms need a break after all the action they've seen."

Tim looked down at his arms. Where there had once been white skin, a chaotic ensemble of ink now resided. His lily-white skin had now been developed into an altogether more eclectic sleeve featuring contemporary tribal blending into graffiti-style colouring. Star was quite proud of what she'd achieved, albeit outrageously unique for a lad's first ink.

Tim moved as if to make for the two travel cases where Star kept all of her gear, constantly refreshed from the shop. Then he stopped, dead, as if some kind of puppet sent in another direction by an invisible string. As Star watched, Tim wandered back outside the station, muttering as he went. She watched in the poor pre-dawn light as he moved through The Rain towards the boneyard, where all of the bodies had been dumped that very first day. Through the station's windows, she watched as the lad unwrapped the pile of bodies, perusing the makeshift grave like a kid in a candy store, before reaching in. His gangly frame strained against the weight of his chosen prey, Tim beginning the laborious and shocking process of dragging the body of a young girl out of the pile and across the tarmac, back into the station.

He presented the body to Star, like a cat with a bird. The Rain, although paling, had spat all over both him and the body dumped before her. "This one looks good," he said, fighting to regain his breath after the exertion. "I want to work on this one."

Eleven

A T PRECISELY 4.30am, ALAN GIBSON FOUND HIMSELF ON THE school football field looking down the barrel of Roy Beggs' SLR rifle. He had been caught by Roy during the early hours as he tried to flee the school with Steve Marshall, no longer keen on sticking around Roy and his ever-loyal militia since that cryptic conversation with Aida Hussein. But it wasn't just that. He'd watched Marshall get side-lined more and more as the days went by. He had noticed the looks of the other survivors each time he opened the door to the classroom to talk with him, the stench of his quarters (or was it a cell?) growing thicker as the broken man's mental health grew weaker. He'd clocked it as huddled groups of survivors suddenly hushed each other as he wandered past them in the canteen, finding himself almost as isolated as Marshall himself.

Rumours had started to circulate. Craggy's hanging around with that nutcase. Craggy thinks Marshall should be allowed out of the classroom, allowed to sleep beside us, eat with us, work with us. Craggy's as mad as Marshall is. But Alan Gibson was a principled man. A good man. He knew that now, despite what anyone else was saying about him. Experience taught him that people like Roy Beggs and Sylvia Patterson, people who operated in ever-narrowing ideologies of black and white, were a danger to themselves and others. He'd suffered at the hands of people like that before, what with the whole Chloe Spence debacle, and he knew how easily the tide of opinion could turn.

The guard, John McElroy, had stopped Gibson at the school's gate as he tried to bundle a doped-out Steve Marshall into Roy's Land Rover. Gibson had stolen the keys from the soldier's bag when he wasn't looking, (having the decency to take only the one to the Land Rover) then replacing the bunch quickly before Roy noticed them gone. He might have been in with a chance of slipping past the dozing sentry was it not for Marshall's boisterous behaviour landing them both in all shades of shit. Rudely awakened, the odious McElroy wasted no time in calling Roy Beggs using his two way radio. McElroy was a smug fucker on the face of it, but underneath all his bravado, Gibson could see that his insecurities ran rampant. Yet Gibson couldn't counsel his way out of this one. Regardless of his own mental health, McElroy was holding all of the cards. He also held the two rebels at gunpoint, seeming to almost be begging Gibson to make a wrong move so he could waste him there and then.

All kinds of thoughts had raced through Gibson's head as he stood there poised like a deer in headlights. He thought of escape. Simply running for it, leaving Marshall behind to whatever fate was in store for him. He didn't like that he had thought this, and wasn't proud of his sudden cowardice, but if he were to be honest, he had to admit this was the first thought that went through his head. He had also looked to the Land Rover, wondering if he could simply overpower his opponent and make a dash for freedom, but with Marshall in tow things were a little more complicated. Even if he himself made it to the Land Rover, somehow able to push aside the wiry but apparently trigger-happy McElroy, he knew that Steve Marshall, in his present doped-out state, would get easily—and mercilessly—gunned down. Then, strangely, he thought of his life. Of the things that used to make him happy before fate had taken a sudden turn for the worse. Before his own mini-apocalypse had descended upon him, forcing him out of his job, out of his marriage, out of his mind. Standing there, staring at the nervous yet smiling eyes of John McElroy, Gibson realised that he hadn't allowed himself to go through the seven stages of grief he had been attempting to guide Marshall through.

It was when Gibson was thinking these things that Roy Beggs appeared, flanked by another two of his militia, the devoutly religious and equally bigoted Trevor Steele and the only Catholic member of Roy's posse, a small, nervous-looking man named Pat Black. All three carried SLR rifles, primed on Gibson and Marshall, as they walked slowly towards them.

"I *told* you, Gibson," Roy said. "I warned you what would happen if you went against my orders and messed about with this freak."

"Orders?" Gibson replied, indignantly. "For Christ's sake, Roy! We're not all soldiers. This man's sick, and whatever you are putting in his food isn't helping matters any."

Roy Beggs looked sincerely baffled by that remark. He looked back at his militia, appearing almost embarrassed by such an allegation. "Careful what you accuse me of, you self-righteous fuck."

Gibson flinched at the soldier's curtness. He needed to choose his words more carefully. He was starting to see the cracks forming in Roy's psyche. This was not a man in full control of himself. "I just think that if we leave, Roy, it'll be best for everyone. We'll leave on foot. We'll take Steve's car. What kind of threat are we to you then, Roy?"

Roy didn't look convinced. In fact,he looked disappointed. It was as if Alan Gibson had betrayed his trust.

"You'll be shot of us," Gibson continued, trying desperately to roll out every take on this he could. "Out of sight and out of mind before dawn. You can get on with building this community, something that you're clearly very capable of doing."

"Don't patronise me," Roy said simply, not seeming to buy the counsellor's placation.

Gibson noticed the other three watching Marshall closely. Reading them, he couldn't be sure if their nervousness would work for him or against him. "We'll leave here. Go to Belfast. You'll never hear from us again," he appealed, looking to each of the men in turn as he spoke.

Roy spoke next. "And what example will that set to everyone else here, eh? What happens if everyone decides to go against the law laid down? The law protects people, and those who rebel against it are dangerous to themselves and others. I've a duty here, Gibson, to all the others back there."

"We're not doing anything wrong, for Christ's sake!" He was losing his patience with Roy. He'd met a lot of unbalanced people through his line of work, but none of them had had a gun trained on him. It seemed to make all the difference.

"Stealing?! What do you call that, eh?" Roy was angry now. "If I let you away with that, how long before everyone's at it? And then comes the rape—the murder. When law breaks down, so too does society. Look at what happened whenever those fuckers from before decided they wanted to take our base. I've a responsibility to—"

Roy was cut off when Marshall suddenly made a dash for the graves of his son and wife, lunging forward like a man possessed. He had been relatively still up until this point, simply standing with his nose high in the air and his eyes closed, like someone smelling freshly cut hay for the first time in their lives. The other three men raised their rifles as Marshall ran off, yet no one fired. They watched Marshall bolt past them, scurrying like some kind of small, excited animal, finally falling to his knees on top of the small mounds of earth marked simply by a makeshift cross.

"Wake up!" he ranted, laughing maniacally. "It's time to get up! Nicky! Time to get up!"

Gibson watched on in horror, open mouthed, as Marshall scratched and pulled at the earth, clawing deeply to reach the body of his son. His eyes were wide and desperate, drool falling from his crooked smile in equal measure to the tears and snot running out of his eyes and nose. He bit and clawed at the black plastic wrapped crudely around the dead child in a close to feral manner, ripping and shredding until the boy's decrepit flesh became visible. Then he stopped, holding the tiny corpse up like some kind of trophy. It looked for a moment like he was going to eat it.

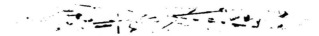

John McElroy started to sweat, realising that the woman, Kirsty, would be unearthed again, her beautiful hair probably still shining despite the earth thrown feverishly on top. His faint stain of cum would no doubt still be fresh on her skin. For an awful moment, McElroy wondered if the feral Steve Marshall might sniff it off her and expose him for the sick, low-life pervert he really was.

From the angle McElroy stood, he saw what happened next more explicitly than anyone else. He viewed the scene, with a clarity and certainty, that caused him to piss himself almost immediately. As Steve Marshall cradled the putrid bundle of flesh that used to be his son, that used to be his reason to get up in the morning, go to work during the day and look forward to coming back home at night, another hand, a hand that's touch Steve Marshall knew all too well, a hand with flesh still pale, lush and angelic, reached slowly towards him from the grave.

McElroy froze.

Roy Beggs didn't wait to find out what the fuck was going on. From his angle, he could only make out the young Steve Marshall bending down over the grave, busying himself in some sick way. With one burst from his rifle, Marshall's carry-on was over. The young man, once an easy-going accounting technician, shook briefly, then fell quietly, a shower of blood and brain escaping from his head. Still clutching the small, rotting body close to his tired, gaunt face, his body slumped awkwardly against the wooden cross. The cross buckled from his weight falling against it, tangling up with the sorry mess that had become the Marshall family grave. The corpse of Steve's wife (whom McElroy was sure had actually reached for him, was sure it hadn't just been some sick game his conscience was playing on him) was once again secluded from view, her husband and son now joining her.

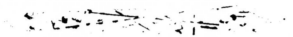

Roy felt a pang of guilt race through him, noting how pathetic the spectacle was. Looking down, he noticed that his hands were suddenly shaking, making his rifle shake too.

He turned to find everyone looking at him. No one said a thing.

(Like that time in court.)

Roy pulled himself together, quickly, remembering bitterly that to let these things go, unchecked, would lead to anarchy. He had a responsibility to take control of these situations, he reminded himself. A responsibility that only he was equipped to do the way it should be done. A responsibility to take action, like he had done during the attack on the school.

"No!" Gibson cried, falling to his knees. "Oh God, no!" His watering eyes filled with rage. His small fists clenched with unspent fury. He had lost all of his professional calmness. "You bastard, Beggs!" he spat, pent up rage turning his face purple. "You bastard!"

"You s-see?!" Roy said, his voice shaking but still much calmer than that of the furious Gibson. Sweat was running down his forehead, meeting his thickening moustache. Like a sponge, the small clump of greying hair above his top lip soaked it all up, its moistness glistening in the pale, pre-dawn light. "How can I trust you now, eh? You'll want revenge. You'll want to kill me now. Didn't I tell you!? That's how it all starts. One person goes doo-lally and the whole fuckin' unit falls apart!" Roy shook his head with genuine sorrow. He wished he could let someone else take care of things. He didn't like being the only one to do this dirty business of policing. But he had to. No one else could do the job right.

Reluctant to do any more killing himself tonight, Roy gestured wordlessly to John McElroy to finish Gibson. McElroy rose his weapon, taking aim. His hands, too, were shaking, suggesting that whilst gung-ho when it came to talk, the racist son of a bitch was slightly less forthcoming when it came to action.

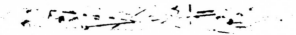

McElroy kept looking at the grave as if he expected something to crawl from it—to come for him, like some old-school zombie flick. The pale, star-lit sky shone upon him, showing up the beads of sweat breaking across his forehead like glitter. His mind was playing tricks on him. That was it. It simply had to be an illusion. The girl was dead. Her husband was a fucking madman. That was the height of it.

McElroy's fingers began to squeeze around the trigger, the barrel of his rifle still shaking, yet trained squarely on Alan Gibson. Finally, as Roy's head remained dipped, a shot rang out.

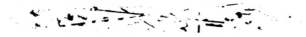

Roy slowly looked up at Gibson, waiting for his body to fall, dead, to the ground. With horror, he realised that instead of Gibson's body crumpling, McElroy had fallen. What the fuck?! Had the silly bastard shot *himself* instead?! He flinched again, jumping as two other shots rang out into the quiet school grounds, Steele and Black crumpling to the ground in a similar fashion.

"You're next, Roy."

As Roy turned, his gaze was met by the familiar, cold stare of Mairead Burns. Her hand remained steady, measured, and undeniably straight as she pointed her handgun squarely at Roy's chest. She was a natural killer. Roy had seen it in her before. Now she stood in defiance against him, having killed three of his men in cold blood with the very weapon he had entrusted her with only weeks ago. Fuck knows why he had let her keep the gun so long. He must have known she would use it against him eventually. He must have known that, especially in a lawless world, Mairead Burns, of all people, would turn against him very quickly.

Why had he let her keep that damn gun? Why hadn't he taken it from her, along with the sniper rifle she had used during the attack on the school?

Something to do with the child, no doubt. Roy knew that Mairead would be able to protect the child better with a weapon, and Clare McAfee was innocent. She was one of those Roy was most keen to protect.

That's what all of this was about, wasn't it? Protection?

Roy let his rifle drop, slowly, to the ground. He had to admit to being scared. He was angry. Very angry. But also very scared.

Watching the scene unfold, the therapist in Alan Gibson was finally able to see Roy Beggs for all that he was. A man who needed to be in control. A man whose own security and self-esteem depended very solely on being able to be King. A man who, when stripped of his thin veneer of self-appointed power, was completely lost. The bettered soldier stood obediently, his eyes wide and moist, his body all hunched over as if he had been caught stealing biscuits from the cookie jar. Painted across his face was a look that made it very obvious that he knew all too well that to show any kind of defiance would wind him up dead. Mairead had wasted no time in executing his men, and Roy failed to see any reason why she would hesitate when it came to putting a bullet in his head too—and he didn't want to die.

Gibson looked to Mairead for permission, before moving, slowly, to take Roy's rifle. The counsellor paused, briefly and vehemently, to spit in the bastard's face before turning his attention to the mess that was the Marshall grave.

It seemed to shock Roy to feel the spray of saliva sprinkle across his face. He probably didn't think Gibson had it in him. A part of him, no doubt, would respect him for having the balls to do that. That's the kind of man Roy Beggs was. Alan Gibson had him diagnosed to perfection.

Gibson walked slowly across the patchy grass of the school grounds towards Steve Marshall's body. He shook his head regrettably on confirming his patient dead.

What a waste!

The smell from the grave was difficult to deal with without throwing up. Marshall's body lay entangled with the rotting and worm-ridden corpse of his baby boy and the simple broken cross that had been marking the grave. The scene looked almost sacrilegious, a brutal and unholy desecration of a simple family grave.

Gibson did the best he could to cover the open ground up again, pushing Steve in further, with shaking hands, before cupping handfuls of earth on top. His nerve finally gave way to nausea and he started gagging, until he got away from the sorry-looking grave in order to throw up violently.

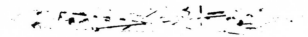

"You going to kill me?" Roy asked, almost oblivious to Gibson's graveside drama.

Mairead turned back towards him, smiling. Her gun still remained trained for a clean shot to Roy's head. She spat, "I'll not even try and pretend that I haven't wanted to do this since I met you, you brit bastard."

Roy closed his eyes tight. He waited for it all to be over. Other survivors were starting to gather at the front entrance of the school, having no doubt heard the shots. Gasps and sudden cries rang out as they saw the bodies, the graveside, the gun trained on Roy Beggs. The full horror of what was happening would be dawning on each of them. It threatened their security. It tore at the thin web of deceit they had spun for themselves, reminding them that all was most certainly not well with the world. Mairead wouldn't care, of course. She would shoot him down in full view of everyone. Roy knew that.

But not in front of the child.

"Mommy!" Clare cried, still in her pyjamas, eyes red and puffed.

Oh God, no, Mairead thought. This wasn't an example she wanted any child to follow. This was exactly what she wanted Clare not to have to see, a side of her that she was trying so very hard to leave behind in the old world. A part of herself that she had almost forgotten. But the truth was that she had been enjoying this way too much. She had enjoyed killing those men. Enjoyed humiliating Roy Beggs. And she would have enjoyed shooting him down, like a dog.

("*It's just a child, Roy!*")

Mairead thought of her own son, and how much of this kind of behaviour must have helped him slip off the straight and narrow. She remembered coming down the stairs one Christmas to find her baby boy with his hands over a stash of firearms as opposed to what Santa had left him. She remembered the look of excitement on his face. The wide-eyed innocence, as his hands caressed the metal.

(*"Mummy is this a real gun? Did Santa leave it for me?"*)

"Clare, go to Mr. Gibson!" Mairead shouted.

The child obeyed, now crying. Gibson, still trying to regain his own composure, put one arm around her, consoling her as she wept. He dried his own eyes, removing his glasses with his free hand before whispering soothing words to the distraught child.

"Keys to the Land Rover," Mairead growled to Roy.

"Gibson has them."

Mairead looked to Gibson, who confirmed this with a nervous nod.

"Okay, let's go," she said simply, backing towards the Land Rover whilst still keeping her pistol trained on the soldier. His look said it all. Through the fear, anger was starting to rise within Roy Beggs' eyes. Mairead sensed it. She knew he would probably hunt them down, hungry for revenge. She knew he wouldn't let the others see him bettered by Gibson or her. She knew that would upset his standing amongst the survivors at the school, challenging his authority, and that wouldn't sit well with the soldier. She knew she should have killed him.

Yet she didn't.

Roy watched as the rebels climbed up into his Land Rover, the very vehicle with which he rescued them some weeks back.

Too bloody soft, he thought to himself. *That's your problem, Beggs, too bloody soft.*

As the military vehicle pulled out, Mairead at its wheel, Roy turned back to the survivors gathered at the door. There they all were. Sylvia Patterson, the cook. Sarah Jenkins, the young student girl. Seamus Moran, the retired bank clerk from Lurgan. Aida Hussein, the beautiful young Egyptian woman. All of them looking at him with fear and trepidation in their eyes. And something else...

Pity.

Twelve

I T WAS BARELY 10am AND MOST OF THE OTHERS, CURRENTLY LIVING between Great Victoria Street Station and the Europa Hotel, had made it out of bed. But not Barry. True to form, he was up to no good, busy dragging the body of a young woman from a red Porsche stalled awkwardly on the silent Great Victoria Street. Chris O'Hagan, a stunningly beautiful Estate Agent in life, looked almost as radiant in death, but Barry didn't pause to consider why that should be, mesmerised by the sheer divinity of not her body, but the ever so smooth body of her car. Its red, polished metal sparkled in the early morning sun. Bold alloy wheels seemed to boast of its power, zero to sixty in mere seconds. A pull-down roof offered that oh-so-sweet feeling of wind through hair that a summer day demanded.

He noticed Caz watching him from the steps leading up to the station, nestling a glass of fruit juice. "Fancy a spin, sweetheart?" he asked, straining to pull the surprisingly well-kept corpse out of the vehicle's open door.

"You can't be serious," Caz replied, running an eye along the long road where other cars lay sprinkled like breadcrumbs. "You'll get yourself killed if you go little-boy-racer up that road."

"I know how to handle a car," Barry boasted, flashing Caz an unashamedly flirtatious grin. He noticed her trying to hide her blushing, shaking her head with pretend incredulity.

"Oh *pleeeeazzze*," she groaned. "Don't come crying to me if you get yourself mangled."

"Oh come on," Barry egged. "If you can't live dangerously when the world's ended, when can you, for fuck's sake?!" He searched inside the dashboard for the ignition. Grabbing the keys with a celebratory rattle, he smiled up at her. "I'll go slow. I'm not a fast driver anyway." Barry gave Caz a look that suggested this last sentence was a lie. It also suggested that he wanted Caz to know it was a lie.

There was something within Barry Rogan that drew the mischief out of anyone he met. And he knew it, too. He knew that it wouldn't take much of his well-stocked charm to convince little-miss-pious to walk on the wild side. Behind those glasses, he could see her cute little eyes just begging to be convinced. "Get the wind in your hair, girl. What do you say?" He smiled, flaunting his 'gift.'

He was about ten years older than her, rough around the edges but definitely good looking. Or so he thought, anyway. He also thought that Caz would almost feel guilty for noticing that. He had known girls like her. They loved their boyfriends, sure, but another part of them, a part of them that they didn't particularly like, would long for a bad boy like him. Someone to take the edge off their boring, humdrum, safe relationships.

"Come on," he egged. "Someone has to work out what the fuck that explosion was about last night. Aren't you even the tiniest bit curious?"

Caz was definitely curious. That was pretty much why she was up so early. She had been staring towards the northern part of the city for the best part of an hour, lapping up the early morning sun and trying to bolster up enough confidence to take a walk to see if she could find anything. The smoke had cleared, giving way to another humid morning. But there still had to be clues as to what had happened, and what it could mean. Yet, curious though she was, Caz didn't want to do anything without first checking in with Tim for the day. Of course, that would be easy if he was about.

"Sure, you can bring your boyfriend too, if you like," Barry said, almost as if reading her mind.

Barry was good. She would have to give him that. But Caz hadn't seen Tim all day. He had withdrawn from her again. After the explosion, he had simply disappeared. Caz blamed herself. She knew it had to be something to do with what had happened the previous night. And she wasn't thinking of the explosion.

(Didn't he say he loved her?)

Caroline Donaldson may have come across as a well-rounded sixteen year old. Wise beyond her years. A conscientious and intelligent girl who almost always did the right thing—whatever that was. But the real truth of the matter was that she was desperately insecure. A part of her needed this attention from Barry, no matter how much she resented it.

"I would have to be back by lunchtime." It wasn't as if she was being disloyal to Tim. Anyway, he spent a lot of time with Star, talking about tattoo designs, learning how to use the machine. Doing all those things that didn't interest a girl like her. A girl who had done her homework on time and cycled to school.

"Sure. We'll be back by noon," Barry replied, playfully grinning at her. He ran one hand over the smooth leather of the steering wheel of Chris O'Hagan's demonic-looking automobile. This baby was going to roar like a tiger. "What about your wee man? Wanna see if he wants to come?"

"I think he's still in bed," Caz lied, hurrying down the steps, setting her glass of juice on the pavement. She knew he had gone into town earlier. She had watched him go from the window of the room where they had slept, longing to follow him but knowing that to do so would set her back about ten squares in the constant game of snakes and ladders she seemed to be playing with him. "We'll probably be back before he wakes."

"Well, let's go then." Barry opened the passenger door to the Porsche, mock-bowing to Caz as she climbed into the car's low seat. Shutting the door with a swing, Barry wasted no time in climbing in beside her and kicking the engine into action. With a couple of revs, the two were soon tearing up the street, Barry dodging the first stalled car with an ease and proficiency that sent a few butterflies rushing through Caz's belly.

On the pavement, at the bottom of the station's steps, the discarded glass and beautiful blonde hair of Chris O'Hagan shimmered together in the sunlight, a gentle breeze lapping playfully at her pretty dead eyes. Perhaps more a trick of the light, one eyelid seemed to flutter briefly before all was still again in the quiet, lifeless city.

Thirteen

GAVIN CUMMINGS SIGHED QUIETLY BEFORE LAUNCHING YET again into another rendition of El Shadi. A ten strong crowd, men and women, stood stoically by the Bandstand at Cornmarket, some with tears in eyes, others with hands raised to the sky, as the twenty-seven year old's gentle acoustic accompaniment oiled over the fact that most people were singing out of tune. Gavin's eyes still followed the *Church Hymns And Chorus* book that The Preacher Man had proudly presented to him on his baptism some weeks ago. Although playing the same songs twice daily since, The Preacher Man's campaign gathering in souls from the tired and frightened survivors seeping out of the dead woodwork, Gavin just couldn't get the chords into his head. Deep down, he hated this banal shite he was playing. Yet after only a couple of weeks under The Preacher Man's charge, Gavin felt guilty even about that.

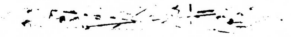

Tim Adamson sat eyeing the whole scene from the shadows of a nearby café. Nestled in one hand was a lukewarm Pepsi. In the other, he fumbled obsessively with his small silver Jesus, given to him only hours ago by Caz. Two yellowed and bloated corpses lay back in the chairs of separate tables within the small patio area at the front. Another girl, head covered by hair, had nose-dived her glass of tomato juice, leaving a trail of red across her table that was more likely to include dried blood as well as tomato. None of these pungent, sickly sweet smells bothered him anymore.

Tim followed every word the desperate choir sang, quietly and reverently. He was waiting for something to happen. They all were. But nothing did. Neither the music nor the fervour with which it was sang stirred anything or anyone, the sparsely talented crowd's racket only seeming to amplify the vast emptiness around them. No trumpet sound blasted through the clouds. No bodies arose, longingly, to dance with angels or cherubs.

(Nothing was the new something.)

Yet still the small band persisted, as they had done all day every day for weeks now. Their voices were hoarse and parched. Their throats were strained and sore. Still they sang, probably because they knew of nothing better to do. Nothing better to say. As Tim watched on every day, they prayed and sang and listened to The Preacher Man simply because he seemed convinced that these were the right things to do. It saved them having to think for themselves.

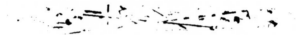

From the south of Cornmarket's spider-webbed streets, another heavy-set man stood silently watching, reverently listening, as the choir sang their glad tidings of woe. He was dressed in full military regalia. A beret rested proudly on his head. His uniform had been washed and ironed and his boots were glimmering in the heat. His head was bowed in silent and respectful prayer. He, too, had a mission.

Picking out no one that he recognised, this man slung his rifle back over his arms, turned, and walked quietly away.

Fourteen

CAZ WAS DREAMING AGAIN. EYES CLOSED, HAIR MASSAGED BY the wind as the open-roofed Porsche raced along the M5 motorway with all the grace afforded by such a luxurious set of wheels. She hadn't daydreamed so indulgently since being on the train the day the world went to hell. Bizarrely, until now, Caz had felt too closed in, too preoccupied with life in an empty world to give any quality time to dreaming. As Barry shifted into 5th gear, tearing the dial up a notch, she felt a sense of freedom kick in along with the speed.

Barry's driving, although at top speeds, was good enough to allow her to concentrate only on the warm summer breeze as it whistled by her face. Despite her guilt about leaving Tim, Caz was really enjoying the drive. Being in a car was one of those things she hadn't realised she would miss, not until it simply wasn't the done thing anymore. Well down the list from showering, but slightly above flying, Caz found being in a car to be a forgotten luxury.

The open road was gloriously empty, save from the occasional Sunday morning spinner who had found themselves and their car slap into one of the motorway's barriers. Carnage was minimal, therefore, as were obstacles. Apart from that, the M5 looked no different to how it always looked. Industry buildings, no longer industrious, provided much of the scenery, along with railway track and the odd field. A stalled train, its few dead passengers still seated randomly throughout, as if sleeping, posed uselessly in the warm, summer glow. Then, within a brief moment, it was gone, lost behind them as Barry's demon-like Porsche tore up the silent motorway. Out of sight, out of mind.

Caz wondered if some of the few survivors' depression stemmed from the fact that the world had ended on a Sunday morning. Notoriously the most hungover day of the week, and not just in terms of alcohol consumption, Sunday was a nationwide come down, shoved into the week after Saturday's revelry to allow a little adjustment time before the horror of another week of school, or work, slowly sank in. Now, of course, most of the world had died, leaving the clock stopped forever at Sunday Morning 11.48am. What could be more depressing?

"Holy fuck!" Barry suddenly yelled, slamming on the brakes.

Caz had almost forgotten why they had taken a drive. The explosion was almost irrelevant now. The two survivors, having covered a good part of North Belfast and finding nothing or nobody, had thrown in the towel. They had slid onto the motorway more for the hell of it than because they thought they would find anything. Yet as the car skidded to a chaotic halt, swinging in various circles, ripping Caz roughly out of her serene daydream, an incredible sight burst into her line of vision.

Dead in front of the two survivors, just as the car came through the roundabout where the M5 met the Shore Road into Whiteabbey, lay the guts and intestines of what had clearly been a helicopter. Pieces of the crashed aircraft spewed across their path like a huge string of metal puke. Wreckage and charred corpses dotted the blackened tarmac of the motorway. Glass had sprinkled across the landscape like fake snow, some of its crystalline, sunlit sparkles tainted by blood red stains. Spat out pieces of baggage and fly-infested body limbs jutted out horrifically from under mangled pieces of propeller and door.

The crash site spread across the entire width of Shore Road, spilling into a nearby grassy area, where its trail of destruction had slaughtered several sheep that had wandered down the empty roads from nearby rural Doagh. A single small lamb grazed casually close to the rotting corpse of its mother, pinned helplessly to a nearby signpost by random pieces of the aircraft's engine. Caz couldn't take in all that she saw, choking back her tears with one hand raised to her mouth.

"*Fuck*," Barry whispered.

This was as explicit as it could get. All the world's death seemed to be summarised here. The quietly polite dying that had gone on across the world was nothing compared to this mess, coughed out uncouthly and painfully. For long moments, Caz sat stalactite still in the halted sports car, its open top and luxurious interiors now meaning absolutely nothing. It was like a ringside seat of misery facing the crash site squarely and vividly.

Minutes passed where nothing was said. Finally, voice suddenly lost, Caz croaked, "Think anyone survived?"

Barry laughed nervously. "Are you bullshitting me, girl?" he stuttered.

Caz couldn't believe he had laughed. "No, but..." She couldn't even finish her sentence. She didn't remember what she was trying to say. She clambered out of the car as if suddenly aware of herself, holding one hand over her mouth, again, half in sheer disbelief and half to try and blot out the sudden whiff of cooked flesh and burned-out oil that swept over her like a polluted sea.

Barry followed her gingerly. "Careful," he warned, noticing huge, brittle chunks of glass and debris scattered throughout the ground.

Caz's eyes were drawn to a single arm, constantly harassed by flies, clad in one sleeve of a dress she had lusted over in Topshop just weeks ago. She still recognised the design of the fabric, even though some of the material had been torn leaving patches of blotchy, sun-raped flesh on display. "I think I want to go home now," she said, hardly able to take her eyes off the frightful image. "This is all... *wrong.*"

"I hear you, girl." Barry wasted no time in returning to the car and kickstarting it into a modest first gear. It seemed like he'd seen enough too. Caz climbed back into the car, quietly and carefully, as if frightened of waking the crudely mutilated dead. Carefully, and almost reverently, as if part of some funeral procession, Barry steered the boastful car away from the crash site. Caz kept her eyes open, staring as the brutality of the sight was lost in the scenery once more, as they made their way back along the motorway into Belfast.

For a long time, neither of them spoke.

THE LAND ROVER HAD PULLED INTO THE BACK OF GREAT Victoria Street Station earlier that morning, but Star was still in bed then. Having vaguely recalled something from Barry about stealing a car and the almost dreamlike sequence of the explosion amidst the revelry of the previous night, Star had chosen not to worry much about any further drama until she had had enough sleep. It was close to lunchtime, therefore, by the time she dragged her arse, once again hungover, out of the hotel bed and into her pair of distressed jeans. Her gut was crying out for something other than booze and coke to digest, and the breakfast bar at the bus station was probably the closest source of all things reasonably healthy.

Staring at her shoes on the way over to the bus station, trying to avoid sunlight as best she could, Star didn't notice the military Land Rover vaguely concealed behind one of the parked buses. The usual smell of the pile of bodies, still festering where she, Tim and Caz had stacked them under the canvas covers, greeted her nostrils, bizarrely reminding her to grab a box of ciggies from one of the shops in the station's small mall. It wasn't til she had swung open the doors by the rear entrance that she noticed that they had company.

Although it didn't surprise Star much to see three strangers at her usual spot by one of the huge, glass-fronted walls, she would have to admit that it did piss her off. She had come to call the station home, especially since Sean and Barry had arrived, rigging the place up with enough electricity to get the coffee machine working and a delightfully spacious party venue made-to-go. Dealing with the sight of a small child and what seemed like her middle-aged parents was not part of the drill for Star's morning routine. She just wasn't that excited about rolling out the welcome mat, especially when feeling so fucking tender.

The male amongst them, a small mousy-looking bloke with glasses and a beard, was the first to notice the tattooist make her shuffling entrance. His face lit up with well-honed affability.

"Hallo!" he shouted, or so it seemed to Hangover Girl, "We... er... just arrived in Belfast today. There's just three of us and we're looking for somewhere to stay that's, you know, *clean*?" He uttered the word 'clean' with a smile that said, *do you know what I mean by that?*, glancing over to the small child as if it were an adults-only secret that bodies were suddenly everywhere, festering in many beds throughout the city.

Star smiled weakly. "You'll find a room in the hotel that's pretty much clean," she replied, over-emphasising the word 'clean' somewhat sarcastically, "and of course, what with our bone yard out back." She thumbed in the general direction of where the bodies from the hotel had been laid out and covered up. "Further 'spring cleaning' is made that little bit more convenient."

Star flicked on the coffee machine, grabbing a cup from the counter of the station's café.

"How many of you are there?" This time it was the woman who spoke, a forty-something bint with a world-weary complexion and heavy eyes that suggested balls of steel. It didn't take Star long to realise that she wouldn't accept bullshit from anyone, especially jumped-up little punks like her. Not that any of that bothered Star. Especially when hungover. The healing steam of coffee caressing her nostrils, she simply leaned back into one of the station's seats, eyeing the woman up suspiciously. "A few," she answered, finally.

"Seen any others in the city?"

"A few happy-clappy god-types seem to congregate in the city centre. You hear them singing their Shine-Jesus-Shine bullshit from time to time. Fuck knows what they have to be shining about, like."

The little girl, who had been glaring at Star since clocking eyes on her, suddenly mouthed shock. "*Awww...*" she whispered dramatically to the woman. "She said a bad word!"

"Oh, dry your eyes," Star whispered under her breath.

The woman pretended not to hear her. "No military presence? " she quizzed in a way that put Star a little on edge. "You know," she elaborated, maybe on seeing Star's bemusement, "trying to mobilise the survivors, hand out rations, that sort of thing."

Setting her coffee down, striking up her first ciggie of the day, Star fixed the woman a look that said it all. "It's everyone for themselves now, doll. Grab a coffee, get yourselves a room, but don't expect any cuddly rescue mission shit happening. This is your lot. Fuck knows you could do worse than a hotel with a free bar."

Again the horrified look on the child's face.

"Do you mind?!" snapped the woman, visibly riled.

"Oh, fuck off," Star retorted, rolling her eyes. "What are you? Some kind of Christian?"

"No. I'm some kind of *parent.*"

Star looked up, silent for a second. Then came the inevitable, sarcy quip. "Well, lighten up, eh? World's ended, honey. Swearing's legal now. Along with thieving, drinking in public and getting absolutely fucking wasted on coke." She exhaled another lung-full of tobacco. "That's kind of our bag here. Eat drink and be fucking merry. Or miserable. Or both. If you don't like it, then feel the fuck free to check into some other hotel. Belfast has a few, I hear. Rates are pretty low, what with it being off-peak fucking apocalypse season."

The woman said nothing, simply staring at her. The child giggled, somewhat nervously, before putting her hand over her mouth on seeing both the woman and Star suddenly glare at her sharply.

"Well," smiled the man, uncomfortably, after an awkward silence was shared, "if you really don't mind, we'll see if we can sort ourselves out with a hotel room, then."

Star eyed up the three, wondering how the hell an entire family managed to remain alive whenever everyone else died so haphazardly. She watched them disappear out the back of the station, making their way towards the hotel. She hadn't even got their names, nor offered hers to them. Names seemed to mean fuck all these days, anyway. Hell, she might even change hers now. Perhaps use a different name every day, just to wind up fuckers like that.

Star drained her coffee then stubbed out her cigarette. She was getting fucking sick of feeling hungover all the time.

Sixteen

BARRY PULLED OFF THE M5, ONTO THE SLIP ROAD LEADING back into Belfast. Neither him nor Caz had spoken a single word since returning from the crash site, their minds still digesting everything they had seen. Barry had been so preoccupied he didn't notice how fucked they were in terms of fuel. The tank read precariously close to empty, and he couldn't be sure there was enough to get them back to Great Victoria Street. He knew there was a petrol station near Carlisle Circus, so he made his way back towards North Belfast instead of following the road into the city centre. He knew that even if the pumps at the petrol station weren't working there might be some cans of petrol laying about, or he could siphon some from the pumps using a piece of tubing. He reckoned the petrol station would be well stocked for both options. Either way, they were also running low on tobacco for mixing with Star's dope. Having cleaned out the station mall's newsagent, he figured it was best to grab some while still on the road. Hell, he needed a fix even more, now, than ever.

"Where are we going?" Caz asked, suddenly aware of the diversion.

"Need some petrol. Don't think we have enough to make it back."

Caz turned back towards the road without saying another word. As they neared Carlisle Circus, the familiar scent of rotting death got a lot more pungent. It hadn't been as pungent on the open road, or as visible.

Here, though, near the housing estates, bodies could be seen festering uncouthly in scattered cars and on the streets. The hum of flies as they gnawed continually at sun-parched flesh competed admirably with the engine of the car to fill the potent silence that remained overwhelming, constantly reminding the few survivors that the living were now very much in the minority.

Barry steered the car gingerly into the petrol station, no longer little-boy-racer with his driving. The fuel pumps stood pretty much as they had since its owner, a man by the name of Dorean Lappen, had fallen behind the counter of the station's small shop while lost in a random daydream about fucking the pretty blonde (Patricia, also now deceased) who usually worked weekends. His fallen body, like that of sweet Patricia, meant nothing to those left alive. Earlier looters had barely noticed him sprawled out awkwardly behind the cash register as they raided his shop of tinned food, chocolates and cigarettes. To Barry, sniffing around the place for cans of fuel, tobacco, rubber tubing and a couple bottles of water, Dorean Lappen was simply another putrid stench amongst a multitude of others. Once nauseating, now simply the norm.

Caz waited outside, her mind still clogged full of nightmarish images from earlier. She thought back to the first body she had seen all those weeks ago. That old lady on the train, who had looked so peaceful, was very much far removed from the burnt-out, bloody mess she had come across earlier. It would have given Caz some comfort to imagine that all of those passengers on the helicopter, torn limb from limb, had fallen as peacefully as the old lady. Blissfully oblivious to their brutal fate. But she knew that hadn't been the case. Somehow, like her, Barry, Tim and the others, they had survived. But how? And where had they come from?

"Nice car, love."

Caz looked around, startled. A small group of survivors hovered close by, shuffling around each other, the car, and Caz. Their legs moved to and fro, almost too spindly for movement. Their faces hung hidden under tipped baseball caps. They were like clones, barely discriminate from each other, hands buried in the pockets of their almost identical jogging bottoms. Their ages were somewhere between 16 and 18. Hungry looks etched into their hollowed-out eyes, bum fluff straining to grow just above their top lips. These pale-skinned wee shits had been known as Spides before the disaster struck. Caz didn't take much solace from the fact that whilst a whole world had died, these little bastards had somehow managed to remain alive—and as dodgy looking as ever.

"My boyfriend's in there," she said, pointing to the petrol station's shop. "He'll be out in a minute." She tried to hide her nervousness, desperately trying to mask it with feigned nonchalance.

"We're not doin' nothing!" one of the pack protested, his whiny voice irritatingly high-pitched and melodramatic. "We're just looking, that's all." It was a well-versed couple of sentences, usually uttered when approached by cops or security guards.

"Go get your own car," Caz snapped, still trying to appear unaffected. "There's loads of them around; you don't even have to steal them now." She looked quickly over to the shop to see where Barry was.

"We're not just looking at the car," another one of the pack said. He seemed to be their leader. There was something about his eyes that immediately terrified Caz. A coldness, maybe. Or callousness that suggested that none of this end-of-the-world shit had affected him the way it should affect a normal human being. Both his eyes stared right through her like glass, as if he was looking at something inside her, something that he very much wanted to rip out.

Caz lunged towards the Porsche's ignition, banging on the car's horn as she realised Barry had the keys.

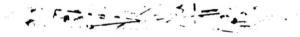

The noise screamed out into the silence like a hoarse banshee, causing Barry to turn quickly from whatever he was doing inside the shop. His eyes widened as he noticed three of the pack light viciously on Caz. She was screaming, kicking and scratching as the spides struggled to hold her down.

Barry felt for his keys, breathing a brief sigh of relief as he found them, his heart then sinking as he noticed the leader of the pack flicking open his knife in order to hotwire the ignition. He knew he could waste no time in getting out to Caz. Within seconds they would be off with her to god-knows-where to do god-knows-what. Quickly grabbing a brush shaft from the shop's storeroom, the only thing vaguely resembling a weapon at short notice, Barry rushed them. As he tore across the petrol station's forecourt, Caz's wide eyes met his, begging for help. She was shrieking, scratching and biting whilst two of the pack held her down, laughing maniacally, one of them even spitting in her face as he goaded her.

Whilst the leader continued to hotwire the Porsche, the third minion came at Barry, aggressively brandishing a flick knife. "Aye! Would ye?!

Would ye?!" he slobbered in his barely legible whine, noticing Barry raise the brush handle with intent.

A keen golfer in days gone by, Barry swung hard and fast, clocking the wee shit squarely in the jaw, slapping his scrawny frame to the ground with ease. "Ah! Fuck!" he screamed, writhing.

Barry sprinted to the car, pausing briefly to lay his toe into his fallen attacker, but by the time he was within range, the engine suddenly was revving up.

The car skidded noisily out of the petrol station and onto the main road, Caz's captors still holding onto her, goading Barry. Although Caz's mouth was held firmly by one of the captors, preventing her from saying anything, her terrified eyes told Barry all he needed to know. Helplessly, he watched the car fly towards the motorway.

"Fuck!" he shouted, kicking a nearby pump.

seventeen

"**S**EAN MAGEE."

"I'm Alan. Alan Gibson. Great to meet you, Sean." Gibson extended his hand amicably. Sean shook it, smiling. It wasn't even tea time, but already the smell of alcohol was heavy on the DJ's breath. Gibson also noticed a slur in the man's voice that suggested more than a couple of beers had been consumed today already. "And this here's Mairead." Gibson gestured across the spacious hotel bar towards the woman and child getting some drinks. "The little one's called Clare. We just arrived in Belfast this morning. A very pleasant young... er... *lady* told us about the hotel."

"Oh, Caz, you mean?" Sean asked. "Pretty wee thing, probably hanging around a lad about the same age."

"Em, she had tattoos."

Sean laughed. "That's our Star, then. Face like an angel and the tongue of a sailor."

Gibson laughed sheepishly. "Yeah. Well, she seems a unique lady, that's for sure."

Sean opened the cap on his hip flask. He cleared his throat. "Want a drink?" he asked.

"No thanks," Gibson replied.

Sean took a swig, reclining back in his chair by the window. He looked out at the first floor view across Belfast's centre. Nothing had changed. Same old lack of activity that there always was, and always would be. Alan Gibson sat quietly opposite him. He smiled constantly, as if Sean was interviewing him for a new job.

"Where did you come from, Alan?" the DJ asked.

"Lisburn. We thought there might be more survivors up here, you know. Maybe some help."

Sean laughed. "I guess you're not religious then?"

"Sorry?"

"No, it's just that the only thing organised up here seems to be a crowd of Holy-Joes over by Cornmarket. You know, in the city centre?"

"Oh, right," Gibson replied. He wondered if Sean had seen any sign of Roy Beggs. Both he and Mairead were expecting the soldier to tail them after what had happened back at the school. "No military, then? Or police taking control?"

Sean laughed again in response. They were not joyous laughs and Gibson noted that. They were too hollow to be anything more than sombre resignation. "Think you been watching too many zombie flicks, mate."

Gibson's English accent was quite obvious, and Sean felt it lent him a certain naïve quality. He realised that, with the exception of the occasional Stones disc he'd spun recently, it had been weeks since he'd heard an English accent. Before the shit had hit the fan, every day was swamped with English accents. Television. Radio. Soaps. They were part of everyday life in Ireland. Now, it seemed, no one talked very much at all, in any accent.

Mairead and Clare came over to join them, setting a couple of drinks in the centre of the table that Sean and Gibson sat at. "Sorry, did you want anything... er...?"

"Sean. Sean Magee," he said, offering his hand. Mairead shook it, weakly, which annoyed him. He never trusted anyone with a weak handshake. It reminded him of the executive types at the radio station. "And, no thanks. Got myself a drink earlier."

Clare sat close to Mairead, glaring up at Sean. He hadn't seen any children alive. Apart from the teenagers, of course. They were as rare as English people, it seemed.

Suddenly the door to the hotel bar opened. Barry, slightly dishevelled-looking, ushered a spidey-looking teenager in. "Sean!" he exclaimed, wide-eyed, and looking around the bar for someone, "Where's your wee man, Tim?"

"Barry!" Sean called out, smiling. "Who's your new friend?" Barry's new 'friend' was literally dragged by the neck over to the table where the others sat. His hands had been tied, and it seemed from the messed-up face that he'd suffered a crack around the head recently.

"This is Joe. Say hallo, Joe!" But Joe said nothing, instead sniffling back tears. Anger and fear seemed to be painted all over his bruised face. "His little spidey mates took off with my wheels, and Caz in tow. We need to get her—" One look at Sean's gormless grin said it all. "Christ, Sean. You're pissed. Fuck, mate, what help can you be?"

Sean's grin turned sour. "What are you on about? Who's took Caz?"

"Never mind," Barry sighed. "Just tell me, is Tim around?"

"Haven't seen the lad all day."

"Good. Don't tell him what's happened. He'd freak."

"Anything I can do?" Gibson asked, eyeing up both Barry and his 'friend' Joe.

Sean watched Barry eye up the five-foot-nothing counsellor. "Probably not," he replied, curtly.

"Wait a minute. Did you say there was a bomb blast last night?" It was Mairead speaking, fixing Barry with one of her looks.

"Well... no, not really." Barry looked impatient. Even drunk, Sean knew that every second wasted talking placed Caz in a lot more danger.

"Well, was there a bomb or not? There either was or wasn't."

"Listen, love..." Barry started, voice raised.

Sean could see the child recoil at the sound of shouting, her short gasp seeming to steady Barry somewhat. He took a deep breath and started again. "Look, it wasn't a bomb blast. Seems to have been a helicopter that has gone down."

"What?" Mairead couldn't contain her excitement. "Don't you know what this means? Where did it go down? Where did it come from?"

Barry sighed, seemingly resigned to a conversation that wouldn't help him. "On the M5. The explosion happened last night, but—"

Suddenly he stopped. Mairead watched a sense of realisation slowly descend upon him. He hadn't given consideration to what the crash could mean. Until now, the very shock of seeing it had been clogging up the cogs in his brain, replaced quickly by the seriousness of his friend's situation. The fact that someone had put an aircraft in the sky weeks after everything had gone to hell was now dawning on him.

Where did it come from? Yeah, the fucking penny drops.

"I'll go with you," Mairead said. "Help you find your friend if you show me that helicopter crash." This was what Mairead had been hoping for all along. Help arriving from somewhere else. A rescue mission, albeit one that had obviously went wrong. It gave her hope that more people like them existed, maybe larger groups of survivors, better resourced and organised. It gave her hope as a parent, wanting to provide a better future for her child.

Barry smiled, patronisingly. It reminded her of Roy. "I don't know about that," he said. "We're talking about—"

Mairead slid a handgun over to Barry, stopping his sentence dead. "Know how to use this?"

Barry's eyes widened. He looked up at Mairead. It was difficult to tell if he was scared or impressed. "Might do," he said, slowly, lifting the handgun up and cocking it.

"We have more guns in our Land Rover," Mairead added. "Now where were these guys headed, did you say?"

"I don't know where they're headed," Barry said, grabbing 'new friend' Joe by the throat and menacingly shoving his newly-acquired handgun in the boy's face. "But you do, don't you, Joe?"

PART
3

"Heav'n has no rage,
   like love to hatred turn'd,
     nor hell a fury,
         like a woman scorn'd."

(from *The Mourning Bride*
by William Congreve)

THE SKIES HAD DARKENED MOMENTARILY AS IF THREATENING to rain. It was an idle threat, though. Everyone knew that the rain only came at night now. Heralded in by a descending cloak of thick, dark cloud, the rain washed away the silence of the day with its sweet pitter-patter. But never before its time. High above the city centre skyline, as the skies darkened, a single white bird darted to and fro as if part of a flock, before making a beeline towards the north of the city. Its solitary cry was almost lost on the dwindled population of Belfast, but not to Roy Beggs.

Across the road from the bus station, seated in a large People Carrier, Roy Beggs watched intently as the bird hovered then fell before swooping north. It was almost as if it had felt a little tension in the air, prepping itself for a shower before realising it was a false alarm.

Roy turned his gaze back to the tall glass building he was parked opposite. He had been watching the comings and goings from the bus station for the better part of two hours, having noticed some activity from it earlier. Roy hadn't expected to strike gold so soon, but a silhouette wandering through the glass-fronted bus station had made him suspicious. It walked the way Alan Gibson did. A worried walk. More of a scuttle, really.

When the Land Rover—his Land Rover—pulled out from behind the large bus depot behind the station's shopping and café area, Roy was sure he was on the money.

Pulling a rifle scope out of his bag, Roy scanned the station. He noticed a young shorn-headed man (or was it a woman?) smoking in the shopping area of the station, downstairs. This person was alone, seemingly. Either way, they were of no real interest to the scorned soldier. Swinging over to the hotel next door, Roy continued to scan each floor. There, on the first floor from what he could see, now more clearly using the scope, he found Gibson, the child, Clare, and an unknown third person sitting by the window.

"Gotcha," Roy whispered, smiling.

He reached into the back of the car towards a bag of assorted weaponry.

two

EVERY MEAL HAD BECOME COMMUNION AT ST. JOSEPH'S Church, mere yards from the city centre base at Cornmarket. The Preacher Man insisted upon it. Breaking of bread preceded every meal, followed by a communal glass of wine being passed around the table. Since running out of fresh bread, oatcakes were being substituted.

For Robert McBride, a man who in days gone by never ventured too far left of pie and chips, oatcakes tasted like soil. But he ate them anyway, regularly and reverently. He drank the wine too, his stomach turning each time The Preacher Man launched into his monologue, dramatically camped up to max the effect, of how communion was to reenact how Christ died on the cross, spilling his blood and shredding his flesh for the salvation of all mankind. To McBride, a man not given to religious hoo-haa before whatever-it-was-that-had-happened had happened, The Preacher Man's graphic retelling of the crucifixion process was harrowing. It hardly surprised him to hear The Preacher Man tell of how some Christians were so mesmerised and consumed by the horrific torture endured by their Lord and Saviour that their hands and feet bled for no apparent reason. McBride suddenly recalled how his mum and sister's periods had regulated whenever they lived together, wondering if blood had a life and soul of its own—a sense of identity and awareness of itself. Was it something that lived and breathed through us, or despite us? Was it possessing us? This was the kind of fucked-up line of thought Robert McBride was finding himself traveling along, of recent.

McBride was himself a man very far from the sort of conviction that would have blood seeping from his wrists, that much was true. If he were to be completely honest, McBride wouldn't be sure what to believe anymore. The Preacher Man simply took his mind off of what was really going on—a drug, if you like, to distract him from the real challenge of dealing with the true horrors of this Brave New World.

Not so for the majority gathered at the table, however. They were hanging on The Preacher Man's every word. Everyone gathered seemed fascinated, almost hypnotised by his personality. His unfaltering faith. His yearning for their salvation—all their salvation. The Preacher Man spoke like a man who was truly in tune with God, truly in love with angels. His passion for his mission was so strong, so wrought with emotion, that he cried almost hourly. Thick, salty tears. Loaded with the holiest of ghosts...

(And rage... And guilt...)

St. Joseph's Church was the base of the mission by night. They returned there once their voices had become hoarse and their backs sore from standing singing all day. Their numbers were growing, yet the church still provided ample room for them all. Pews acted as beds. Food could be kept in the spacious kitchen, mostly tins as the power had long died on the fridge. The Preacher Man had his own study to pray and read scripture at during the night, sporadically sleeping whenever his fervour allowed him. And, of course, they had the communion table, the focal point of every meal and communion.

With the exception of McBride, an apathetic man, never given to any strong feelings, the numbers gathered in the church truly believed in every word The Preacher Man spat. His dramatic use of Olde English only seemed to add spunk to his message of woe, warning of a final calling for all who were Saved. The Preacher Man begged and pleaded for his followers to dig deep within their souls for assurance of their undying and unquestioning faith. Like that of a child for its father. That, and that alone, would save them. That, and that alone, would decide whether they were to be among the Sheep (those gathered at the throne of their Heavenly Father) or the Goats (those whose faith waned, leaving them shunned by a demanding God).

Gavin Cummings felt he could never measure up. He listened as The Preacher Man demanded unfaltering faith, as he spoke of lesser men, characters in the Bible like Lot, who lost their bottle at the last moment, ending in their doom. As he strummed that guitar daily, often to the point of his own hands bleeding (but not through the wounds of the stigmata) his heart struggled with the words being sung. How could he have faith like those he heard The Preacher Man talk of? People like Moses and John The Baptist? Primal men, whose sheer, unkempt love for God would drive them to do the most incredible things. Yet all Gavin could do was strum his guitar, often missing a chord, still having to follow on with the *Hymn And Chorus* book.

As The Preacher Man started onto another rant-like sermon, like some great monarch dishing out death sentences, Gavin's hand began to shake suddenly and violently. He was feeling it. Feeling *it*! Sin was in his veins now, racing through his flesh, its raw danger threatening to completely consume him. It was like The Preacher Man said—every breath, every thought, every idea was riddled with temptation. Curdled with sordid intention. It was as if God in the sky could actually smell the failings within him, sniffing out his fear and insecurity like some great divine bloodhound. And now The Preacher Man, eyes filled with knowing, was staring intently at him as he spat out each and every fiery word.

Suddenly Gavin felt very aware of himself, very aware that everyone could see right through his skin as if it were invisible and read his every hellish thought. Gavin shoved his offending hand roughly between his legs and prayed for the shaking to stop.

THE LAND ROVER PULLED UP BY THE EDGE OF THE RUN-DOWN North Belfast housing estate. It was the most animated place any of the survivors had seen since the disaster struck. Pavements and lampposts screamed out with red-white-and-blue glory. Wall murals, one reading simply "TAIGS OUT" clearly stated who was and who wasn't welcome in the area. Rows and rows of identical houses, some with mahogany windows and doors, others run-down looking to the point of squalor stood like dominoes. Like the residents who once lived here, hard-faced and paranoid, the houses had a weather-beaten look of pride about them, as if primed to march through the streets of Belfast, defiantly waving their colours and murals and roughly pruned gardens.

This was inner-city Belfast at its most grim. A place caught in a political time-warp since the seventies. It stood for everything Mairead stood against, and yet, bizarrely, her own house would have stood in a very similar fashion to this, only with a different colour scheme. As Mairead slipped a fresh clip into her SLR rifle, her bottom lip curled. Even in the Brave New World, where none of this could matter a fuck, it still antagonised her to see a place like this.

"You sure this is the place?" They were looking straight at one of the many terraced council houses sprawling through the estate like cells. Barry stuck his handgun in Joe's ear, reminding him of the consequences of telling porky pies.

"Aye! Fuck ye," Joe replied, sweating like a whore in heat.

"Okay, remember the plan then, Joey. Up to the door. Call out to your mates. Wait for them to open the door, then walk in." Barry emphasised the next bit clearly, as if Joe was a naughty child. "*Leave. The door. Open.*"

Joe nodded, looking from Barry and then to Mairead, clearly terrified. There was a stain in his trackie bottoms, where he'd obviously soiled himself, the smell thankfully masked by the stifling stench of death ever rampant throughout the dead city.

"Any messing about and I'll put you down like a manky dog," Barry warned, poking Joe in the back with his gun. Mairead said nothing. But one look in her eyes was enough to see what she would do to Joe were he to step left of centre.

Joe's eyes darted about like a startled animal, staring back fearfully as he climbed out of the vehicle. They had parked some distance from the house where Joe and his mates had been holed up for the last few weeks. It had been Joe's home. He had lived with his mother there, and his sister Tracey, since he had come out of foster care last year. Now the lads all stayed there together. Although the Porsche was nowhere in sight (*Probably burnt out in some waste ground,* Barry mused) beer cans and broken bottles littered the lawn. Whilst Joe's mother had been very house proud, the lads' standards of hygiene were less than lacking.

Joe banged on the door, calling out a couple of names. There was no reply. Looking behind him, worriedly, Joe once again called to his friends. Still no answer. He looked across to where Barry and Mairead were standing, having slowly climbed out of the Land Rover. Barry motioned for him to go on inside. Joe tried the door, surprisingly finding it unlocked. That meant the others had to be inside. Although there hardly seemed much point in a relatively dead world to be security conscious, the lads usually locked up before going out. There were too many spoils in the house, (beer and narcotics, mainly) and being thieving little shits themselves, the lads were wary of making it easy for other looters to raid their gaff.

Stepping inside the small hallway of the two-up-two-down terraced house, Joe called out again. "Sammy! Billy! I'm back! Your man cleared off and left me! Where are ye's?!"

Silence. Well, almost.

From the upstairs room, Joe could hear an odd sound of commotion. Kind of like someone eating noisily. Occasional sniffing. He figured it must have been one of the lads.

"That you Sammy?" Bizarrely, there was no reply. The house, usually full of chatter and banter when the lads were in, seemed uncharacteristically sombre. Just that sound of chewing again. And then a slight whimper. For his own sake, Joe hoped that the sounds he was hearing weren't what he thought they were.

"Mackers? You in, mate?"

They had taken other girls back. Him and the lads. Random, frightened loners who were wandering around aimlessly whenever the shit had hit the fan. People from the shadows. Sammy liked them young, so they aimed for girls who were in their early teens. Promised them all sorts to come back with them. Food. Shelter. Booze. Drugs. Anything at all to make it easier. Anything to keep them quiet for as long as they needed to dope them out, usually adding pills to their drinks or food. That made them very drowsy. Drowsy enough to rape them.

Sometimes they had held competitions—seeing which one of them could finish the job the quickest, the slowest to shoot off being the one left to dispose of the girl when they'd all had enough of her. Usually that person had been Joe. And that pissed him off to no end. He had got them the house, right? Sure, it had been his ma's house, but he lived there too. When his ma and Tracey had fallen, (along with millions of others), he had thrown their bodies in the shed out the back and opened the place up to them. Surely that should have counted for something, no?

A shuffling... from the main upstairs bedroom. Gingerly, Joe climbed the stairs. "Quit muckin' about, lads," he said nervously, aware of Mairead and Barry stealthily coming through the door behind him. The sounds continued.

(Shuffling, sniffing, eating?)

As Joe neared the door, an awful thought came into his mind. What if they had left the girl for dead, obviously attacked and abused. What if the sounds he could hear were her, tied up and fucked up. There was no way her friends, those two behind him with their guns pointed up his arse, were going to let him live then. His mind began working overtime. Maybe if he got inside the room quickly, somehow, he could clean up the worst of the mess. Maybe he could even escape, himself, out of the window, sprint up the Antrim Road into another estate. They'd never find him if they didn't know the area.

He was at the door now. From behind it, the sounds were louder. He could hear breathing, broken and strained. Joe pushed the door open.

His eyes widened at the grim view that spread before him.

The main bedroom looked every bit the typical forty-something woman's haven. Gaudy wallpaper clung tightly to each wall, seamlessly applied. A few framed pictures dotted the walls, one of Joe, his mother and sister, side by side, serious-faced as they stood by a passing loyalist band parade. A large, messy duvan bed stood centre place in the room, tall, golden bedposts sparkling in the afternoon sun's invasion through partially open Venetian blinds.

There was blood everywhere.

A young girl lay, shaking profusely, on the bed. Another girl sat huddled in the corner, hair hanging over her face as she worked busily at something in her hands.

The sniffing had been Sammy, his mutilated torso, half alive, shivering deliriously in the corner. Blood spilled from where his leg used to be attached to his body, now just a gnawed bone, hanging from a bloody, bile-soaked stump. His eyes darted about, closing then opening again as he slid in and out of consciousness. The contents of Sammy's stomach—and what seemed to be the stomach and gut itself—spread out from his belly like a crushed slug. Occasionally Sammy would gag, clotting blood gargling out of his throat, his left hand shivering as it reached forth to nowhere. It seemed to be the only limb actually capable of moving now.

Joe puked all over Sammy, adding to the various bodily fluids and parts already seeping out of him. He started to cry, sobbing like a terrified child on his first day at school. Wiping his mouth with the sleeve of his sports top, he went to move away from the mess that was still, somehow, alive. Still, somehow, his friend Sammy.

That was when Joe tripped over Mackers. Or what was left of Mackers. Sammy's right-hand man was in three parts, savagely torn apart like a victim at the centre of a bomb blast. He was barely human-looking anymore, one sordid mess of him indeterminable from another, only now recognisable from his ever-present (now stained red) gold, marijuana leaf necklace.

Joe cried harder on seeing this new horror. He could hear the sound of his heart racing in his chest, that and his own whimpering drowning out the weak, dying rasp as Sammy, in the farthest corner of the room, drew a final breath before choking on his own bloody mucus.

But Joey-boy hadn't seen the worst of it yet.

The girl stooped in the corner, now visibly chewing on the mangled corpse of the youngest of the lads, Billy, seemed to be his sister. Tracey! Her eyes were pure black, and her lips and body scarlet-red with blood. Her long dark hair shone in the sun, sprinkling through the half-closed blinds. She wore her pyjamas, the ones she was wearing whenever Joe had dragged her corpse out of bed that morning everything had went to hell. Although Joe didn't want to believe what he was seeing, it was most certainly his sister, in the corner, beautiful and intelligent in life, now seemingly feral in death, like some kind of fucking zombie from a movie.

What the?!

Only still looking every bit his beautiful sister.

"Oh, fuck no!" Joe screamed, pathetically, almost choking on the floods of tears heavy on his face. "Fuck no! Tracey!"

She looked up at him, keenly attentive to the noise. As Joe watched on, she stopped eating, her head tilting to one side. She drank his appearance in, and unknown to Joe, began the process of checking his face against the many dark memories in her primal brain, searching for any link to the awful things that the mangled boys on the bedroom floor had once put her through. Her eyes, wide and jet black, seemed to suddenly flick between various different colours. It was like a slot machine spinning, flipping from black to red, to white, then back to black again. As they changed, a rough papery sound could be heard, as if someone was flicking through a book.

Joe choked and coughed violently. His sister returned to her meal. She hadn't found him guilty of anything. In reality, he wasn't aware of any of the atrocities his so-called mates had put his sister through behind his back.

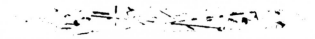

Barry was next through the door, eyes and gun at the ready. What with hearing all the commotion whilst climbing the stairs, Mairead wasn't far behind him, her rifle raised to eye level like a trained marine. The whole scene opened out before their eyes, a rampant mess of carnage.

Barry ignored the other bodies, his eyes clapping on the badly-beaten girl on the bed. He winced at the sight of her abused body. It was Caz. Her virginity was obviously in tatters. Save from a grubby t-shirt, she was naked, blood having trickled down her legs, hardening on the bedclothes. The only signs of life from her were sporadic whimpering and constant shivering. For Barry Rogan, in a room full of explicit and violent death, the small, curled-up child on the bed was the most horrific part of a very fucked up scene. Yet, in some ways, it was a very familiar sight to him.

Reluctantly, his eyes moved to the bedside table nearby. There he saw the all too familiar bottle of pills he knew only to be Retinol, his drug of choice once. Barry swallowed hard as the familiar wave of dark guilt and shame washed through him. He knew deep inside that these little fuckers, now somehow mutilated, had done no worse to Caz than he had done to those three women, their faces still etched clearly in his own mind. Barry had thought that the new world provided a fresh chance for him to be a new person. A better person. Free of the sins of the past, the sins of another life before everything had changed. But nothing changed as long as people were still around. Humanity, like leopards, had acted predictably throughout its long history. Breeding, killing, invading each other...

Raping.

There was no escape from human nature. From feral urges. The animal within only roared louder, unchecked in this new, unruly world. It roared within Barry even now. Fearfully, and tearfully, Barry fought dark inner demons as he felt, amongst the more forgivable emotions of shame, guilt and shock, a powerful and all consuming feeling of arousal.

"Jesus," Mairead whispered, lowering her weapon. She noticed Caz on the bed and immediately ran to her. "You're okay, pet," she soothed. "No one's going to hurt you."

The young, broken girl shook violently and let loose a scream, as if possessed. Mairead held on tight, rocking her to and fro. She couldn't begin to imagine what she would have done were this to be Clare lying on the blood-stained bed. She couldn't begin to imagine what kind of sick fuck would even do this kind of thing. She looked over at Barry Rogan, hoping for some kind of support, but he seemed to have zoned out. Suddenly Mairead stopped, still holding the girl tight but attention now fixed on the other girl backed into a corner nearby.

This other girl was chewing on a torn-off limb.

"Fuck," Mairead breathed. "B-Barry... What the fuck?!"

One look at Barry was all Mairead needed to realise he wasn't operating on all cylinders. His eyes were locked in a thousand-yard stare, almost lending the normally cocky young man an ethereal look. His whole body was shaking and his breathing and heartbeat were audibly speeding up, as if he were about to explode. Behind him, their prisoner Joe lay slumped against the wall, his head buried in his hands.

Mairead watched, frozen, as the young blood-thirsty girl in the corner looked up at her, smiling, then turned her gaze towards Barry, her head cocked slightly to the side. Her eyes, jet-black against her pale face, flicking to a shade of red, then back to black, narrowed menacingly as they lingered on the man.

Dropping the chewed body part from her stained hands, the young girl lunged at him suddenly with all the speed of a wild cat, long-nailed fingers outstretched, snarling with feral rage. On impact, she was ripping and shredding at Barry's chest and throat, then his arms as they automatically raised to defend himself.

Mairead acted quickly. Dropping Caz back onto the bed, she picked up her SLR rifle, aiming and firing in quick succession. The first burst of firepower, due to her shaking hands, went slightly left of her target, tearing a clean hole through the chest of the cowering Joe in the corner.

"Shit!"

Quickly firing again, the next burst of firepower tore through the head of the feral young woman on top of Barry. The wildly psychotic girl shook violently and briefly, stepping back as if shocked, before finally falling.

Four

THE SWISH-LOOKING PIANO BAR IN THE EUROPA HOTEL sprawled decadently across the first floor. High walls met beautifully carved coving, framing the blank ceiling, emphasising the roominess of the bar. The dark, wooden piano stood elegantly by the main window, looking across the skyline of Belfast's city centre. Perhaps in reaction to the pungent loneliness, spreading like a tattoo throughout the hotel's pristine, empty corridors and golden staircases, the survivors at the hotel had always chose to sit by the window. They probably felt less alone there. Even though the city usually stank of silence, its occasional voice, random car or droll chorus of Shine-Jesus-Shine would offer at least some comfort.

Alan Gibson was glad of the simple luxury of company. Sean Magee was a man of a similar age to himself, a man with something to say, even if it was mainly about his ex-wife. It was something, and after weeks of nothing, the survivors at the school having left him to fester alongside the barely alive Steve Marshall, Gibson wasn't going to turn his nose up at anyone.

He had started on orange juice, but Sean's continual tempting with the distinctively off-perfume scent of vodka finally became too much to resist. The counsellor gave in, perhaps having buried his last ounce of hope and direction in the Marshall family's crude grave. Alan Gibson no longer saw any reason to deny himself, and he wasn't alone with that one. In the days that had passed, many survivors who had once smoked, once drank, once jacked off to porn or shoveled junk food into their gobs, returned to their respective vices with devil-may-care resign. Gibson was no different. He no longer saw the point of abstinence. His last refusal of Sean's offer of vodka had resulted in a 'why not?' look from the DJ, leading him to wonder why not, indeed?

Before long, the mild-mannered counsellor was diving into the vodka with admirable fervour, downing sizable shots with ease and comfort. Years away from alcohol hadn't done much to his ability to stomach it. Nor had it quelled his thirst for it. Like every recovering alcoholic, when Alan Gibson fell, he fell hard and fast. As the drink went down, the words poured out, Gibson relaying his own tales of woe to a partially alert Sean. The two men swayed and pointed at each other as they spoke like two pantomime pirates sharing a bottle of rum.

Gibson continued speaking, caring not that Clare, fixing herself a drink in the corner, unchecked, could hear every sordid and child-unfriendly detail of his story of the young girl who had made allegations against him. Yet it hardly mattered what Gibson said to the man opposite. Gibson could have been Ted Bundy and Sean would have still offered him grace and vodka in equal amounts.

"You're one in a million, Alan," he had said, almost tearful with drunken sincerity. "Don't you let anyone tell you otherwise, eh?"

Now Gibson found himself in an awkward embrace with the man opposite him, meeting halfway between a messy table full of drinks and empties. In the drunken gesture, he found some comfort from the pent-up confusion and fear that had been buried, in shallow graves, somewhere beyond realisation. It was survival instinct alone which had kept such unkempt fear from bubbling over, and continued to do so even when filthy drunk. But through the language known only to drunken men, Alan Gibson shared a universal truth with Sean Magee:

Everything's fucked up and I'm afraid.

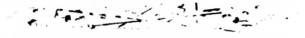

Clare looked on from the next table, rather confused. Although supposedly under the care of Gibson, neither he or the other adult had offered as much as a glance since the vodka bottle had come out from behind the hotel bar. Clare had found her own drink, a blue bottle of something called WKD. She liked the colour and, although a little odd at first, its sugary taste seemed to hit the spot. She was beginning to feel a little dizzy as she neared the bottom of the bottle, but it wasn't a bad dizzy.

She looked up, head spinning, as the door near her slowly opened. As her eyes steadied, hoping to find Mairead coming through, Clare discovered someone else she knew. Roy Beggs, gun raised, full combat regalia tucked in to perfection. He was like a cowboy coming into a saloon, like they did in those old movies her daddy used to watch. The kind of entrance that would have demanded a DANGER-theme tune to kick in.

It seemed that only she had noticed him. The two adults across the room were lost in their own world to the point where everyone else had become invisible. Clare remembered seeing her mummy and daddy coming in after a night out, getting on in a similar way. Drunk. Her granny used to babysit her when they went out to the pub. When they got back, Granny and her would seem invisible to them in the same way Roy was invisible to the other two men. Sober people, it seemed, played minor roles in the drunken world. Ever-present, yet ever-ignored. Forgotten as soon as they were seen. Or maybe even before they were seen, as was the case with Roy Beggs.

Clare was confused. She was glad to see Roy, a familiar and sensible face. The man who gave her choclate bars and told her not to tell anyone else. She knew that Mairead had fallen out with Roy, the two of them shouting at each other and pointing guns in a way which had made Clare cry, but she still liked Roy. He had made her feel safe, secure— and that was important to her in a world without certainty. She loved Mairead the same way she loved her real Mummy, but she had felt safe knowing Roy was around as well.

Sneaking through the door, Roy smiled at her, quickly raising his finger to his mouth in a gesture that let her know to be quiet. Although unsure as to what she should do, Clare played along. She watched as he looked over at the other men, maybe deciding whether to say something to them. Then he looked down at her, and seemed to decide against it. He quietly ushered Clare down the plush, carpeted staircase towards the front entrance to the hotel. Within moments, both Clare and Roy Beggs had left the hotel.

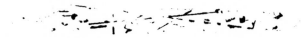

Suddenly Gibson's eyes narrowed as if struck by an important thought. He looked inquisitively at Sean before the penny dropped.

"Oh fu..." he uttered. He looked about him, panicked. "Where's Clare?!"

Sean looked at him, totally baffled. "Who?"

"Clare!" Gibson emphasised, irritably. "The child! We—I was meant to be looking after her!"

Sean still seemed to have no idea what was going on. Gibson recalled, earlier, before Sean had produced the bottle of vodka from behind the bar and persuaded him to take just one wee drink, Mairead leaving him strict instructions to keep Clare hidden and safe. Fuck knows, the south Armagh bred woman wasn't going to be too pleased when she returned. He looked to Sean, hoping for some help or enlightenment. He got neither. Only nausea had washed over his friend, causing him to suddenly gag, puke dribbling out of his nostrils then mouth as he became violently sick all over the table.

BARRY SAT IN THE BACK SEAT OF THE MILITARY VEHICLE WITH Caz buried in his arms. He was still bleeding from where the crazed girl had bitten him. Caz was catatonic with the shock of whatever the hell had been done to her, but Barry felt every bit as broken. Everything raced through his mind. The fucked-up girl's attack. The bodies—how could they have been so cut up like that?

The faces of three girls, in particular, started to form clearly in Barry's delirious head. Colours and lights seemed to be swimming around his vision, swaying from side to side with almost mocking treachery. The picture of a night club was forming. A local spot he used to frequent some years back. Barry rubbed his eyes, trying to snap out of whatever trance he was slipping into. He continued to bleed, blood slowly seeping out and collecting against his shirt.

A moment of clarity swept him back to reality. "W-what was wrong with that girl?" he asked, voice shaking. His eyes were wide and manic-looking. He was hardly even listening for an answer, simply having asked the question to try to distract himself from the strange vision that was threatening to consume him.

"Don't know," Mairead answered, curtly. "But you need to pull yourself together. That girl needs you."

Barry looked down at Caz, suddenly aware of her again. Her eyes were shut tight as if trying to keep the dam of tears welled up inside her from gushing free. Her bare legs were covered now with an old blanket they had found in the house. She shivered constantly, her shakes almost rhythmic, keeping time to some attempt at self-deluding distraction playing out in her mind, far away.

"F-fuck," he said, slamming a fist against the window.

Mairead turned to look at him, her face hard and devoid of sympathy. "You've got to keep it together," she repeated, coldly.

"That girl!" Barry began, yelling at first. "That girl... she bit me! She was trying to do to me what she did to those..." His words trailed off, his throat hoarse. His face was beetroot red. Beads of sweat were beginning to glisten on his forehead. The colours returned, swirling in around him, like stars in some cartoon where someone had been hit on the head. He fought them, swaying in and out of the same vision as before. "She pulled them apart! She was fucking eating them!"

Barry was losing it. A kind of dizziness was dragging him in and out of consciousness. The sweat was streaming down his face now, breaking out all over his body as if he were somehow evaporating. He felt as if he were slipping into some form of outer-body experience.

In the vision, he was talking to a girl. Pretty. Blonde. The type he liked. As she excused herself and left for the bathroom, Barry saw his own hand hover, briefly, over her drink. He watched a small pill drop from his hand into her glass. The same scene repeated itself, two other girls sitting across from him with each repeat.

He swayed back into reality, with all the motion of an out-of-control pendulum. Mairead had turned to look at him, her eyes darting back and forth from the road.

"Barry, keep it together."

But Barry was losing it.

SIX

A SMALL, PETITE HAND PUSHED THROUGH THE DIRT AND STONES, pausing as the weight of her husband stalled her for a few seconds. Before long, however, Kirsty Marshall clambered from her crudely constructed grave, her face pale and nonchalant as she threw her husband's body aside with ease and a distinct absence of emotion. Her hair shone in the afternoon sun, blonde highlights glistening in beautiful contrast to her almost coal-like eyes. Even though pieces of the black bin bag she had been wrapped in still stuck to her bare legs, glued uncouthly with semen from John McElroy's one-for-the-road ejaculation over her, Kirsty still looked absolutely gorgeous. Dead for several weeks now, she looked every bit the young bombshell she was in life. Perhaps even better.

She walked across the grass like a fucked-up angel, the black bin bag trailing in her wake like some kind of gothic bridal train. Her mind was a chaotic collage of undigested images, faces and names. Although emotionless, Kirsty still operated with purpose, as if fuelled by primal urges. Yet there was no passion. Kirsty wanted violence—specific violence—but she didn't know why.

She walked through the open door to the school, elegantly, as if it were the front door to her palace. Her filthy torn clothes and shreds of black bin bag did little to distract from her catwalk swagger. As if dressed head-to-toe in prada, the twenty-something ex-teacher strolled up the main corridor of the school. Her black eyes searched for something.

For someone.

Aida Hussein had been cleaning up in the canteen, washing down the tables after the last few stragglers had finished their lunch. When the door opened she simply expected it to be some straggler wanting his or her dinner after everyone else had eaten everything. That always pissed her off.

"I'm sorry, we're cleaning up now..." Aida began, only looking up to finish her sentence. Her words hung, uselessly, in the still air. A beautiful mess stood in front of her, its chaotic beauty stunning her as much as the cold terror in its black eyes. The young Egyptian dropped her cloth. Her lips moved to say something, yet stopped short of an actual word leaving her mouth.

Kirsty sided up to her, her black eyes seeming to look somewhere above her rather than at her. It was as if she was blind. Suddenly Aida could hear a sound not unlike flapping wings. To her horror, the dead Marshall woman's eyes were switching from one colour to another. Her lips were slightly parted, her body swaying. She was lost in some kind of daze. It was almost as if she were in the middle of one fucking good orgasm, only in slow motion. Suddenly she stopped, dead, her eyes a very definite shade of white. They stared straight at Aida, her nostrils drawing close to the Egyptian woman's skin. She sniffed once, twice in succession. Then she smiled.

After but a moment, the young woman—the creature—turned, no longer interested. She moved past Aida. She was after someone else. Someone who was close by. Someone who she would know when she found them, but not before.

Her trail of black bin bags caressed the smoothly polished canteen floor, swerving around the various tables and chairs, neatly laid out, with the grace and precision of a ballet dancer. Aida looked on, still frozen to the spot, her cloth still lying on the ground where it had been dropped. As she watched, Kirsty approached the kitchen, the only part of the school with any power. An electric light shone from behind the corrugated shutter, half drawn to discourage hungry survivors from disturbing the post-lunchtime cleanup. Kirsty Marshall halted in front of the shutter.

From the inside, the sounds of hustle and bustle could be heard. Kirsty's head cocked to one side, her mind drinking in every detail of each image, making sense of it in order to plan her next move. One hand reached to pull up the shutter, revealing what she had been looking for all along: the large frame of Sylvia Patterson. Chief cook and all-round provider for the group, Sylvia had comforted, fed, watered and nurtured the survivors in a way which helped many of them deal with their respective losses. She had held them as they cried, soothed them as they grieved, put food on their plates and tea in their mugs. She had helped organise the survivors as they generated a little power to keep the kitchen running. She had taken control of things when Roy Beggs left to reclaim the child that had been taken away from them, slipping smoothly into a leadership role because, whilst Roy Beggs wouldn't have admitted it, she had been leading just as much as he had, all along. Sylvia Patterson had achieved what Roy Beggs could never achieve. She had gained the survivors' full and unquestionable respect and support. Whilst Roy could provide security and structure for the survivors, Sylvia provided comfort—but she poisoned Steve Marshall, adding progressively lethal quantities of rat poison to his every meal.

As Sylvia's eyes met Kirsty's, she could hear what sounded to her like a kitchen fan. To her horror, Kirsty's eyes flicked from white to red, finally finding a very deep, dark black. The cook didn't recognize her, having only met her husband—the man she had poisoned—as opposed to the entire Marshall family. Sure, she had watched them be buried, but only Roy Beggs—and the insidious John McElroy, tasked with preparing the Marshall family's bodies—had actually seen Kirsty's body. But Sylvia knew that whoever this strange woman-like being was, this beautiful shadow of what was once human, but now beyond human— and the very constraints of humanity—had ill intentions towards her. Of that she was sure.

The cook reached quickly and fearfully for a large kitchen knife on the table, but Kirsty got there first, lifting then turning the blade on Sylvia in one complete movement. It sliced through Sylvia's throat as if it were wet paper, spraying the clinically clean, white walls of the kitchen with a jet of bright red and separating her head from its body. The cook's full-figured body fell heavily to the ground, leaving the cleanly decapitated head held, by the hair, in the left hand of her beautiful young assailant. The pristine white kitchen floor, usually polished within an inch of its life, now ran red with its chief cook's life. The decapitated corpse of Sylvia Patterson continued to puke blood onto the tiles, the red liquid at first running along the grooves of each tile before finally pooling across the entire floor like some thick quilt of revenge.

Kirsty Marshall stood silently as if unsure what to do next. She was operating on raw passion, yet still seemed uncertain how to express such. After a few seconds of lull, she suddenly leaned her beautiful face towards the severed neck hanging from her hand, drinking greedily from the throat's many veins, shoving torn flesh into her small mouth as if it were a jam pastry.

seven

"MAYBE I SHOULD WAIT FOR MOMMY," CLARE SAID, seeming a little anxious and confused. Her parents split before the disaster had struck, meaning she was accustomed to a tug-of-war between adults concerning her welfare. Yet now both mummy and daddy had gone completely off the map of her life, leaving the child desperately alone. Mairead had been a good replacement for her mummy and in the Brave New Fucking World, her father figure might as well be a man like Roy Beggs. Unlike the softer Gibson, Roy actually seemed to have an interest in her and seemed strong enough to protect her. When the reset button was hit, basic needs like protection meant a hell of a lot, especially to a child. Especially to Clare.

Roy looked at her and winked, gesturing for her to be quiet by drawing one finger over his mouth. It was as if their escape was like a big secret that only him and her knew about. She liked that feeling. A feeling of being included, playing a part in some game with the adults. Truth be told, she was happy to go with him. She didn't like this new place, nor the people who lived in it. She had never been to Belfast before, and even in post-apocalyptic emptiness, the Big Smoke still seemed overwhelming to her. Buildings seemed too tall, roads too wide. The starkness of the world seemed a lot more explicit here than in the school.

But she didn't want to leave Mairead, her new mummy.

"I want to wait for mummy," she whispered, still playing the game even if unsure what were.

"Erm... we'll meet her back at the school," Roy chanced, hurrying the child away from the hotel, across the normally busy road to where his car was parked.

"I don't think she likes the school." Clare looked up to Roy, saucer eyes blemished only by a redness that suggested a few nights sleep had been missed, of late.

"Sure she does," Roy coaxed, flashing a cheesy grin that made him look a lot like a teddy bear. Clare had giggled the first time she had seen that grin. Now it was strangely comforting.

"Where is she then?" Clare persisted. "If mummy likes the school, she'll come back with us, won't she?"

"She'll follow us later," Roy snapped under his propped-up smile.

"No she won't. She doesn't like it there. She doesn't like you." She had tested Roy and found him lacking. Everyone knew that Mairead didn't like the school. Clare may have been a child, but she knew as much as that and, like most children, she didn't take too well to being patronised.

Roy got down on his hunkers, stroking Clare's hair with paternal love she had always thought non-existent. "What's most important is making sure you're safe, isn't it?"

Clare nodded agreeably. Her face was approaching the kind of pout that might lead to a stubborn strop.

"Well, I'm here to bring you back to the school. You know, where you went when your mu—I mean when everything became weird, eh?"

Clare nodded. She did like the school. It was where she had spent a lot of her days over the last few years. She didn't feel too scared there. It even smelt right, Sylvia's canteen cooking reminding her of that noon feeling that lunch was on its way, and home-time would follow swiftly afterwards. The timetable of it all, steadfast and sure, was comforting.

Perhaps that was the attraction of the school for all the survivors. Perhaps that was why none of them, apart from Gibson, Mairead and Clare, had made any moves to leave it. The small school brought them back to a place where things were more predictable, less volatile. It reminded them of routine, of stability, of structure. It reminded them of authority, and how much they needed that in their lives to feel safe. These were the things that were ripped from them on that fateful day, just over three weeks ago.

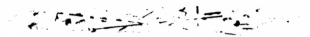

Roy gestured for Clare to get inside the car. She did so obediently. He turned on the car's CD player, sliding in a disc he thought might appeal to the child—some pop shite that his niece used to listen to. Still smiling, his face almost hardened into that stupid grin he used especially for Clare, Roy closed the car door and allowed himself to frown. He took a moment to lean back on the side of the car and feel the calm breeze blow against his face. It seemed even quieter now than it had before.

Roy had some nasty business to take care of before they left. Never a man who took being scorned lightly in days gone by, the self-appointed lawmaker wasn't going to let someone like Gibson, the middle-class tosser that he was, get away with what he had done. He cringed when he thought of how humiliated he had been, how much of a fool he had been made to look—especially in front of the others, the people he had sworn to himself he would remain strong for. Gibson had to be punished for what he had done. It was that simple.

Calmly, the soldier reached inside his bag for add-ons to the rifle he had slung across his shoulder. Whistling nonchalantly, he screwed a telescopic scope onto the top of the rifle. Once satisfied with that, taking a moment to aim through the lens, following the hotel wall until it reached the window where Sean and Gibson still sat, he looked again in his bag, feeling around for something else. In the thick, heavy silence it seemed even more important to muffle a noise as obnoxious as a rifle shot. Roy found what he was searching for, fixing the long, top-heavy length of metal onto his rifle's tip. It was a silencer.

Checking again to make sure everything was well aligned, Roy loaded the rifle with three bullets.

Three strikes and you're out.

He winked at Clare, who was looking out at him through the car window.

"Won't be a moment, sweetie," he mouthed into the silence, flashing that grin again.

eight

THE LATE AFTERNOON SUN CUT LIKE A KNIFE THROUGH THE grey clouds. With the evening, the rain would come, shunning the sunlight like a condemned man. Last night's rain had been particularly heavy and Cornmarket's cobbled streets and ornate bandstand still bore the fruits of its labour. The marble of the band stand, of late almost golden with the kiss of sunshine, was an off-beat grey colour. Drips of moisture ran down each of the brass legs of the structure, meeting the cobbled streets in small pools, gradually paling as the streets meandered like the points of a compass throughout the more antiquated parts of Belfast's city centre.

It would have lent the area something of a gothic feel even if The Preacher Man hadn't been there. His small congregation stood almost stalactite, their sombre sincerity and bowed heads almost choking the already Victorian atmosphere. For the twenty-third night running they prayed the same prayer, ad-libbed to various shades of melodramatic by The Preacher Man. It started with a low moan and built to a shrill whimper before spiraling dramatically and then peaking to an enormous roaring finale. The Preacher Man's body would theatrically curl up, spring forward then open up like a flower, arms outstretched and head raised, to bring proceedings to an explosive crescendo. Yet regardless of how it was done, The Preacher Man was always praying for the same thing: for angels to come and claim their souls.

Tonight their prayers were answered.

Like rats from woodwork, those beautiful creatures seeped out of the city. From north, south, east and west they descended upon the holy throng, their gentle approach peeking open an occasional eye amongst the pensive crowd. The angels poured towards them in unison, as if choreographed, their beautiful, luminous faces cocked slightly to the left as they approached. Like holy ghosts they almost glided across the cobble-stoned ground, each picking out their respective target calmly and elegantly. Then they stopped. From a distance of exactly five metres from the group, the beautiful creatures slowly raised their faces. As if searching for TV channels, their eyes flicked back and forth between various colours—red, black and white and various shades of such. It was as if they were fine-tuning into their feelings. As the eyes flicked back and forth, a sound not unlike the clicking of fingers broke against the reverent silence of prayer. Up to this point, almost every member of the group, even skeptical freeloader Robert McBride, had really hoped them to be angels. Really hoped them to be the salvation they had each prayed fervently for. Another reality dawned upon them, however, as a different set of eyes, finally tuned into their respective colours, stared upon each face in the group. They had been praying for angels, yet what they saw before them was even better.

Gavin Cummings looked upon the beautiful, freckled face of his wife, Kory. For Robert McBride, it was his mistress Patricia, and the tearful, wide eyes of Jackie McCrory met with the dark, tiny, narrow face of his stepdaughter, Barbara.

It was Gavin who cracked first. His hands, shaking like wings, reached forward to touch the face of his beautiful Kory, his eyes wide and fraught with disbelief. He just couldn't understand what was going on. Was it some kind of trick? A test, maybe, from God or The Preacher Man? Thoughts and emotions blended together like paint in a palette as his quivering hands finally reached the face of his wife, each fingertip feverishly sending the same message to his brain. This was Kory. This felt like Kory. Only better. Everyone followed suit, their hands feeling all over the bodies of their respective loved ones, some of the men snatching them close as if scared they might be taken from them again. It was a moment charged with raw, passionate energy. An electric orgy of love and loss, played out in front of the one man who stood alone:

The tall, dark Preacher Man.

And then it changed. Almost as if sick of the feverous affection heaped upon them by their respective men, as if the groping and grabbing and embracing had made them suddenly and violently claustrophobic, something within the women assembled cracked.

Within a split second, each beautiful creature had lunged for their former lover, greedily scooping clawfuls of flesh and sinewy vein from their throats, barely leaving the victims time to gasp a breath, never mind a tearful hallelujah for the miraculous resurrection of their fallen dearest. Soon the screams of each man was tearing through the dead weight of silence, shredding any kind of serenity they had struggled to achieve through their prayer.

In the middle of the onslaught, each man falling quickly and theatrically on the scarlet-stained cobblestones, The Preacher Man remained unchallenged, his eyes drinking up the sight with fascination, his sandwich board hanging limp and ridiculous around his neck, spelling out 'JESUS SAVES'.

Staring as every splash of blood and slice of body part slopped out around him, The Preacher Man showed little emotion, stepping through the carnage as if this was all part of some bigger, divine plan. A part of him believed it was. Another part of him feared it wasn't. Yet as he moved, the weight of his sandwich board bearing down upon each soft step forward he made, it seemed as if the violence parted before him, a red sea of death and carnage happening around him, beside him, (because of him?) yet not *to* him. As terror and mayhem spilled into his wake, staining the cobblestone damp with seven shades of bile, The Preacher Man waded, gradually, away from the Bandstand.

It was then that he spotted Tim Adamson.

The lad's awkward, gangly frame sent a raw stab through The Preacher Man's heart, a mixture of joy and pain, Love and disgust. The boy was shivering, yet sweating at the same time. Tears ran freely down his face, shimmering in the sunshine like precious stones.

Jaw to the floor, The Preacher Man stopped briefly, only long enough to drink in the sight of Tim standing in front of him. He wondered if the boy had been in the crowd all along, perhaps standing at the back or in one of the shadows that seemed to cast themselves over the congregation at Cornmarket like cliffs. It was barely a second The Preacher Man had stopped, but it was long enough to allow one of the angels, a large, full-figured beauty with her husband's blood smeared over her lips like crudely-applied lipstick, to reach for him, catching a lock of his unkempt hair. The Preacher Man was dragged to a standstill, his eyes wide now with real terror. He froze, his large frame and imposing stature dragged to a standstill by the most beautiful of assailants. He was trapped.

Scared.

Yet the terror was not from the cold, clammy touch ebbing its way through his hair for a tighter grip, nor was it from the doom that such a grasp would truly spell for him. Instead his terror came from looking again upon this boy's face—*his* boy's face. A face not washed with the disdain and venom that should have been there, but with *love*.

The Preacher Man—Samuel Adamson by name—felt his heart break in unison with the sharp pain of teeth sinking into his neck, tearing veins open like wrapping paper. His life blood spilled onto his dark grey suit and sandwich board, the back print ironically reading, 'THERE'S POWER IN THE BLOOD'. Samuel reached one long, powerful arm out towards his boy, flailing wildly for a last touch. A last embrace. His eyes closed, smarting with pain as the creature's teeth tore again through his grey-toned skin. Deeper. He felt himself slipping away, an all-consuming dizziness swamping his mind. Golden dreams swirled around his head, seeming to almost search for an opening. There was none. There was only this.

And then it happened.

Samuel heard what sounded like a gunshot ringing out. He felt his attacker falling dead, a single bullet tearing through her beautiful face. He looked up with disbelief, finding his son, gun outstretched, staring back. A sudden tear ran down Samuel Adamson's face.

His son had saved him!

Hallelujah?

The Preacher Man—Samuel—had prayed for the salvation of everyone, including himself, so many times that he had lost count. He had rinsed out the sinner's prayer more times than he cared to even fathom, his own guilt and self-loathing stocking up more sackcloth to don than he could keep up with. He had looked everywhere for an answer to his rampant inner demons—a cure to sate his dark, bile-stained lust for everything that he stood against—yet he never expected that very answer to come from the very person who had seen the absolute worst of him. A single, enlightened tear trickled down his cheek. This was what life was about. It wasn't about death.

It was about grace. Real grace.

That very look sealed Samuel's doom. It was too much for Tim Adamson. His hate for his father quickly overwhelmed any trickles of love seeping from his heavy heart. Tim aimed his weapon, the same gun he had taken off the policeman's body that very first day, squarely at Samuel, pulling the trigger with a surety that was rare for a sixteen year-old firing his second ever bullet. It tore a clean hole through his father's heart with almost marksman precision.

Within seconds, Samuel Adamson's life was ended, his soul simply evaporating into the ether. Tim was quite sure that no pearly gates welcomed his monster of a father, no flames of hell licked at his feet. Instead, his daddy-dearest left the world as simply as he had, no doubt, entered it.

Tearstained eyes closed. Flailing arms searching, wildly.

Tim's own eyes blurred with fraught and raw emotion. His gun dropped to the cobbled street, now a paddling pool of blood and flesh. His thousand-yard stare met with a bloody face, beautiful and dark-eyed. The face cocked to the left, almost drinking in Tim's raw emotion, before it fine-tuned a heavenly shade of white. As the beautiful yet deadly angel moved towards Tim, stains of violence in every finger reaching, his eyes closed. He felt no fear. Relief's anaesthetic soothed him. One cold hand clasped around his neck, snapping for his silver crucifix, but he held on to it, strong, his fingers bleeding as he strained to keep hold of his little shiny Messiah. The creature persisted, reaching next for his face. As sleek, perfectly-manicured fingers tore at his hair and eyes, gouging out each pupil as if scooping out ice cream, Tim was left only with memories to look upon. Memories of the most beautiful sight he had ever seen in his sixteen short years:

The face of Caroline Donaldson.

Nine

THE FIRST SHOT SHATTERED THE FRONT WINDOW OF THE HOTEL bar, dragging the two middle-aged drinkers out of their alcoholic stupor, but failing to actually kickstart their brains quickly enough to take cover before the second shot. It followed the first within a second, cutting through the empty window frame to slice a lethal hole in Alan Gibson's head. The pissed-up counsellor, barely conscious before the second bullet violated him, lost all signs of life immediately, his small, rotund body hitting the bar floor like a burst football.

"Christ!" Sean hit the deck, covering his ears for some unknown reason. As he stumbled to the floor, an entire table of glasses and bottles fell on top of him, smashing theatrically. Sean closed his eyes as the booze and glass showered him. "Fuck!" Quickly recovering, he looked over to Alan Gibson. A thick, dark liquid now oozed, slowly, from the man's head, a man Sean had only seconds ago offered another drink to. Seconds ago, this man could talk. Now his brains were seeping out of his head like lentil soup.

This was fucked up.

Sean could almost feel the sights of the sniper rifle search for him. It had got Gibson. Now it would want him. Desperately, he scrambled under the nearest bar table. He listened, straining to hear some sign or clue as to what the sniper's next move was going to be, over his own heavy breathing and racing heart.

Nothing. Just The Silence.

Who the fuck would do such a thing? Sean had heard very little commotion over the weeks as he downed the drinks. An occasional shout or burst of a window, looting now being as common and inoffensive as shopping. The kickstart of an engine or rev of a car. Random music, the distant, sombre singing of the Cornmarket god-botherers. But little violence. He'd heard the others talk about having seen the odd scuffle, burning out quickly as if too embarrassed to continue to a logical conclusion. In the New World, it seemed The Silence would do most of the policing. Like the wagging finger of God, burned within a penitent sinner, The Silence was ever present. Ever watching. Ever measuring.

Until now. Something had burst through with lethal insolence, ripping a hole in the chest of Alan Gibson, and Sean knew that whoever was responsible would most probably seek him out, too.

His eyes fell upon the only entrance to the bar. One half-ajar door dead in front of him. The sniper's next move might be to search him out on foot. Sean didn't know what to do. He felt too drunk for sensible, reasonable action. He was in a bar, for Christ's sake! What the hell could he do to defend himself in a bar?!

Roy Beggs was almost sure he had struck gold with his second shot. He thought he saw someone fall, and from the angle he was shooting from, and the shape of the silhouette that his bullet was aimed at, he was about ninety-nine percent sure he had hit Gibson. He was about ninety-eight percent sure that his bullet had hit the right spot to make the pious wee fucker a dead man. But not one hundred percent. And Roy had to be one hundred percent.

Turning, he looked in at the small girl in his car. She hadn't heard any of the commotion, the silencer having muffled Roy's shot and whatever shite CD he had given her doing a fine job of masking the sound of the window shattering. There was no reason that Clare wouldn't be safe for another few minutes, just until he checked things out in the hotel—made sure he had finished the job properly.

Roy sighed, heavily. A part of him regretted that it had come to this. He wished there were others who could share the responsibility for keeping things under control, protecting the innocent and punishing those who could be a threat to his small community. Shouldering his rifle, he felt inside the bag at his feet, finding a semi-automatic. Checking the weapon was loaded and cocked, the heavy-set soldier moved, cautiously, towards the hotel's front entrance.

ten

THE CREATURE THAT, IN LIFE, HAD BEEN KIRSTY MARSHALL, and in afterlife/death/un-death was something *similar* to Kirsty Marshall, sat by her own self-desecrated grave. The body of her husband, Steve, lay somehow entwined in the simple cross that had been thrown together by one of the survivors, a decent man named Phillip, who now lay face down in his own blood and spittle somewhere on the school's football pitch. He had been the last one Kirsty had managed to kill, succumbing to her bloody hands just after the young student girl had been torn down. The others, terrified, defenceless and disorganised, had spilled messily out into the streets of Lisburn, caring not for each other or the ones they left behind. Their bubble of security, a façade created by the uniform of Roy Beggs and the routine of Sylvia Patterson, had been burst open like a fallen egg carton. Now they were just scared children again, running from the school that had nurtured them for the last number of weeks.

Kirsty didn't need to chase them. She had achieved what she set out for, anything else being a bonus. She was sated with the blood of Sylvia Patterson hardening on her full-bodied lips, lips Steve Marshall had begged to have around his cock on many occasions.

Some part of Kirsty remembered that, and became aroused.

Sitting cross-legged on the unkempt lawn of the school, Kirsty ran her hand roughly through Steve's hair. It was filthy. Uncombed and greasy. The hair of a man who had given up caring about life well before any bullet reached him. Kirsty felt a draw towards him. His smell, masked a little by the sun-scorched decay that had already set in, seemed vaguely familiar. Attractive, in some way. It touched a very basic, primal part of Kirsty. A cocktail of raw emotions raced through her chaotic head. Somewhere between hunger and passion she found love, then loss, her head cocking to the side as she searched her post-life brain for an appropriate reaction. Her eyes flickered again as she searched, finding red—for passion—before they settled on the purest white they could be, a purity that equalled the love she had shared for her Steve. For a moment Kirsty's arms flailed wildly at the body of her husband, tearing skin from bone like peel from an orange. Water gathered in her eye for a reason lost to her. Her tears twinkled, like tiny stars, in the sunlight. Her eyes turned from its pure white, to red, and finally to a deep almost blue colour. A low, heart-wrenching moan escaped from her lips, ripping through the stifling silence like a bird through sky.

Grief.

Dipping like a child bobbing for apples, Kirsty Marshall sank her teeth into the skinless chest of Steve Marshall, tearing chunks of flesh and bone with raw passion, the crystal tears seeping from her red eyes mingling with the broken heart spilling onto her lap.

From close by, the solitary figure of Aida Hussein watched on, terrified and broken-hearted in equal measure. She knew now who this woman was. This vicious, desperate woman who had been so badly scorned. A tear caressed the Egyptian woman's cheekbone, shed in regret for the very emotions that Kirsty Marshall's crude, violent brain was discovering.

Aida moved slowly towards the confused, ravenous creature. As she approached, Kirsty gave no credence to her, lost in the bittersweet ritual of feasting upon her husband's remains. Aida reached a shaking hand towards the creature's glistening mane of hair, gingerly running her long, slender fingers through. Kirsty stopped, for a moment. She looked up at the Egyptian woman, her eyes flicking slowly from one colour to another with the same steady rhythm as a paper fan on a bicycle wheel. She was searching for a suitable feeling. An appropriate emotion. Somewhere deep inside she remembered tenderness. She remembered what it was like to be stroked, and pushed her head into the waiting caress of Aida Hussein's hands.

Professor Herbert Matthews sat in the armchair across the room from his wife, Muriel. He was holding a shotgun he retrieved from his garden shed. His hands trembled as the woman he had spent over forty years with—now looking remarkably young—climbed out of the armchair she hadn't moved from for a number of weeks.

She had been dead, and in many ways still was. The larger part of Herb understood that. A small part of him, however, wanted to embrace this new Muriel no matter how deadly such an embrace might be.

Instead he snapped open his shotgun.

As he loaded one of the barrels with a shell, Herb noticed the colour of Muriel's eyes. They had once been a very pale blue so ethereal that Herb often wondered if she had elfin blood in her veins. Now those same eyes raged red—a deep, passionate red that Herb could only translate as aggression. The fact that pure, condensed love fuelled their intensity was lost on him. Herb only saw the danger and their very definite feral intent towards him.

She rushed him, moving extremely fast for a woman who hadn't as much as scratched her head in the last month. But Herb was ready for her. Still in his armchair, he aimed the shotgun at head height and blasted her at close range. The sound was deafening, ringing out obnoxiously through the quiet country air. The contents of Muriel's head were splattered over Herb in a violent wave of blood. The remainder of her body immediately hit the floor.

Herb took a moment to gather himself before removing, cleaning, and replacing his glasses. A moment was all he needed. He had mourned his wife many times since her death—her *real* death. He didn't need to mourn her again.

He slowly got to his feet, his dressing gown heavy with her blood. He sat the gun down and moved towards his desk, stepping over Muriel's desecrated body. He switched on the power of the amateur radio and lifted the mic.

"Terry? You there?"

Pzzt. "Professor? That you? Thank God you're still okay. We've had some... incredible developments—"

Herb squeezed his mic, blotting out what the Englishman was going to tell him. He didn't want to hear what was coming next. He had worked out for himself that nothing good could come from the dead returning to life. Herb had let the end of the world pass him by, but he wasn't going to be fooled anymore. Hence, he had waited for the inevitable to happen, sitting in vigil by his wife's side as she became the girl he fell in love with once more before becoming... *something else.*

Then he did what he had to do.

"It's okay, Terry. I'm safe. Muriel... she came back for me... but I attended to her in the proper manner. "

Pzzt. "Professor Matthews... I'm sorry. I really am. If there was anything I could have done... anything I can do now..." *Pzzt.*

"Thank you, Terry. I appreciate it. This is difficult for all of us. I'm sure you have lost people too."

For a moment there was nothing but fuzz on the radio.

Pzzt. "Professor Matthews. I know it's a difficult time but we're going to need you to do something for us. With these new developments, time is of the essence. I know it's a lot to ask someone as... er... mature in years as yourself, Professor, but we're going to need your help. You're the only hope for Northern Ireland." *Pzzt.*

"What do you need me to do?" Herb asked.

Pzzt. "We need you to go to Belfast. Spread the word. But you have to be clear on some matters before you do so." *Pzzt.*

Herb's ear pricked up on hearing the word 'Belfast'. He hadn't been to Belfast since retiring.

"Go on," he said to his radio friend.

As Terry explained to Herb exactly what he needed him to do, exactly what message he needed him to take, Herb looked to the front door of his two-storey cottage, remembering what had happened before when he tried to leave. He thought back to all those years ago to the last time he was in the outside world, a time whenever his condition wasn't quite as serious as it eventually got. He was listening to Terry's each and every word, yet he couldn't help but be distracted by the things in his home, the things he had come to know and love and... fear?

Herb looked behind him at the bloody mess on the carpet. Muriel would have hated that mess. He would have to clean it up, of course, before he went anywhere.

Pzzt. "Professor? Are you still there? Professor Matthews?" *Pzzt.*

"I'm still here, Terry," Herb said, squeezing the mic. "And, yes, I'll go to Belfast. God help me, I'll go."

His hand was shaking profusely. Herb didn't know what was making it shake the most, the shock from blowing his undead wife's head off, the excitement from what Terry had told him, just then, on the radio, or the fear from knowing that, in order to execute their plan, he'd have to go out that bloody door again.

S TAR WATCHED THE SERIES OF EVENTS UNFOLD FROM THE
relative safety of Great Victoria Street Station. The girl, Clare,
being led to the car by a stranger in camouflage. The sounds
of splintering glass and distinctive flash of muzzle as said
stranger, evidently a soldier, quickly constructed a sniper
rifle and opened fire on the hotel bar, where she knew Sean would be.
She knew this because, frankly, Sean did nothing else, of late, except
drink.

The DJ's obsession with lost love had got too much for the tattooist,
leading to her withdrawing from him. She had found herself spending
a lot more time with the quiet, introspective Tim Adamson, the two of
them diving into all things tattoo. Tim didn't have a lot of talent in the
area, but nevertheless Star encouraged him as he dreamed up weird
and (frankly) creepy designs, then practised applying them on false skin.
More recently, Tim moved to real skin—the skin of the dead. It was a
little distasteful, one might have thought—*might have*, that was, before
thinking of such things (or thinking much of anything) became less of
an issue. The body they had been using seemed strangely well preserved,
and whilst Star and her young apprentice both clocked that, neither
had said so to the other. They needed skin, and this skin was as good as
you could get, for whatever reason. The dead had become inanimate, in
a way. Almost invisible in this godforsaken city.

Tim had fucked up his first few attempts, drawing too much blood
from the corpse, digging too deep into the skin, inking lines so crooked

they looked like zig-zags. But the boy was coming on—or had been, anyway.

As for Sean, he continued to drink, regardless of whether or not he had company. If anything, his intake had risen. At times Star would have joined him, (last night for example) but the wild all-nighters were fast becoming a one-man show. Sean, and Sean alone, would be found sitting in the piano bar, spinning discs on his portable CD player until its batteries ran out, downing shots of vodka like a broken man. Sometimes he could be heard crying, his drunken tears and rants almost part of the décor of the hotel now, as if it were haunted.

As Star had watched the whole scene outside the hotel, she wondered what the drunken DJ had done to piss off Green Beret dude. Was it something to do with that weird family she had seen earlier? Hadn't they been asking strange questions about military presence? Barry had gone somewhere with the woman earlier, but she hadn't seen the other, creepy guy with the beard leaving. Maybe he was with Sean? Maybe the military guy was after him instead of Sean? Fuck knew what kind of politics were at play here, but Star didn't like to see Sean getting drawn into it, and with the hairy bastard having not surfaced from the bar today, she was starting to worry about more than just his liver.

She lit up a cigarette. She needed to think about this. As she smoked, she watched the soldier make his way towards the hotel. Probably moving in to finish the job. Star didn't know what to do. She wondered about the child in the car. Why was the soldier interested in her? A shudder went through her as she thought the worst. Grown women (as Barry often reminded her through his many drunken passes) were a little scarce these days. Would-be-predators now had a free hand to practise whatever sick games they played out in their minds, before the shit had hit the fan, in full Technicolor depravity. A lawless society had its perks to a woman like Star, but there were very definite drawbacks for those more vulnerable.

Star had to do something. She didn't like children, but no part of her was going to sit back and watch something like this happen. Stamping her cigarette out, before lighting up another, she grabbed hold of a large kitchen knife (the only thing even resembling a weapon,) pulled open the front doors of the station and made her way across the road to the parked car. The army guy had gone inside. She had a few moments grace.

As the doors swung closed again, behind her, something else stirred from behind the counter of the coffee shop.

Her crudely tattooed mannequin was moving.

Twelve

THE LAND ROVER SCREECHED TO A HALT BY CARLISLE CIRCUS. It was a local name for the roundabout bringing together North Belfast's Crumlin Road and Antrim Road. It was a flashpoint of sorts, two communities meeting where the roads did. Flags could be seen within a stone's throw of the beginning of each road, proudly yelling out their paranoid tribalism as if to ward off the 'wrong kind.' This place was no stranger to riots and clashes with police involving both sides of the divide.

Strange, then, to see a steady stream of women march suddenly from the houses on each side of divide, meeting at the roundabout to file on into the city centre as peacefully as sand pouring through an hourglass.

Mairead wound down her window to get a clearer look. There was something not quite right with the scene. First of all, where the hell had so many survivors come from? Without actually counting, Mairead would have reckoned on there being two hundred of the women. Which was the second thing that didn't quite add up. Why were they all women? And fucking gorgeous women, at that?

Manic laughter came from behind her. It was Barry, delirious and flipping out. Shivering in the corner beside him, now a little more with it (*thankfully*, thought Mairead) was the girl they had rescued. Her eyes were darting about, catching her bearings. Wondering, no doubt, why the hell she was in the back of a military Land Rover with a nut-job like Barry Rogan. Mairead ignored Barry, reaching a hand to the girl instead.

"You okay, pet?" she asked, her normally hardnosed face curled up into an expression of pity. "Can you remember anything?" The girl seemed startled at her touch, backing further into the back seat of the Land Rover.

"What's going on? Who are you?"

"It's okay, sweetie," Mairead fawned, her natural maternal instinct kicking in seamlessly.

The girl looked to Barry. His eyes were swimming around his head as if he were drugged. Some kind of fever was breaking on his brow. "Barry? What's wrong with him?"

Mairead looked at the young man. He had gone completely awol after being attacked by that... Then it hit her.

Turning slowly back to the crowd of women pouring into town, Mairead caught sight of three of the creatures staring in through the windscreen. These weren't women. Not anymore. Their eyes were switching ethereally between red and black as if some form of fucked-up traffic light. One of them was naked. The other two wore unflattering pyjamas. They were clearly of the same messed-up ilk as the 'girl' they'd encountered at Joe's house. And with the middle one suddenly taking it upon herself to ram the palm of her hand wildly against the bulletproof windscreen, Mairead figured they were more than likely equally as violent as the last creature.

Because 'creature' is what Mairead had decided these things were. Not girls, not women—not even humans. They were something other-worldly, the likes of which you would normally see in one of those horror films that her husband used to love watching. Something primal and deadly.

Something that could be attacking her little Clare, right about now.

Mairead sank her foot onto the accelerator, knocking the three girls in front of her across the bonnet of the military Land Rover. Dodging a stalled car, still in possession of its now rotting driver, Mairead aimed the Land Rover straight for the crowd of creatures in front of her, advancing towards the city centre. She wasn't going to let this bevy of bitches keep her from her little girl.

As the Land Rover connected with half a dozen creatures, struggling as it mangled a few under its rough terrain wheels, Barry suddenly sobered from his drugged-like daze, his eyes drawn towards the three girls picking themselves up behind him. Their faces were more than familiar. They were etched into his mind. Tattooed with guilt-ridden ink upon his conscience. The blonde one was called Nuala. Barely out of her teens, Barry had met her at a club in the city centre, notorious as being a haunt for off-duty hairdressers. The brunette was a German student named Simone. The red-haired girl had been his first. He couldn't even remember her name, even though her face, drugged and innocent, was burned into his memory. He had drugged, then raped them all. Now they were coming for him. Barry knew it was that simple.

And he was scared.

The Land Rover fought on through the crowd, some of which were now clawing uselessly at the reinforced glass and heavy doors of the vehicle. Blood had sprayed onto the Land Rover's windscreen, presumably from the bitches Mairead had driven over. The wheels spun menacingly, the engine revving in anger as more and more of the beautiful monsters fell foul of the heavy duty machine's progress. Although seeming to be on the winning side in terms of safety, the three humans inside the vehicle were completely surrounded by the elegant yet deadly females. The constant chaos of noise as each creature scraped and clawed, punched, kicked and even bit at the windows and doors of the vehicle was unnerving. The commotion at the back window was particularly gruelling. The three girls who had seemingly taken an interest in Barry were shrieking like banshees. It was difficult to know which were screaming the loudest—them or Barry.

"Fuck! They're coming for me! They want me!"

Barry's progressively more high-pitched and embarrassing whine was, perhaps, pissing Mairead off even more than the creatures outside. A dark part of her considered opening a window and feeding Barry to them just to shut him the fuck up.

The girl, suddenly alert, climbed in beside Mairead.

"Don't worry!" Mairead yelled above the collage of noise and activity, as the Land Rover rocked and jolted against the deadly sea. "They can't get in!"

The girl looked incredulously at her. "They?!" she yelled back, over the noise, suddenly more aware of her surroundings than she'd like to be. "What the hell are they?!"

Mairead looked sternly at the teenager beside her. The girl's young face was hard again, her mouth pulled down into its usual on-edge sneer. Mairead didn't answer her question, instead pointing to the door on the passenger side of the vehicle where the young girl now sat. "Make sure it's locked!"

The teenager checked the lock. Twice. Then again. She really wanted to be sure the door was shut down tight. Numerous black eyes stared in at her from the road, competing with one another as they clawed and scraped at the window. Their outstretched and bloody fingers, nails splitting and smearing against the window, were less than ten centimetres away from tearing her pretty young eyes out. Even their teeth scraped against the window, some cracking and bleeding as they dragged across the tough glass repeatedly.

A feeling of terror crept up her spine, a warm dampness that seemed to settle somewhere in between her skin and backbone. "They can't get in, can they?!"

Mairead didn't answer. She was ignoring the difficult questions now, it seemed.

Suddenly Barry's voice rose to an even more manic level. It was enough to make both women look immediately behind them.

And that's when they saw it: A crack creeping across the rear window. The hand of a red-headed creature pounding upon it, blood seeping out of her broken fingers. Barry, now entirely beyond reason, raising his handgun and firing, blowing chunks out of both damaged window and red-headed creature.

Thirteen

ROY CONFIDENTLY STEPPED THROUGH THE DOORS OF THE hotel bar. His weapon, the semi-automatic, was readied. His eyes carefully scaled the entire view of the bar, still lavish-looking despite the remnants of many a night's drinking having gone on. Most of the tables looked as if they hadn't even been used, a thin coating of dust shimmering against the light now pouring in from the broken window at the front. The bar itself stood proud and dapper in the centre of the room, well stocked with all manner of spirits and fine wines, some drained more thirstily than others. Vodka, it seemed, was the drink of choice for those most recently resident here.

Roy stepped a little closer to the broken window. Gibson's body lay on the floor, shreds of glass coating it like diamonds. There was no sign of anyone else. He figured the other guy who was drinking with Gibson must have bolted, running like a scared little girl when his friend had hit the floor. Roy caught a strong whiff of alcohol as he bent towards Gibson's body, just to make sure the job had been finished. The little cunt must have been drinking from early morning, the strength of the alcohol almost overwhelming. Then he noticed something a little odd. Gibson's body was soaking wet. That's why the smell was so strong. It was as if he'd not only been drinking booze, but swimming in it.

Like a glorious, drunken phoenix the ginger mop of Sean Magee rose from behind the bar, a lighter in one hand, flaming bottle of sambucca in the other. With one fluid motion and all the skill of a West

Indian fast bowler, the flaming bottle left Sean's hand, hurtling towards Roy Beggs. The bottle smashed against the soldier, coating his uniform with its contents, immediately catching fire from the burning rag at its neck. The flames licked up the heavy coating of booze, soaking Alan Gibson, sending up a chorus of fire that almost drowned out the hoarse screech emitting from Roy Begg's mouth as his raw flesh fried like a slice of steak. His gun reacted against the sudden and immense heat, shooting off wildly against his own torso, lifting and hurling his whole body out through the broken window like a firecracker.

As Star watched on, mouth agape, a human fireball jettisoned out of the first floor window of the hotel bar, seeming to move in slow motion as it sailed through the air towards the street. The man was blazing, bullets slicing through the windows of shops and offices on the opposite side of the road from the hotel. A stray bullet tore through the car window, Star immediately diving for cover. Finally the body hit the ground with a slap that seemed to almost echo throughout the city. The gun quietened, the flames dying down almost immediately. A potent smell of cooked flesh seeped into the air that reminded Star of chicken.

Then came the women.

Fourteen

"**F**UCK."

Mairead said it more calmly than was demanded of the situation. They were entirely surrounded by the creatures, stuck in a Land Rover that's only saving grace was reinforced glass and armoured doors. Those bitches had done enough scraping, biting, punching and head butting to make an impression upon the rear window, but it was Barry's sheer stupidity, in the midst of all the panic, that changed their situation from grim... to *very* grim.

It seemed like a hundred arms were reaching through the window as Barry scrambled backwards, still shooting, into the already occupied front seats of the Land Rover. Bullets tore through each arm of his assailants, shredding skin and splintering bone as they showered the window and rear seats with scarlet red. Yet still they reached. Frantically feeling for something to tear, something to drag into their beautiful but lethal sea. Soon, one of them, a blonde-haired girl with eyes black as hell itself, had pushed her whole upper torso through the windscreen and was straining to grab hold of Barry, now sitting on top of Mairead.

"Fuck! Fuck! Fuck!" Mairead spat, more animated. She pushed Barry over to the seat that Caz was curling up in, eyes welded to the dramatic danger inching towards them in the suddenly overcrowded vehicle. Grabbing Barry's gun away from him, Mairead turned herself towards the rear window. With one shot, aimed precisely at the creature's blonde locks, she had split the damned thing's head open, pieces of bloody brain and hair showering the three humans. Each shot at the advancing horde, scrambling and competing against each other for Barry Rogan, or anyone else who stood in their way, ended with more bile and blood soaking them. Mairead was spitting out pieces of flesh after each shot, then wiping her face before unleashing another. Some blood had got into her eyes and she was struggling to maintain the vision she needed to shoot with precision.

Caz yelled directly into the terrified lad's face, "Barry, do something!" But it was no good. Barry was crying, tears mixing messily with the gore splashing across his face with every shot fired.

He reached shakily for the SLR rifle that was nestled in behind her seat, feeling the flailing hands of the bitches, inching closer, scratching at his skin, grabbing for his cock. Screaming with effort and terror, Barry dragged his hands back, keeping hold of the weapon. Undoing the safety, he opened fire indiscriminately on the back seat, shattering the remainder of the window along with half a dozen heads.

Caz reached her foot into Mairead's seat, pressing down hard on the accelerator. They could make more headway, many of the creatures having streamed towards the back of the vehicle and its broken window. Progress was still slow, but they were inching though the crowd a little more promisingly.

Barry continued firing wildly, his bullets tearing open skulls and breasts in equal measure, the fruits of his labour lapping back against him. A fever was building again on his forehead, his mind struggling to stay focused. He felt a mixture of dizziness and nausea sweep over him, disturbing his aim. Before he knew it he was pumping a round of ammunition, at close range, through the side window next to Mairead.

"Fuck sake, Barry!" she yelled, grabbing the barrel of his gun with her free hand, scalding herself in the process, moving it away. The heavy din of weapons firing so close to her ears had deafened her and with the constant shower of blood clogging her vision, Mairead neither heard nor saw the window beside her give against Barry's firepower and the incessant sea of deadly beauty before it was too late. Arms reached in, grabbing her hair roughly, dragging her towards the street. Although she fought it, shooting her handgun randomly, Mairead's whole upper body was in the open air within seconds.

Fifteen

THE BEAUTIFULLY SUITED-AND-BOOTED CHRIS O'HAGAN HAD no recollection of her former glories as a businesswoman, making over twice her weekly target each day, affording her respect and Porsche alike. She had no memory of her endless quest down at the Gym each evening, after a gruelling ten hours in the office, sweating profusely against the lack of sleep, food, and constant popping of antidepressants (stress was what she had told her doctor) to make even more targets. She cared even less for her family (long since broken down after the murder of her brother all those years ago) and longsuffering boyfriend (now dead, his corpse having decayed textbook-style) as her dead eyes flickered open and her mind slowly kicked into a most basic form of action. Chris' only target now was fuelled by dark, raw emotion.

Vengeance.

As she rose to her feet, rather awkwardly at first, finally standing tall, svelte and elegant, her senses kicked into overdrive. Her vision flickered between colours, white at first, then black as her hatred simmered to boil. Her sense of smell—this most primal of sense—sought out the blood of the man who had ruined her brother's life, made her the girl she was today, beautiful, successful, barely human.

Miserable.

Its very distinctive odour (like her expensive perfume) filled her delicate nostrils. That very smell was all around her. Everywhere! It filled the air, slightly more pungent due to its current state—cooked.

Her dark eyes fell upon the body of Roy Beggs, remembering him sitting so defiantly in the dock as the verdict of 'innocent' was read out and her life shifted into a new, cold, emotionless gear. Not sated by his brutal death filling her nostrils, Chris sauntered over to his burned-out husk, the barbecued flesh reminding a deep, distant part of her of all-too-familiar hunger pangs from days gone by.

And she fed.

The over-inked naked form of Sonya Bailey, her body bearing the marks of Tim Adamson's crude, childlike attempts at tattooing, stumbled, then steadied herself. Her face pressed against the window of Great Victoria Street Station's front doors, staring down to meet with the disbelieving eyes of Tim's some-time sensei, Star.

From every corner, every nook and cranny, every street and alleyway throughout the quiet, dead city, more beautiful women emerged, swanlike in their almost musical approach. A sea of dark-eyed, ravenous vixens. Some came from Cornmarket, blood hungry with the taste of their loved ones still fresh from their scarlet lips. These ones appeared more feral, it seemed, than others.

Star looked this way and that, her neck almost breaking with the speed at which it turned to drink in this incredible yet sinister sight. She looked to the car where Clare remained, eyes glued to the approaching women, palms pressed upon the window.

"*Fuck me royal,*" she whispered, more to herself than anyone else. In The Silence, still omnipresent in the still late afternoon sunshine, even her whisper seemed to growl. Star dragged on her cigarette, grabbing the car door and shaking it violently.

"Open the fuck up!" she cried.

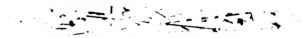

Clare looked out, her distrust of the uncouth young woman hesitating her from opening the door. She wondered where Roy had got to, having missed his glorious exit from life while she was dancing in her seat to the loud music blaring out from the CD. Now the music was turned down, seeming an almost irreverent soundtrack for what she saw happening all around her.

They're all so pretty, Clare thought, having not seen or smelled anything less than gruesome since The Great Whatever some weeks ago. The women reminded her of fairies. Overgrown, wingless, but still graceful. They washed towards the car like a shoal of mermaids, a choir of angels, a toy store's worth of dolls, their pretty hair shimmering in the fairytale sunshine.

"Open the fucking door, you stupid wee bitch!"

Sixteen

BARRY GRABBED HOLD OF MAIREAD'S LEGS, WEDGING HIS FOOT against the side door as leverage. His lean, tall frame sprawled messily across the driver seat, obscuring Caz's view as she continued grinding the Land Rover against the thick, fearless crowd of beautiful women swarming thickly around them. She felt a little give, continuous bitch casualties seeming to bear the brunt of her sinking foot on the accelerator, blood squirting against the window as the Land Rover's large wheels churned against flesh and bone, bumpily negotiating the fallen, mangled beauties.

"Fuck... these... bitches!" Barry screamed, straining to keep hold of Mairead's legs, sweat continuing to pour down his forehead.

Mairead fought valiantly, trigger finger busy, her gunfire tearing through the masses. But it was useless. Like vultures they pecked and tore at her abdomen, her freshly-spilled blood splashing in against Barry and Caz. Mairead's legs kicked violently with the pain, catching Barry in the face with a high-heeled boot. He almost lost his grip, yet scrambled again to keep hold of her. He fought against the almost overwhelming urge to let go, to give into the fever, slipping back into his drugged state.

Finally Mairead's spine gave way, the creatures having gnawed at her like a dog would a bone. She snapped, upper body disappearing out the window, lower body falling against Barry as he fell against Caz. The two of them screamed blue hell, the legs, lower abdomen and fleshy spine of their friend shaking and jittering against them as if still alive.

Soon the doll-like creatures were scurrying like ants on the roof of the vehicle. Like bees around a hive they closed in, pushing, stretching, snapping at each other in a passion-fuelled drive to reach the distinct cocktail of blood and sweat filling their nostrils. A horde of arms stretched into the vehicle, grabbing, pulling and ripping at anything they could grip. They tore the remainder of Mairead out into their mass, fighting over her flesh and bone like starving dogs.

Beautiful starving bitches.

And then they came for Barry. The one they had wanted from the start. Led by the two remaining 'girls' he had recognised—raped—they scrambled forward, pushing a screaming Caz aside to get hold of him. They dragged him out, tearing him mercilessly across the jagged edges of the torn windscreen. Grouping together like a mad pack of hungry animals, they held him down in chaotic unison as the red-haired beauty whose name he couldn't remember—his first victim—strode across him like a lap dancer. Tearing the belt from his jeans with one fluid movement, she went down on him, her mouth wide open. Barry screeched like a newborn puppy as her teeth sunk into his cock.

Seventeen

FROM HIS VANTAGE POINT BY THE DEVASTATED WINDOW, BY the first floor bar of the Europa Hotel, Sean Magee looked down upon the fantastic sight of hundreds—maybe thousands—of beautiful young women swarming onto Great Victoria Street. They came from everywhere, pouring out like marbles from a tin, their dense numbers and choreographed approach somehow lending both an erotic and sinister quality to their mass. A part of Sean thought he was dreaming, perhaps having fallen into his daily drunken coma earlier in the day than normal. He was still shaking from the Roy Beggs incident. Still trying to take in the fact that he'd murdered a man, albeit a violent, deluded bastard like Beggs. The aging DJ ruffled his mop of unkempt grey hair in an expression that could only say 'what the fuck?!'

This couldn't be real. And yet the women continued to come, their numbers and density swelling like punters at a Football Cup Final.

At the centre of the mass, almost the very reason for the direction of its swarm, stood the shorn-headed and comparatively uncouth-looking Star, poised on top of a People Carrier-type car parked opposite the hotel. She was lying on the roof, beating the front windscreen passionately. This was beyond fucking odd.

"Star!" Sean called, his voice seeming to harmonise Star's incessant beating of the window, breaking the weird and incessant Silence.

"What the fuck?! Sean! Jesus... Sean!" She seemed genuinely elated to see him. It was as if she had thought him dead.

Sean looked again at the dramatic sight of thousands of drop dead gorgeous women swarming towards her, rubbing his eyes to make sure the beer goggles weren't working at some accelerated rate to make a crowd of spides/soldiers/terrorists somehow appear beautiful.

Nope. Still there.

He fought for an appropriate and eloquent way of expressing himself. "What the *fuck* is going on?!"

(...and failed.)

"Sean!" Star yelled back. "You've got to help me here, mate!"

"How?! What's going on?!"

"I... they... fuck! Sean! These... women... there's something not right about them!"

"How do you know?! Talk to them! See what they say!" A large part of him couldn't believe that anything so collectively beautiful could be so dangerous. Another part of him was so pissed he couldn't see anything wrong with the world at all, and yet another part of him was still reeling in post-traumatic, drunken shock from disposing of Roy Beggs so dramatically.

"Sean!" she yelled, now understandably frustrated with the DJ, "Their eyes are fucking black!"

Sean bent down a little to look closer, still unable to see clearly from his height. He watched as some of the women looked up at him, a few turning their direction from the main herd in order to move towards the hotel's front entrance. He wondered if the doors were open.

Star turned her attention back towards the approaching horde. She looked in all directions, met only by hundreds of black eyes looking back at her.

She took Sean's advice, mainly because she was flat out of any other options. "H-h-hey..." she stuttered, heart racing at a speed which would have worried her doctor. "Look... Can any of you, like, speak?"

There was a unanimous lack of reaction. Star looked all around, for anyone—anything—which could resemble communication from them. Only the eyes... Flickering. Blending colours. Narrowing. Star's heart sank, realising that whatever was happening all around her wasn't going to be talked down. Nervously, she lit up a cigarette. There was no response from them. Finally, they collectively ignored her, turning their attention back towards the People Carrier she stood upon.

From inside, palms still pressed against the windows of the car, the small, delicate eyes of the child, Clare McAfee, stared back at the doll-like creatures swarming towards her. She was overawed by their sheer loveliness. Perhaps something to do with her childlike innocence or inert trust for everything that sparkled, or maybe just because of her longing for something—anything—bright and beautiful to rescue her from this new, broken and grey world, she wasn't able to see the very definite malice in their hellishly-black eyes.

It wasn't long before Sean Magee was able to see first hand exactly why Star was so freaked out by the women suddenly swarming from everywhere. They had breached the hotel, drawing towards him and the hotel bar like flies to meat.

Their eyes... so empty. So very black...

Suddenly Sean felt very sober. Very alone. Very afraid. Since his whole world had turned itself inside-out, he'd been responsible for the deaths of two people (three if you were to count his ex-wife, Sharon— which Sean would, no doubt). He had always thought of himself as a lover-not-a-fighter, but something about this (brave, new) world had changed him. Fucked him up. Maybe the same something that had created whatever insanity he was witnessing now.

The inhuman-looking women filled the room, quickly and quietly. Their mouths remained incredibly expressionless. Their beautiful faces, each as different to each other as they were the same, seemed almost radiant. Apart from their eyes, they were the picture of health and catwalk-quality beauty. Sean's eyes fell on one in the middle of the crowd as they approached. She was naked, and one of her breasts was so stained with blood that it looked as if someone had thrown a tin of paint around her. Sean couldn't take his eyes off her. She was beautiful and repulsive all at once, like some kind of strangely beautiful yet horrific fetish. She led the slow, calm charge towards him.

Sean backed away, inching closer towards the broken window. He weighed up his options. They were extremely limited. He could either wait for them, or walk towards them. There were too many of them, and they were too close to him for him to try walking around them. The final option involved climbing out onto the window ledge and trying to find some escape from there. That was only going to delay the inevitable, of course, as they were now literally everywhere.

It was useless. Sean lifted his glass, tipped it to the approaching horde and drank deeply. Dutch courage.

They say that your life flashes before your eyes just before death.

Sean's eyes closed as he heard the familiar low-ebbed guitar sound and brash voices of the Sabbath gig he had been at in '77. It was the most energetic night he could remember, with pogo dancing and head-banging so extreme that he left with a bloody nose to go with the smile across his sweaty face. It was the first time Sean had stage dived into the crowd. He had loved the experience, chasing the thrill of it several times during the night, higher each time until Ozzy himself had pushed him into the waiting fans, hands raised to lift and carry him both gently and gruffly back to ground level.

Turning towards the window, the aging DJ hurled himself forward into the throng of beautiful women below.

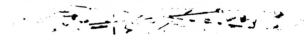

All of a sudden they were shaking and clawing at the People Carrier with a fury that seemed demonic to her. Almost instantaneously the windows shattered, and what seemed like a million pairs of arms reached in.

Star stood, poised on the roof of the vehicle. As they moved in, she sprung into action, swiping and kicking at them as they approached, swarming around her like a plague of locusts. Her weighty Doc Marten boots acted as the ideal weapon to land some of their beautiful mass on the ground, blood pouring from gashes in their pretty heads. Others felt the wrath of her cigarette, now a weapon to be thrust into their sadistic eyes, still flapping from one colour to another as they flocked in. Those assaulted fell back, embers, puss, and blood staining their porcelain cheekbones as others thrust forward in their place. Yet still they ignored her, her frantic violence against them hardly even acknowledged. Their faces, elegant and hungry, shone in the late afternoon sun as they fought forwards to the prize inside the car. That of the child.

From inside, Clare stared at one of the creatures in particular, her bright, innocent eyes twinkling as tears began to build up. The broken glass had showered her like snowflakes, several shards slicing her soft cheeks and leaving a trail of bright red to blend painfully with her rich, salty tears. The hands kept reaching forward, then pulling back, some of them managing to tear at her long blonde locks, freshly washed and conditioned in the hotel earlier. Yet she ignored these creatures. She was interested in only one of them. Clare McAfee smiled, tearfully, as the face of her mummy—her real mummy—seemed to draw nearer to her. The crowd of fairies seemed to be parting, allowing mummy to glide towards her as if on a cloud. Her face seemed more expressive than the other fairies, her eyes whiter than snow. Clare felt the love beaming in at her, like sunlight. She reached towards her mummy, arms outstretched, blood and tears streaming down her cheeks.

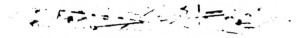

"No! Get away from her, you fucking whores!"

Star was in the middle of the crowd, screeching and clawing like a mad banshee. Her kitchen knife came out of her pocket, the blade flashing in the sun as she ripped skin from bone, digging into flesh with an animal thirst. She swung and sliced with a fervour beyond sanity, her voice cutting through the air like a siren.

She was suddenly taken back to the horror of that first day, whenever she had seen the corpse in the pram. That stained innocence had stung her deep, making her feel as if her heart had been pickled from the inside out. She couldn't let this fucked-up world steal another innocent soul.

Her boots were kicking out as several of the creatures attempted to grab her before meeting with leather sole. Half in the crowd, half on top, she fought like a wild cat, trying in vain to reach the little girl as the creatures passed her, some gently, others scraping and clawing at her as she moved through their ever-swelling numbers. It was useless. There were just too many of them. Before long, the child was lost within the sea of beauty, the only trace of her being the bloodstained tears that had dripped like raindrops from a petal onto each of the creatures as she passed over them and through them. Some of the blood even fell upon Star. She was so close, yet so very far away.

Yet still Star screeched, arms still flailing, feet still swinging as the creatures turned their full attention towards her, their eyes flashing a colour so dark that it almost hurt to look upon. She grinned maniacally back at them. They were going to pay for what they did, all they stole. They were going to pay for all the death that had happened since that first day when this fucked-up world had creeped up against her, sliding into life at a time whenever things were looking up for once. All of a sudden these glamorous, shiny monsters represented everything fucked-up in life, everything that had ever stood in Star's way. They were the drugs that had messed up her mental health, spitting her from one fucked-up situation to another in the arsehole of London, some years ago. They were the people she knew then, users like her. Abusers and veterans of self-destruct who knew no boundaries in their relentless thirst for hedonism. These callous bitches represented the very essence of 'wrong' to Star. Like ghosts, beautiful and chaotic ghosts from her past, they pressed against her again, their primal rage ignited.

Star licked her knife clean of the blood that she had already spilled. A small splash of blood trickled from the side of her mouth. She was ready for them. Ready to face her demons...

It was then that they turned to look at her, their eyes flicking back and forth between various colours, finally stopping at red.

"Come on you bitches," she spat, smiling sinisterly.

They swarmed her like angry wasps.

Then came The Rain.

Eighteen

IT RAINED HARD AND FAST, THE SKIES TURNING ALMOST BLACK WITH cloud. The water mingled with blood, streams soon flowing through the streets like watered-down wine. The rain came heavy, its monotonous patter breaking The Silence like glass. Soon it was joined by thick and deep moans of thunder, blurting out uncouthly. It was as if Great Mother Nature had finally decided to mourn its loss, crying out in gut-wrenching heavy tears. It was Her turn to grieve, and grieve heavily.

A storm swept through the whole of Ireland like a huge facecloth, wiping clean every street and field. Its fury beat upon the flesh and bones of fallen animals, broken down cars and half-decayed corpses. Little escaped its touch as riverbanks gave way to rising tides, floods soon invading every hill and incline. Buildings were beat upon, billboards stripped clean. Corpses, some still untouched, others half-eaten by beautiful ex-lovers and family, were sterilized. Where there was Silence everywhere, now there was just Rain.

Nineteen

SEAN AWOKE, DELIRIOUS WITH BOOZE AND FEAR. ADJUSTING his eyes to the poor light (it must have been night time), he looked around him, for a second, still too shaken to actually get off the ground. He was lying on the road by the hotel. It was dark and wet, yet the rain seemed to have cleared.

His arms had been pecked at, as if by birds, leaving long strips of tender flesh bleeding freely. His hair had been ripped out by the handful, leaving ginger-grey clumps dotted around where he lay. But he had clocked none of this. Sean fought, for a moment, to remember all that had happened. Yet he had forgotten everything. Every sordid event that had taken place since the end of *Whiskey In My Jar* and the start of his new life without a microphone. Everyone he had met, the motley crew he had fallen in with at the hotel and bus station. He had forgotten everyone and everything, his brain perhaps finally giving way to the years of alcohol abuse he had subjected it to.

But then it all came crashing back to him.

Looking to his left, Sean saw the half-devoured, charred corpse of the soldier who had attacked him. To his right was the car the soldier had come in, the People Carrier he had last seen Star standing on top off.

He didn't see her now.

Sean struggled painfully to his feet. Something was broken, something on his right side. He wasn't sure if it was an ankle or the foot, but something failed to work properly when he put weight on it. He grabbed hold of a nearby streetlight to steady himself.

The rain must have fallen hard and heavy on him whilst he was out cold. He was soaking wet, and even though the evening was quite humid, he felt very cold. Yet he didn't mind. The coldness had a distinctly sobering effect and, hell, Sean needed to be sober. He ran one hand through his long hair.

More pain.

It was as if someone had driven a combine harvester along his head, such was its mess. Blood from a gouge on the crown had mixed in with the rainwater and it was smarting as he touched it. A clump of hair and flesh fell out, suddenly unsettled by his hand. Then came more blood.

"Jesus," he muttered to himself. "Why aren't I dead?"

Maybe he was dead. Maybe this was heaven, or hell. A grimmer version of Earth. A fucked-up mirror image of the post-apocalyptic mess that had been his world for the best part of a month. A world with free vodka, as much as you wanted. A world with no work, no responsibility.

A world without Sharon.

Straining his eyes against the dampest, darkest evening ever recorded for summer, Sean tried to find any sign of the creatures which had attacked them. Whilst they had been swarming in their hundreds, clogging up Great Victoria Street like the entrance to some huge rock concert, now there wasn't a single one, alive or dead, to be seen. Every last one of them had vanished as if they had never been there in the first place.

Where the fuck had they gone?

He heard the sound of an oncoming vehicle.

What the fuck, now?

Soon it came into view, moseying down Great Victoria Street as if on a pleasant Sunday afternoon stroll. The vehicle (Sean realising it to be a beat-up white van as it drew closer) pulled up by the hotel, its worn-down rubber tires rolling over the charred remains of Roy Beggs as if they weren't even there. Its front windscreen remained intact, regardless of a large stain of blood, diluted somewhat by the recent fall of rain. The van ground to a clumsy halt as if the driver was still learning how to drive.

For an uncomfortable amount of time, nothing happened. Sean stared at the vehicle's windows, too damp with dirt and rain and blood for him to actually make out anyone inside. He was just about to approach when the driver's door opened and a rather scruffy-looking elderly man climbed slowly out of the car. He carried a shotgun under his arm and, curiously, Sean noticed, he seemed to be wearing a bizarre ensemble of pyjamas, dressing gown, and work boots.

Shutting the car door, the old man walked towards Sean, his head bowed low.

"Good evening, sir," he said, still avoiding eye contact. "My name is Herbert Matthews. I've just had the most horrendous journey and I really could do with a glass of bourbon." At this point he paused, looking up at the bloody mess that was Sean Magee. "And by the looks of you, my good man, I reckon you should join me."

Sean was lost for words. He felt tears build up in his eyes, the shock of all that had happened finally kicking in. A drink was exactly what he *didn't* need. A drink was exactly why he had ignored all the fucked up chaos surrounding him, wallowing in his own self-pity. And drink was probably the only reason he wasn't dead yet, those murderous whores too repulsed by his pickled mess of a body to bother much with him.

Within seconds Sean was sobbing, the salty tears smarting against his recent wounds.

The old man looked shocked, his mouth agape. Then, before Sean's misty eyes, the man began fumbling in the pockets of his dirty dressing gown, finally presenting the DJ with a blackened handkerchief. It was clearly not clean, but Sean took it anyway, thanking him, then blowing his nose loudly.

"So," the old man said, his face looking rather kindly and paternal upon the younger DJ, "about that drink..."

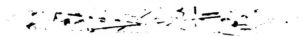

The rain had pounded hard and fast upon the scarlet-stained cobblestones at Cornmarket, cleaning the violently torn bodies of the bandstand's daily worshippers with an almost clinical precision. Pink water still pooled densely in pockets throughout Belfast's whole city centre, an indication perhaps that many of the shadow people had also fell foul of the beautiful young women's lethal and feral charms. Whatever number of survivors remained since The Great Whatever, that number had almost certainly become as diluted as the blood, leaving humanity in Belfast an incredibly endangered species.

Star's eyes had awoken before the rest of her, Cornmarket's whole brutal scene spreading out before her like modern art. Her hearing returned next, droplets of rain from the bandstand's ornate roof splashing delicately into the pink puddles below. She drifted almost blissfully back into consciousness, the gentle splish-spash noise whispering into her ear like a lullaby, a soundtrack for the scarlet-washed, cobblestoned landscape before her. But then it all came crashing back, the art before her suddenly morphing into the picture of carnage that it truly was, the young tattooist longing for unconsciousness to reclaim her again.

She couldn't remember much of what had happened since those bitches had decided, all of a sudden, to take an interest in her. She didn't know why she was in Cornmarket, slightly east of Great Victoria Street. She saw no sign of the child she had tried in vain to protect. All she knew was that she was alive, albeit covered in blood (seemingly not her own), and the rain seemed to have washed more than just the sunshine away.

Those beautiful and deadly whores, all several hundred of them, were currently nowhere to be seen.

Star ran an eye over the sterilized chaos before her. The bodies of several men, (*the God-lovers*, she reckoned,) lay spread-eagled before her. A sandwich board proclaiming 'THERE IS POWER IN THE BLOOD' was itself stained pink. Bones jutted out obtusely from the bodies, some of the men having enough of their faces left to allow Star a little glimpse of the pain and sheer terror they were experiencing before death.

As far as she could look to the east, west, south and north of Cornmarket's compass centre, Star saw nothing but devastation. Cars, once just abandoned, were now ravished with the same ferocity afforded the bodies. Shop windows lay in glittering pieces up and down every street. Even advertising billboards, their models seemingly too beautiful for chaos, couldn't escape the carnage. Strips of paper hung lifelessly from their corporate nests, ripped down by violence or the rain—or both.

But Star saw something else in the half-baked twilight, something twinkling differently to the shards of glass littering the damp streets like glitter. Something that stood out like a gem, its precious nature all too poignant. Her heart skipped a beat as she realized what it was that had caught her eye.

"Oh God, no," she whispered, a tattooed hand rising to cover her mouth.

Star walked, slowly and tearfully, towards the slender, half-devoured body of Tim Adamson. As she approached, her stomach turning with every footstep she made, she was able to see the full atrocity of the lad's final seconds. Both arms and legs had been torn greedily from his torso, leaving ragged stumps of bone and vein. His hair, having grown a little emo since she had first met him, had been ripped out in clumps. But worst of all was the expression on his face.

He was smiling.

Bending down, Star noticed the last tattoo she had worked on with Tim, still perfectly intact despite the desecration of the boy's corpse. It was a small black and white star shape, wrapped in Celtic characters forming a circle. It was one that Tim had worked on for himself.

He had told her that it represented hope.

She noticed the thing that had attracted her eye to him in the first place. There, lying close to Tim's corpse, was the small silver crucifix that Caz had recently given him. Star picked it up, running one finger over its tiny, longsuffering Jesus. She didn't mean to compare them, but looking back at Tim, she noticed how the position of his body's head (cocked slightly to the right) wasn't dissimilar to that of silver Jesus'.

And for some reason that unnerved her.

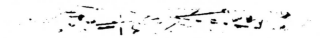

Professor Herbert Matthews was thoroughly enjoying his first bourbon in quite a while, its dark and bitter taste sliding down his dry throat like velvet.

His new friend, a curious looking fellow by the name of Sean, had needed some assistance into the nearby bus and railway station, an architectural anomaly of glass and steel that seemed way too modern looking for the likes of Herb. They made it over to the coffee shop area of the station's mall, Herb setting himself down by the window whilst Sean, like the gentleman he was, reached behind the bar area for an untouched bottle of bourbon. He then helped himself to a glass from an already well-tested bottle of vodka before falling into a seat beside the professor.

For a moment or so the two men had sat, wordless, downing sizable gulps of their respective nectars. Now steadied by the drink, its warm comfort caressing every tingling nerve within their shell-shocked bodies, Herb began to talk and Sean began to listen.

Herb told Sean of the day he woke up, removing his glasses to wipe a damp eye, as he described how he had found Muriel, dead on the couch, covered with crumbs. He then spoke of his old HAM radio, informing Sean that it was one of only two items he had taken with him on his journey to Belfast (the old shotgun being the second) and how its use was to prove paramount for the future survival of the human race. As his scruffy friend listened intently, pouring himself another vodka, Herb explained how, with the use of his radio, he had made contact with an Englishman named Terry who was planning something very clever to put some kind of structure back into people's lives. A structure that, Herb surmised by looking at his new friend, humanity could really do with right about now.

His audience's gaze was suddenly disturbed, seemingly alerted by the door opening behind them. As Herb turned around, an even more curious looking individual walked in. In her one hand was a cigarette, its embers shaken to the ground with the absolute minimum of respect. The other was holding a silver chain—a crucifix—if Herb's eyes could be trusted. Her appearance was almost tribal, blood having hardened in patches around her strange tattoos and piercings. Dark shadows of make-up swirled messily around her wide, hungry-looking eyes. Her boyish clothes were torn in a fashion almost unseemly to a man of Herb's mature years.

Yet this frightful appearance didn't deter Sean from extending to the young woman a most hearty of welcomes.

"Star! You're alive! Thank God!" The wounded survivor, himself quite the battle-worn mess, was beaming, suggesting to Herb that the curious young lady was a friend of his. He tried to get up, an attempt to greet her properly, and failing as he painfully fell back into his seat.

But Herb felt intimidated by the newcomer. A cold sweat ran up his spine reminding the Professor of his age-old 'condition.' This was why he stayed indoors. This was why his doctor had prescribed the quiet, rural plains of Ballyclare to him instead of his old city haunts. The city could be quite unpredictable, bringing you into contact with all kinds of folk you wouldn't want to meet.

"Sean," the young woman said, simply, a look of bemusement scribbled across her shorn and chaotic face. "I can't believe you made it, man... Fuck." Turning to Herb, she added, "Who's the old man?"

Herb couldn't abide ill manners, especially from young people, but he didn't pass the comment, instead standing up to introduce himself.

"My name is Professor Herbert Matthews," he politely began, despite his chronic nervousness, "and it's an absolute—"

"Where did you come from? Did you see any of those bitches on your travels?" the young lady snapped back, apparently unconcerned for politeness in any context.

Herb began to feel his hand shaking. He tried desperately to maintain his composure as he spoke. "I came from Ballyclare and 'those bitches', as you so very eloquently describe them, swarmed me briefly before the rain seemed to chase them away. We haven't quite worked out why that is the case."

"*We*? Who's we?" the impertinent woman snapped.

"He's been talking to some bloke from England, Star. Apparently they have been studying those... *things*," Sean chipped in, a lot more politely. "What more do you know about them, Professor?"

Herb turned to Star. "The team at Manchester have made contact with others across the world, people that have survived this damned plague, or whatever it is. They tried to send a helicopter here, to search for survivors... but, sadly, they lost contact with it."

"That's got to be the one Barry was talking about! It crashed, Professor, on the M5... Didn't you notice it coming from Ballyclare?"

"Dear boy, motorways are a curse to me. I came by the back roads."

"Forget this bullshit. Any word from Barry?" It was the young woman again.

Herb ignored her. He hated it when people tried to knock him off track, simply glaring at her before continuing.

"Terry's people are trying to organize themselves against the new threat... the threat of our own people returning from the dead. I can see by your appearance, young lady, that you've fallen prey to such, already."

"Wait a minute," she snapped back, "are you trying to tell me that those bitches are some kind of fucking zombies? Cause I, for one, am not going to buy any of that Hammer Horror bullshit, Granpa."

Herb's voice suddenly rose as he turned towards the uncouth girl who had interrupted him once too many. "You'll watch your mouth, young lady," he said, sternly, "especially when talking of the dead." His heartbeat was speeding up so he took a moment to calm down, sitting himself back in his chair and reaching for his glass of bourbon. "I'll have you know that those creatures are much more than mindless zombies."

"What are they, then?" she snapped back. "Come on! You have all the answers, old man. What are they?!" She was seething now, her rage, pent up to overflow, pouring out like lava from a volcano.

Her sudden aggression startled Herb, the old man retreating back into his seat. But she came after him, spitting and shouting.

"What the fuck are they?!"

Herb cowered, Sean struggling to get out of his own seat to come between them. As his aggressor's face drew closer, wide-eyed with rage,

Herb could see that tears were building in her eyes. Her voice was cracking with emotion. For a minute it looked like she might grab the old man, but then she turned away, perhaps becoming aware of how raw terror had twisted her.

Herb fought for breath, chasing the pending panic attack. Sean was shouting at the young woman, telling her (in colourful language) to calm down. She didn't seem to be listening, simply leaning against the station's glass wall, her appearance all too visible to the Professor.

She was crying quite uncontrollably.

For a moment no one spoke. Herb, too, was quiet, fighting against his condition, trying desperately to hold onto his own composure and calm. He needed to be strong not only for his own sake, but for Terry's sake and the sake of the two damaged survivors he was trying to win over to his cause. A cause that was vital to the very survival of Northern Ireland's dwindled population.

"They used to be human, like you and me," Herb began again, once he had reclaimed his breath. He took a swig of bourbon, swallowing hard before continuing. "Now they're more than that."

"What do you mean by that, Professor?" Sean asked, pouring himself another vodka with shaking hands.

"What we're seeing here is evolution, dear boy. I don't know much about the human body, but I'm led to believe that it's a machine quite like any other machine. And machines are something that I know quite a lot about." Herb's voice suddenly morphed to that of his lecturer persona, his vocal cords exercising in ways which hadn't been heard in a long time. He was focusing on the young lady, Star, as he spoke. "You see, my dear, in order to make any machine better you have to turn it off, take it apart. Then you put it back together again, perhaps adding some new and innovative parts to make it work more efficiently. That is precisely what has happened with the human machine. Great Mother Nature has turned the majority of the human race off—unplugged us from the wall, if you like—before beginning the whole process of reinvention." He chuckled before adding, ruefully, "And it seems that the age-old cliché of the superior 'Y' chromosome is right after all! It's the women that seem to have been evolved while the men waste away in the gutter."

"So these women… the ones that are returning…" It was Sean speaking again, Herb noticing what seemed to be a longing look in his unkempt face. "Is there anything left of what they were before?"

Herb paused, solemnly recalling that harrowing moment whenever his dear wife had reanimated. He remembered the photograph he had displayed on his mantelpiece, the picture of Muriel in her prime, all those years ago. He smiled and turned to address the unkempt man at the table nearby.

"A little, perhaps," he answered, quietly, "and in time, perhaps, they could show a lot more of the thoughts and feelings that they once had. But they are a deadly threat to our continued survival as a species now. We have to take the greatest of care when dealing with them. Research from Terry's team suggests that they feed not only on flesh, but on the very fabric of humanity itself. My friends, these creatures both thrive and feed on our emotions—the most raw and fundamental part of us. We must therefore take the greatest of—"

"They didn't attack me."

The young lady turned back towards Herb. She was clinging to the small silver crucifix she had been holding, and blood was beginning to seep through her fingers where she gripped it. Her hard exterior had been broken, her defense mechanism now short-circuited. Herb felt his feelings towards her change. She was as broken-hearted as the rest of them. Deep beneath the hardened and violent front she had erected was a whole reservoir of grief that was only now becoming visible.

"They didn't attack me because I feel *nothing*! I feel nothing for myself or anyone else." She was sobbing hard. She banged her fist against the wall of the station, its dull thud doing no damage to the strong glass. "I'm hardly fucking human. That's why they left me, like some fucked-up and unwanted ragdoll."

Herb looked at her as she shivered and cried before his very eyes, opening up to him like some rare flower. It was as if this release of unspent emotion was her first real expression in a very long time. Herb could see that, where the hard and well-oiled exterior had crumbled, a beautiful and fragile young woman appeared. She even looked pretty, an angelic and vulnerable face hidden underneath all of the blood, tattoos and make-up.

Herb walked over to her, pausing briefly before using a sleeve of his dirty dressing gown to wipe away her tears. She didn't resist.

A good touch.

"Still waters run very deep, my dear child," he whispered, softly to her, unclenching her fist. "Those bitches just aren't smart enough yet to see what a beautiful and wonderful young woman you are."

He smiled at her before turning again so he could address Sean as well. "They only sense raw emotion. The heart that we wear on our sleeves. They, themselves, seem fuelled by that very same primal energy, according to Terry, possibly leading to them seeking out those who they feel... *felt*... their deepest connection with in life. Those who would have drawn the most primal of emotions from them, for whatever reason."

Herb was on fire now, unleashing his theories with eloquence and ease. "Of course, we can hide our feelings from them, protect ourselves. It would be possible, but in a broken down world like this, a world where those few of us who have survived are wide-eyed and raw, our cover is well and truly blown. They smell those feelings off us like blood." Herb's face turned very serious. "And it draws them to us like wild dogs."

Another sudden interruption led all three survivors to turn their gaze towards the huge glass walls of the station looking out upon the bus depot. Straining his tired old eyes, Herb noticed upon looking out what seemed to be a small line of bodies, all decomposing, half-covered by a canvas sheet. Some of their number had already risen to join the unholy throng of beautiful creatures he had watched retreat from the rain and Herb thought, for a moment, that another was rising to join their ranks.

But this most recent interruption hadn't come from there. It was something else. As Herb's eyes adjusted to the growing darkness outside, peering through the huge glass walls, he noticed a beat-up Land Rover stuttering to a standstill by the station's side entrance.

EPILOGUE

THE RAIN DIDN'T RETURN THAT NIGHT, ITS FAMILIAR PITTER-patter being missed by the shell-shocked survivors at the bus station, all too aware of The Silence again. They had thought that without the rain the creatures might return, so no one had even tried to sleep. Instead, under new leadership, they made ready for their new mission—a mission introduced to them by Herbert Matthews—that of setting up base and communications at Belfast's International Airport, making Northern Ireland an established country again.

Whilst the others worked silently and carefully, gathering supplies and jump-starting one of the smaller buses in the depot, Caz remained in the bus station's waiting area, tending to the delirious Barry Rogan. His wounds were extensive, those callous bitches having mauled him in places that would really hurt... but Caz didn't feel any embarrassment. She felt very little of anything. She tended to Barry with a clinical approach, wrapping what was left of his penis in sterile bandaging, tending to the bloody sockets that had been his eyes, recently brutally torn from his very face. She was making his shivering mess of a body as comfortable as possible yet she did it all without any emotional attachment to the young man. A man who had lost his dignity, and just about everything else, in order to rescue her.

Caz nursed Barry with apathy, doing it out of duty and loyalty than concern. All of her innocence had been torn mercilessly from her and it had left her devoid of feelings now. A mere shell, devoid of hope.

She hadn't even as much as shed a single tear as Star had handed her the small blood-stained crucifix, her present to Tim Adamson. For a short moment she simply ran her finger along its round edges, reading it like Braille that told the story of Tim's last moments, his final smile on thinking about her.

Then she simply placed it in her pocket.

Three hours ago, just before dawn, the others had set off. The darkness was beginning to recede and the Professor had thought it best for them to get on the road sooner rather than later. There had still been no sign of the creatures from the day before, but they decided to leave early, while the coast was clear.

They had gathered up a small amount of supplies, all from within the station's small mall. Barry was wrapped up in warm blankets, his shivering having continued from the previous night. He hadn't said a word. Nothing, except the occasional guffaw of disturbed laughter had come out of his mouth. They weren't sure how much he was aware of, or how bad his injuries were. Once at the airport, they intended to make contact with Terry's team in Manchester to get Barry some medical help.

Sean didn't leave with them, deciding that he had other business to attend to, business that was long overdue. Despite the protestations of the others, Star in particular almost furious with his decision, the DJ refused to change his mind. He really didn't have much left to go with them for. All this talk of mobilization was scaring him. It had taken the most of what he had in terms of energy to do his little part in preparing the others for their mission, hobbling about with his broken foot, scraping bottles of water and chocolate bars together for their journey. Sean wasn't a man of action, he was a man of passion—a passion that had been ripped from him twice.

And now there was a chance of reclaiming it.

Sean Magee sat in the bus station's coffee bar where he had racked up yet another vodka, leaving a gin and tonic at the seat beside him. He'd been playing one particular song on repeat, changing the batteries on the CD player to those high-powered, expensive ones to make sure it wouldn't run out. He tried to brush his hair as best as possible, despite the pain, washed and shaved for the first time in weeks, and put on a nice new shirt he picked up in the shopping mall.

He stayed behind because he knew that people—women—were coming back from the dead. He knew that they were returning a little different, perhaps, than they had been before, but they still looked similar, and smelt similar, and felt similar. And Sean needed to look and smell and feel his Sharon again.

So there, at that oh-so-familiar bus station mall, he waited. He played their song on repeat and waited, changing Sharon's drink twice in that time to make sure it was as fresh as possible.

He waited with a tear in his eye and memories in his heart. He waited with a flowing sense of hope and an ebbing sense of despair. She would come back to him and she would love him again, despite what she had become.

He waited a little longer before she did, indeed, return to him.

Acknowledgements

There are a lot of people I'd like to thank, each having contributed in some way to helping me puke this delightfully nasty little ditty onto the pages before you...

Travis Adkins (The Man With The Words), Jacob Kier (The Boss), Michael Brack, Tariq Sarwar (The Website Wizard), Elaine (Bitemark Clothing), Gracie (Torture Couture), Heidi (Pretty Scary), Frenchy (Kitten Koffin Zombies), Kriscinda Meadows, Jude (ATZ), Dave Moody, Andre Duza, Jan and Chris O (Identity), Chris Crooks (White Dragon), Jackie Coupe, Jo Harrison (Modern Body Art), Dan Henk, The Bloody Messy Girls, Chris 'fuckin' Jones (Physical Graffiti), Pete Leathley and Steve Vold (fellow HOO-HAAs!), Geoff at Revenant (The Other Boss), Ryan (The Workmate With The EMO haircut), Crazy Michael, Geoff (The Bro), Dougal, EMO, Stumpy, Huffy-Boldfish, Zombie, Dwagon (The Children), Satan, The Devil, Anton LaVey, King's X, Andy and Hannah at Mr & Mrs Nutter Promotions, Insomnia Magazine, Ian and Mark at Free Talk Live, All the Tattoo Jammers, Snoopy and Eve, Arch Enemy, Rob Zombie, Motley Crue, Hole, The Ramones, George Romero (The Inspiration), Everyone at Permuted Press/ Allthingszombie/Horror Express/Pretty Scary/anywhere else I've loitered with intent, Anyone else I've forgotten (sorry!) ...and, of course, my very own DROP DEAD GORGEOUS Rebecca xo

Hang in there for *Drop Dead Gorgeous: Doll Parts*!

Permuted Press

delivers the absolute best in **apocalyptic** fiction,
from **zombies** to **vampires** to **werewolves**
to **asteroids** to **nuclear bombs** to
the very **elements** themselves.

Why are *so* many readers turning to

Permuted Press?

Because we strive to make every book
we publish feel like an **event**, not
just pages thrown between a cover.

(And most importantly, we provide some
of the most fantastic, well written, horrifying
scenarios this side of an actual apocalypse.)

DYING TO LIVE
LIFE SENTENCE
by Kim Paffenroth

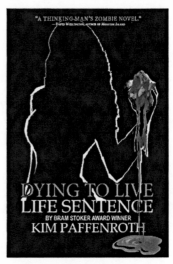

At the end of the world a handful of survivors banded together in a museum-turned-compound surrounded by the living dead. The community established rituals and rites of passage, customs to keep themselves sane, to help them integrate into their new existence. In a battle against a kingdom of savage prisoners, the survivors lost loved ones, they lost innocence, but still they coped and grew. They even found a strange peace with the undead.

Twelve years later the community has reclaimed more of the city and has settled into a fairly secure life in their compound. Zoey is a girl coming of age in this undead world, learning new roles—new sacrifices. But even bigger surprises lie in wait, for some of the walking dead are beginning to remember who they are, whom they've lost, and, even worse, what they've done.

As the dead struggle to reclaim their lives, as the survivors combat an intruding force, the two groups accelerate toward a collision that could drastically alter both of their worlds.

ISBN: 978-1934861110

AFTER TWILIGHT
WALKING WITH THE DEAD
by Travis Adkins

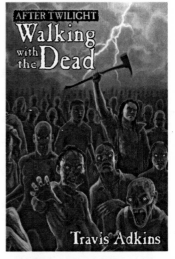

At the start of the apocalypse, a small resort town on the coast of Rhode Island fortified itself to withstand the millions of flesh-eating zombies conquering the world. With its high walls and self-contained power plant, Eastpointe was a safe haven for the lucky few who managed to arrive.

Trained specifically to outmaneuver the undead, Black Berets performed scavenging missions in outlying towns in order to stock Eastpointe with materials vital for long-term survival. But the town leaders took the Black Berets for granted, on a whim sending them out into the cannibalistic wilderness. Most did not survive.

Now the most cunning, most brutal, most efficient Black Beret will return to Eastpointe after narrowly surviving the doomed mission and unleash his anger upon the town in one bloody night of retribution.

After twilight,
when the morning comes and the sun rises,
will anyone be left alive?

ISBN: 978-1934861035

Permuted Press
The formula has been changed...
Shifted... Altered... Twisted.™
www.permutedpress.com

BY WILLIAM D. CARL

Beneath the dim light of a full moon, the population of Cincinnati mutates into huge, snarling monsters that devour everyone they see, acting upon their most base and bestial desires. Planes fall from the sky. Highways are clogged with abandoned cars, and buildings explode and topple. The city burns.

Only four people are immune to the metamorphosis—a smooth-talking thief who maintains the code of the Old West, an African-American bank teller who has struggled her entire life to emerge unscathed from the ghetto, a wealthy middle-aged housewife who finds everything she once believed to be a lie, and a teen-aged runaway turning tricks for food.

Somehow, these survivors must discover what caused this apocalypse and stop it from spreading. In their way is not only a city of beasts at night, but, in the daylight hours, the same monsters returned to human form, many driven insane by atrocities committed against friends and families.

Now another night is fast approaching. And once again the moon will be full.

ISBN: 978-1934861042

EDEN

A ZOMBIE NOVEL BY TONY MONCHINSKI

Seemingly overnight the world transforms into a barren wasteland ravaged by plague and overrun by hordes of flesh-eating zombies. A small band of desperate men and women stand their ground in a fortified compound in what had been Queens, New York. They've named their sanctuary Eden.

Harris—the unusual honest man in this dead world—races against time to solve a murder while maintaining his own humanity. Because the danger posed by the dead and diseased mass clawing at Eden's walls pales in comparison to the deceit and treachery Harris faces within.

ISBN: 978-1934861172

Permuted Press

The formula has been changed...
Shifted... Altered... Twisted.™

www.permutedpress.com

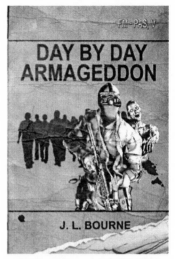
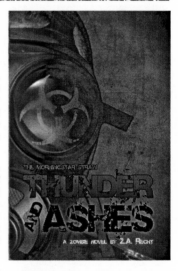

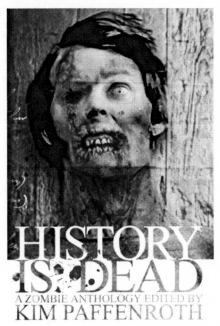
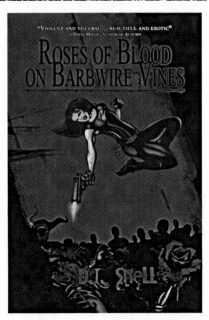

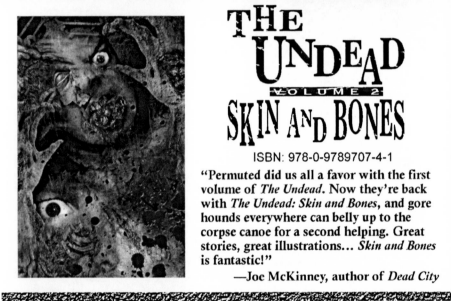

Printed in the United States
207146BV00001B/112-531/P